DC SUPER HERO GIRLS™

OUT OF THE BOTTLE

a graphic novel

WRITTEN BY
Shea Fontana

ART BY
Marcelo DiChiara,
Agnes Garbowska,
AND **Mirka Andolfo**

COLORS BY
Silvana Brys
AND **Jeremy Lawson**

LETTERING BY
Janice Chiang

COVER BY
Yancey Labat and Monica Kubina

MARIE JAVINS Group Editor
BRITTANY HOLZHERR Editor
DIEGO LOPEZ Assistant Editor
STEVE COOK Design Director - Books
AMIE BROCKWAY-METCALF Publication Design

BOB HARRAS Senior VP - Editor-in-Chief, DC Comics
BOBBIE CHASE Executive Editor, Young Reader & Talent Development

DIANE NELSON President
DAN DiDIO Publisher
JIM LEE Publisher
GEOFF JOHNS President & Chief Creative Officer
AMIT DESAI Executive VP - Business & Marketing Strategy, Direct to Consumer & Global Franchise Management
SAM ADES Senior VP & General Manager, Digital Services
MARK CHIARELLO Senior VP - Art, Design & Collected Editions
JOHN CUNNINGHAM Senior VP - Sales & Trade Marketing
ANNE DePIES Senior VP - Business Strategy, Finance & Administration
DON FALLETTI VP - Manufacturing Operations
LAWRENCE GANEM VP - Editorial Administration & Talent Relations
ALISON GILL Senior VP - Manufacturing & Operations
HANK KANALZ Senior VP - Editorial Strategy & Administration
JAY KOGAN VP - Legal Affairs
JACK MAHAN VP - Business Affairs
NICK J. NAPOLITANO VP - Manufacturing Administration
EDDIE SCANNELL VP - Consumer Marketing
COURTNEY SIMMONS Senior VP - Publicity & Communications
JIM (SKI) SOKOLOWSKI VP - Comic Book Specialty Sales & Trade Marketing
NANCY SPEARS VP - Mass, Book, Digital Sales & Trade Marketing
MICHELE R. WELLS VP - Content Strategy

DC SUPER HERO GIRLS: OUT OF THE BOTTLE. Published by DC Comics, 2900 W. Alameda Avenue, Burbank, CA 91505. GST # is R125921072.

Printed by Cenveo, Richmond, VA, USA. 8/1/18. ISBN: 978-1-4012-7483-2

SUSTAINABLE FORESTRY INITIATIVE
Certified Chain of Custody
Promoting Sustainable Forestry
www.sfiprogram.org
SFI-00484

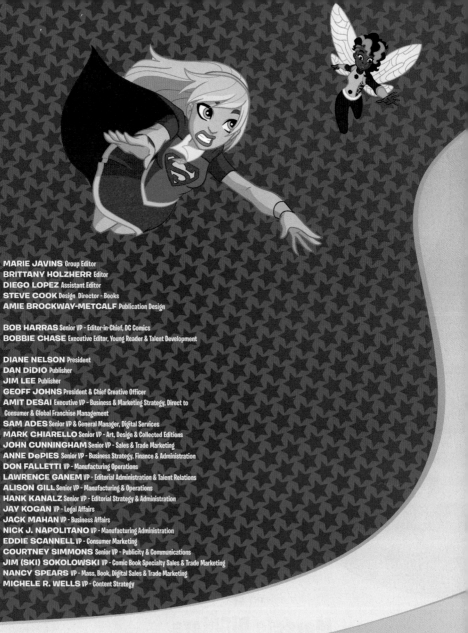

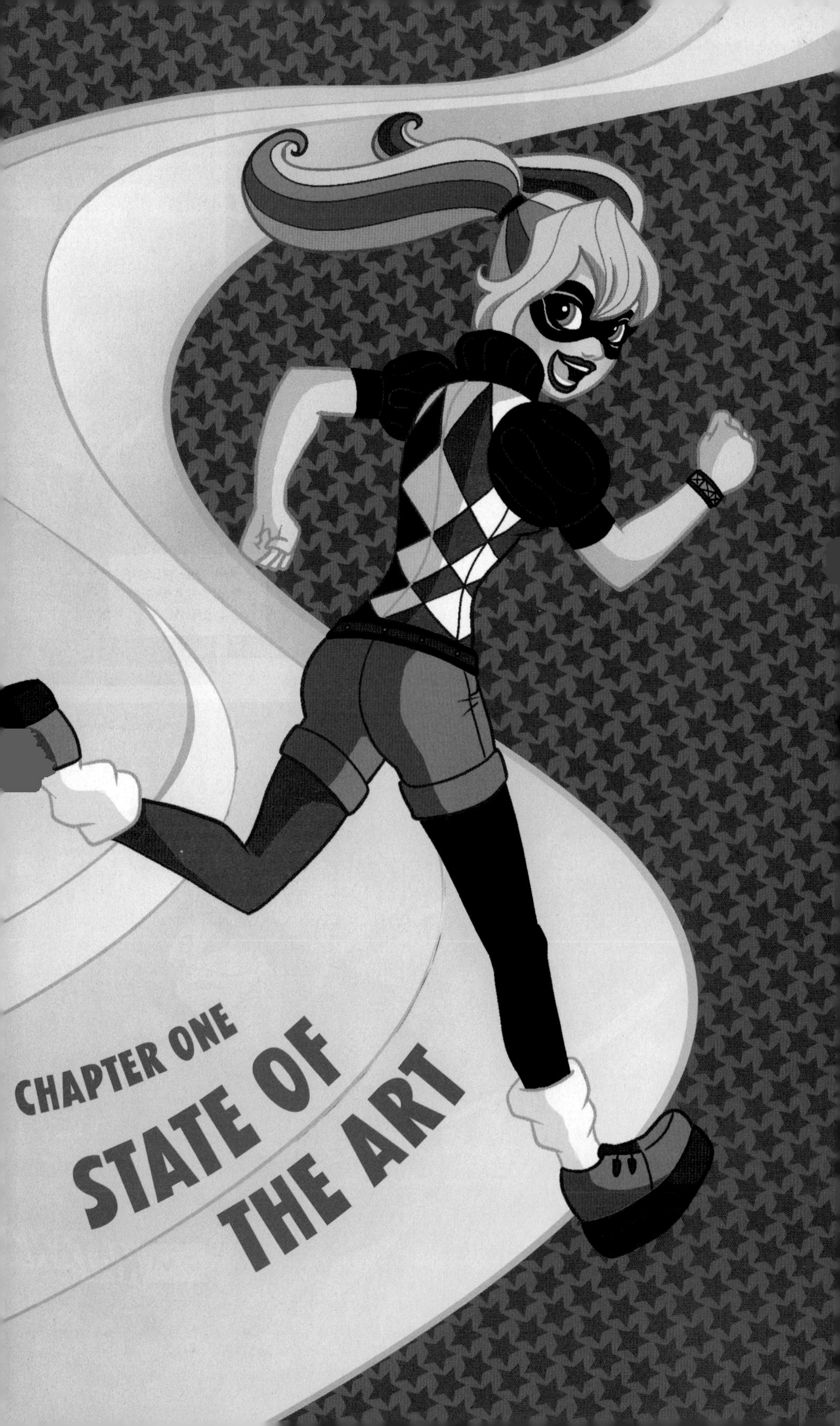

CHAPTER ONE
STATE OF THE ART

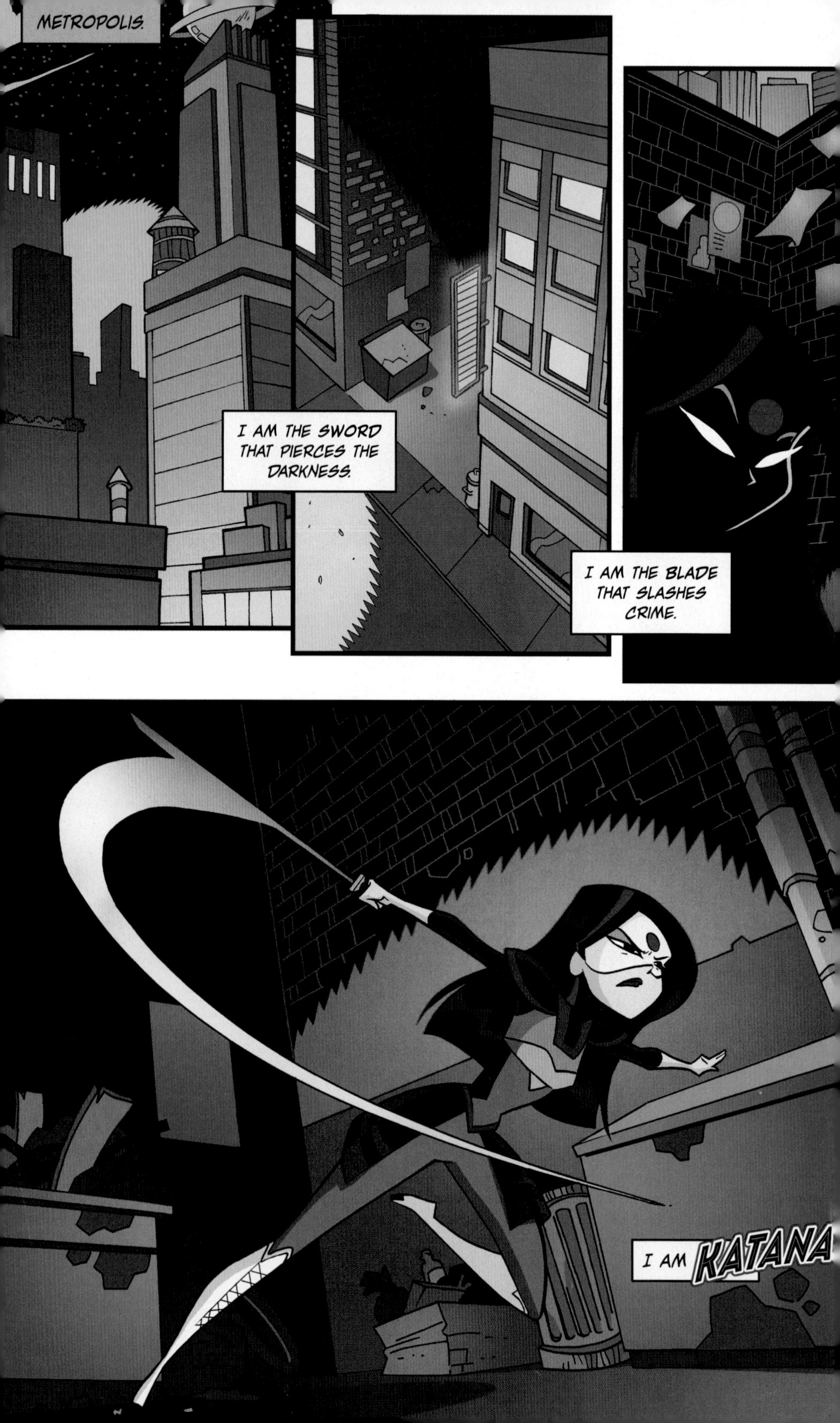
METROPOLIS.
I AM THE SWORD THAT PIERCES THE DARKNESS.
I AM THE BLADE THAT SLASHES CRIME.
I AM KATANA

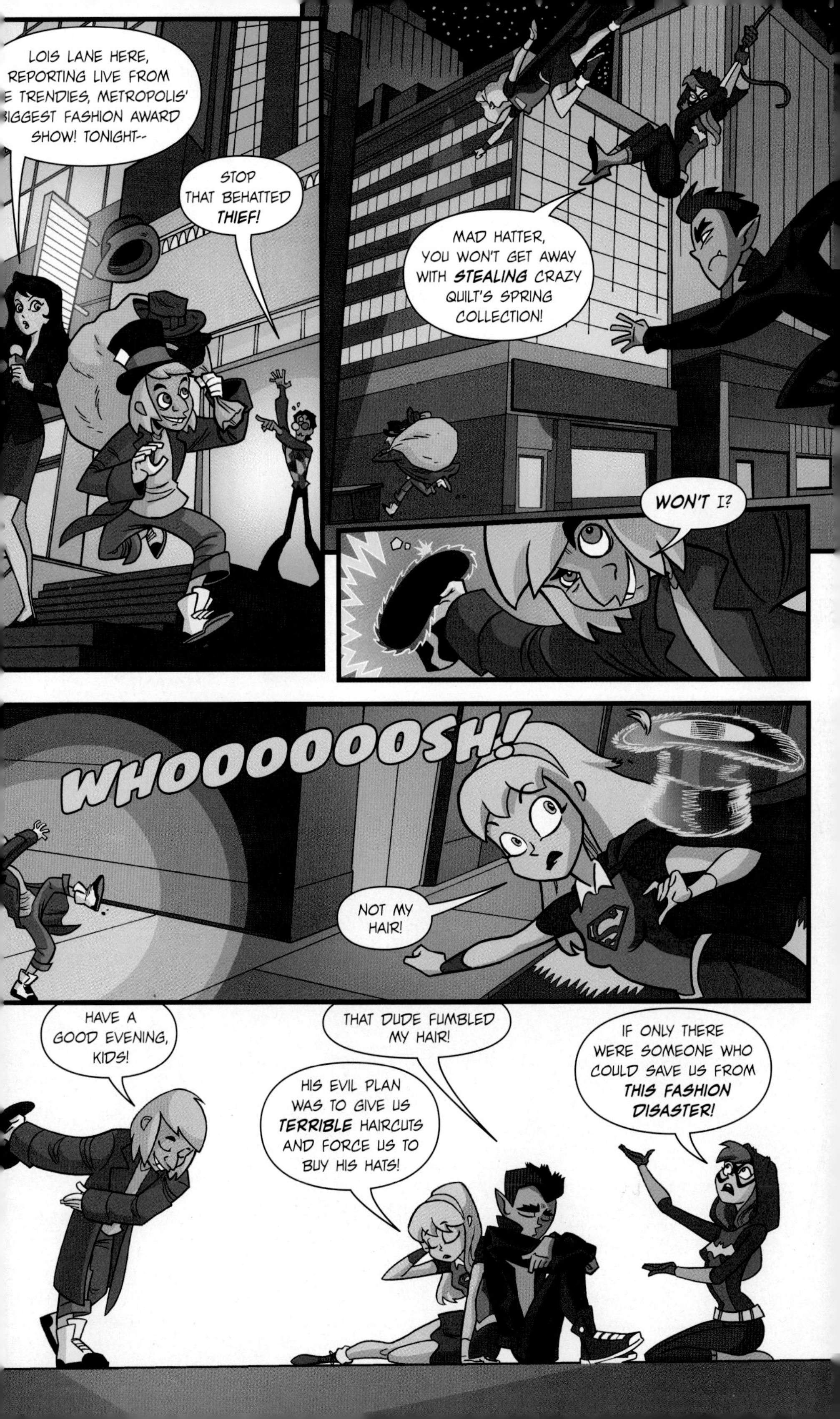
LOIS LANE HERE, REPORTING LIVE FROM E TRENDIES, METROPOLIS' BIGGEST FASHION AWARD SHOW! TONIGHT--
STOP THAT BEHATTED ***THIEF!***
MAD HATTER, YOU WON'T GET AWAY WITH ***STEALING*** CRAZY QUILT'S SPRING COLLECTION!
WON'T I?
WHOOOOOOOSH!
NOT MY HAIR!
HAVE A GOOD EVENING, KIDS!
THAT DUDE FUMBLED MY HAIR!
HIS EVIL PLAN WAS TO GIVE US ***TERRIBLE*** HAIRCUTS AND FORCE US TO BUY HIS HATS!
IF ONLY THERE WERE SOMEONE WHO COULD SAVE US FROM ***THIS FASHION DISASTER!***

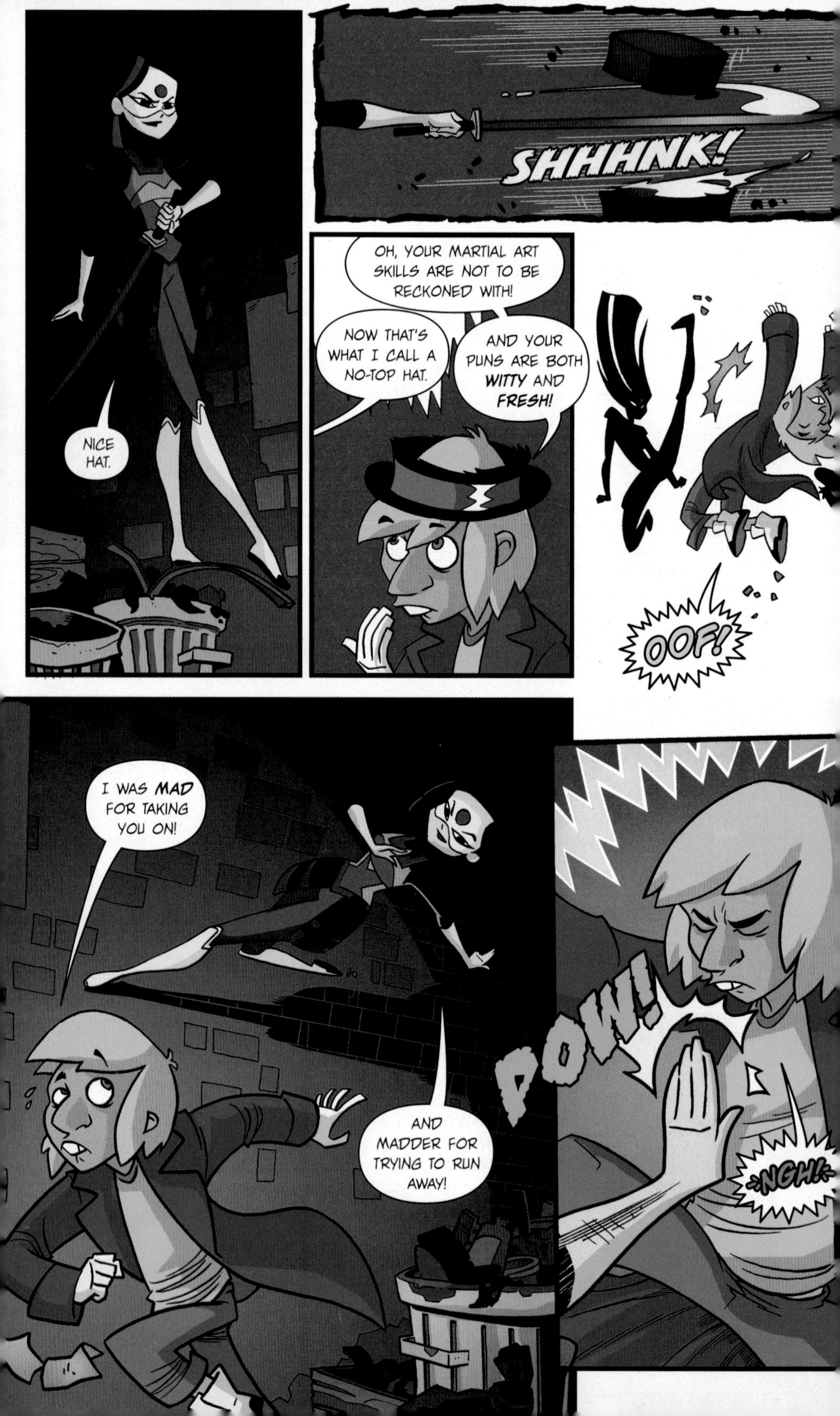

NICE HAT.
SHHHNK!
NOW THAT'S WHAT I CALL A NO-TOP HAT.
OH, YOUR MARTIAL ART SKILLS ARE NOT TO BE RECKONED WITH!
AND YOUR PUNS ARE BOTH **WITTY** AND **FRESH!**
OOF!
I WAS **MAD** FOR TAKING YOU ON!
AND MADDER FOR TRYING TO RUN AWAY!
POW!
NGH!

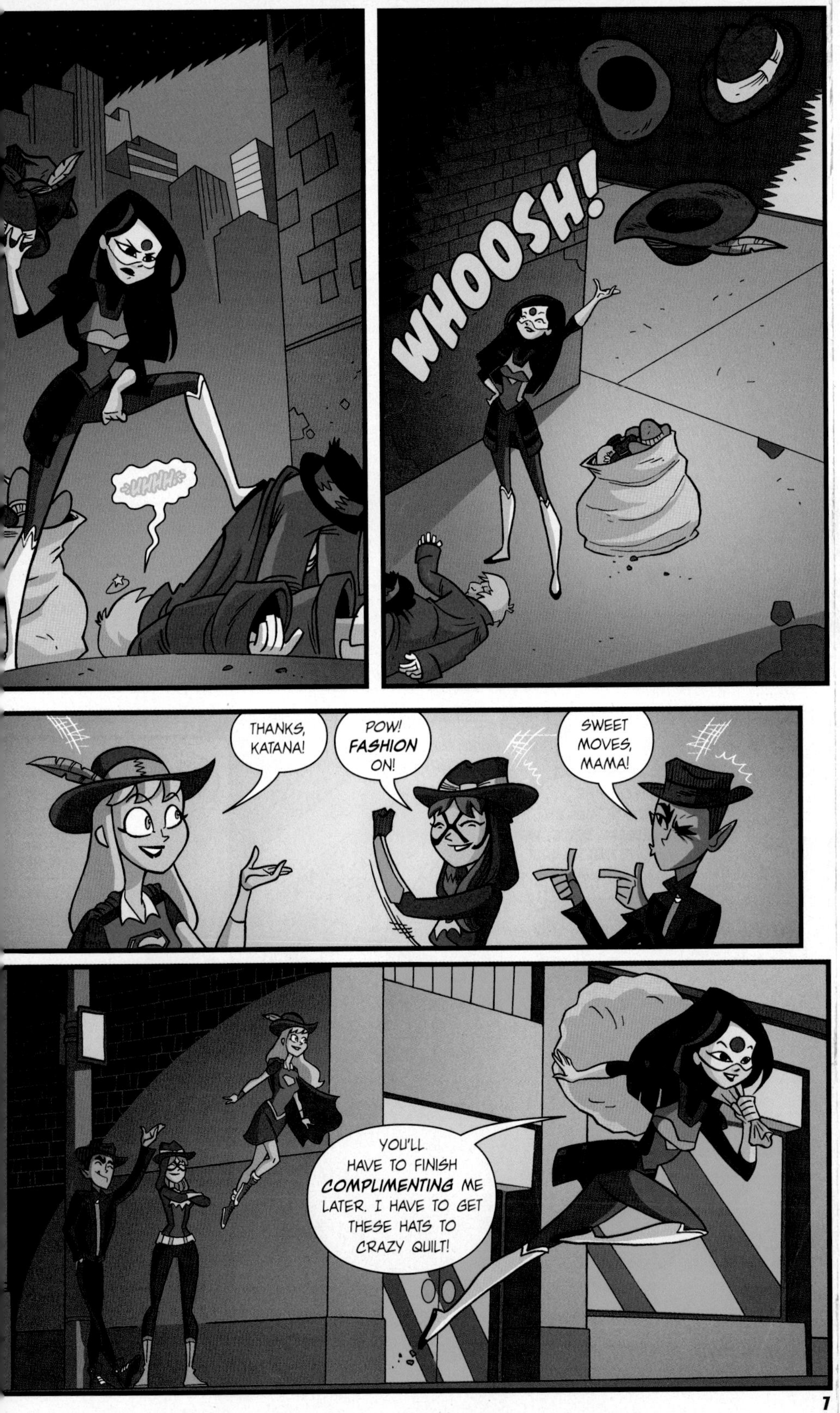
WHOOSH!
THANKS, KATANA!
POW! FASHION ON!
SWEET MOVES, MAMA!
YOU'LL HAVE TO FINISH COMPLIMENTING ME LATER. I HAVE TO GET THESE HATS TO CRAZY QUILT!

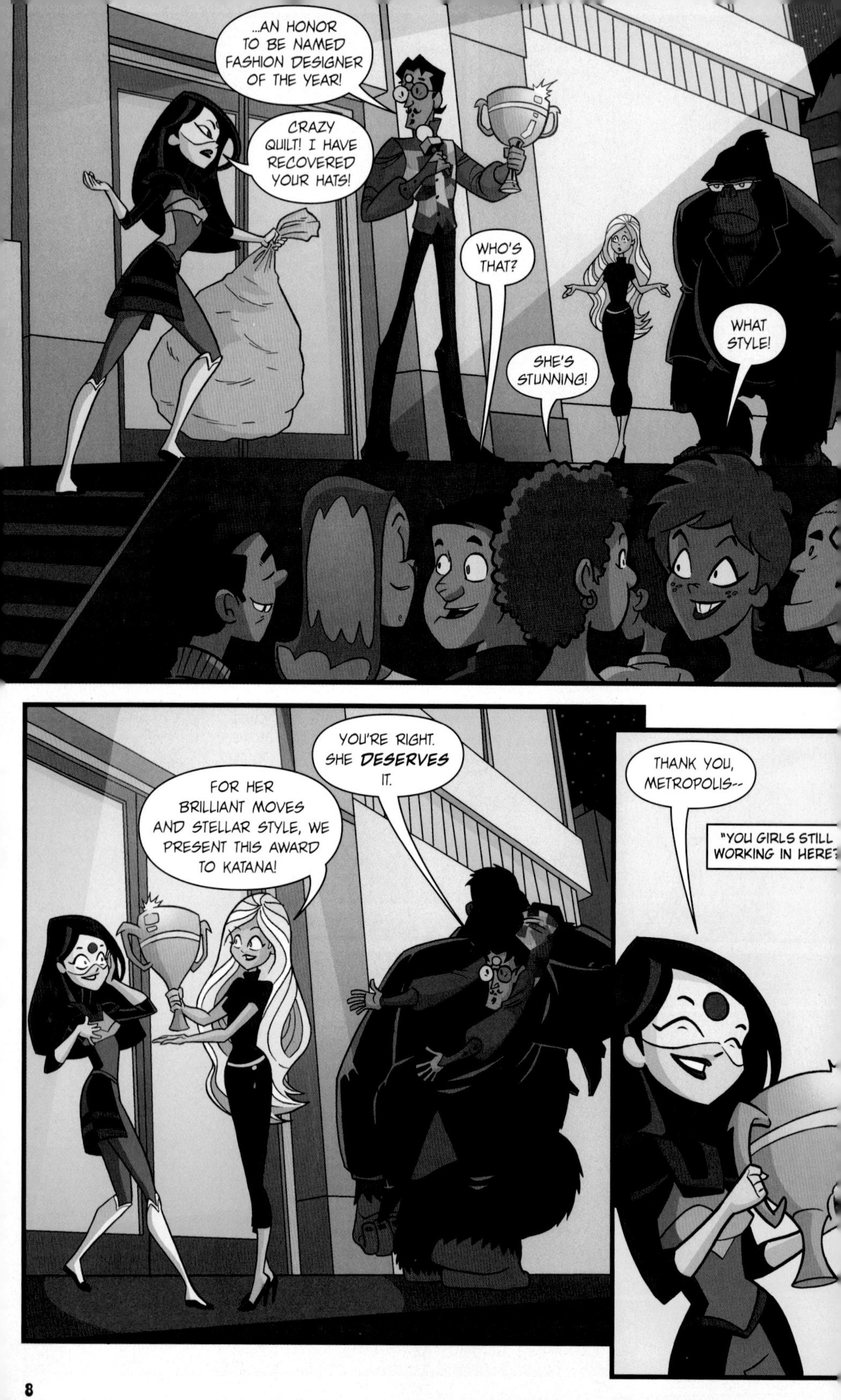

...AN HONOR TO BE NAMED FASHION DESIGNER OF THE YEAR!
CRAZY QUILT! I HAVE RECOVERED YOUR HATS!
WHO'S THAT?
SHE'S STUNNING!
WHAT STYLE!
FOR HER BRILLIANT MOVES AND STELLAR STYLE, WE PRESENT THIS AWARD TO KATANA!
YOU'RE RIGHT. SHE **DESERVES** IT.
THANK YOU, METROPOLIS--
"YOU GIRLS STILL WORKING IN HERE?

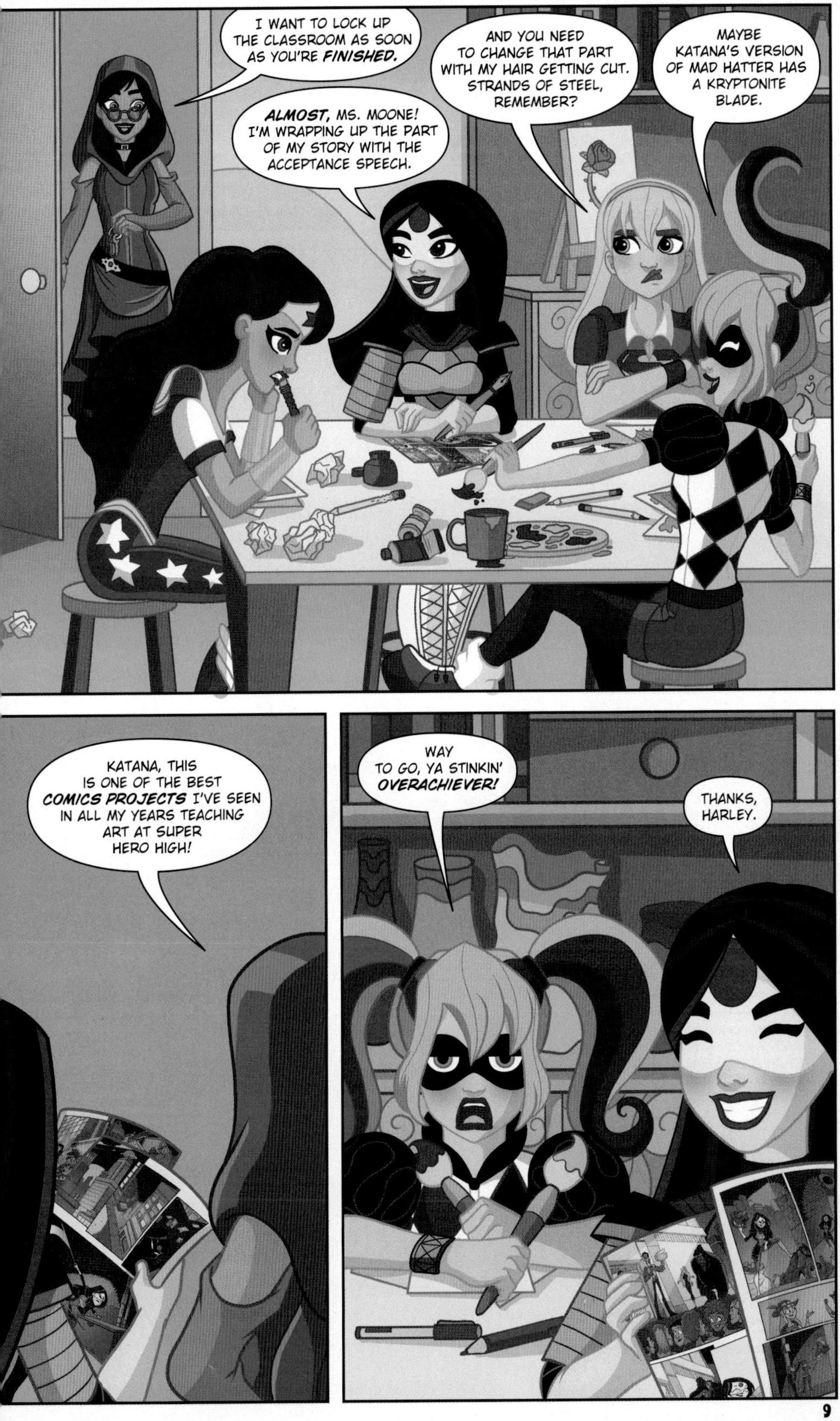
I WANT TO LOCK UP THE CLASSROOM AS SOON AS YOU'RE FINISHED.
ALMOST, MS. MOONE! I'M WRAPPING UP THE PART OF MY STORY WITH THE ACCEPTANCE SPEECH.
AND YOU NEED TO CHANGE THAT PART WITH MY HAIR GETTING CUT. STRANDS OF STEEL, REMEMBER?
MAYBE KATANA'S VERSION OF MAD HATTER HAS A KRYPTONITE BLADE.
KATANA, THIS IS ONE OF THE BEST COMICS PROJECTS I'VE SEEN IN ALL MY YEARS TEACHING ART AT SUPER HERO HIGH!
WAY TO GO, YA STINKIN' OVERACHIEVER!
THANKS, HARLEY.

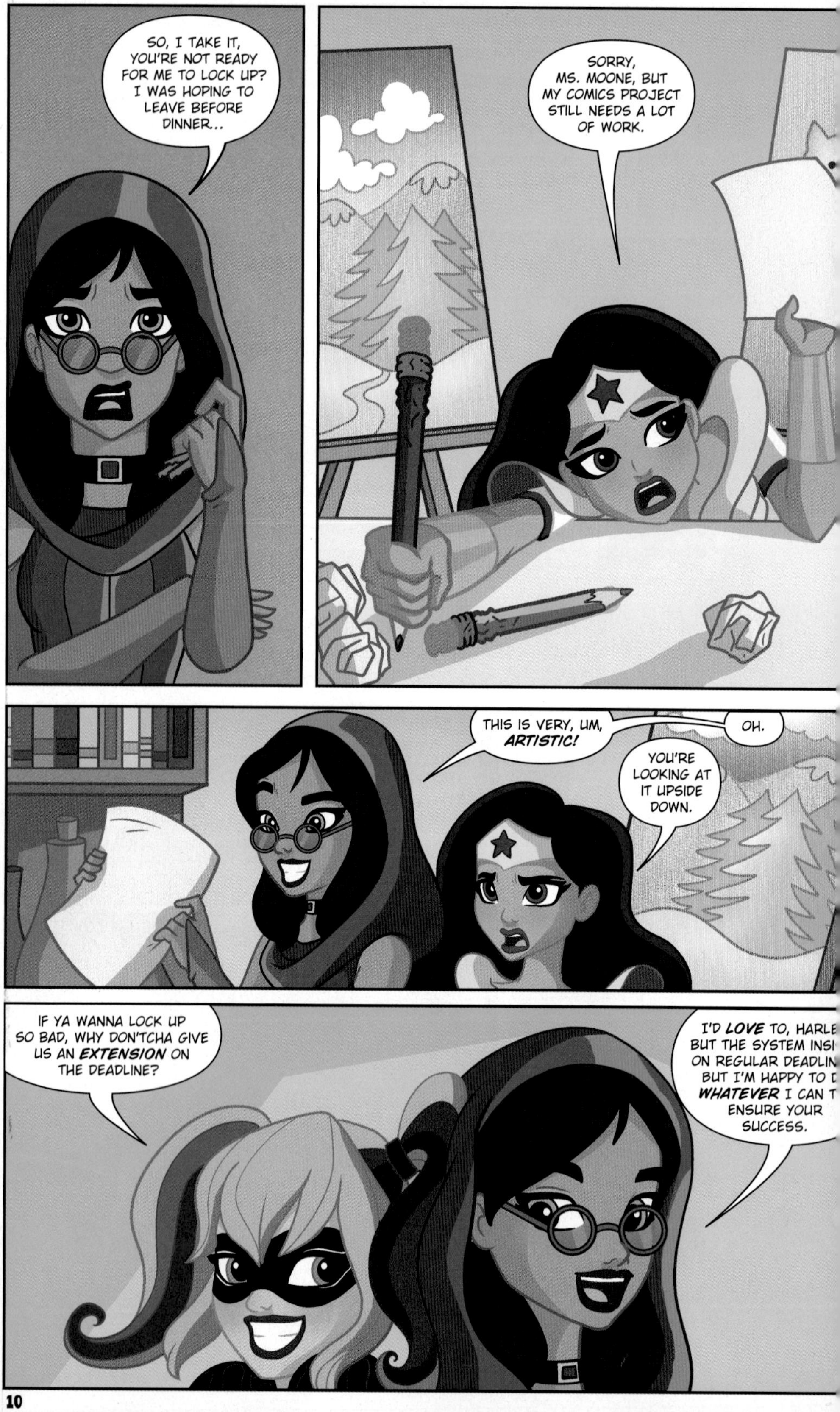
SO, I TAKE IT, YOU'RE NOT READY FOR ME TO LOCK UP? I WAS HOPING TO LEAVE BEFORE DINNER...
SORRY, MS. MOONE, BUT MY COMICS PROJECT STILL NEEDS A LOT OF WORK.
THIS IS VERY, UM, ***ARTISTIC!***
OH.
YOU'RE LOOKING AT IT UPSIDE DOWN.
IF YA WANNA LOCK UP SO BAD, WHY DON'TCHA GIVE US AN ***EXTENSION*** ON THE DEADLINE?
I'D ***LOVE*** TO, HARLE BUT THE SYSTEM INSI ON REGULAR DEADLIN BUT I'M HAPPY TO D ***WHATEVER*** I CAN T ENSURE YOUR SUCCESS.

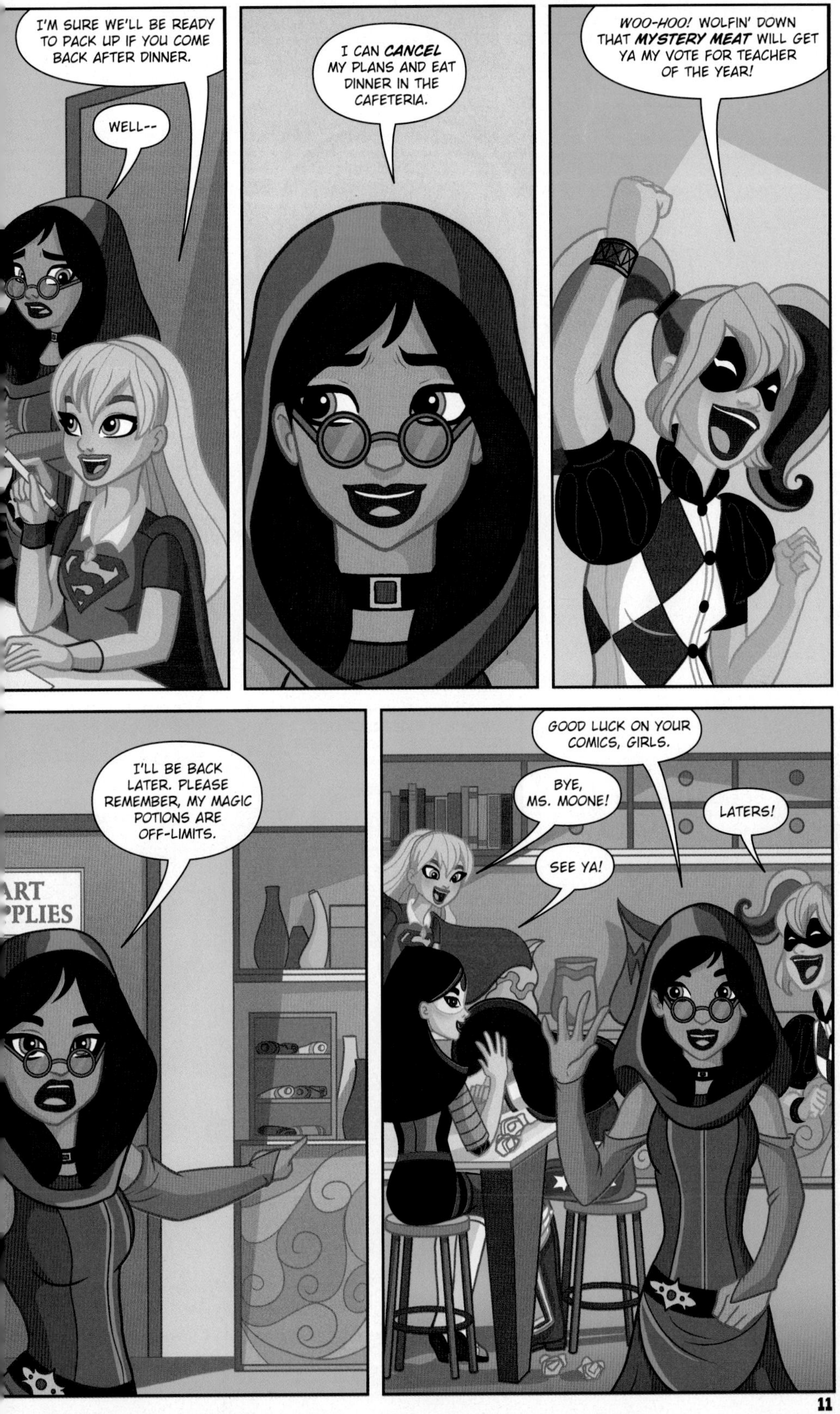
I'M SURE WE'LL BE READY TO PACK UP IF YOU COME BACK AFTER DINNER.
WELL--
I CAN **CANCEL** MY PLANS AND EAT DINNER IN THE CAFETERIA.
WOO-HOO! WOLFIN' DOWN THAT ***MYSTERY MEAT*** WILL GET YA MY VOTE FOR TEACHER OF THE YEAR!
I'LL BE BACK LATER. PLEASE REMEMBER, MY MAGIC POTIONS ARE OFF-LIMITS.
ART
PLIES
GOOD LUCK ON YOUR COMICS, GIRLS.
BYE, MS. MOONE!
SEE YA!
LATERS!

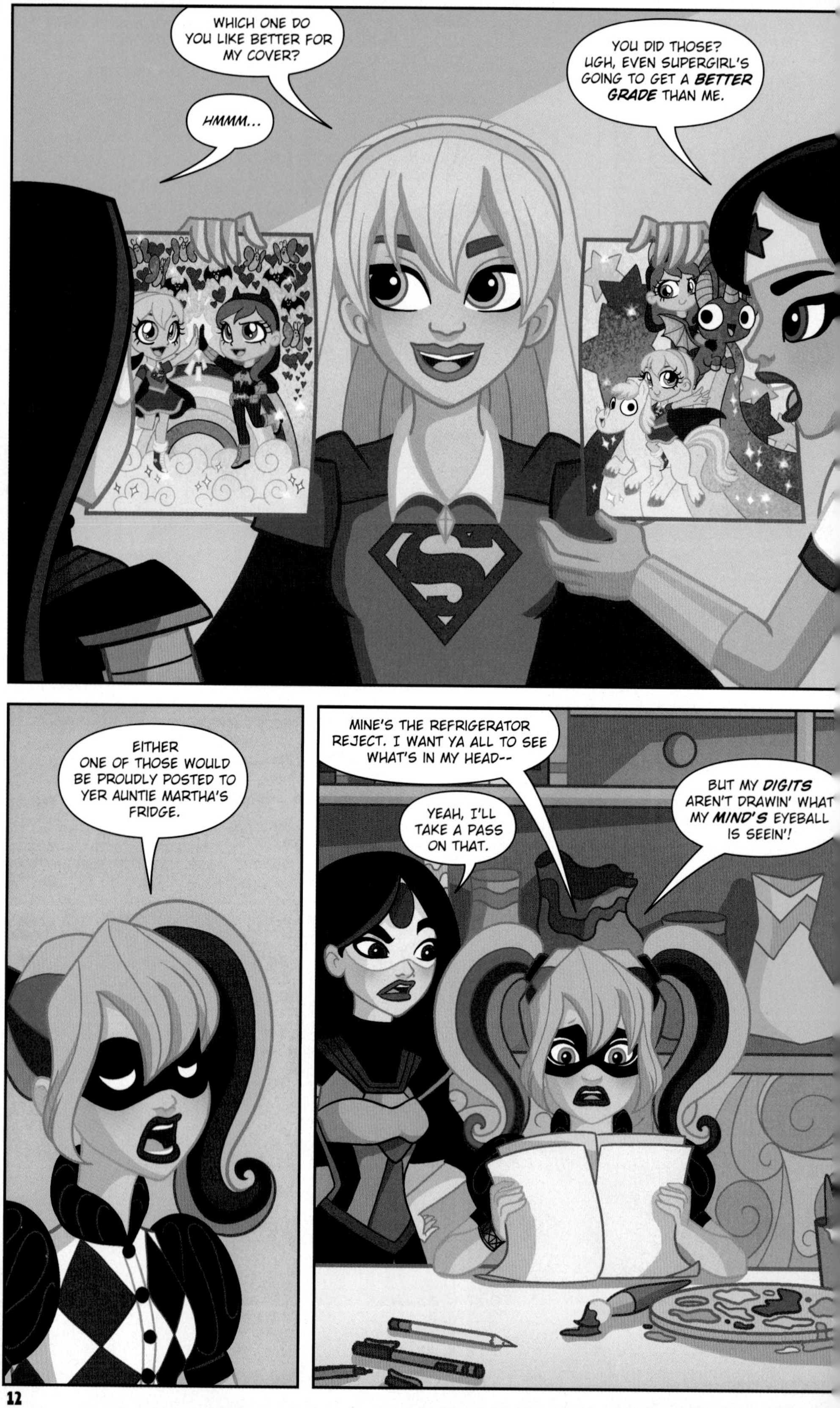
WHICH ONE DO YOU LIKE BETTER FOR MY COVER?
HMMM...
YOU DID THOSE? UGH, EVEN SUPERGIRL'S GOING TO GET A ***BETTER GRADE*** THAN ME.
EITHER ONE OF THOSE WOULD BE PROUDLY POSTED TO YER AUNTIE MARTHA'S FRIDGE.
MINE'S THE REFRIGERATOR REJECT. I WANT YA ALL TO SEE WHAT'S IN MY HEAD--
YEAH, I'LL TAKE A PASS ON THAT.
BUT MY ***DIGITS*** AREN'T DRAWIN' WHAT MY ***MIND'S*** EYEBALL IS SEEIN'!

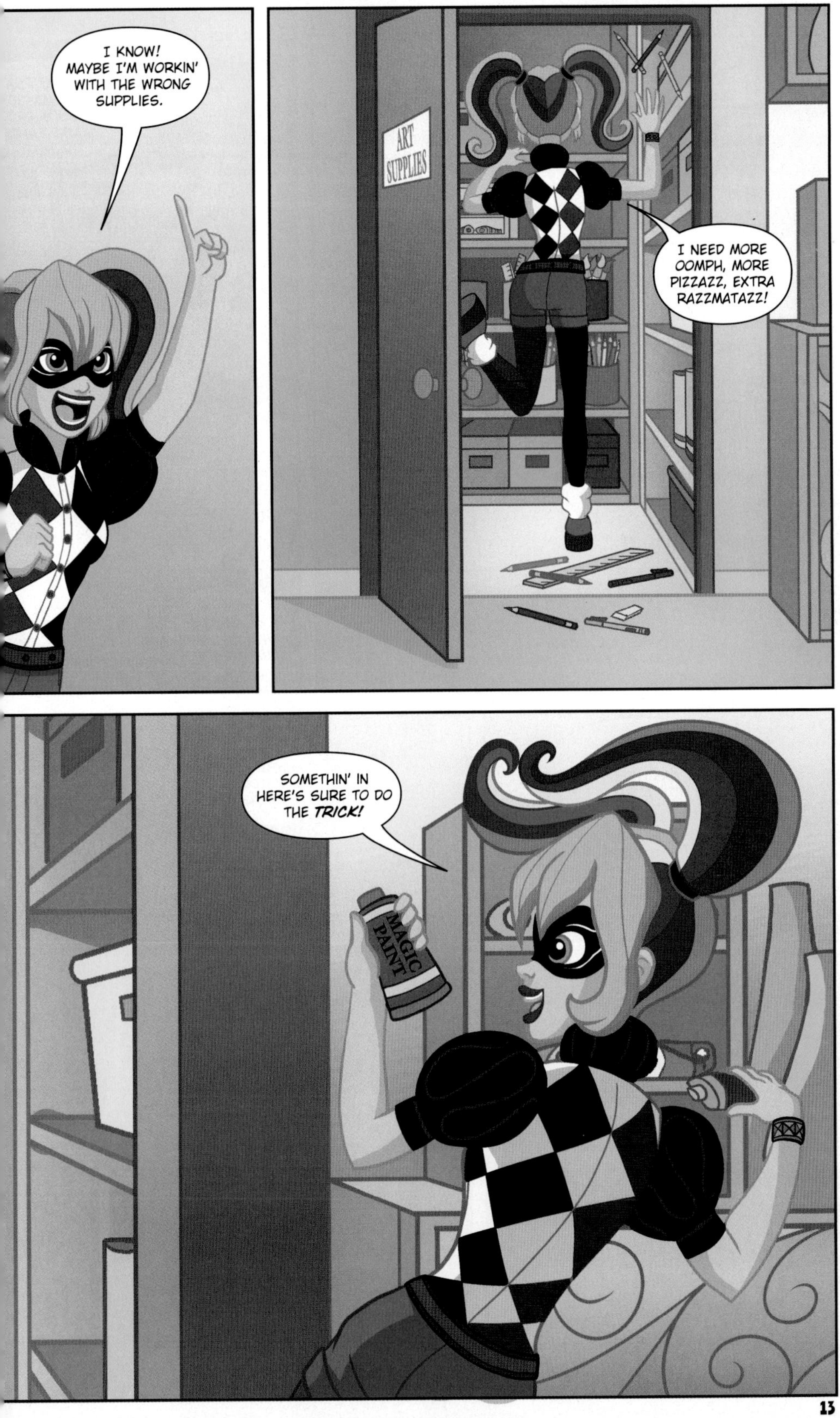
I KNOW! MAYBE I'M WORKIN' WITH THE WRONG SUPPLIES.
ART SUPPLIES
I NEED MORE OOMPH, MORE PIZZAZZ, EXTRA RAZZMATAZZ!
SOMETHIN' IN HERE'S SURE TO DO THE *TRICK!*
MAGIC PAINT

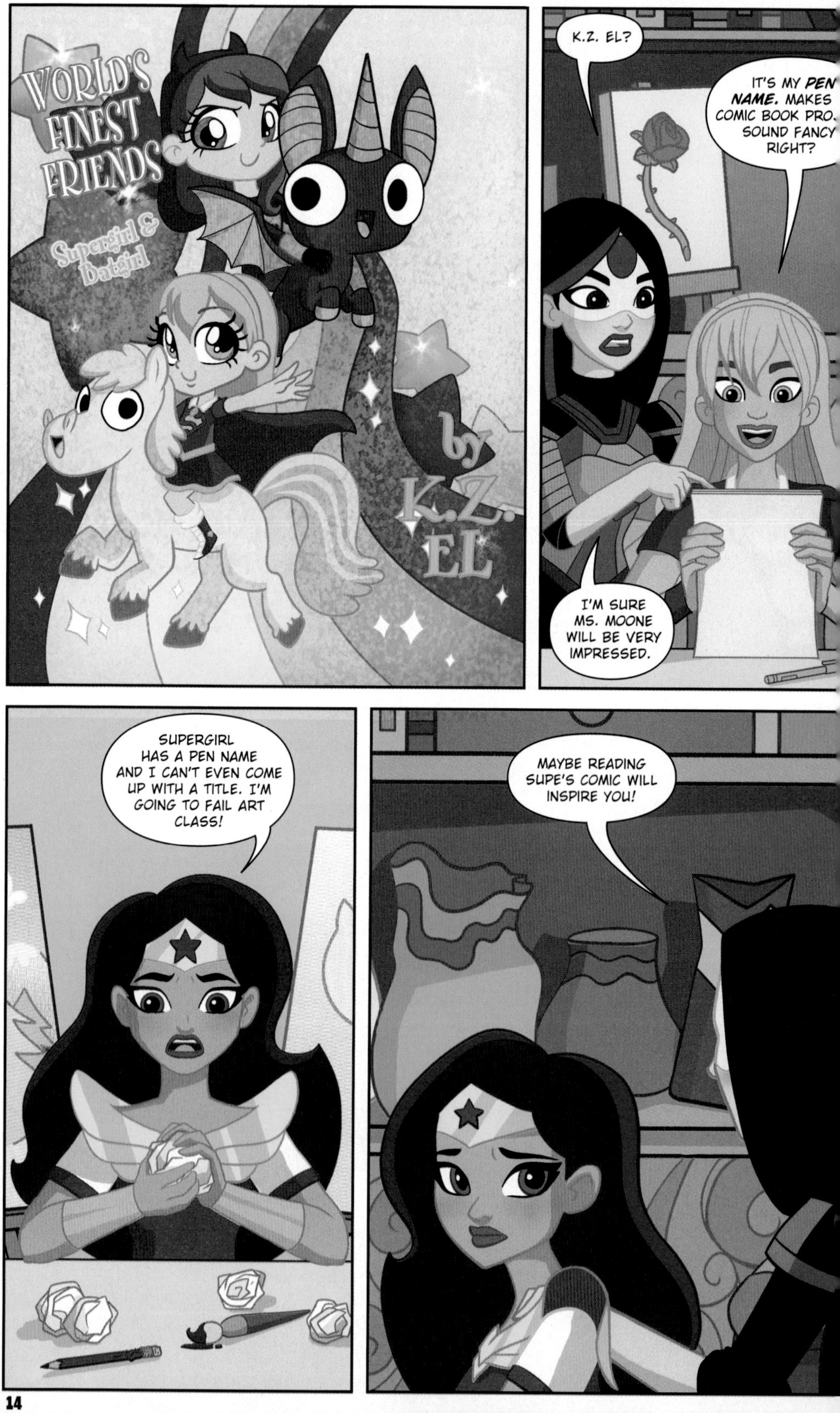
WORLD'S FINEST FRIENDS
Supergirl & Batgirl
by K.Z. EL
K.Z. EL?
IT'S MY **PEN NAME.** MAKES COMIC BOOK PRO. SOUND FANCY RIGHT?
I'M SURE MS. MOONE WILL BE VERY IMPRESSED.
SUPERGIRL HAS A PEN NAME AND I CAN'T EVEN COME UP WITH A TITLE. I'M GOING TO FAIL ART CLASS!
MAYBE READING SUPE'S COMIC WILL INSPIRE YOU!

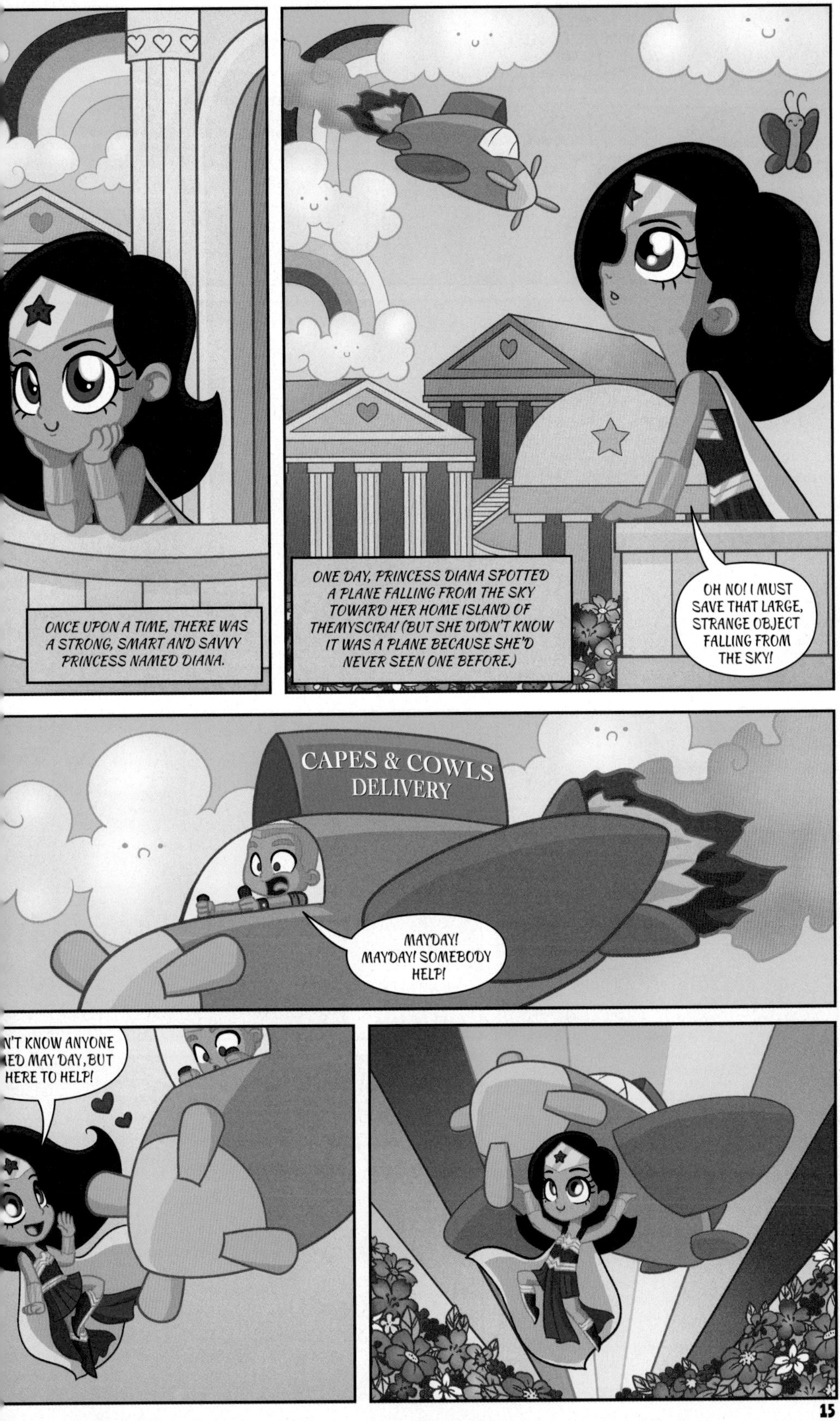
ONCE UPON A TIME, THERE WAS A STRONG, SMART AND SAVVY PRINCESS NAMED DIANA.
ONE DAY, PRINCESS DIANA SPOTTED A PLANE FALLING FROM THE SKY TOWARD HER HOME ISLAND OF THEMYSCIRA! (BUT SHE DIDN'T KNOW IT WAS A PLANE BECAUSE SHE'D NEVER SEEN ONE BEFORE.)
OH NO! I MUST SAVE THAT LARGE, STRANGE OBJECT FALLING FROM THE SKY!
CAPES & COWLS DELIVERY
MAYDAY! MAYDAY! SOMEBODY HELP!
N'T KNOW ANYONE
ED MAY DAY, BUT
HERE TO HELP!

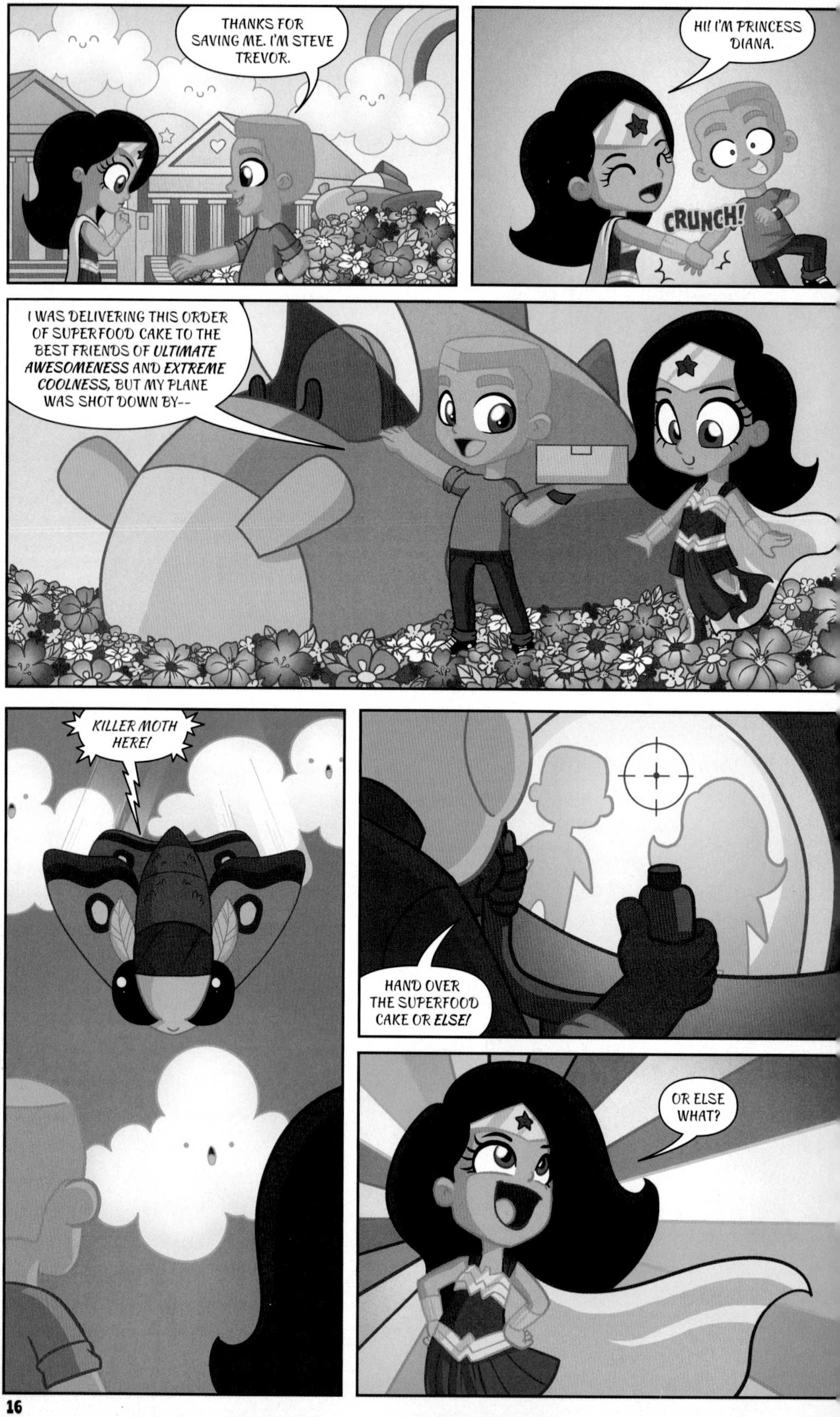
THANKS FOR SAVING ME. I'M STEVE TREVOR.
HI! I'M PRINCESS DIANA.
CRUNCH!
I WAS DELIVERING THIS ORDER OF SUPERFOOD CAKE TO THE BEST FRIENDS OF *ULTIMATE AWESOMENESS* AND *EXTREME COOLNESS*, BUT MY PLANE WAS SHOT DOWN BY--
KILLER MOTH HERE!
HAND OVER THE SUPERFOOD CAKE OR *ELSE!*
OR ELSE WHAT?

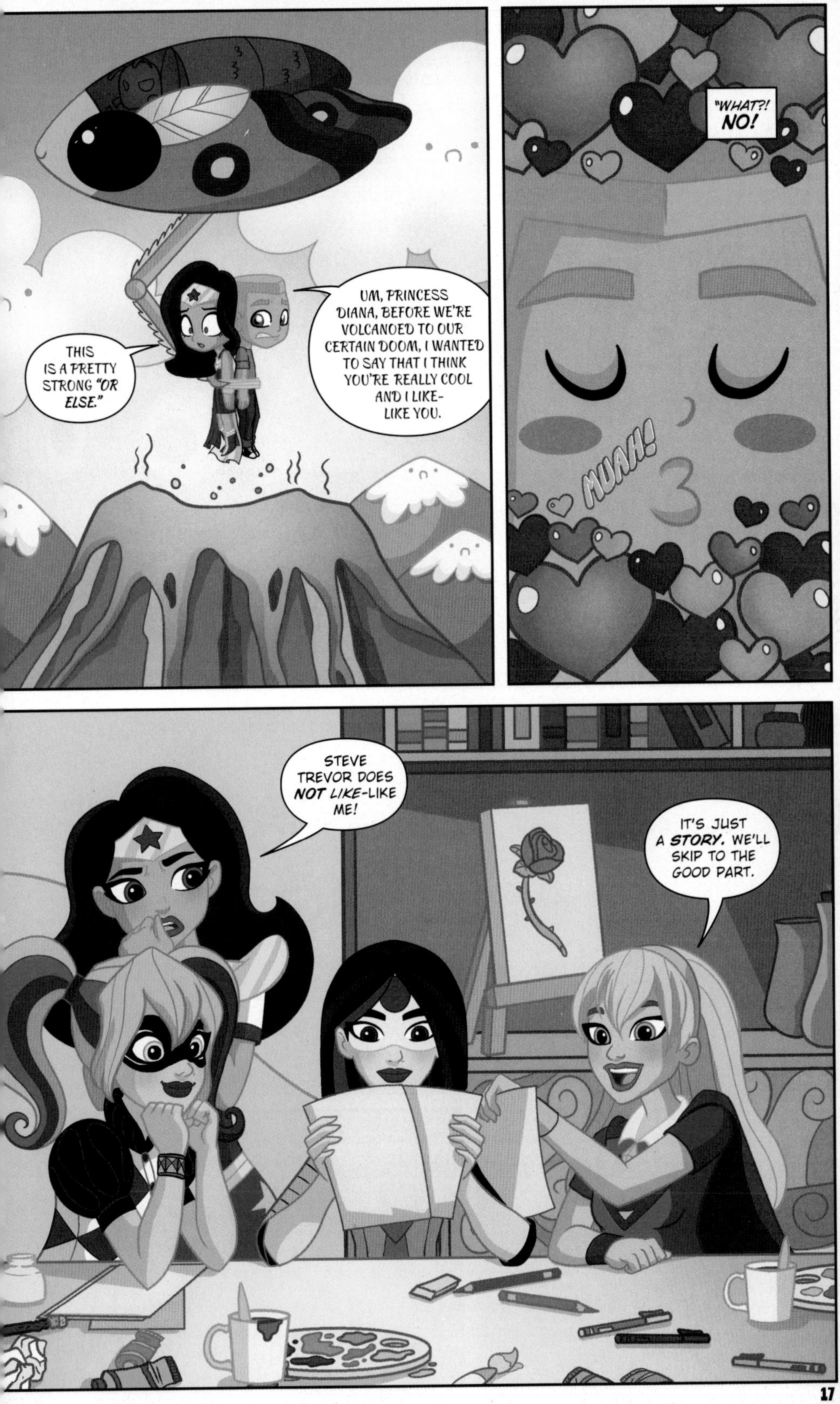
UM, PRINCESS DIANA, BEFORE WE'RE VOLCANOED TO OUR CERTAIN DOOM, I WANTED TO SAY THAT I THINK YOU'RE REALLY COOL AND I LIKE-LIKE YOU.
THIS IS A PRETTY STRONG *"OR ELSE."*
"WHAT?! **NO!**
MUAH!
STEVE TREVOR DOES ***NOT*** *LIKE*-LIKE ME!
IT'S JUST A ***STORY.*** WE'LL SKIP TO THE GOOD PART.

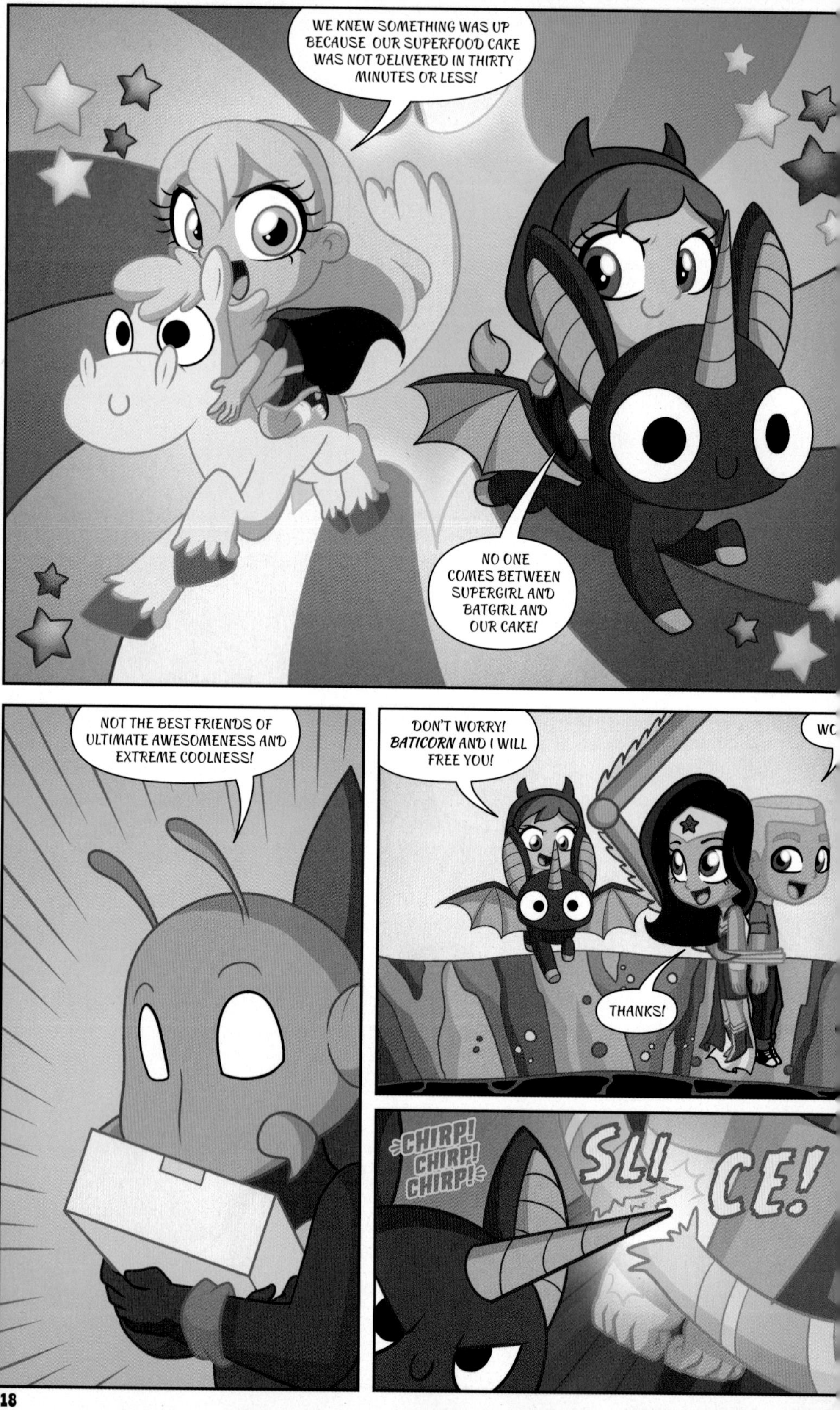

WE KNEW SOMETHING WAS UP BECAUSE OUR SUPERFOOD CAKE WAS NOT DELIVERED IN THIRTY MINUTES OR LESS!
NO ONE COMES BETWEEN SUPERGIRL AND BATGIRL AND OUR CAKE!
NOT THE BEST FRIENDS OF ULTIMATE AWESOMENESS AND EXTREME COOLNESS!
DON'T WORRY! *BATICORN* AND I WILL FREE YOU!
THANKS!
CHIRP! CHIRP! CHIRP!
SLI CE!

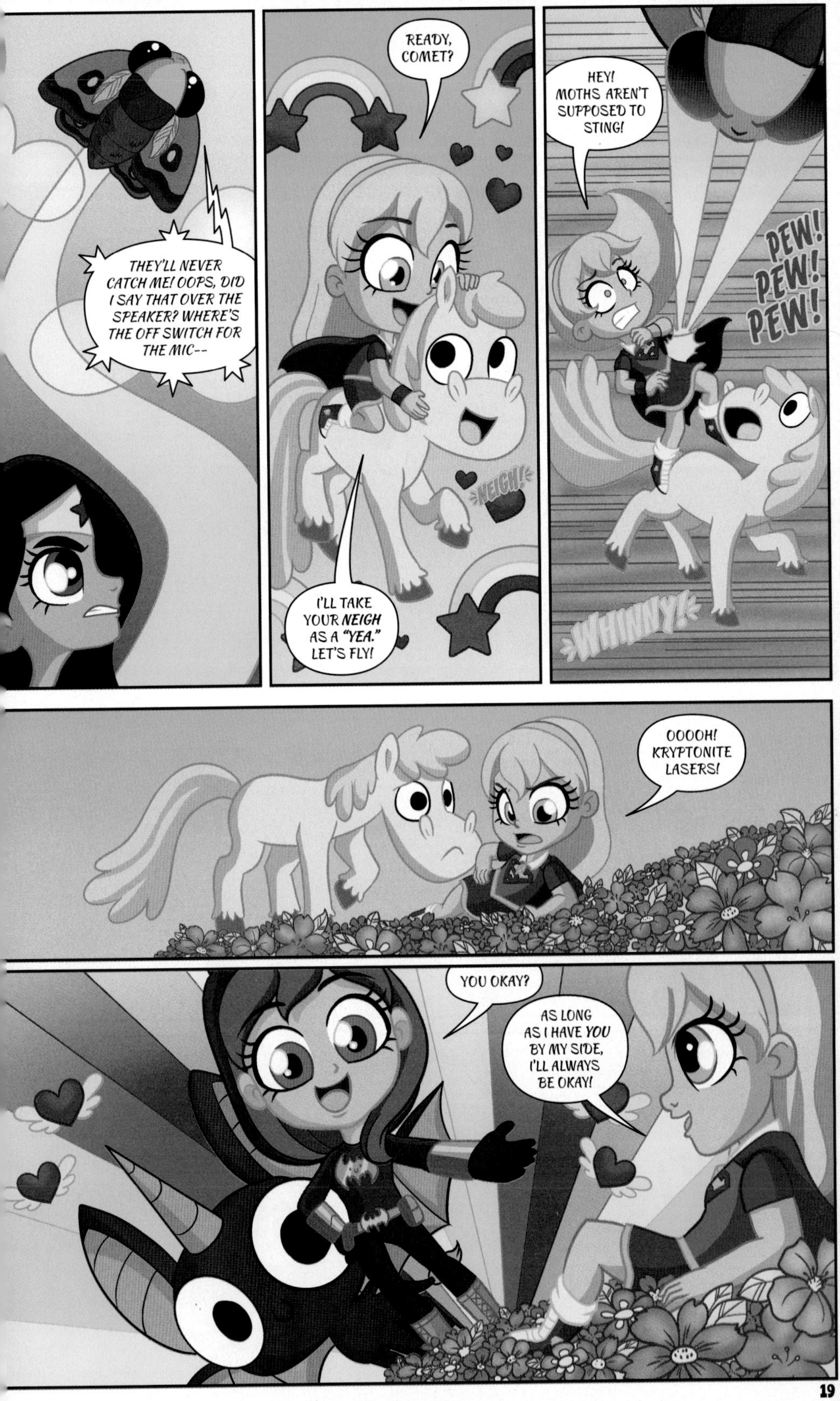
THEY'LL NEVER CATCH ME! OOPS, DID I SAY THAT OVER THE SPEAKER? WHERE'S THE OFF SWITCH FOR THE MIC--
READY, COMET?
NEIGH!
I'LL TAKE YOUR *NEIGH* AS A *"YEA."* LET'S FLY!
HEY! MOTHS AREN'T SUPPOSED TO STING!
PEW! PEW! PEW!
WHINNY!
OOOOH! KRYPTONITE LASERS!
YOU OKAY?
AS LONG AS I HAVE *YOU* BY MY SIDE, I'LL ALWAYS BE OKAY!

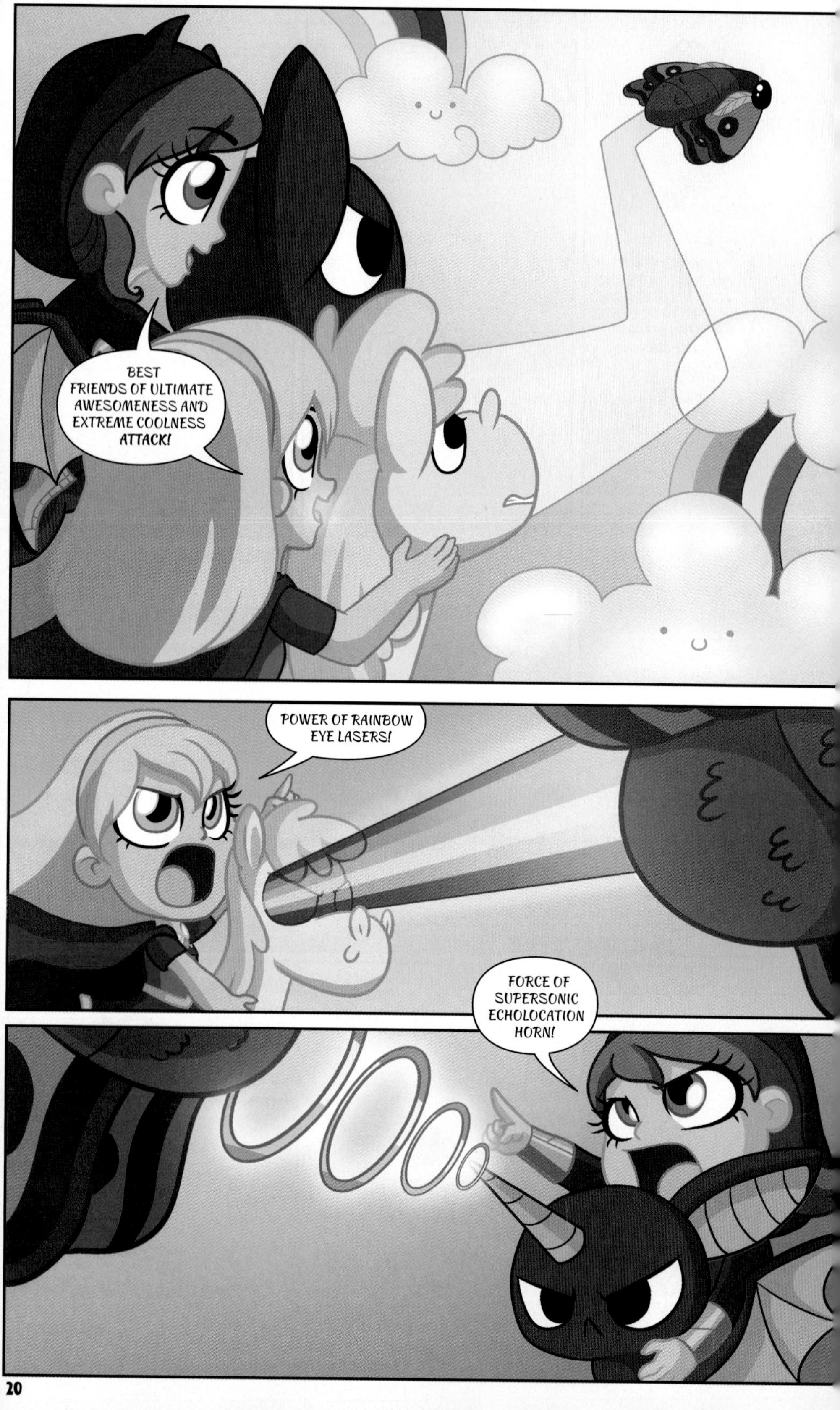
BEST FRIENDS OF ULTIMATE AWESOMENESS AND EXTREME COOLNESS ATTACK!
POWER OF RAINBOW EYE LASERS!
FORCE OF SUPERSONIC ECHOLOCATION HORN!

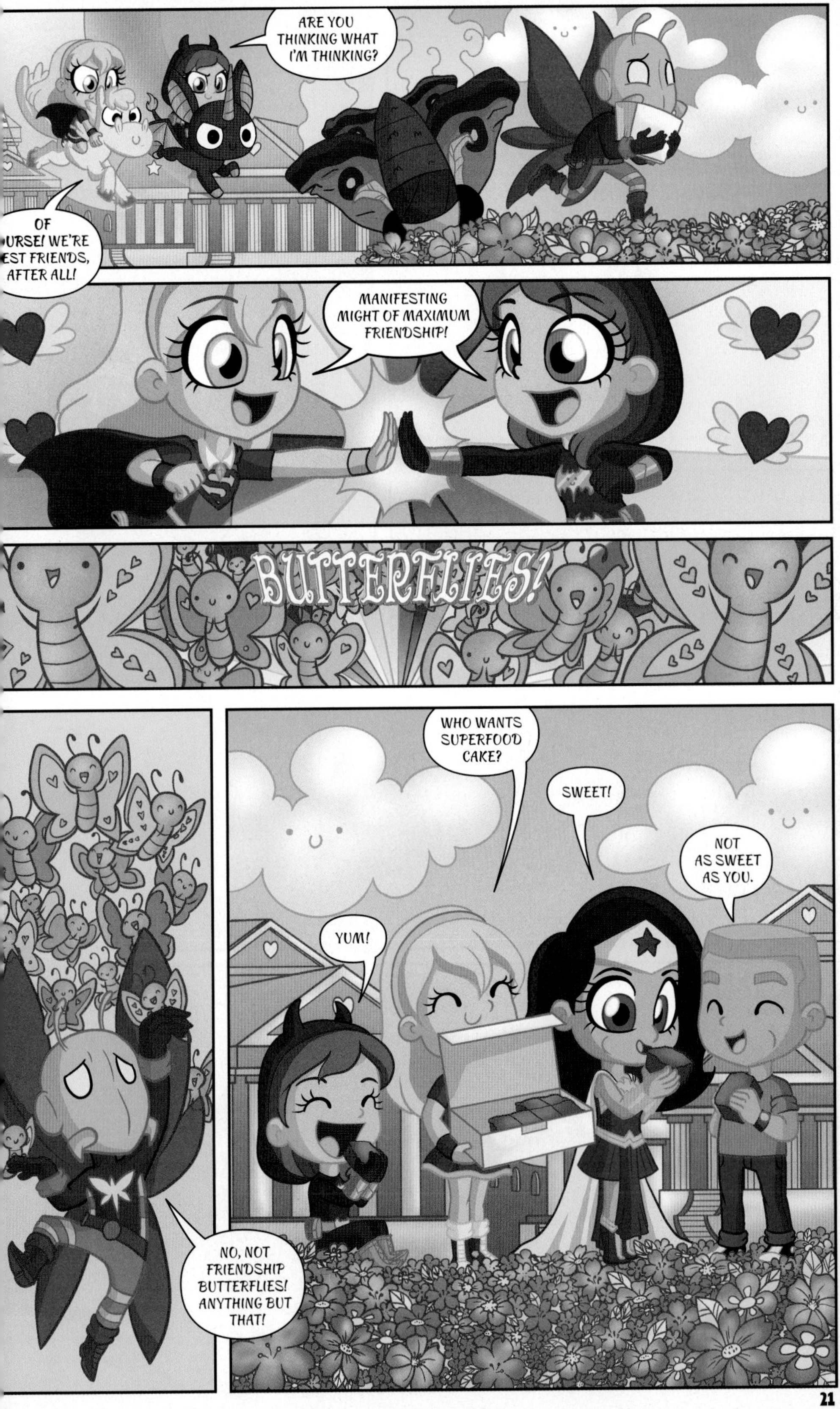
ARE YOU THINKING WHAT I'M THINKING?
OF URSE! WE'RE EST FRIENDS, AFTER ALL!
MANIFESTING MIGHT OF MAXIMUM FRIENDSHIP!
BUTTERFLIES!
NO, NOT FRIENDSHIP BUTTERFLIES! ANYTHING BUT THAT!
WHO WANTS SUPERFOOD CAKE?
SWEET!
NOT AS SWEET AS YOU.
YUM!

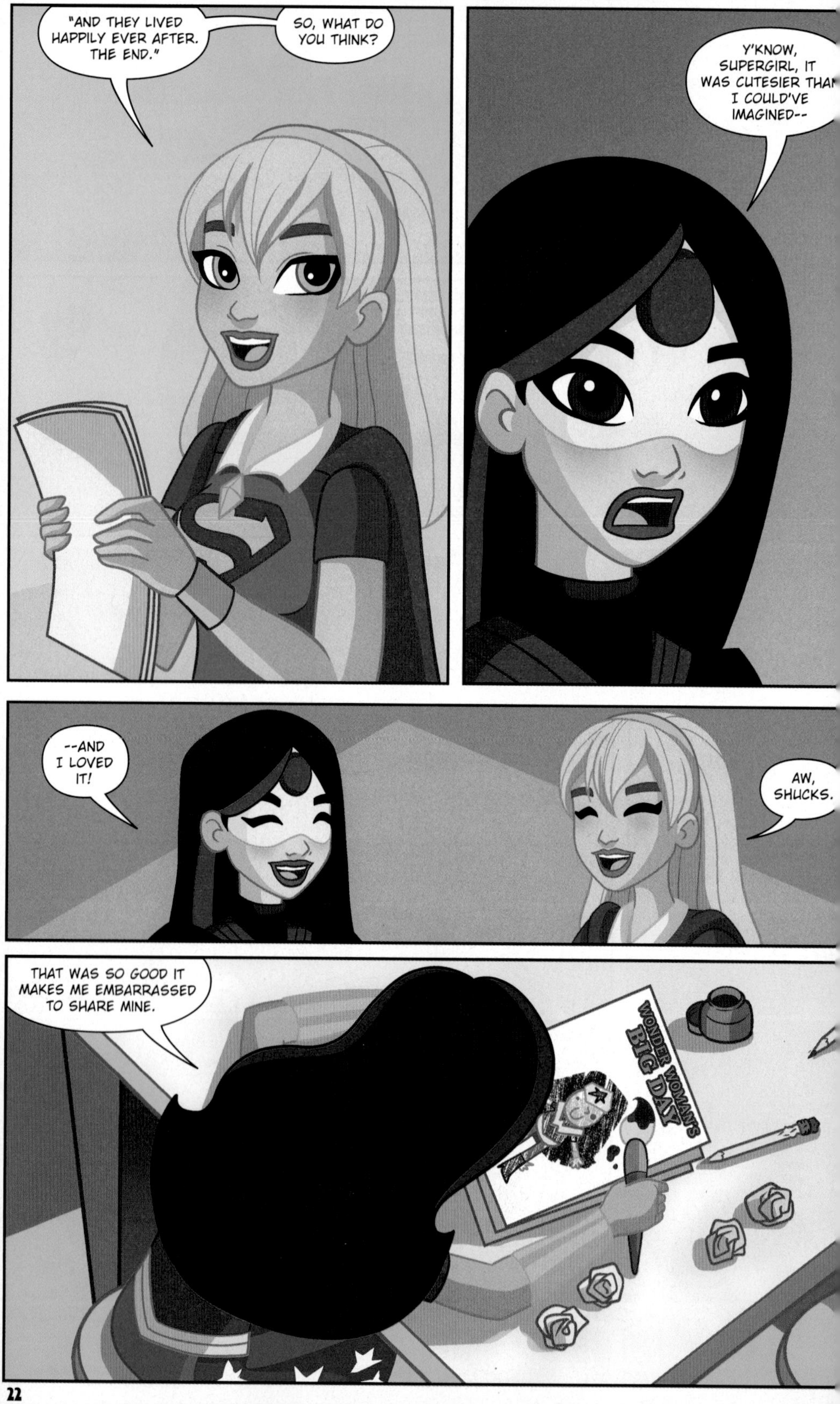
"AND THEY LIVED HAPPILY EVER AFTER. THE END."
SO, WHAT DO YOU THINK?
Y'KNOW, SUPERGIRL, IT WAS CUTESIER THAN I COULD'VE IMAGINED--
--AND I LOVED IT!
AW, SHUCKS.
THAT WAS SO GOOD IT MAKES ME EMBARRASSED TO SHARE MINE.
WONDER WOMAN'S BIG DAY

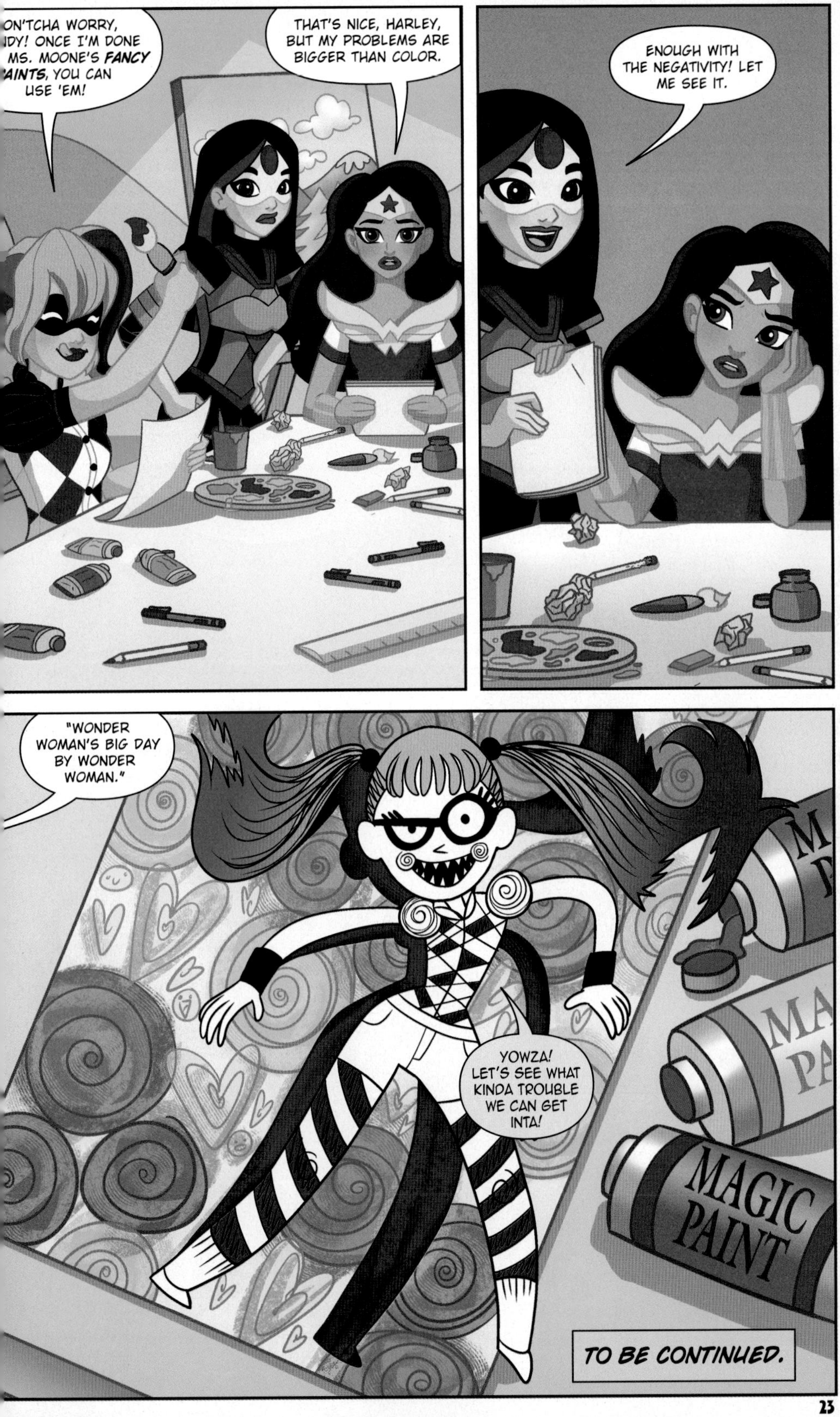

ON'TCHA WORRY, NDY! ONCE I'M DONE MS. MOONE'S FANCY AINTS, YOU CAN USE 'EM!
THAT'S NICE, HARLEY, BUT MY PROBLEMS ARE BIGGER THAN COLOR.
ENOUGH WITH THE NEGATIVITY! LET ME SEE IT.
"WONDER WOMAN'S BIG DAY BY WONDER WOMAN."
YOWZA! LET'S SEE WHAT KINDA TROUBLE WE CAN GET INTA!
MAGIC PAINT
TO BE CONTINUED.

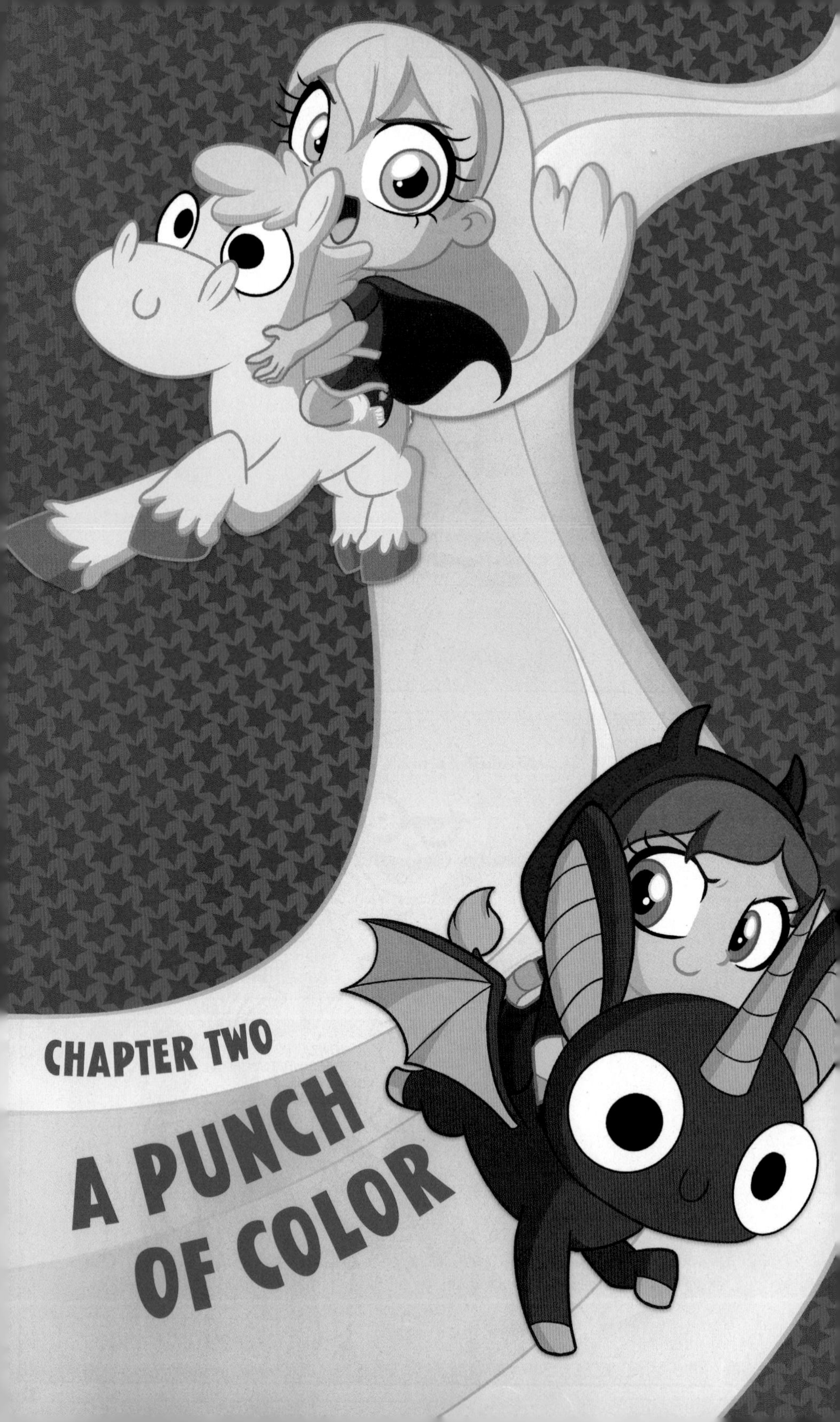

CHAPTER TWO

A PUNCH OF COLOR

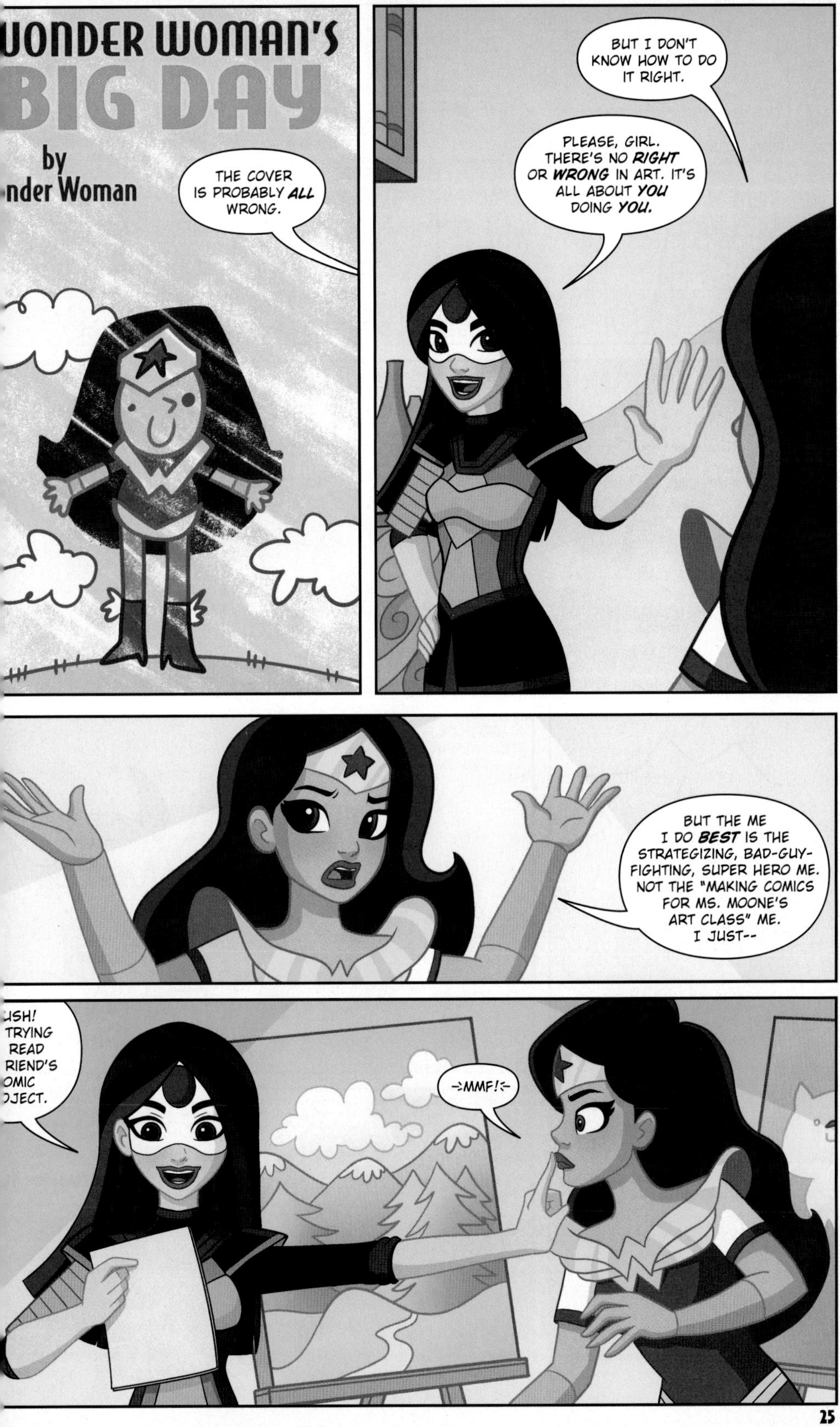
ONDER WOMAN'S
BIG DAY
by
nder Woman
THE COVER IS PROBABLY *ALL* WRONG.
BUT I DON'T KNOW HOW TO DO IT RIGHT.
PLEASE, GIRL. THERE'S NO *RIGHT* OR *WRONG* IN ART. IT'S ALL ABOUT *YOU* DOING *YOU.*
BUT THE ME I DO *BEST* IS THE STRATEGIZING, BAD-GUY-FIGHTING, SUPER HERO ME. NOT THE "MAKING COMICS FOR MS. MOONE'S ART CLASS" ME. I JUST--
USH! TRYING READ RIEND'S OMIC OJECT.
MMF!

I AM WONDER WOMAN. I AM A SUPER HERO.

LOOK! THERE ARE SUPER VILLAINS WHO THREATEN THE CITY OF METROPOLIS!

POW!

TAKE *THAT*, MRS. CLAYFACE!

GO BACK TO THE *UNDERWORLD*, TRIGON!

BAM!

BUSTED

ECLIPS(AND DARK (YOU'RE GO TO JAIL

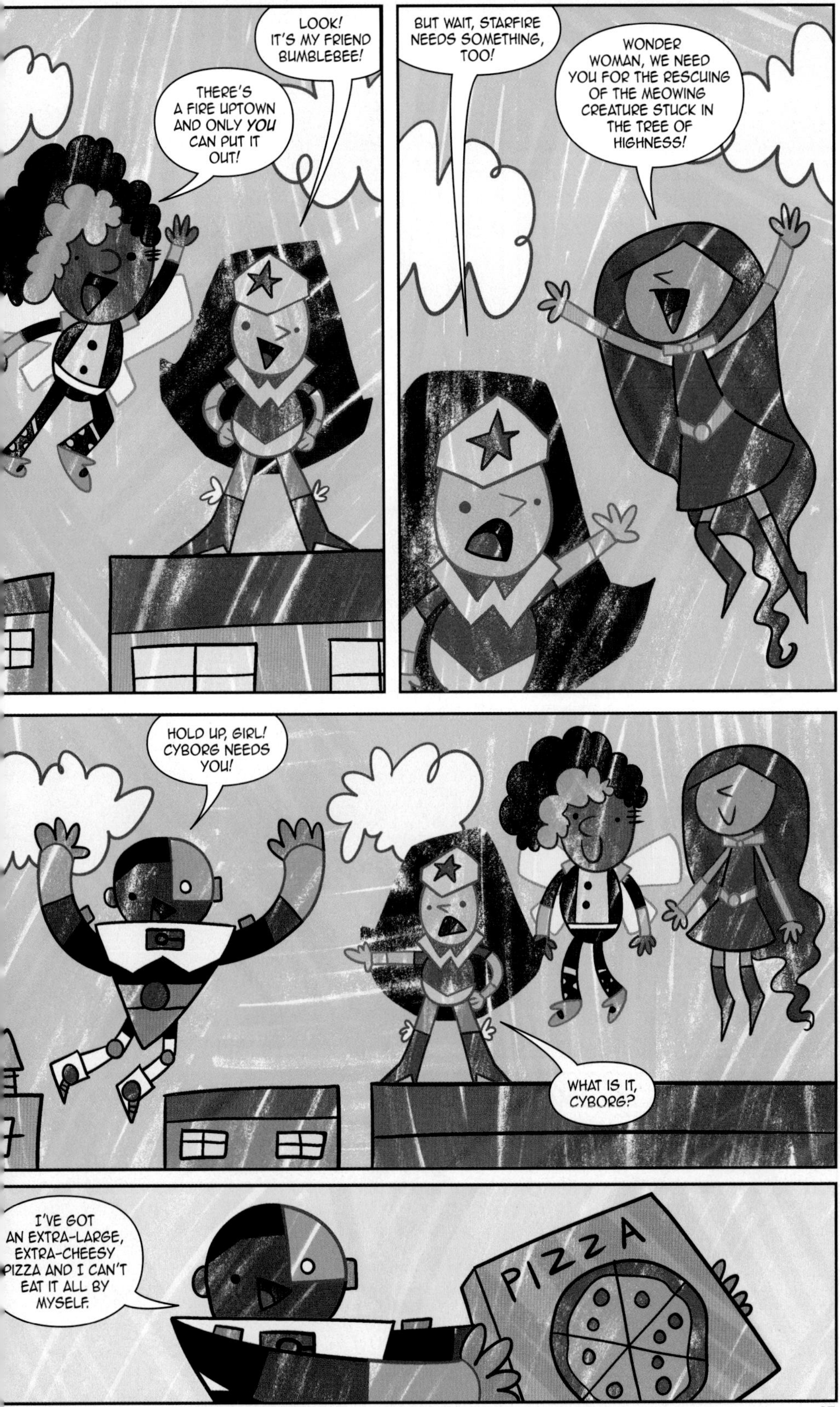
LOOK! IT'S MY FRIEND BUMBLEBEE!
THERE'S A FIRE UPTOWN AND ONLY *YOU* CAN PUT IT OUT!
BUT WAIT, STARFIRE NEEDS SOMETHING, TOO!
WONDER WOMAN, WE NEED YOU FOR THE RESCUING OF THE MEOWING CREATURE STUCK IN THE TREE OF HIGHNESS!
HOLD UP, GIRL! CYBORG NEEDS YOU!
WHAT IS IT, CYBORG?
I'VE GOT AN EXTRA-LARGE, EXTRA-CHEESY PIZZA AND I CAN'T EAT IT ALL BY MYSELF.
PIZZA

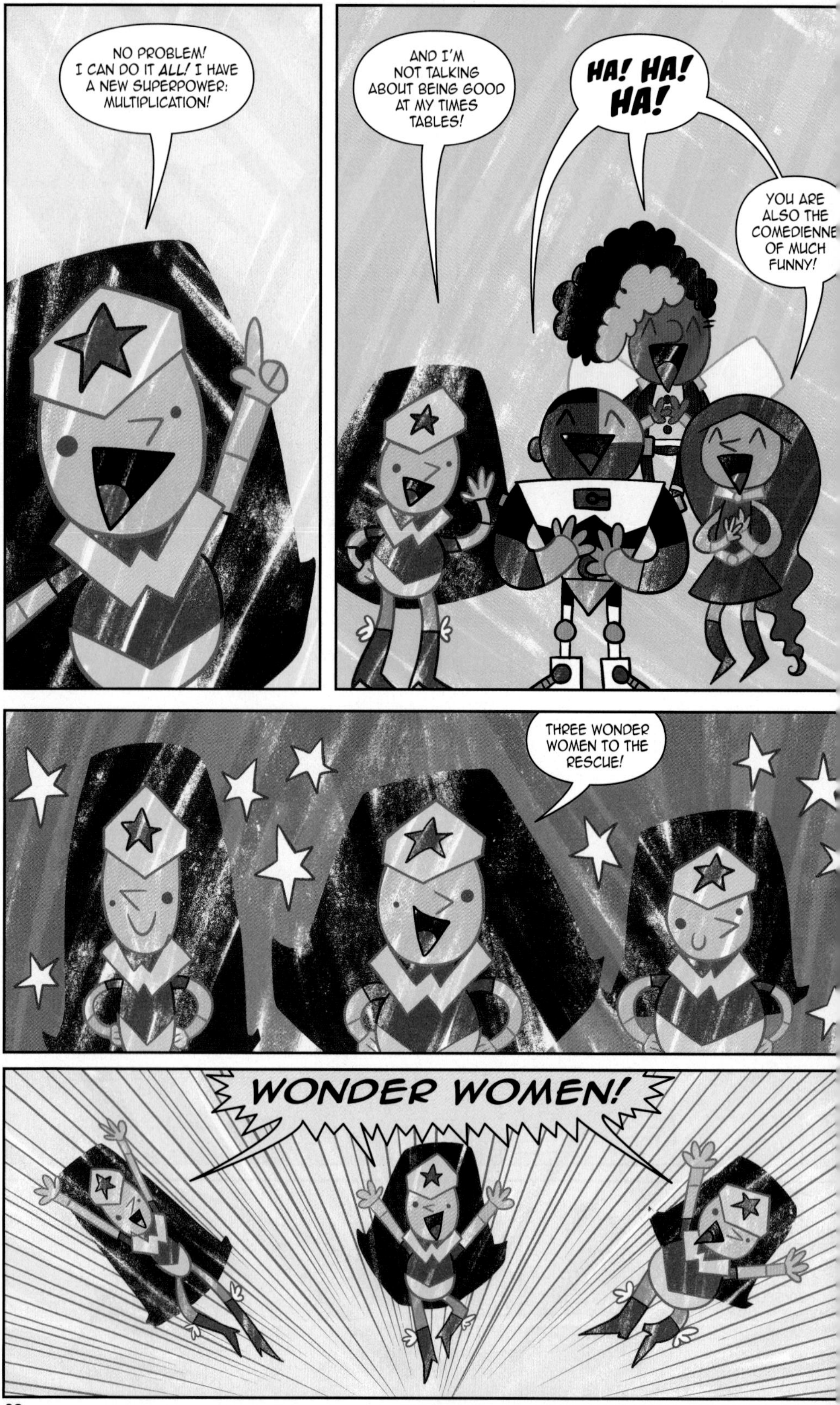

NO PROBLEM! I CAN DO IT ALL! I HAVE A NEW SUPERPOWER: MULTIPLICATION!
AND I'M NOT TALKING ABOUT BEING GOOD AT MY TIMES TABLES!
HA! HA! HA!
YOU ARE ALSO THE COMEDIENNE OF MUCH FUNNY!
THREE WONDER WOMEN TO THE RESCUE!
WONDER WOMEN!

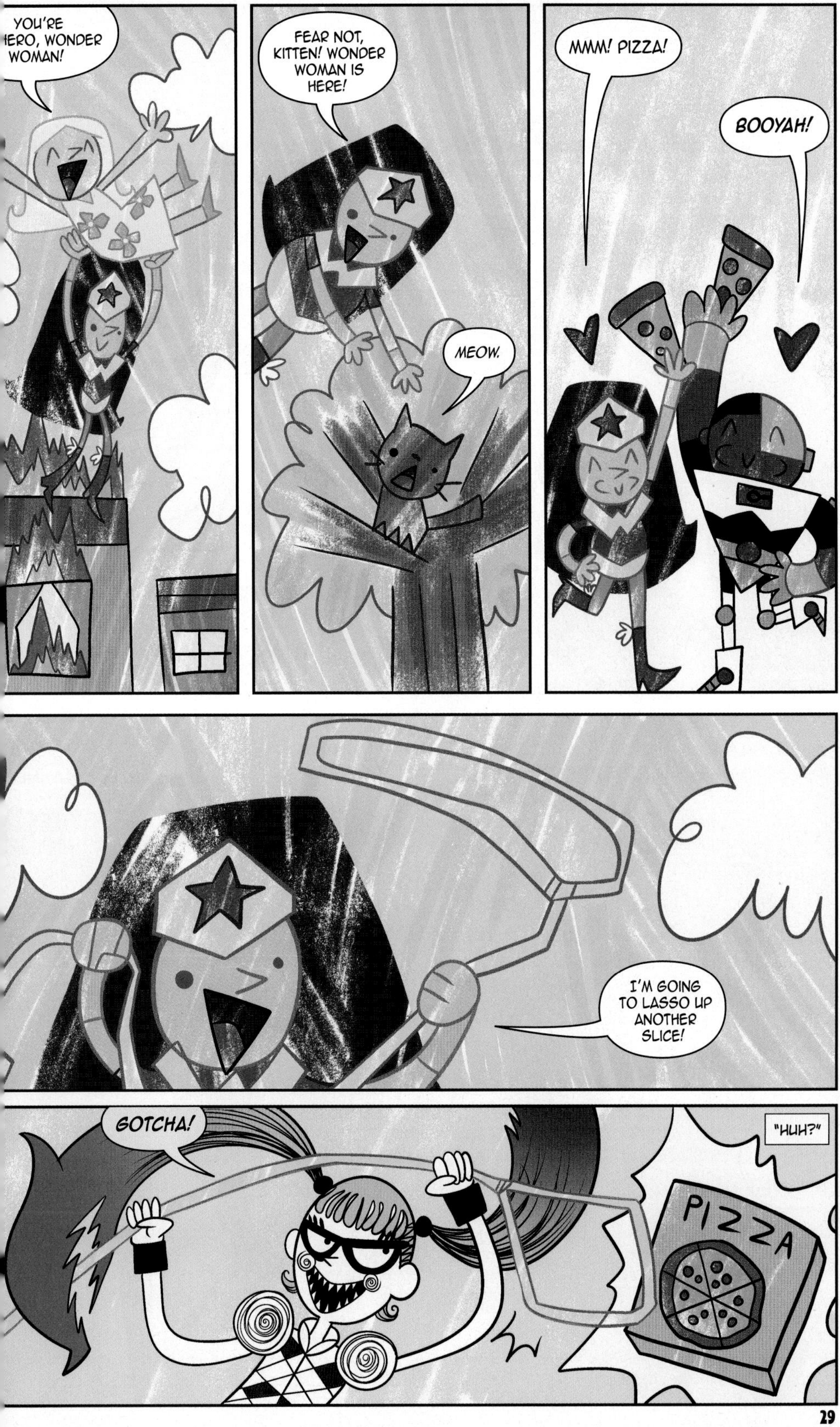
YOU'RE
HERO, WONDER
WOMAN!
FEAR NOT, KITTEN! WONDER WOMAN IS HERE!
MEOW.
MMM! PIZZA!
BOOYAH!
I'M GOING TO LASSO UP ANOTHER SLICE!
GOTCHA!
"HUH?"
PIZZA

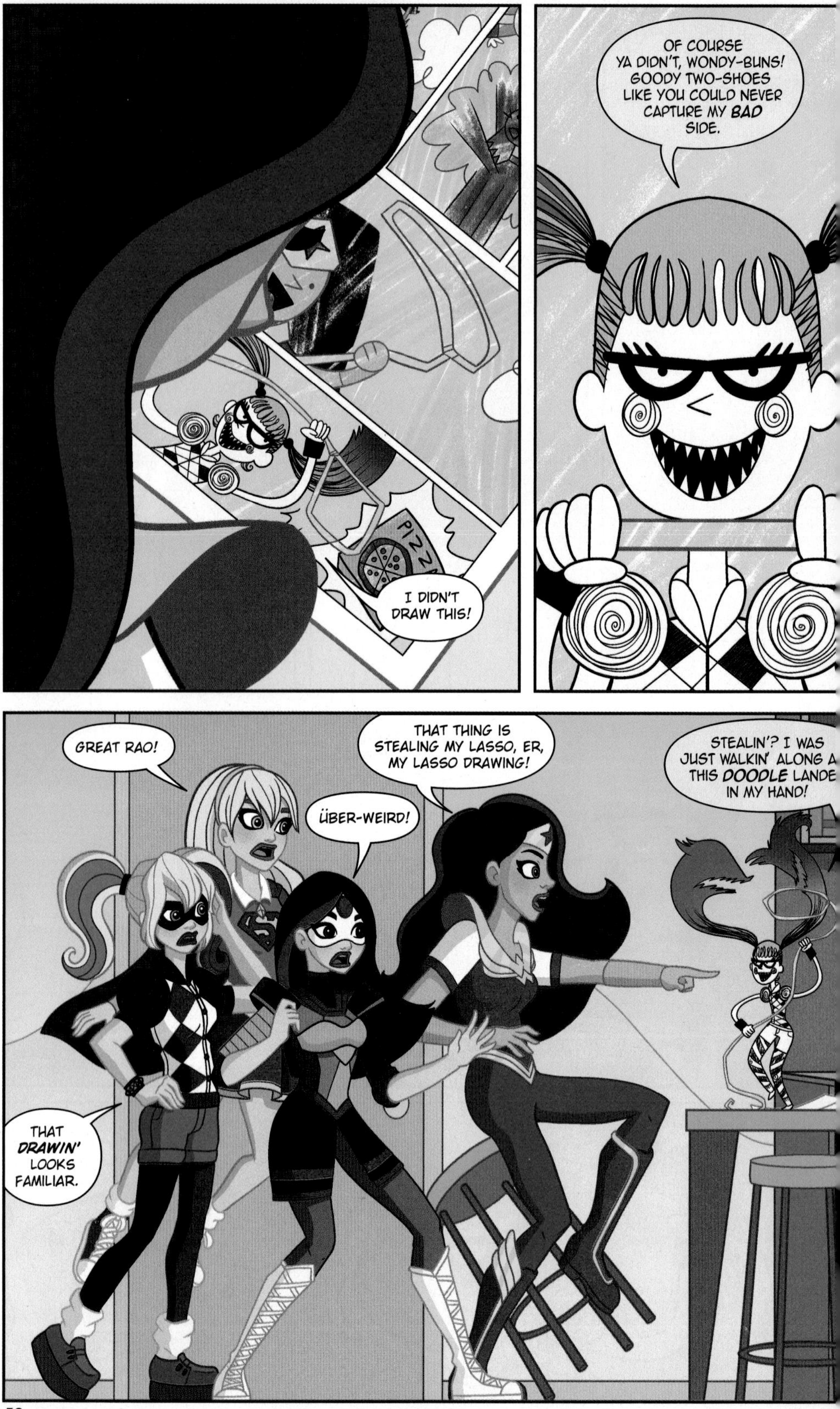
I DIDN'T DRAW THIS!
OF COURSE YA DIDN'T, WONDY-BUNS! GOODY TWO-SHOES LIKE YOU COULD NEVER CAPTURE MY BAD SIDE.
GREAT RAO!
ÜBER-WEIRD!
THAT THING IS STEALING MY LASSO, ER, MY LASSO DRAWING!
STEALIN'? I WAS JUST WALKIN' ALONG A THIS DOODLE LANDE IN MY HAND!
THAT DRAWIN' LOOKS FAMILIAR.

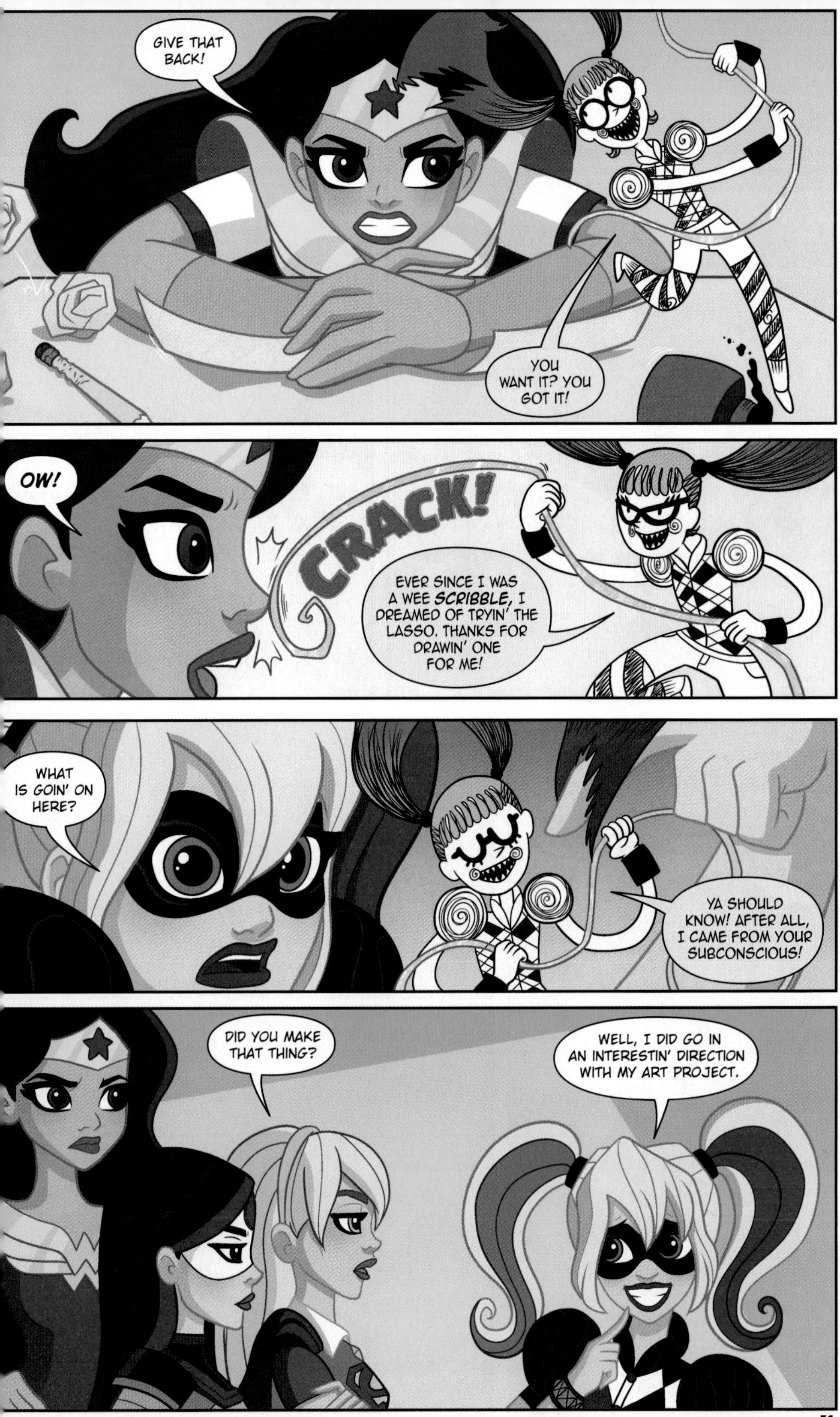
GIVE THAT BACK!
YOU WANT IT? YOU GOT IT!
OW!
CRACK!
EVER SINCE I WAS A WEE SCRIBBLE, I DREAMED OF TRYIN' THE LASSO. THANKS FOR DRAWIN' ONE FOR ME!
WHAT IS GOIN' ON HERE?
YA SHOULD KNOW! AFTER ALL, I CAME FROM YOUR SUBCONSCIOUS!
DID YOU MAKE THAT THING?
WELL, I DID GO IN AN INTERESTIN' DIRECTION WITH MY ART PROJECT.

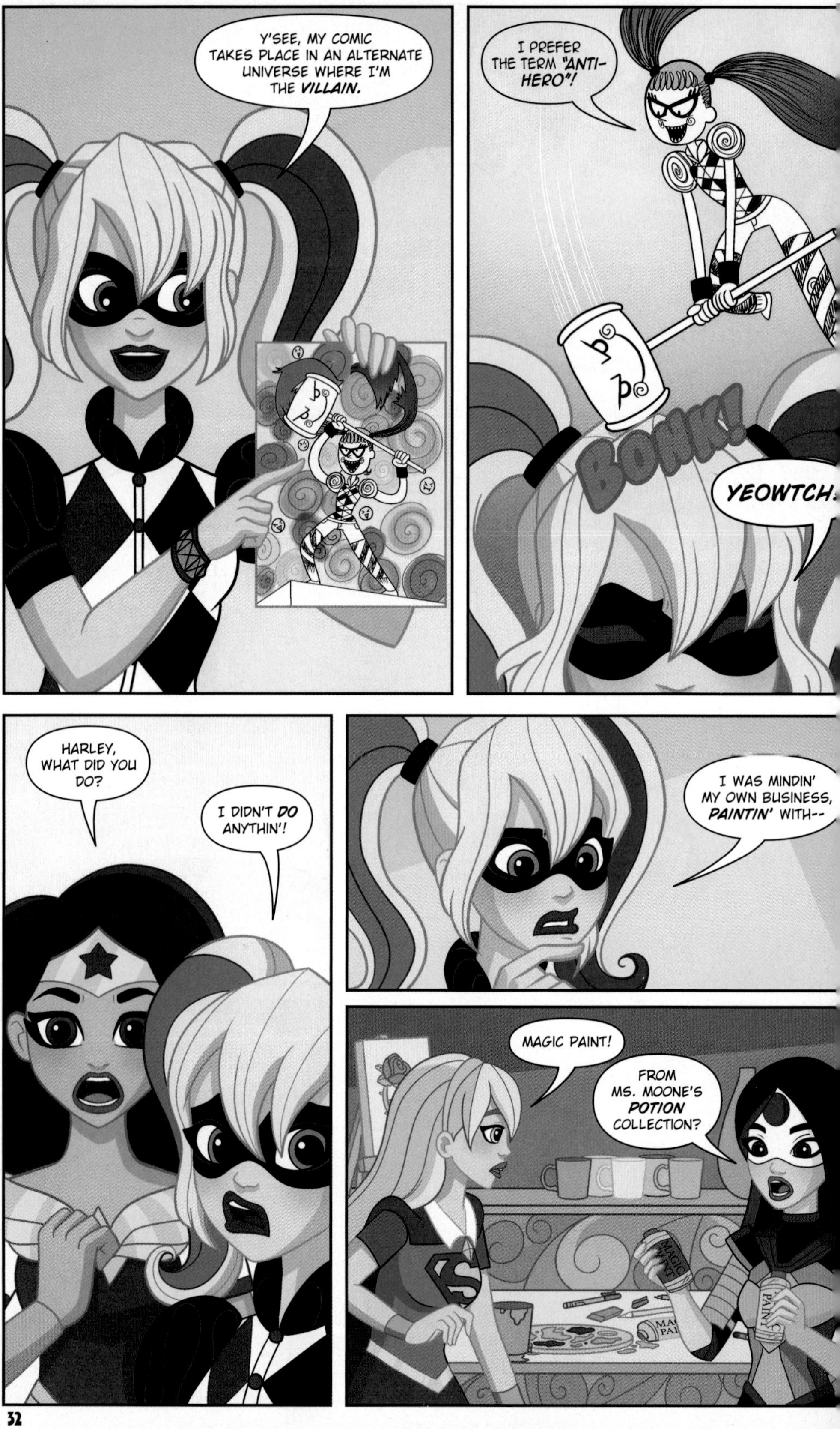
Y'SEE, MY COMIC TAKES PLACE IN AN ALTERNATE UNIVERSE WHERE I'M THE VILLAIN.
I PREFER THE TERM "ANTI-HERO"!
BONK!
YEOWTCH!
HARLEY, WHAT DID YOU DO?
I DIDN'T DO ANYTHIN'!
I WAS MINDIN' MY OWN BUSINESS, PAINTIN' WITH--
MAGIC PAINT!
FROM MS. MOONE'S POTION COLLECTION?

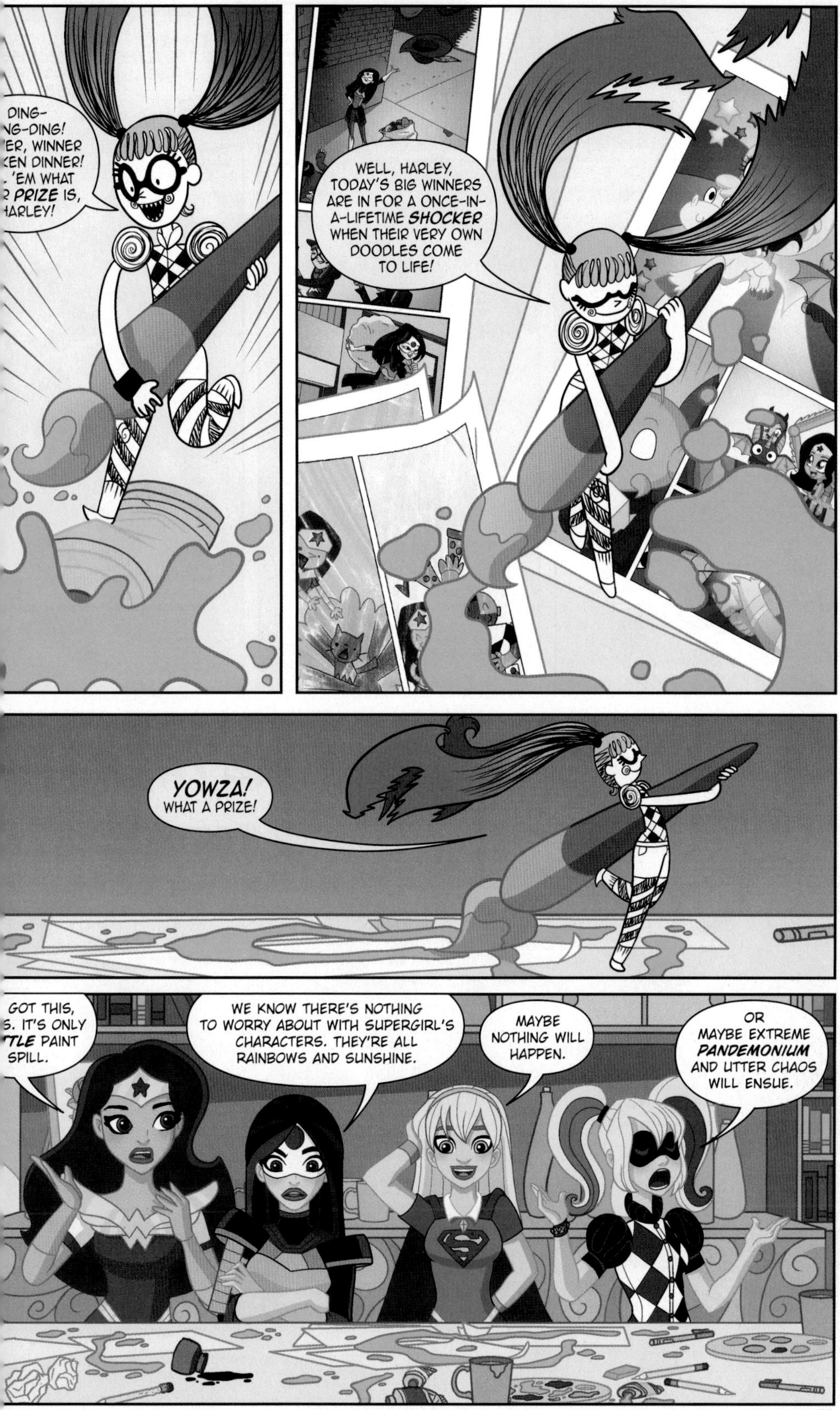

DING- NG-DING! ER, WINNER KEN DINNER! 'EM WHAT R PRIZE IS, HARLEY!
WELL, HARLEY, TODAY'S BIG WINNERS ARE IN FOR A ONCE-IN-A-LIFETIME SHOCKER WHEN THEIR VERY OWN DOODLES COME TO LIFE!
YOWZA! WHAT A PRIZE!
GOT THIS, S. IT'S ONLY TTLE PAINT SPILL.
WE KNOW THERE'S NOTHING TO WORRY ABOUT WITH SUPERGIRL'S CHARACTERS. THEY'RE ALL RAINBOWS AND SUNSHINE.
MAYBE NOTHING WILL HAPPEN.
OR MAYBE EXTREME PANDEMONIUM AND UTTER CHAOS WILL ENSUE.

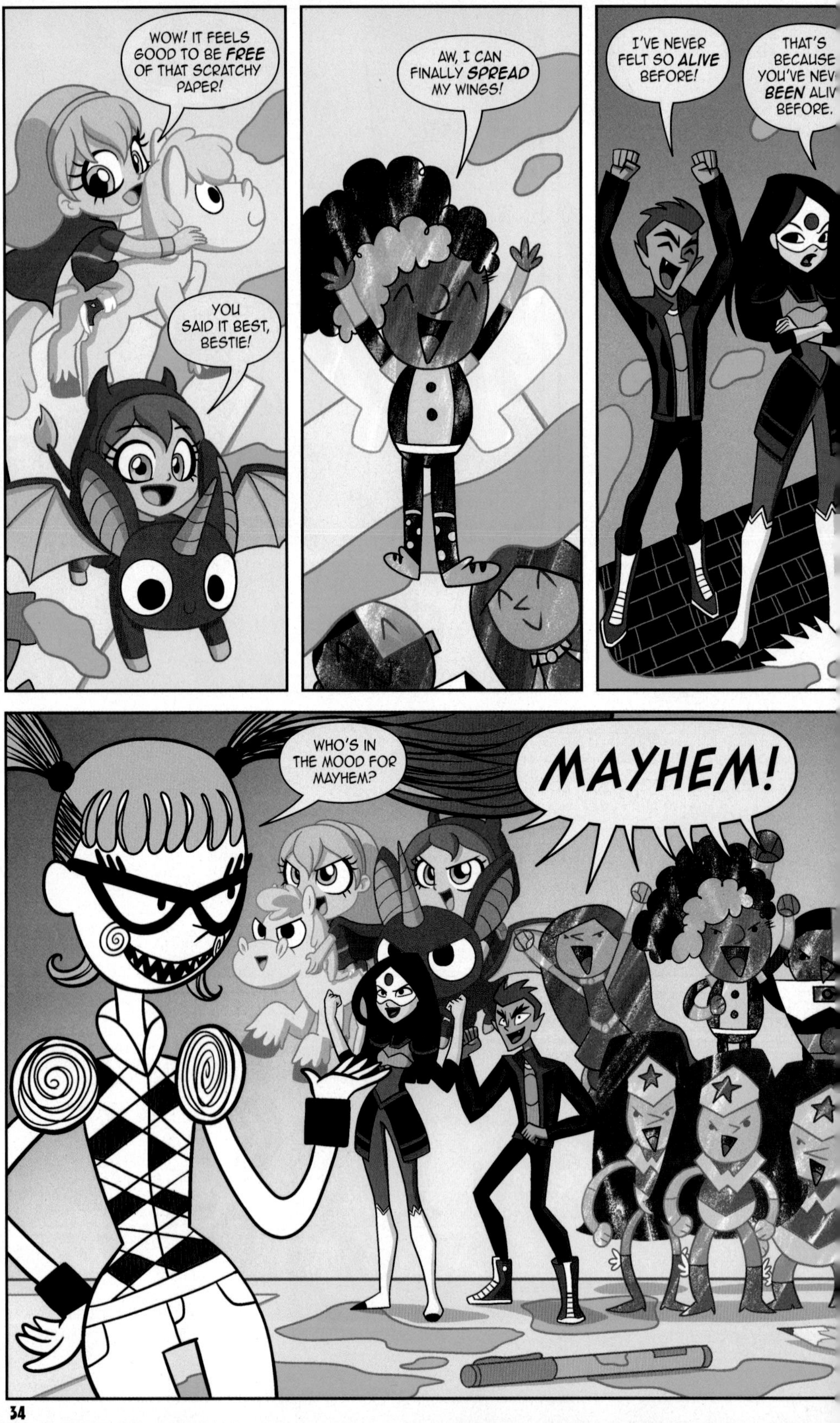

WOW! IT FEELS GOOD TO BE FREE OF THAT SCRATCHY PAPER!
YOU SAID IT BEST, BESTIE!
AW, I CAN FINALLY SPREAD MY WINGS!
I'VE NEVER FELT SO ALIVE BEFORE!
THAT'S BECAUSE YOU'VE NEV BEEN ALIV BEFORE.
WHO'S IN THE MOOD FOR MAYHEM?
MAYHEM!

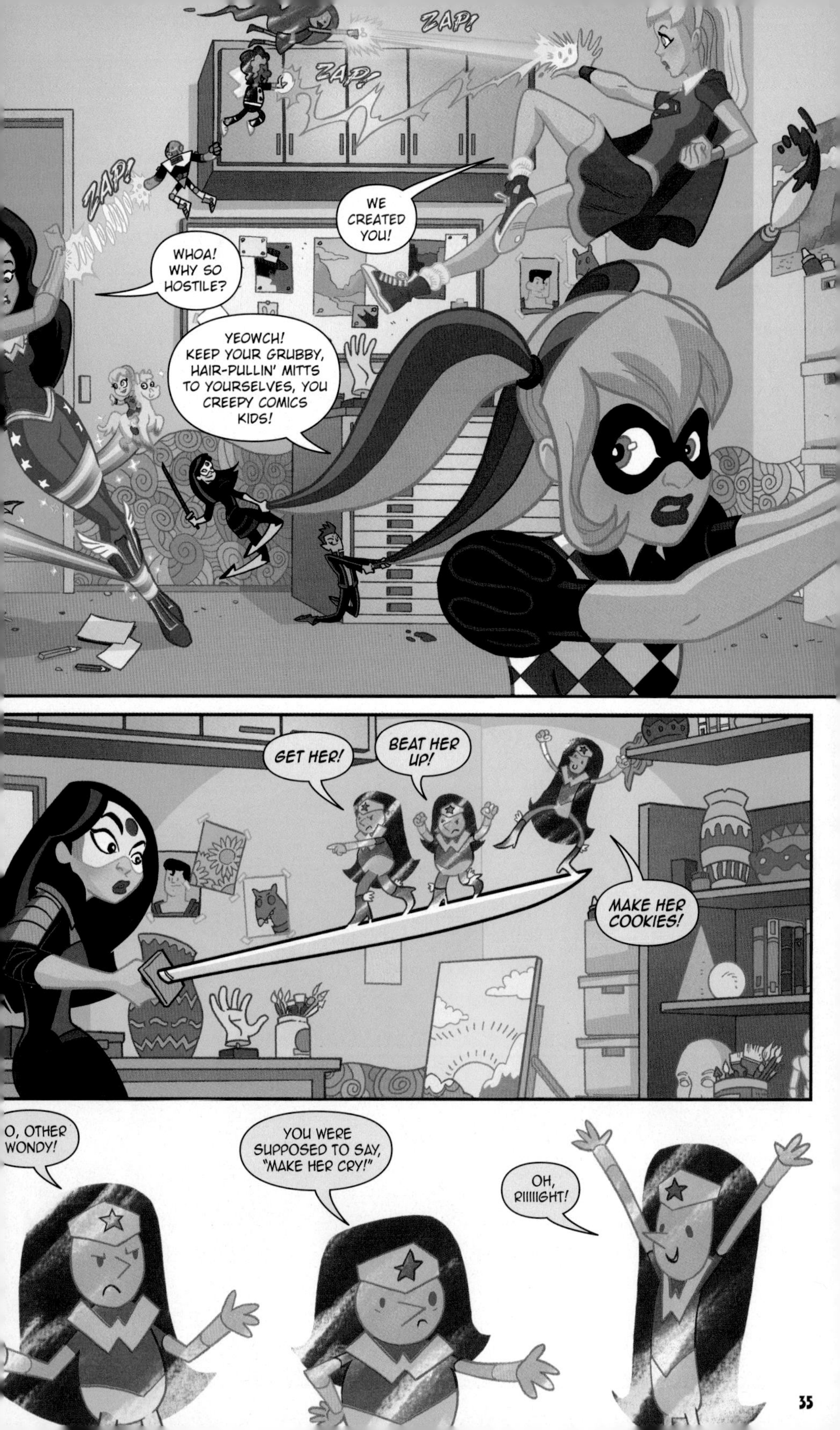
ZAP!
ZAP!
ZAP!
WE CREATED YOU!
WHOA! WHY SO HOSTILE?
YEOWCH! KEEP YOUR GRUBBY, HAIR-PULLIN' MITTS TO YOURSELVES, YOU CREEPY COMICS KIDS!
GET HER!
BEAT HER UP!
MAKE HER COOKIES!
O, OTHER WONDY!
YOU WERE SUPPOSED TO SAY, "MAKE HER CRY!"
OH, RIIIIIGHT!

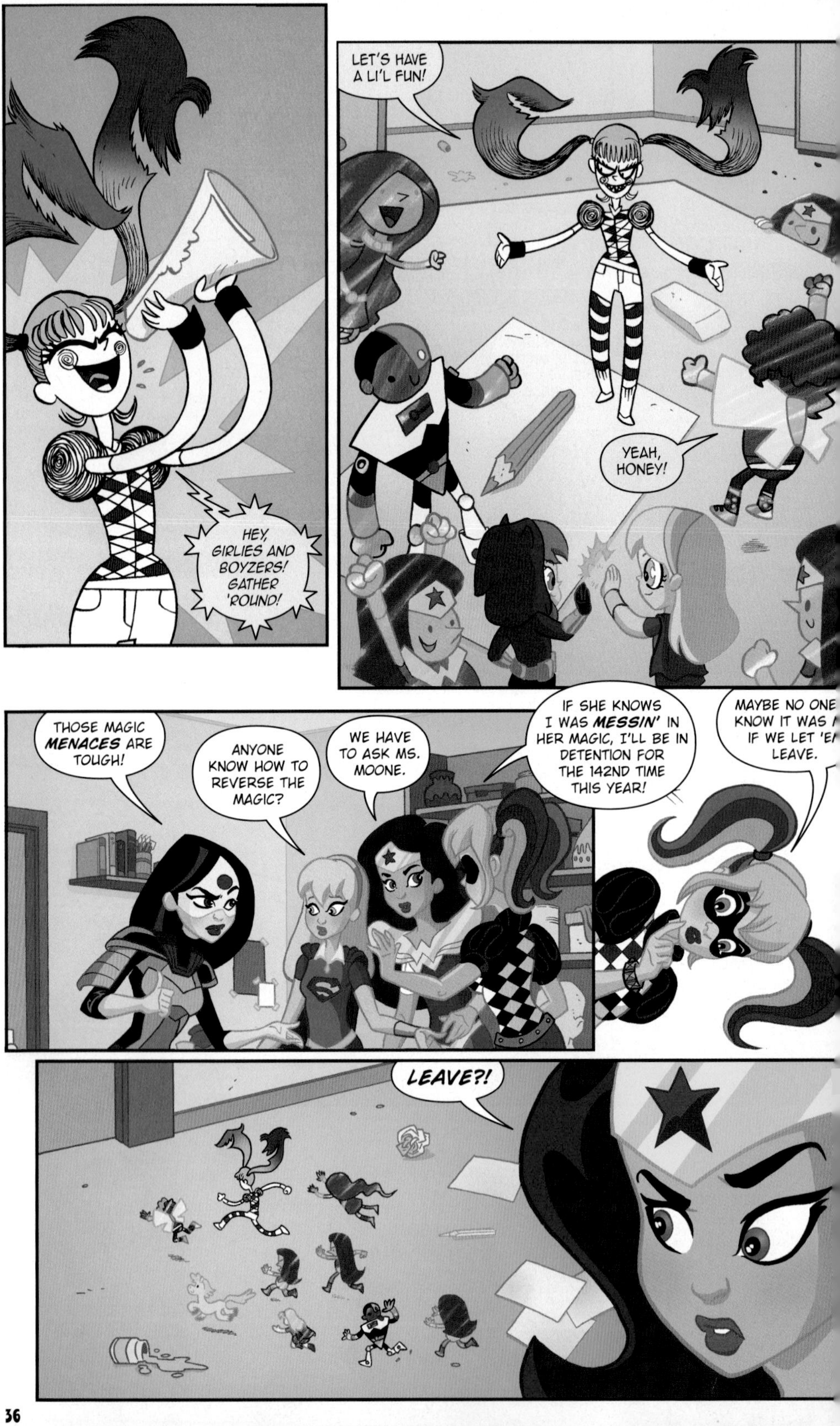

HEY, GIRLIES AND BOYZERS! GATHER 'ROUND!
LET'S HAVE A LI'L FUN!
YEAH, HONEY!
THOSE MAGIC *MENACES* ARE TOUGH!
ANYONE KNOW HOW TO REVERSE THE MAGIC?
WE HAVE TO ASK MS. MOONE.
IF SHE KNOWS I WAS *MESSIN'* IN HER MAGIC, I'LL BE IN DETENTION FOR THE 142ND TIME THIS YEAR!
MAYBE NO ONE KNOW IT WAS IF WE LET 'E LEAVE.
LEAVE?!

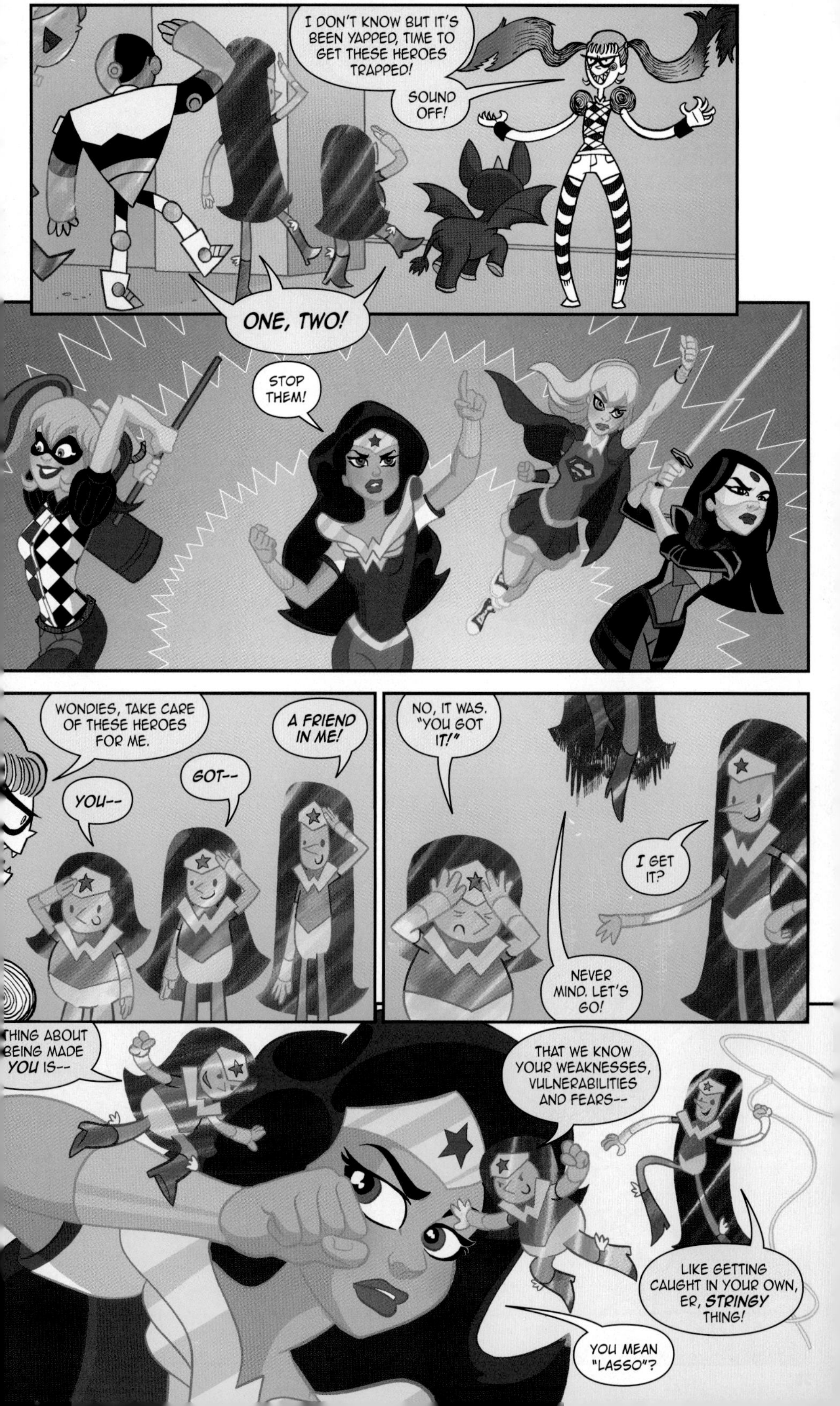
I DON'T KNOW BUT IT'S BEEN YAPPED, TIME TO GET THESE HEROES TRAPPED!
SOUND OFF!
ONE, TWO!
STOP THEM!
WONDIES, TAKE CARE OF THESE HEROES FOR ME.
YOU--
GOT--
A FRIEND IN ME!
NO, IT WAS. "YOU GOT IT!"
I GET IT?
NEVER MIND. LET'S GO!
THING ABOUT BEING MADE YOU IS--
THAT WE KNOW YOUR WEAKNESSES, VULNERABILITIES AND FEARS--
LIKE GETTING CAUGHT IN YOUR OWN, ER, STRINGY THING!
YOU MEAN "LASSO"?

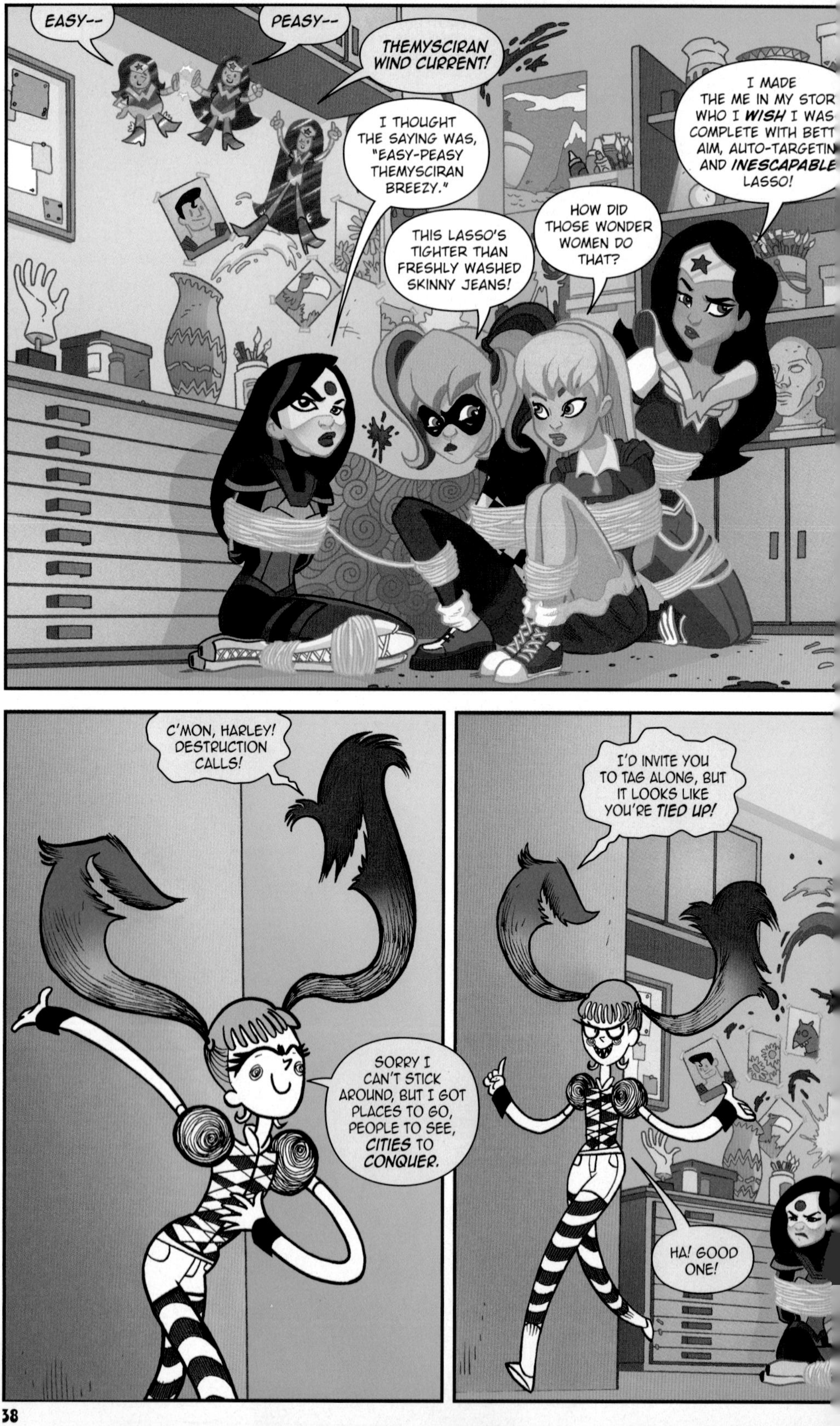

EASY--
PEASY--
THEMYSCIRAN WIND CURRENT!
I THOUGHT THE SAYING WAS, "EASY-PEASY THEMYSCIRAN BREEZY."
THIS LASSO'S TIGHTER THAN FRESHLY WASHED SKINNY JEANS!
HOW DID THOSE WONDER WOMEN DO THAT?
I MADE THE ME IN MY STOR WHO I WISH I WAS COMPLETE WITH BETT AIM, AUTO-TARGETIN AND INESCAPABLE LASSO!
C'MON, HARLEY! DESTRUCTION CALLS!
SORRY I CAN'T STICK AROUND, BUT I GOT PLACES TO GO, PEOPLE TO SEE, CITIES TO CONQUER.
I'D INVITE YOU TO TAG ALONG, BUT IT LOOKS LIKE YOU'RE TIED UP!
HA! GOOD ONE!

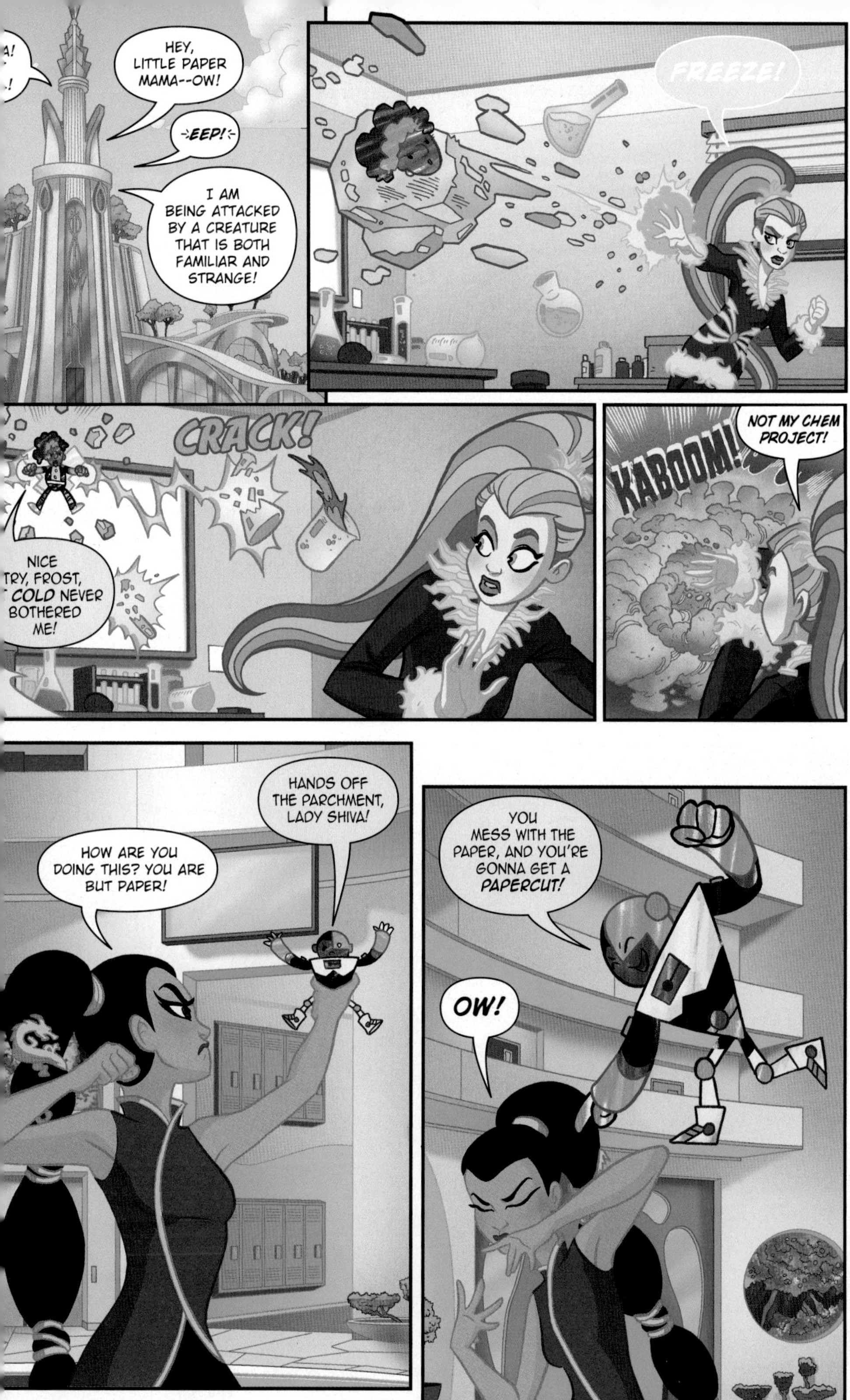

HEY, LITTLE PAPER MAMA--OW!
EEP!
I AM BEING ATTACKED BY A CREATURE THAT IS BOTH FAMILIAR AND STRANGE!
FREEZE!
CRACK!
NICE TRY, FROST, COLD NEVER BOTHERED ME!
KABOOM!
NOT MY CHEM PROJECT!
HOW ARE YOU DOING THIS? YOU ARE BUT PAPER!
HANDS OFF THE PARCHMENT, LADY SHIVA!
YOU MESS WITH THE PAPER, AND YOU'RE GONNA GET A PAPERCUT!
OW!

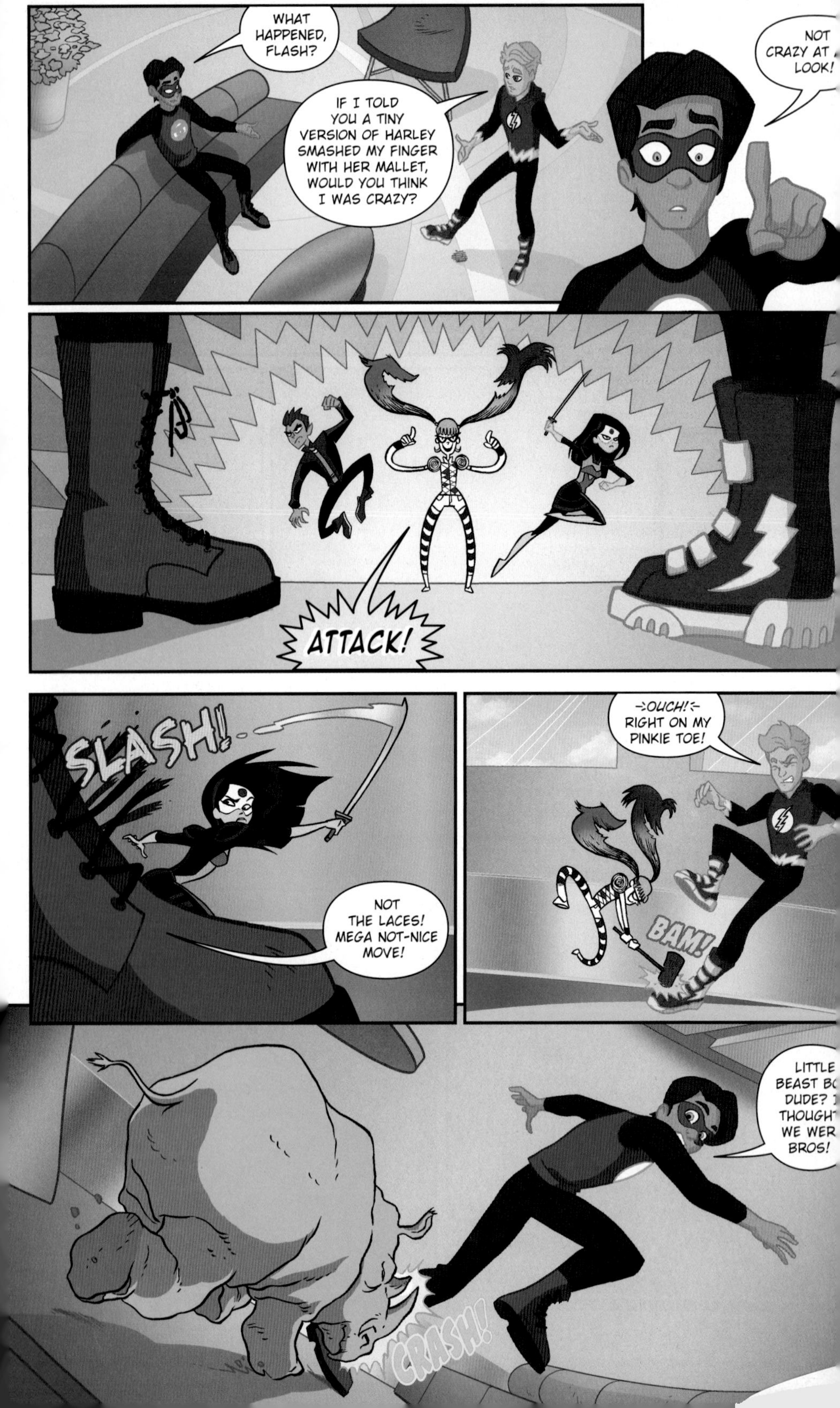
WHAT HAPPENED, FLASH?
IF I TOLD YOU A TINY VERSION OF HARLEY SMASHED MY FINGER WITH HER MALLET, WOULD YOU THINK I WAS CRAZY?
NOT CRAZY AT LOOK!
ATTACK!
SLASH!
NOT THE LACES! MEGA NOT-NICE MOVE!
OUCH! RIGHT ON MY PINKIE TOE!
BAM!
LITTLE BEAST DUDE? THOUGHT WE WER BROS!
CRASH!

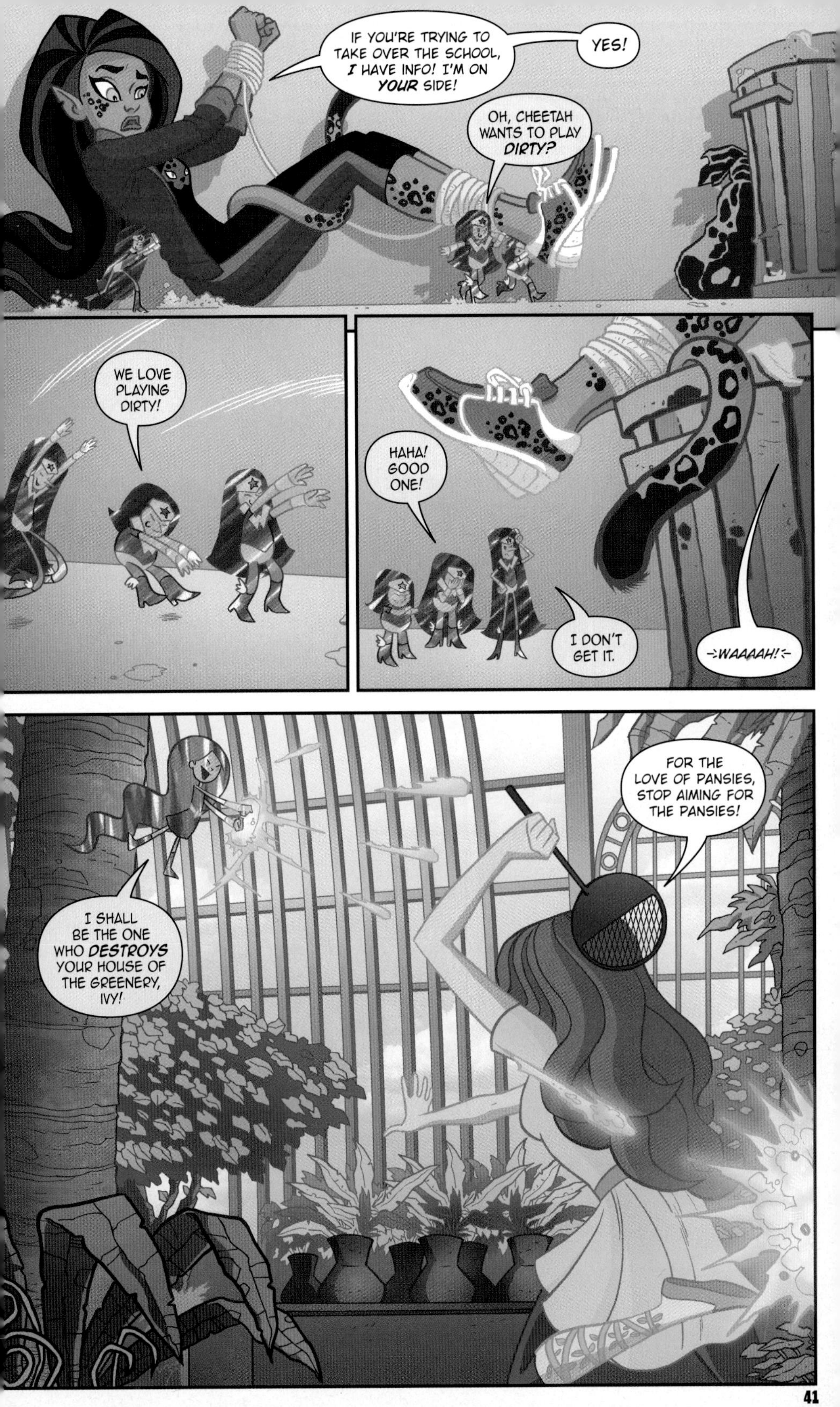

IF YOU'RE TRYING TO TAKE OVER THE SCHOOL, *I* HAVE INFO! I'M ON ***YOUR*** SIDE!
YES!
OH, CHEETAH WANTS TO PLAY ***DIRTY?***
WE LOVE PLAYING DIRTY!
HAHA! GOOD ONE!
I DON'T GET IT.
WAAAAH!
FOR THE LOVE OF PANSIES, STOP AIMING FOR THE PANSIES!
I SHALL BE THE ONE WHO ***DESTROYS*** YOUR HOUSE OF THE GREENERY, IVY!

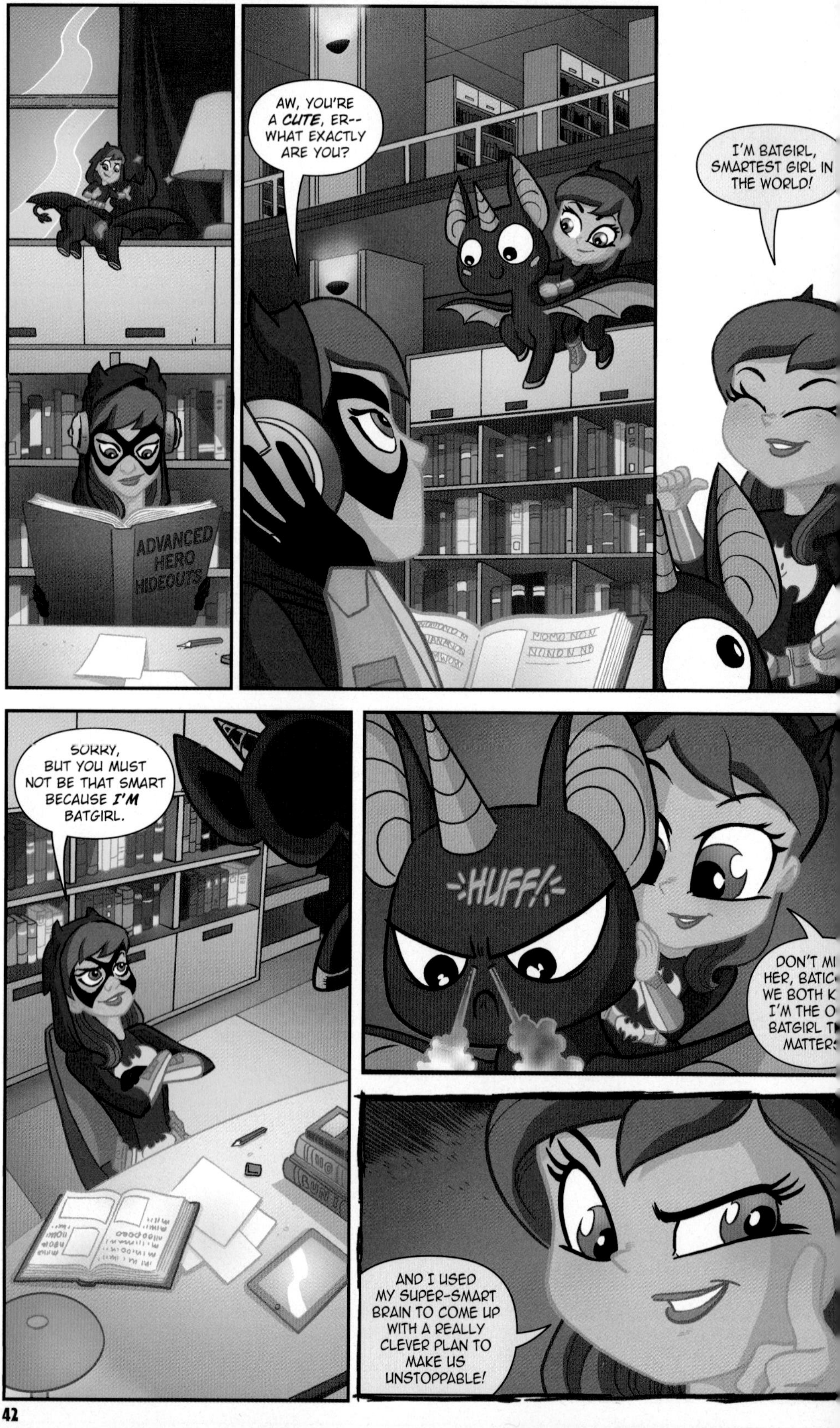
ADVANCED HERO HIDEOUTS
AW, YOU'RE A *CUTE*, ER-- WHAT EXACTLY ARE YOU?
I'M BATGIRL, SMARTEST GIRL IN THE WORLD!
SORRY, BUT YOU MUST NOT BE THAT SMART BECAUSE *I'M* BATGIRL.
HUFF!
DON'T MI HER, BATIC WE BOTH K I'M THE O BATGIRL T MATTER
AND I USED MY SUPER-SMART BRAIN TO COME UP WITH A REALLY CLEVER PLAN TO MAKE US UNSTOPPABLE!

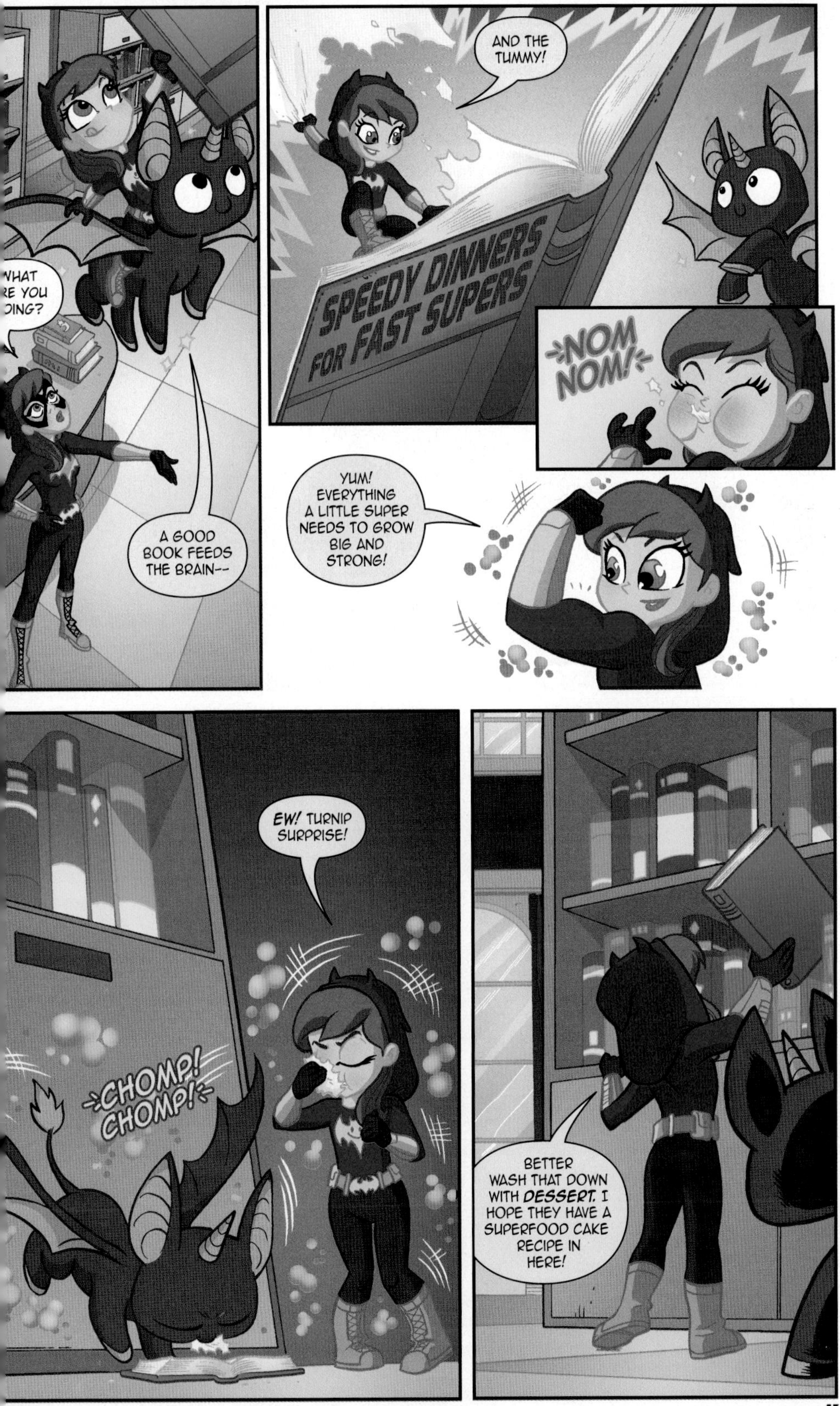
WHAT
RE YOU
DOING?
A GOOD BOOK FEEDS THE BRAIN--
AND THE TUMMY!
SPEEDY DINNERS FOR FAST SUPERS
NOM NOM!
YUM! EVERYTHING A LITTLE SUPER NEEDS TO GROW BIG AND STRONG!
EW! TURNIP SURPRISE!
CHOMP! CHOMP!
BETTER WASH THAT DOWN WITH DESSERT. I HOPE THEY HAVE A SUPERFOOD CAKE RECIPE IN HERE!

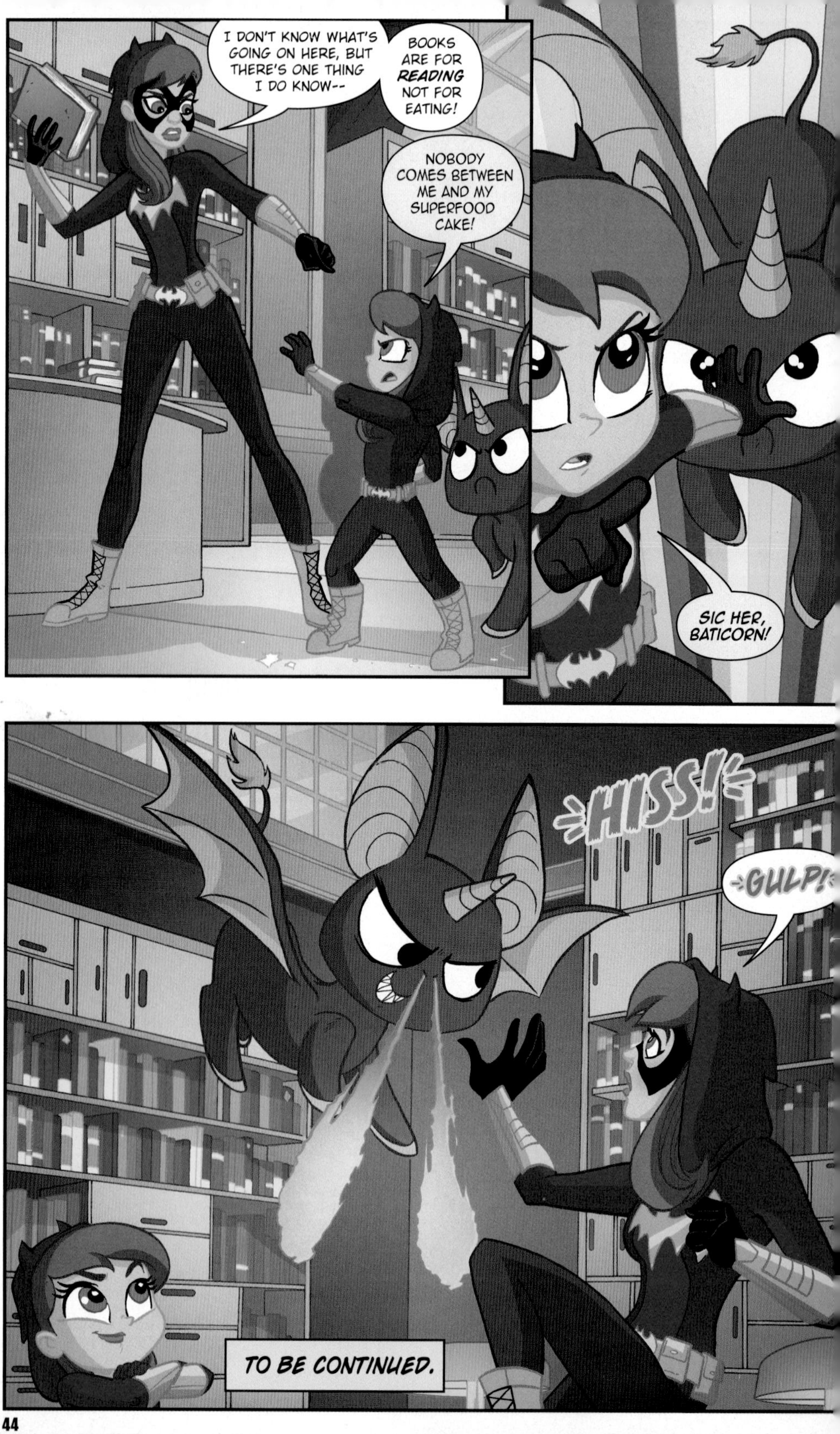
I DON'T KNOW WHAT'S GOING ON HERE, BUT THERE'S ONE THING I DO KNOW--
BOOKS ARE FOR *READING* NOT FOR EATING!
NOBODY COMES BETWEEN ME AND MY SUPERFOOD CAKE!
SIC HER, BATICORN!
HISS!
GULP!
TO BE CONTINUED.

CHAPTER THREE

EVERY TRICK IN THE BOOK

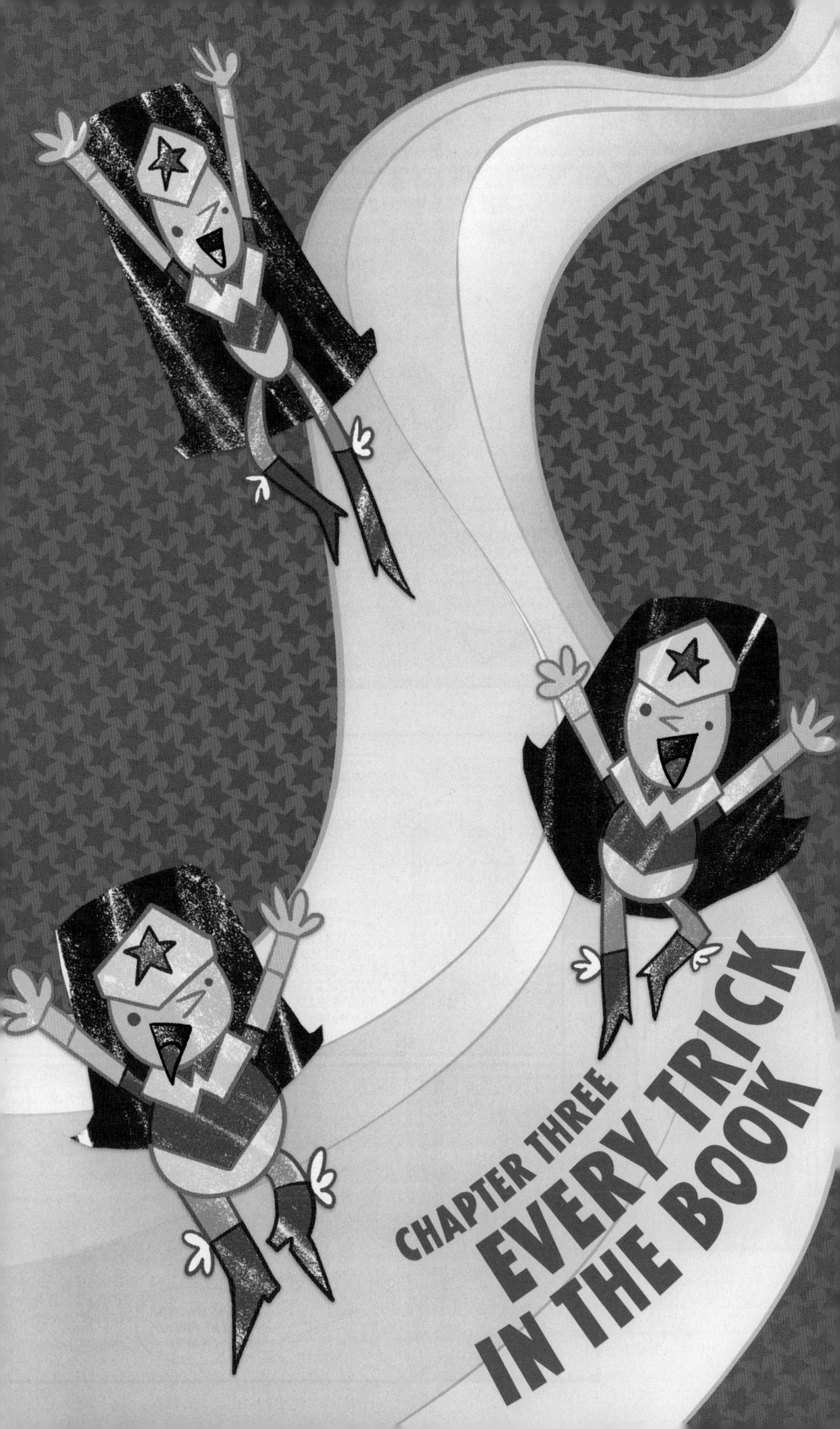

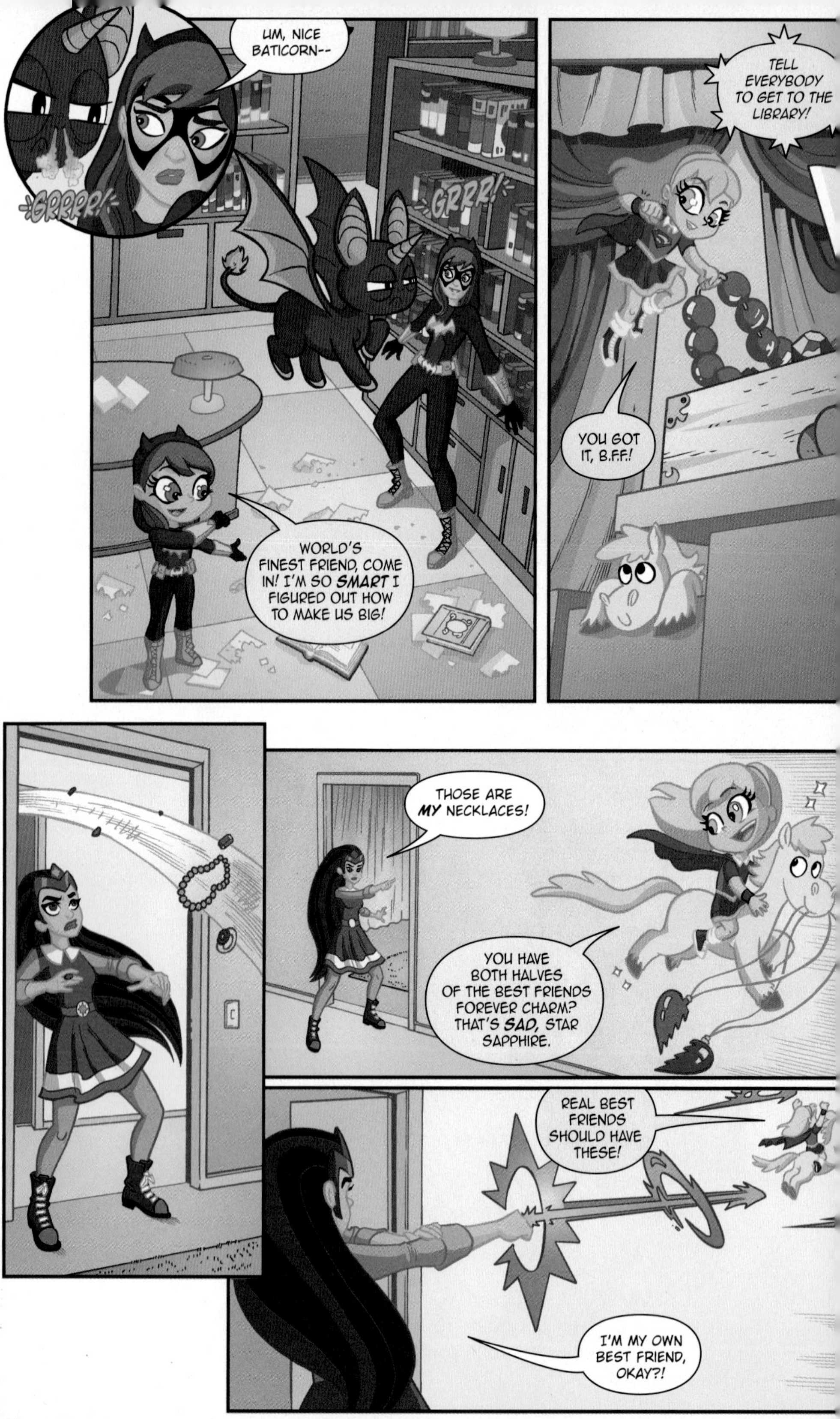
UM, NICE BATICORN--
GRRRR!
GRRR!
WORLD'S FINEST FRIEND, COME IN! I'M SO **SMART** I FIGURED OUT HOW TO MAKE US BIG!
TELL EVERYBODY TO GET TO THE LIBRARY!
YOU GOT IT, B.F.F.!
THOSE ARE **MY** NECKLACES!
YOU HAVE BOTH HALVES OF THE BEST FRIENDS FOREVER CHARM? THAT'S **SAD,** STAR SAPPHIRE.
REAL BEST FRIENDS SHOULD HAVE THESE!
I'M MY OWN BEST FRIEND, OKAY?!

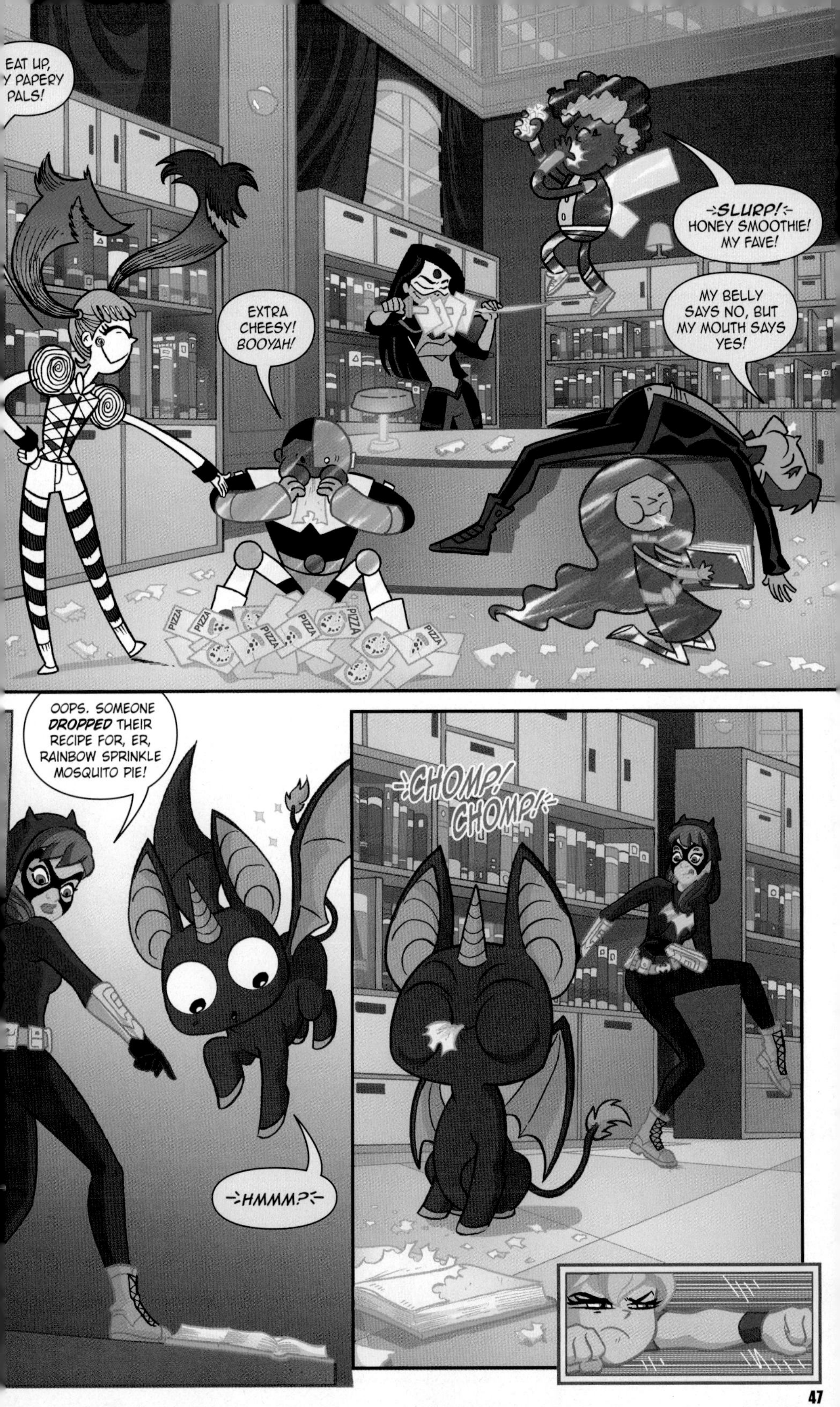
EAT UP, Y PAPERY PALS!
EXTRA CHEESY! BOOYAH!
-SLURP!- HONEY SMOOTHIE! MY FAVE!
MY BELLY SAYS NO, BUT MY MOUTH SAYS YES!
OOPS. SOMEONE DROPPED THEIR RECIPE FOR, ER, RAINBOW SPRINKLE MOSQUITO PIE!
-HMMM?-
-CHOMP! CHOMP!-

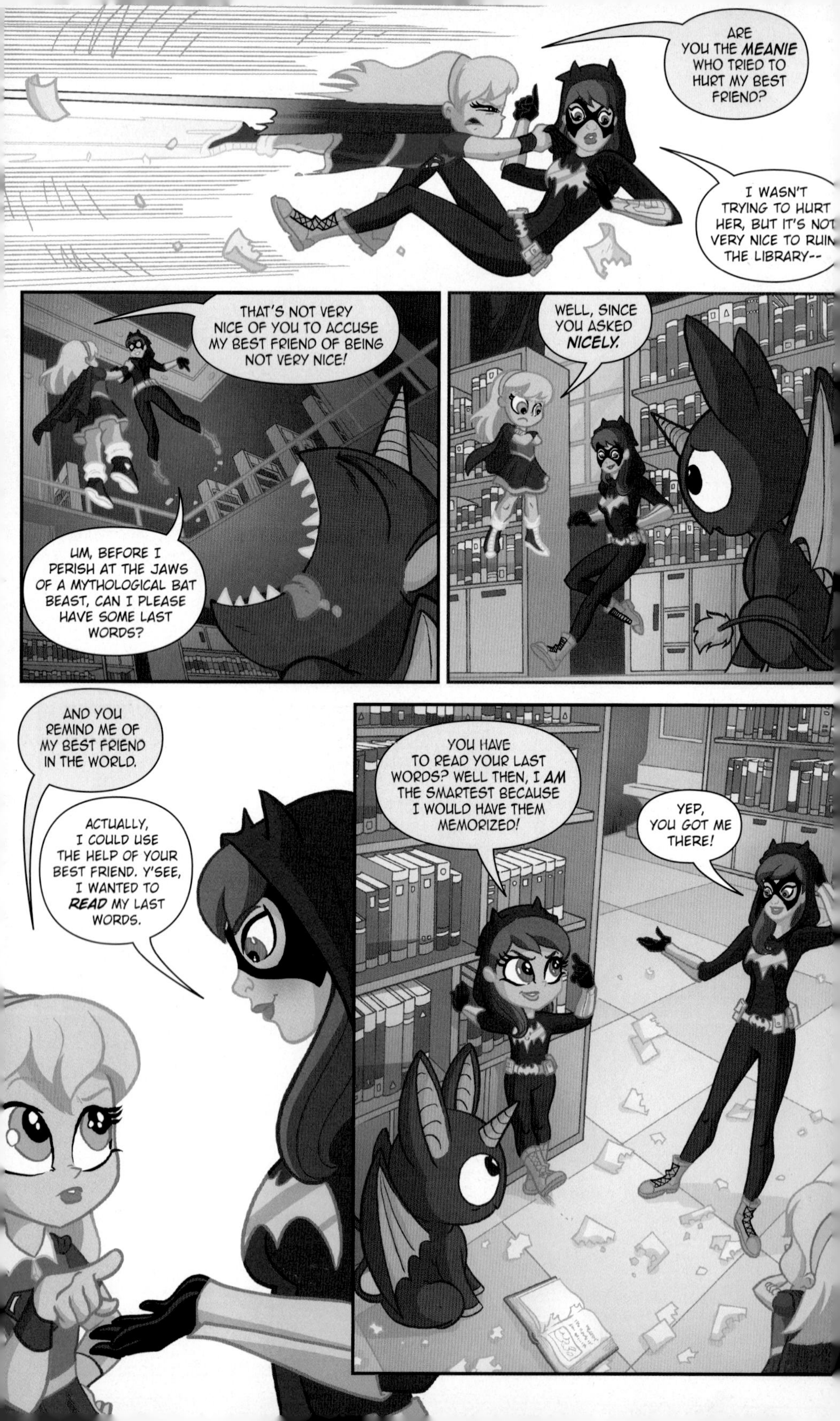
ARE YOU THE *MEANIE* WHO TRIED TO HURT MY BEST FRIEND?
I WASN'T TRYING TO HURT HER, BUT IT'S NOT VERY NICE TO RUIN THE LIBRARY--
THAT'S NOT VERY NICE OF YOU TO ACCUSE MY BEST FRIEND OF BEING NOT VERY NICE!
UM, BEFORE I PERISH AT THE JAWS OF A MYTHOLOGICAL BAT BEAST, CAN I PLEASE HAVE SOME LAST WORDS?
WELL, SINCE YOU ASKED *NICELY.*
AND YOU REMIND ME OF MY BEST FRIEND IN THE WORLD.
ACTUALLY, I COULD USE THE HELP OF YOUR BEST FRIEND. Y'SEE, I WANTED TO *READ* MY LAST WORDS.
YOU HAVE TO READ YOUR LAST WORDS? WELL THEN, I *AM* THE SMARTEST BECAUSE I WOULD HAVE THEM MEMORIZED!
YEP, YOU GOT ME THERE!

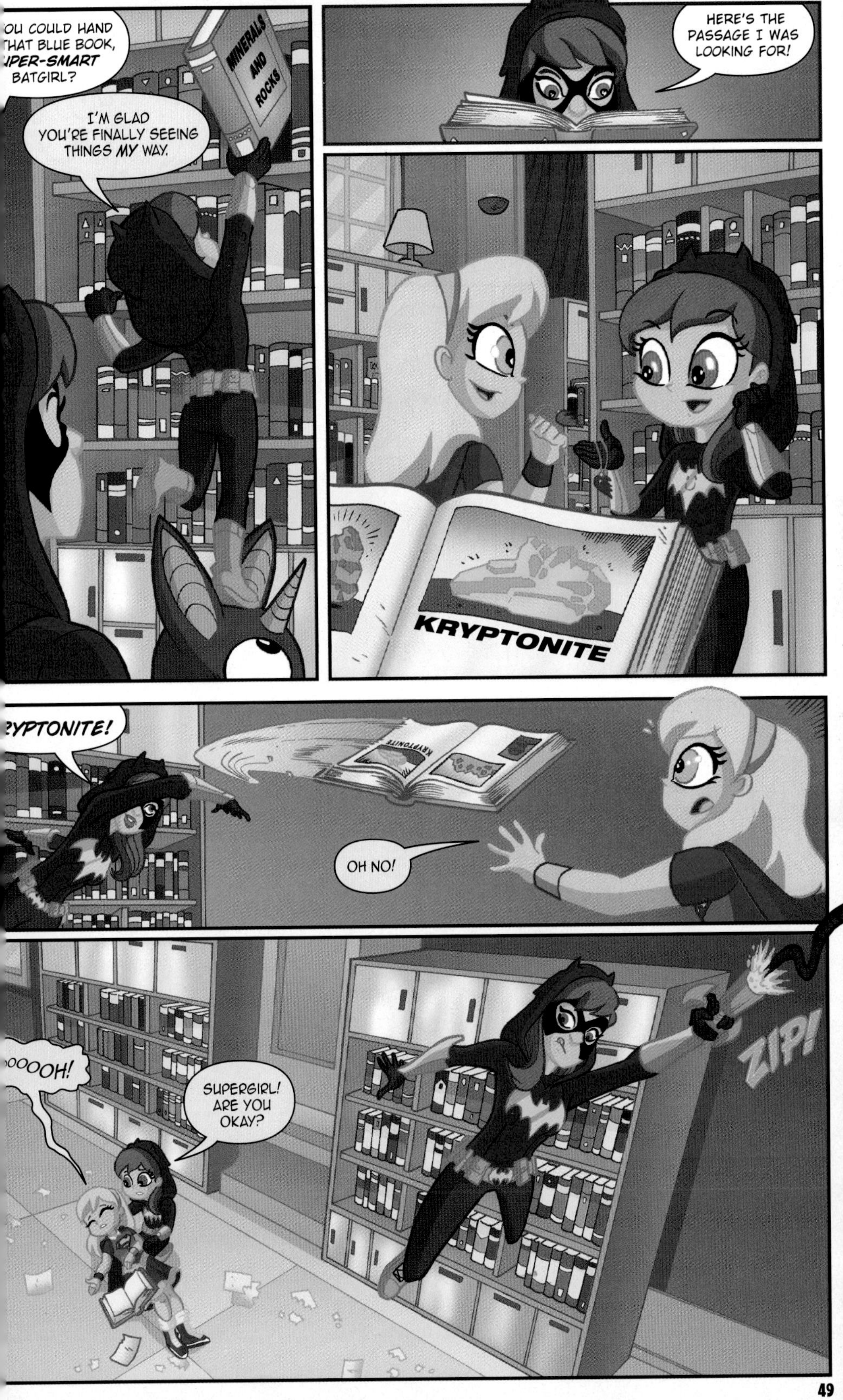
OU COULD HAND THAT BLUE BOOK, UPER-SMART BATGIRL?
MINERALS AND ROCKS
I'M GLAD YOU'RE FINALLY SEEING THINGS MY WAY.
HERE'S THE PASSAGE I WAS LOOKING FOR!
KRYPTONITE
RYPTONITE!
KRYPTONITE
OH NO!
OOOOOH!
SUPERGIRL! ARE YOU OKAY?
ZIP!

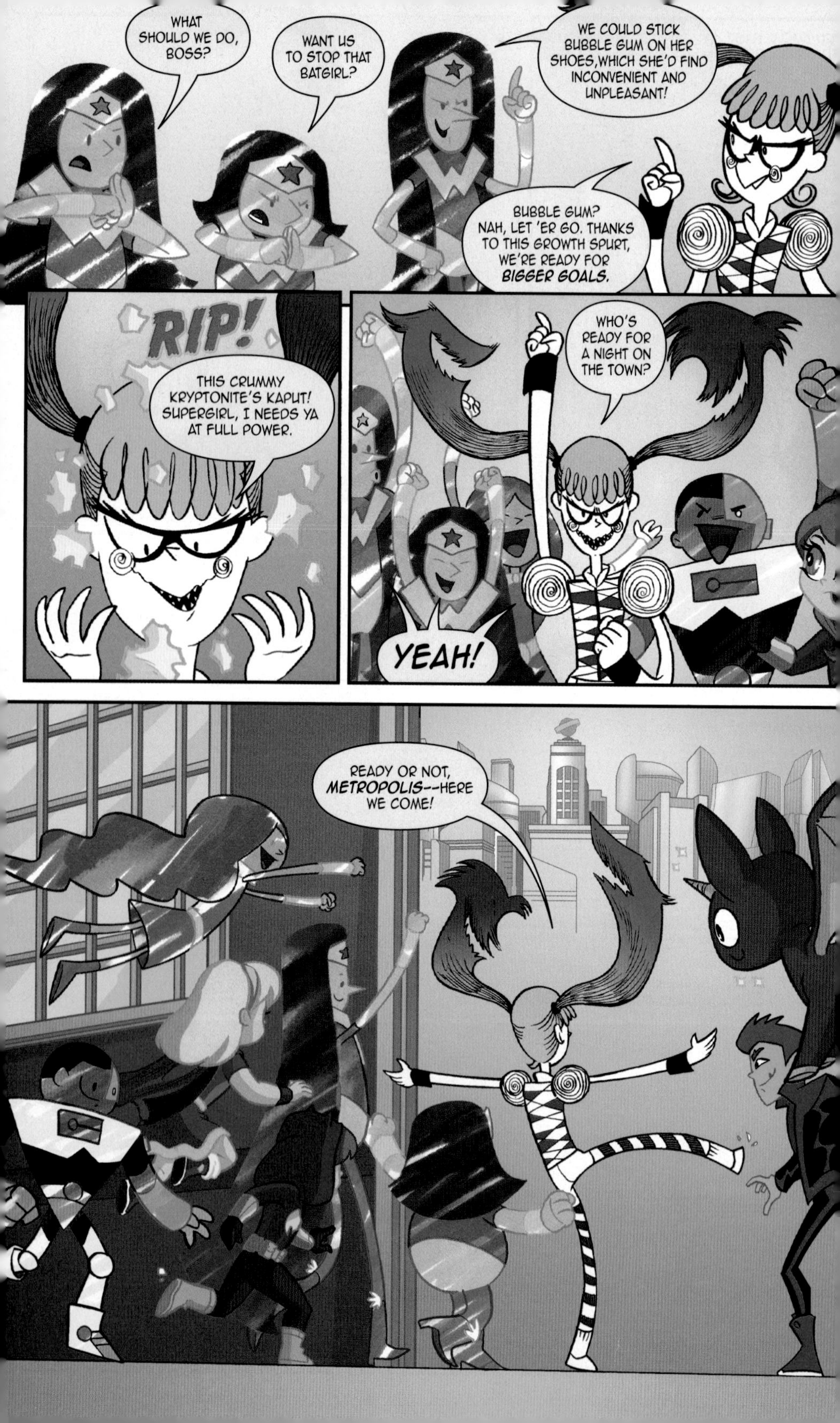
WHAT SHOULD WE DO, BOSS?
WANT US TO STOP THAT BATGIRL?
WE COULD STICK BUBBLE GUM ON HER SHOES, WHICH SHE'D FIND INCONVENIENT AND UNPLEASANT!
BUBBLE GUM? NAH, LET 'ER GO. THANKS TO THIS GROWTH SPURT, WE'RE READY FOR BIGGER GOALS.
RIP!
THIS CRUMMY KRYPTONITE'S KAPUT! SUPERGIRL, I NEEDS YA AT FULL POWER.
WHO'S READY FOR A NIGHT ON THE TOWN?
YEAH!
READY OR NOT, METROPOLIS--HERE WE COME!

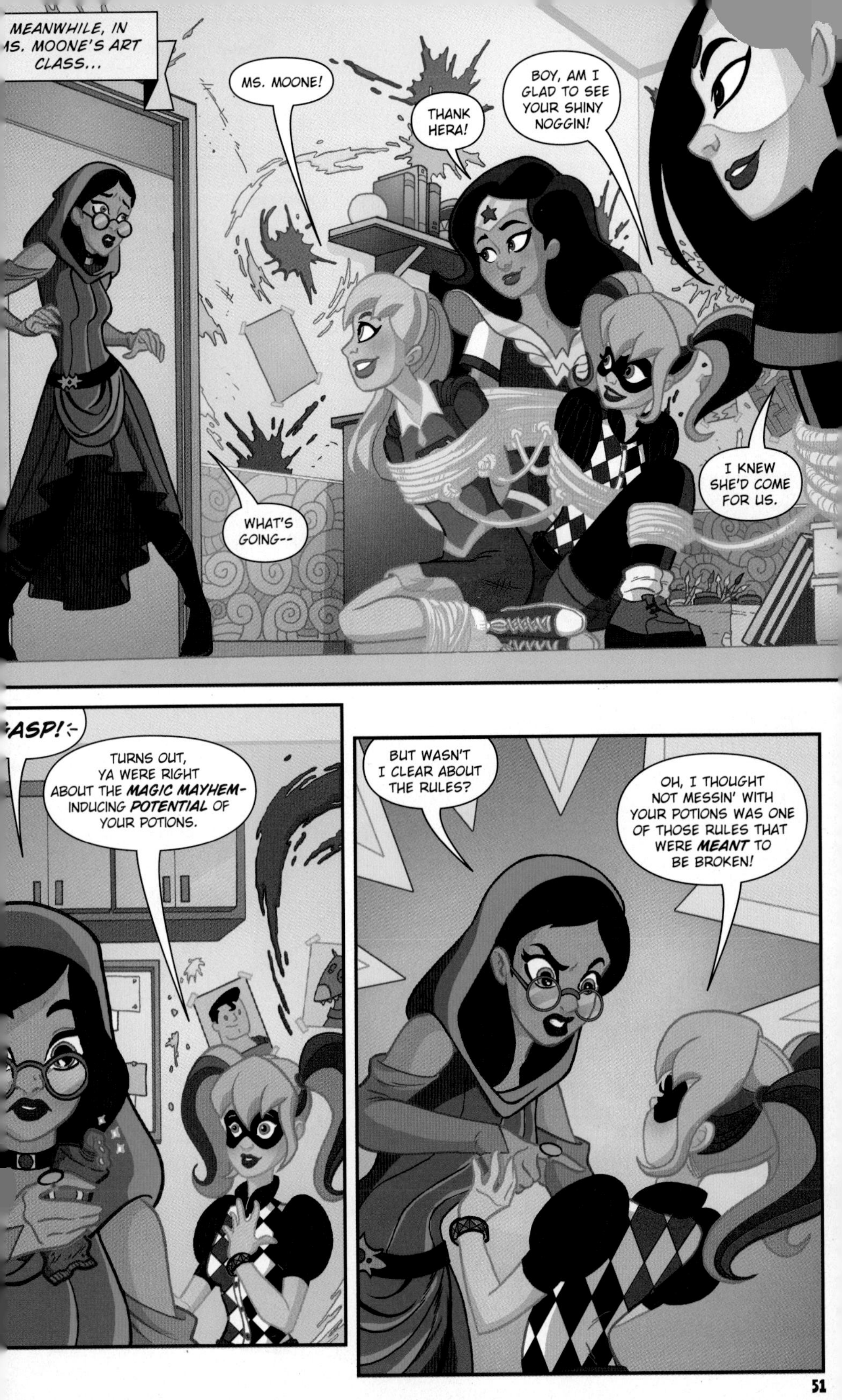

MEANWHILE, IN MS. MOONE'S ART CLASS...
MS. MOONE!
THANK HERA!
BOY, AM I GLAD TO SEE YOUR SHINY NOGGIN!
WHAT'S GOING--
I KNEW SHE'D COME FOR US.
GASP!
TURNS OUT, YA WERE RIGHT ABOUT THE MAGIC MAYHEM-INDUCING POTENTIAL OF YOUR POTIONS.
BUT WASN'T I CLEAR ABOUT THE RULES?
OH, I THOUGHT NOT MESSIN' WITH YOUR POTIONS WAS ONE OF THOSE RULES THAT WERE MEANT TO BE BROKEN!

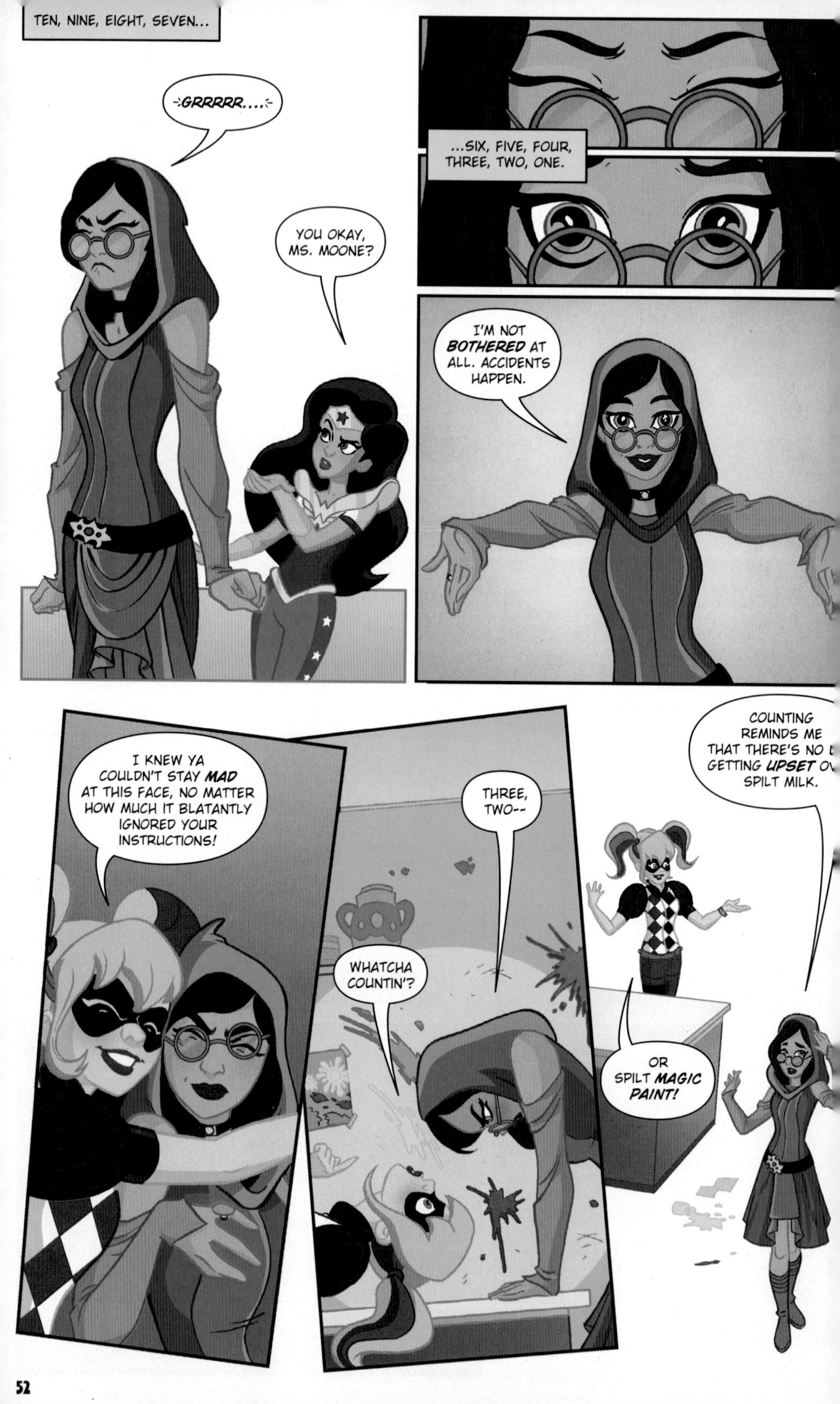

TEN, NINE, EIGHT, SEVEN...
GRRRRR....
YOU OKAY, MS. MOONE?
...SIX, FIVE, FOUR, THREE, TWO, ONE.
I'M NOT **BOTHERED** AT ALL. ACCIDENTS HAPPEN.
COUNTING REMINDS ME THAT THERE'S NO
GETTING **UPSET**
SPILT MILK.
OR SPILT **MAGIC PAINT!**
WHATCHA COUNTIN'?
THREE, TWO--
I KNEW YA COULDN'T STAY **MAD** AT THIS FACE, NO MATTER HOW MUCH IT BLATANTLY IGNORED YOUR INSTRUCTIONS!

...N DID THAT PAINT ...NG OUR COMICS TO LIFE?

AND WHY ARE THEY ÜBER EVIL?

THE WAY OF THE MAGIC PAINT IS A MYSTERY.

BUT I KNOW THAT THEY'RE "ÜBER-EVIL" BECAUSE THEY DON'T HAVE THE *HUMANITY* THAT ALLOWS THEM TO BE GOOD OR *HEARTS* THAT CARE FOR OTHERS.

WHAT SHOULD WE DO?

YOU MUST STOP THE CREATURES BEFORE PRINCIPAL WALLER *FINDS OUT--*

I MEAN, BEFORE THE CREATURES CAUSE ANY *HARM.*

I KNOW THIS MIGHT SOUND CRAZY, BUT THERE WERE THESE ART THINGS LED BY THIS HARLEY PAPER-THING, WHO'S A BAD VERSION OF OUR HARLEY!

NOT CRAZY. *WHERE* ARE THEY NOW?

...RLS, ...ME, ...CK!

THEY'RE GOING TO METROPOLIS!

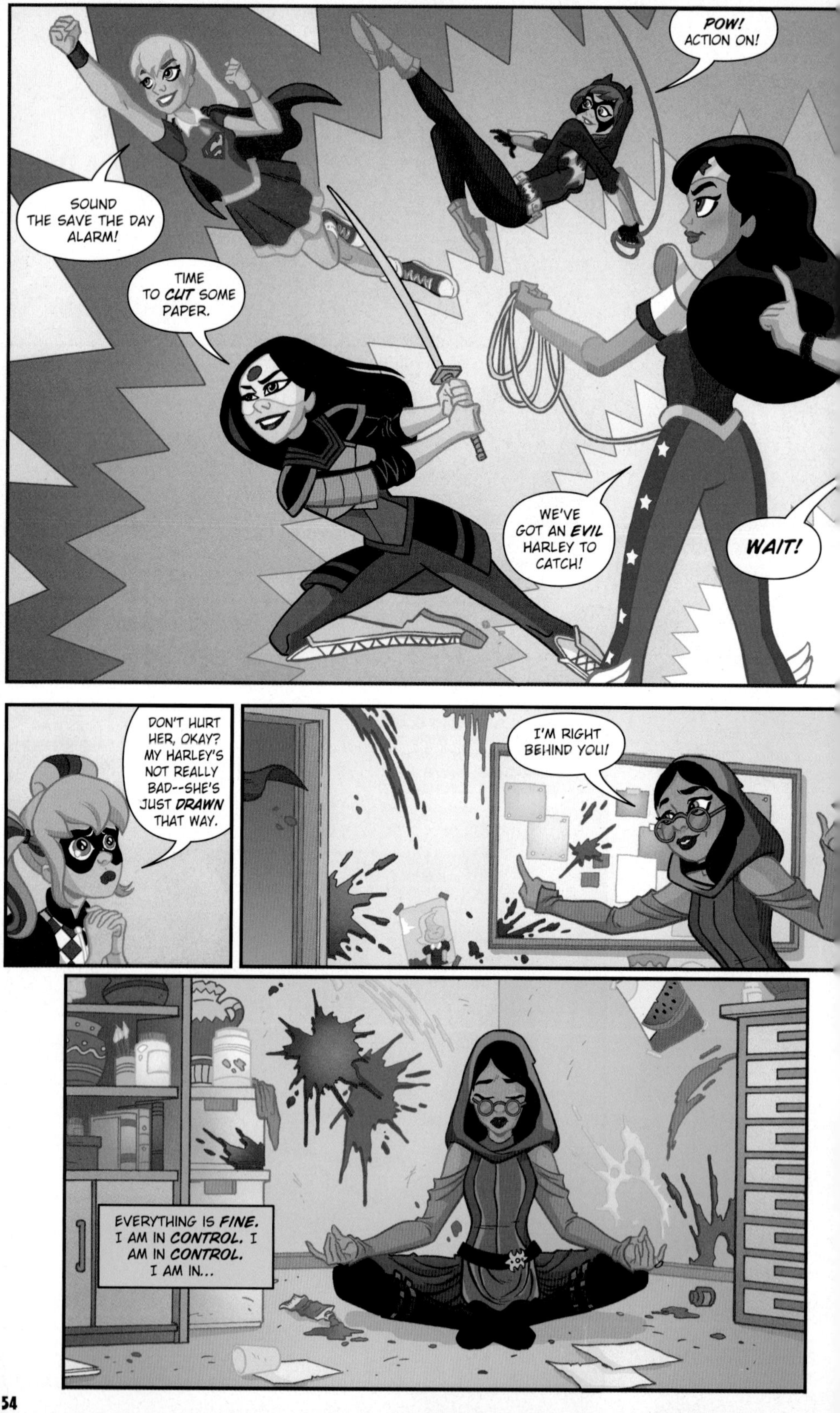
POW! ACTION ON!
SOUND THE SAVE THE DAY ALARM!
TIME TO CUT SOME PAPER.
WE'VE GOT AN EVIL HARLEY TO CATCH!
WAIT!
DON'T HURT HER, OKAY? MY HARLEY'S NOT REALLY BAD--SHE'S JUST DRAWN THAT WAY.
I'M RIGHT BEHIND YOU!
EVERYTHING IS FINE. I AM IN CONTROL. I AM IN CONTROL. I AM IN...

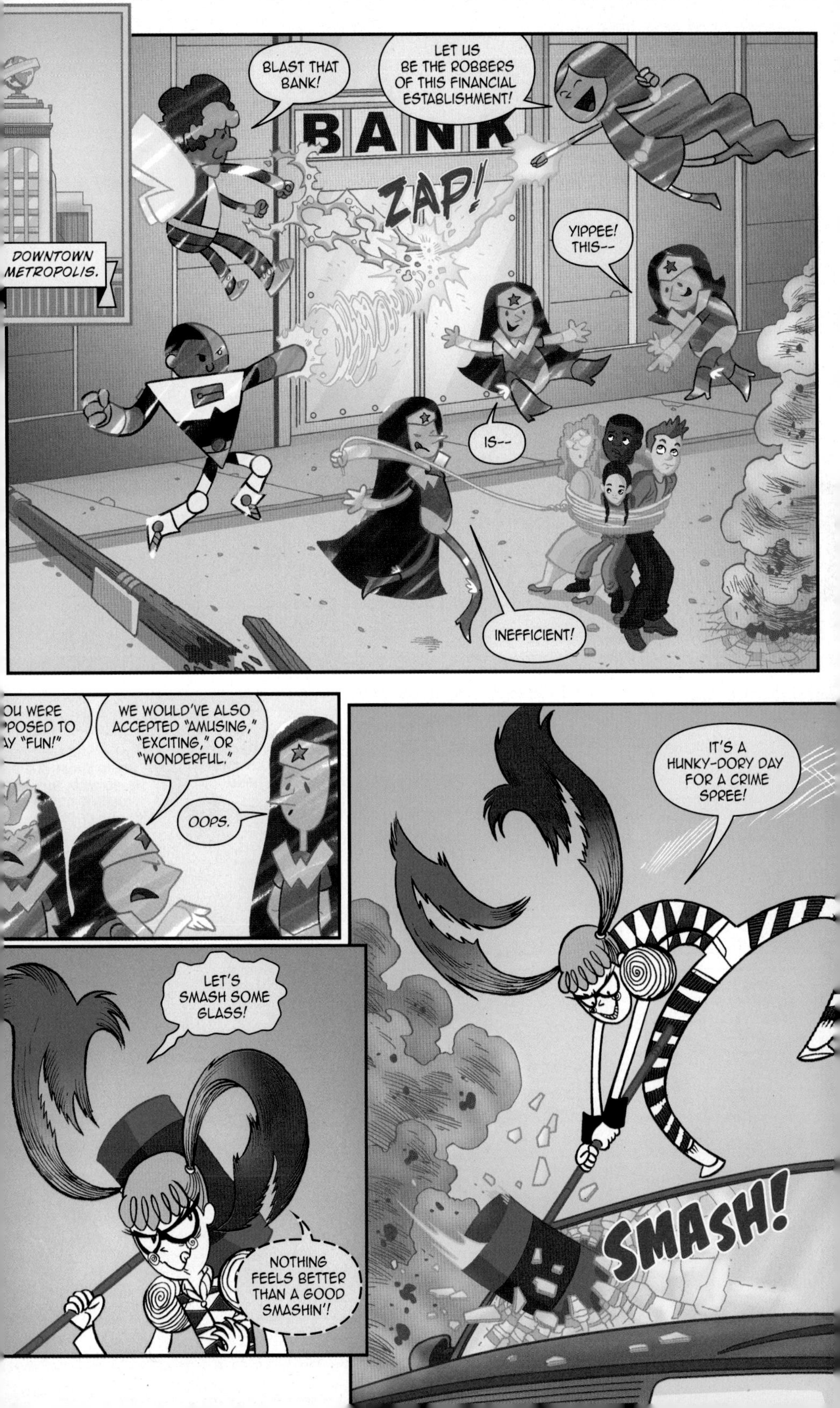
DOWNTOWN METROPOLIS.
BANK
BLAST THAT BANK!
LET US BE THE ROBBERS OF THIS FINANCIAL ESTABLISHMENT!
ZAP!
YIPPEE! THIS--
IS--
INEFFICIENT!
OU WERE PPOSED TO AY "FUN!"
WE WOULD'VE ALSO ACCEPTED "AMUSING," "EXCITING," OR "WONDERFUL."
OOPS.
LET'S SMASH SOME GLASS!
NOTHING FEELS BETTER THAN A GOOD SMASHIN'!
IT'S A HUNKY-DORY DAY FOR A CRIME SPREE!
SMASH!

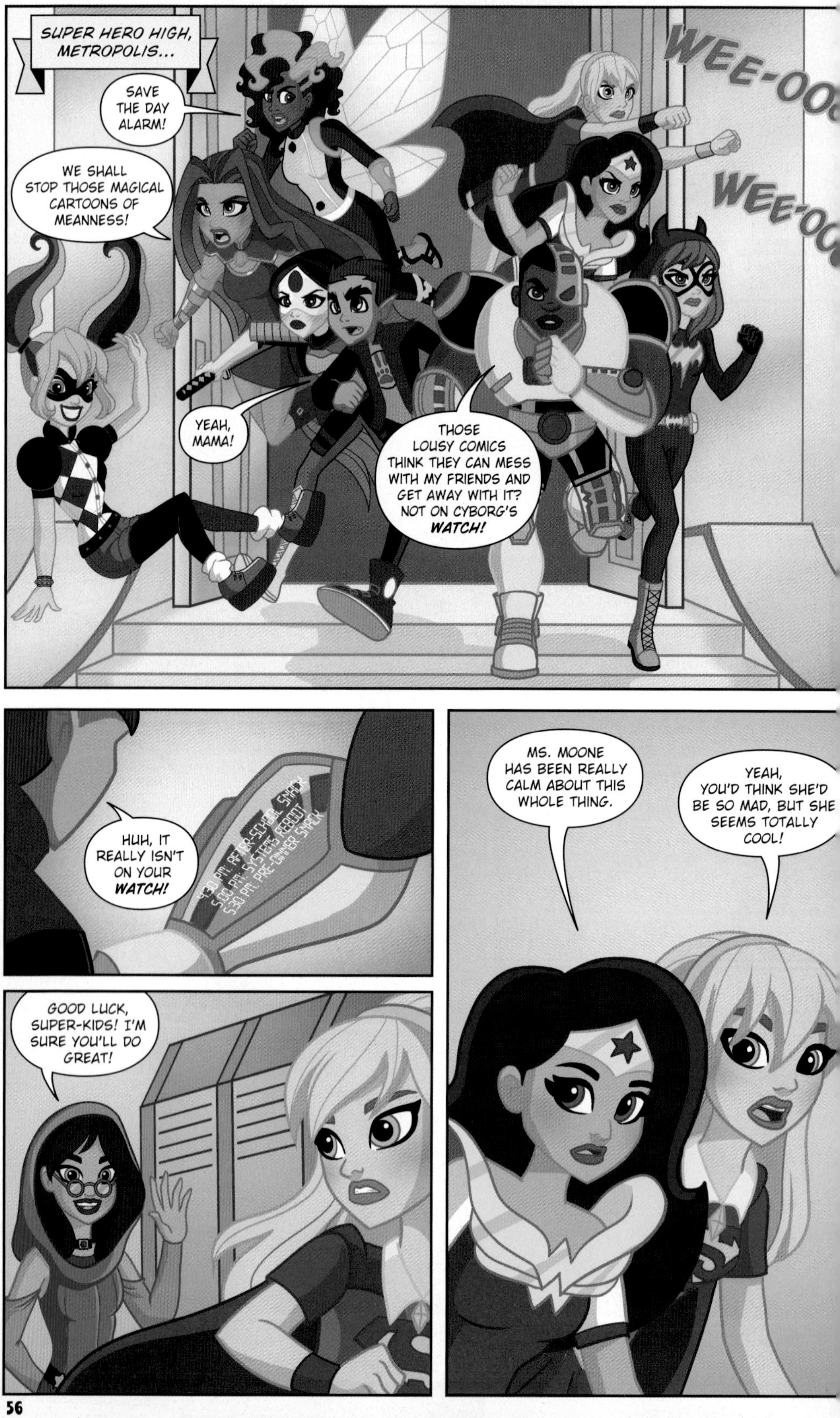
SUPER HERO HIGH, METROPOLIS...
SAVE THE DAY ALARM!
WEE-OOO
WEE-OOO
WE SHALL STOP THOSE MAGICAL CARTOONS OF MEANNESS!
YEAH, MAMA!
THOSE LOUSY COMICS THINK THEY CAN MESS WITH MY FRIENDS AND GET AWAY WITH IT? NOT ON CYBORG'S **WATCH!**
HUH, IT REALLY ISN'T ON YOUR **WATCH!**
4:30 PM: AFTER-SCHOOL SNACK
5:00 PM: SYSTEMS REBOOT
5:30 PM: PRE-DINNER SNACK
GOOD LUCK, SUPER-KIDS! I'M SURE YOU'LL DO GREAT!
MS. MOONE HAS BEEN REALLY CALM ABOUT THIS WHOLE THING.
YEAH, YOU'D THINK SHE'D BE SO MAD, BUT SHE SEEMS TOTALLY COOL!

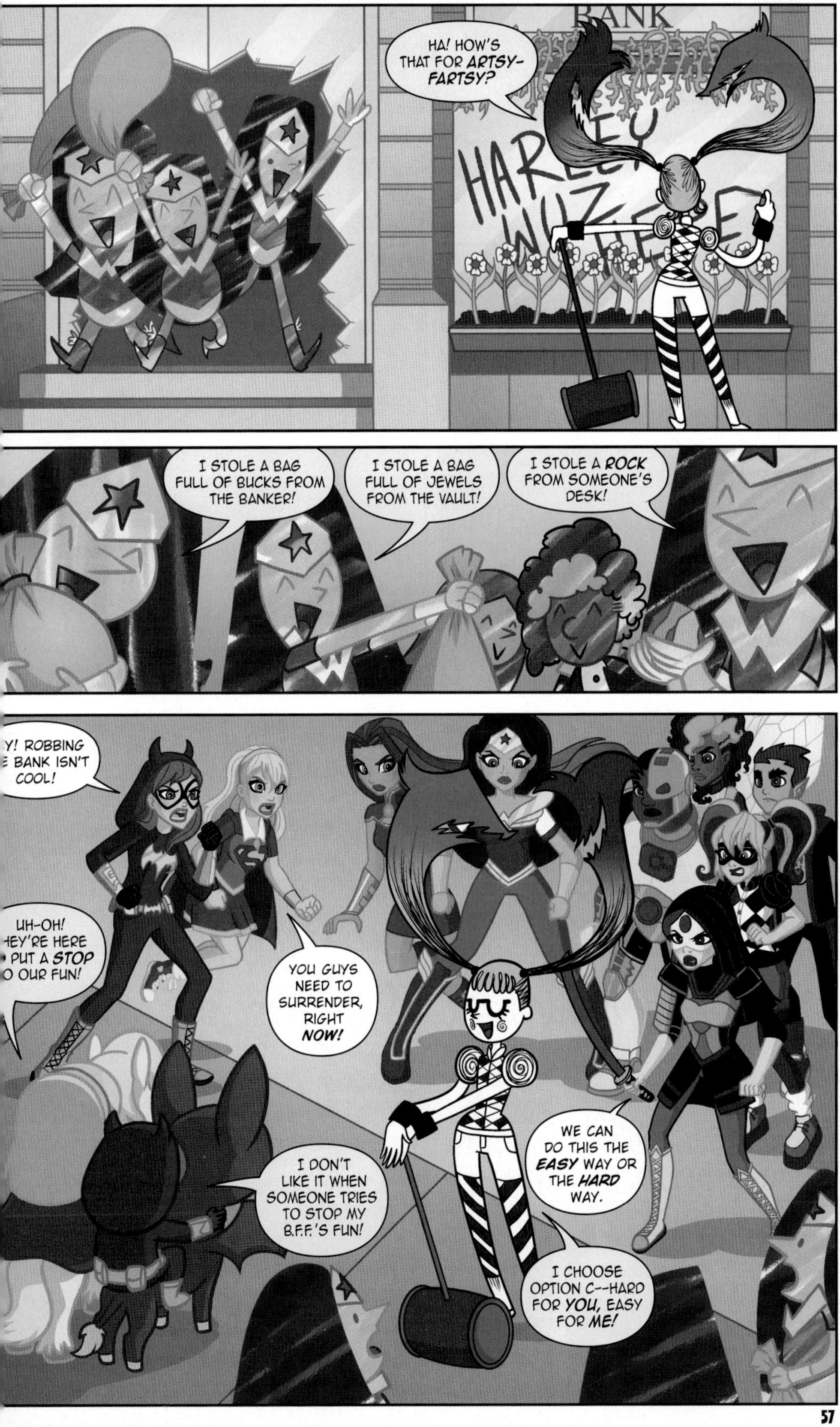
BANK
HA! HOW'S THAT FOR ARTSY-FARTSY?
I STOLE A BAG FULL OF BUCKS FROM THE BANKER!
I STOLE A BAG FULL OF JEWELS FROM THE VAULT!
I STOLE A ROCK FROM SOMEONE'S DESK!
Y! ROBBING E BANK ISN'T COOL!
UH-OH! HEY'RE HERE PUT A STOP O OUR FUN!
YOU GUYS NEED TO SURRENDER, RIGHT NOW!
WE CAN DO THIS THE EASY WAY OR THE HARD WAY.
I DON'T LIKE IT WHEN SOMEONE TRIES TO STOP MY B.F.F.'S FUN!
I CHOOSE OPTION C--HARD FOR YOU, EASY FOR ME!

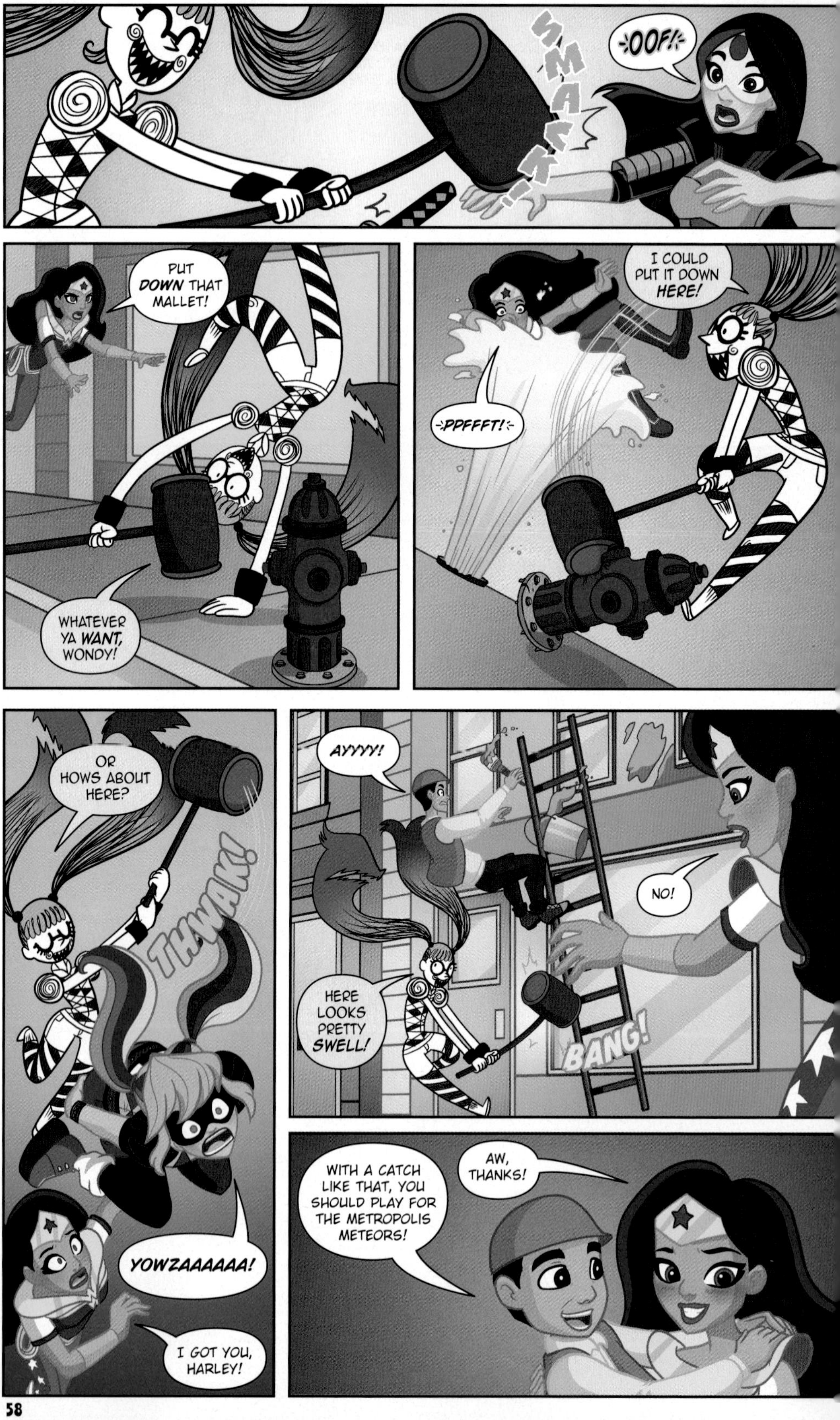
SMACK!!
OOF!
PUT DOWN THAT MALLET!
WHATEVER YA WANT, WONDY!
I COULD PUT IT DOWN HERE!
PPFFFT!
OR HOWS ABOUT HERE?
THWAK!
YOWZAAAAAA!
I GOT YOU, HARLEY!
AYYYY!
NO!
HERE LOOKS PRETTY SWELL!
BANG!
WITH A CATCH LIKE THAT, YOU SHOULD PLAY FOR THE METROPOLIS METEORS!
AW, THANKS!

IS ACTION NOT OF THE GOODNESS!

I AM NOT THE GOOD!

ZZZING!

I AM OF THE BADNESS UNTO MY BONES!

YOU ARE MADE OF THE PAPER! YOU DO NOT HAVE THE BONES, YOU SPINELESS THING!

WHOA! HARSH WORDS FROM STARFIRE!

I CALL THE THINGS THAT ARE LIKE UNTO WHICH I AM SEEING! AND I SEE THAT SHE IS MAKING ME VERY ANGRY!

YOU GO, GIRL! WHEN IT COMES TO FEELINGS, HONESTY IS THE BEST POLICY!

HA! ARMS OF STEEL!

BIND HER STEEL, BEAST BOY!

K-TINK!

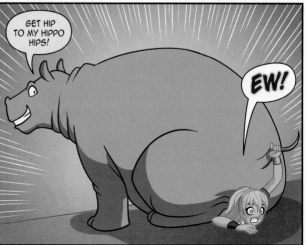

GET HIP TO MY HIPPO HIPS!

EW!

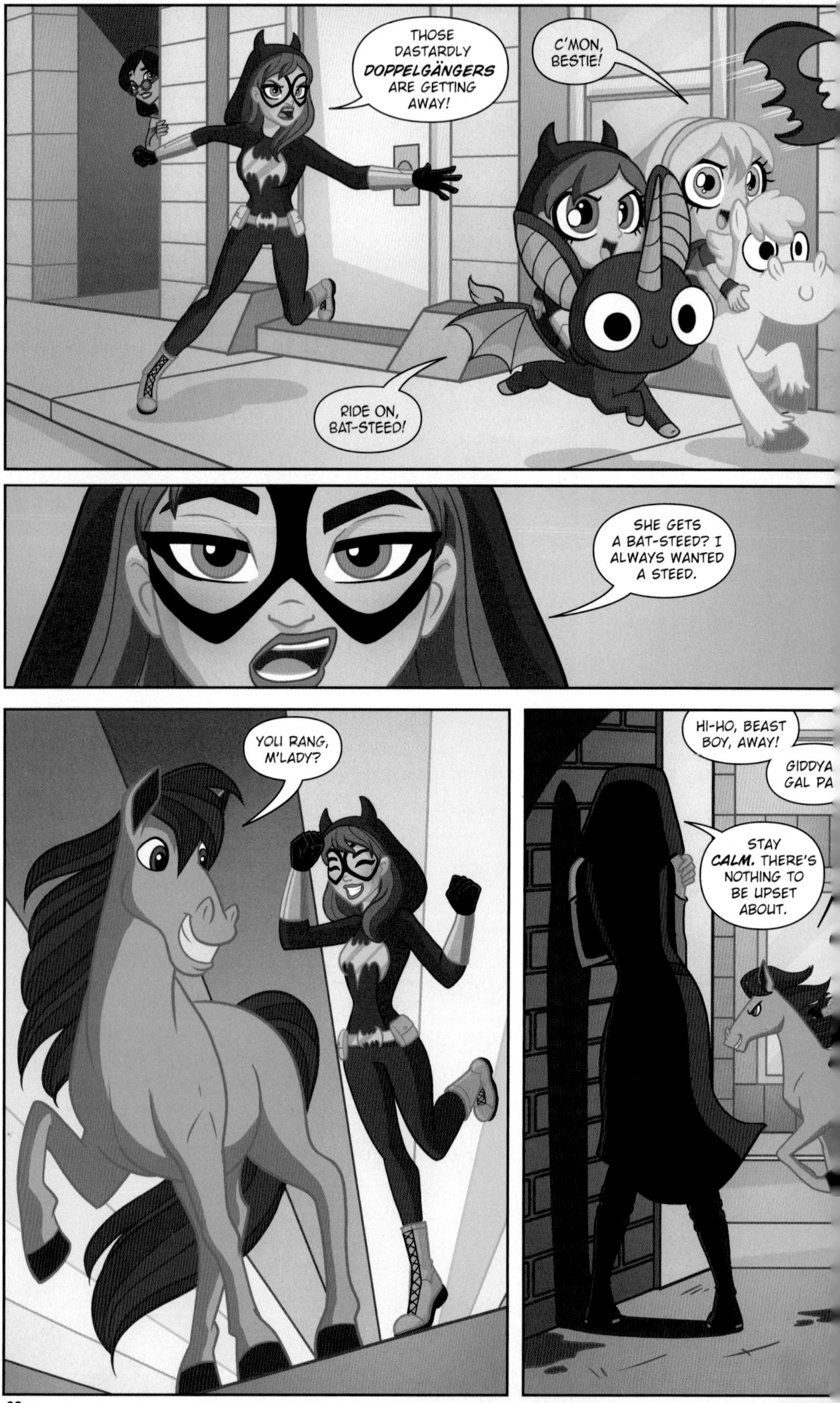
THOSE DASTARDLY DOPPELGÄNGERS ARE GETTING AWAY!
C'MON, BESTIE!
RIDE ON, BAT-STEED!
SHE GETS A BAT-STEED? I ALWAYS WANTED A STEED.
YOU RANG, M'LADY?
HI-HO, BEAST BOY, AWAY!
STAY CALM. THERE'S NOTHING TO BE UPSET ABOUT.

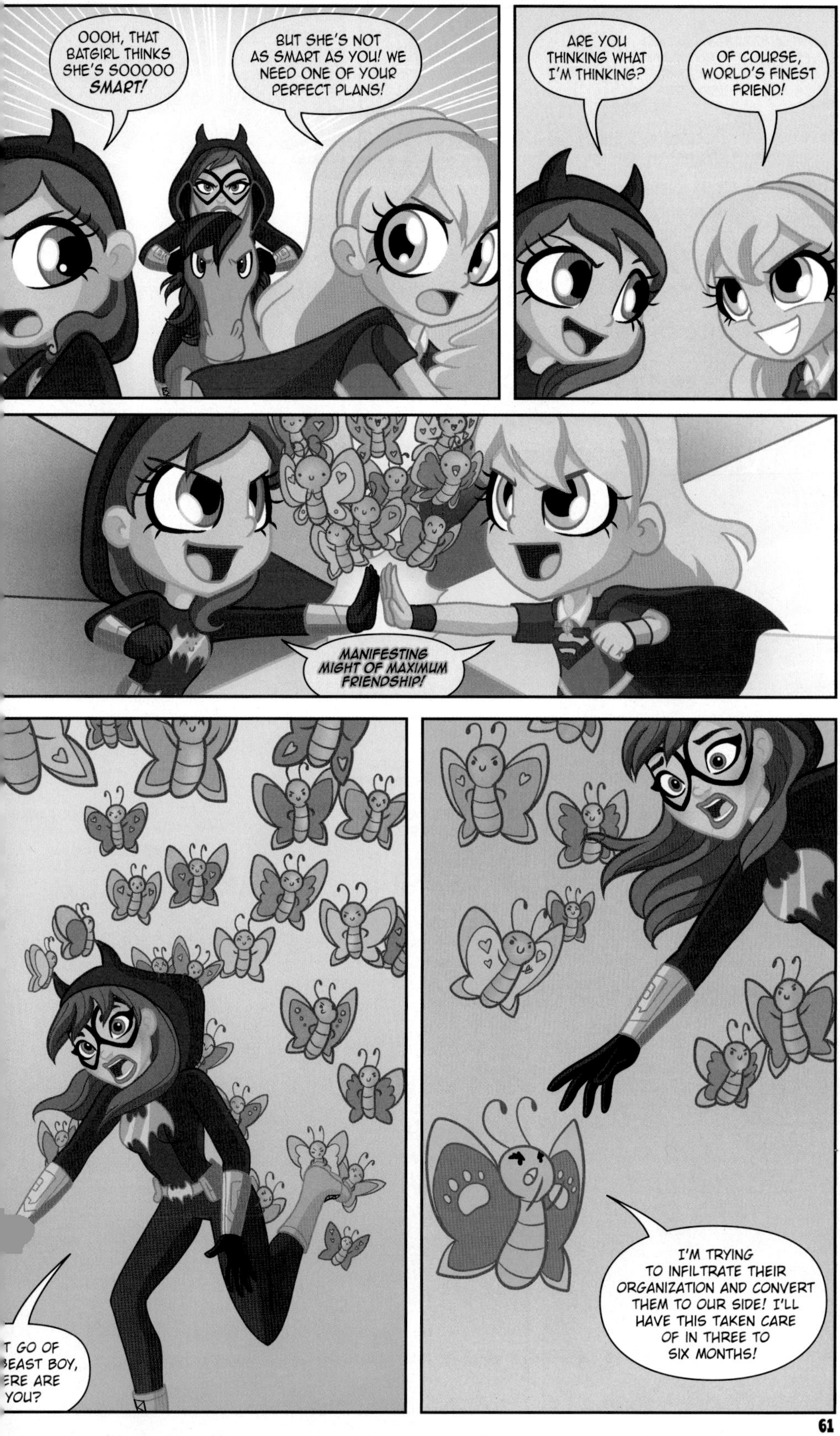

OOOH, THAT BATGIRL THINKS SHE'S SOOOOO SMART!
BUT SHE'S NOT AS SMART AS YOU! WE NEED ONE OF YOUR PERFECT PLANS!
ARE YOU THINKING WHAT I'M THINKING?
OF COURSE, WORLD'S FINEST FRIEND!
MANIFESTING MIGHT OF MAXIMUM FRIENDSHIP!
T GO OF BEAST BOY, ERE ARE YOU?
I'M TRYING TO INFILTRATE THEIR ORGANIZATION AND CONVERT THEM TO OUR SIDE! I'LL HAVE THIS TAKEN CARE OF IN THREE TO SIX MONTHS!

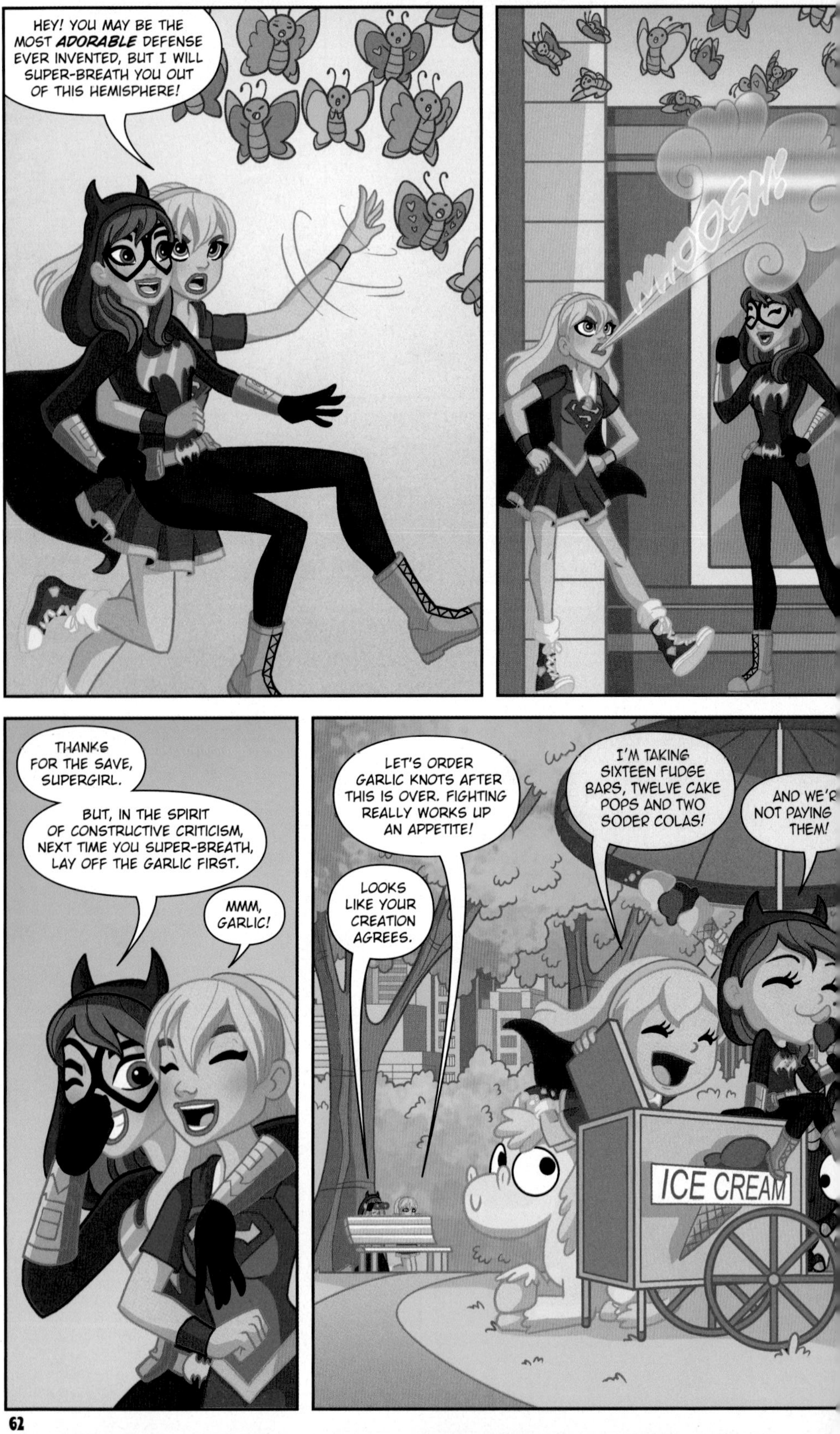
HEY! YOU MAY BE THE MOST ADORABLE DEFENSE EVER INVENTED, BUT I WILL SUPER-BREATH YOU OUT OF THIS HEMISPHERE!
WHOOSH!
THANKS FOR THE SAVE, SUPERGIRL.
BUT, IN THE SPIRIT OF CONSTRUCTIVE CRITICISM, NEXT TIME YOU SUPER-BREATH, LAY OFF THE GARLIC FIRST.
MMM, GARLIC!
LET'S ORDER GARLIC KNOTS AFTER THIS IS OVER. FIGHTING REALLY WORKS UP AN APPETITE!
LOOKS LIKE YOUR CREATION AGREES.
I'M TAKING SIXTEEN FUDGE BARS, TWELVE CAKE POPS AND TWO SODER COLAS!
AND WE'R NOT PAYING THEM!
ICE CREAM

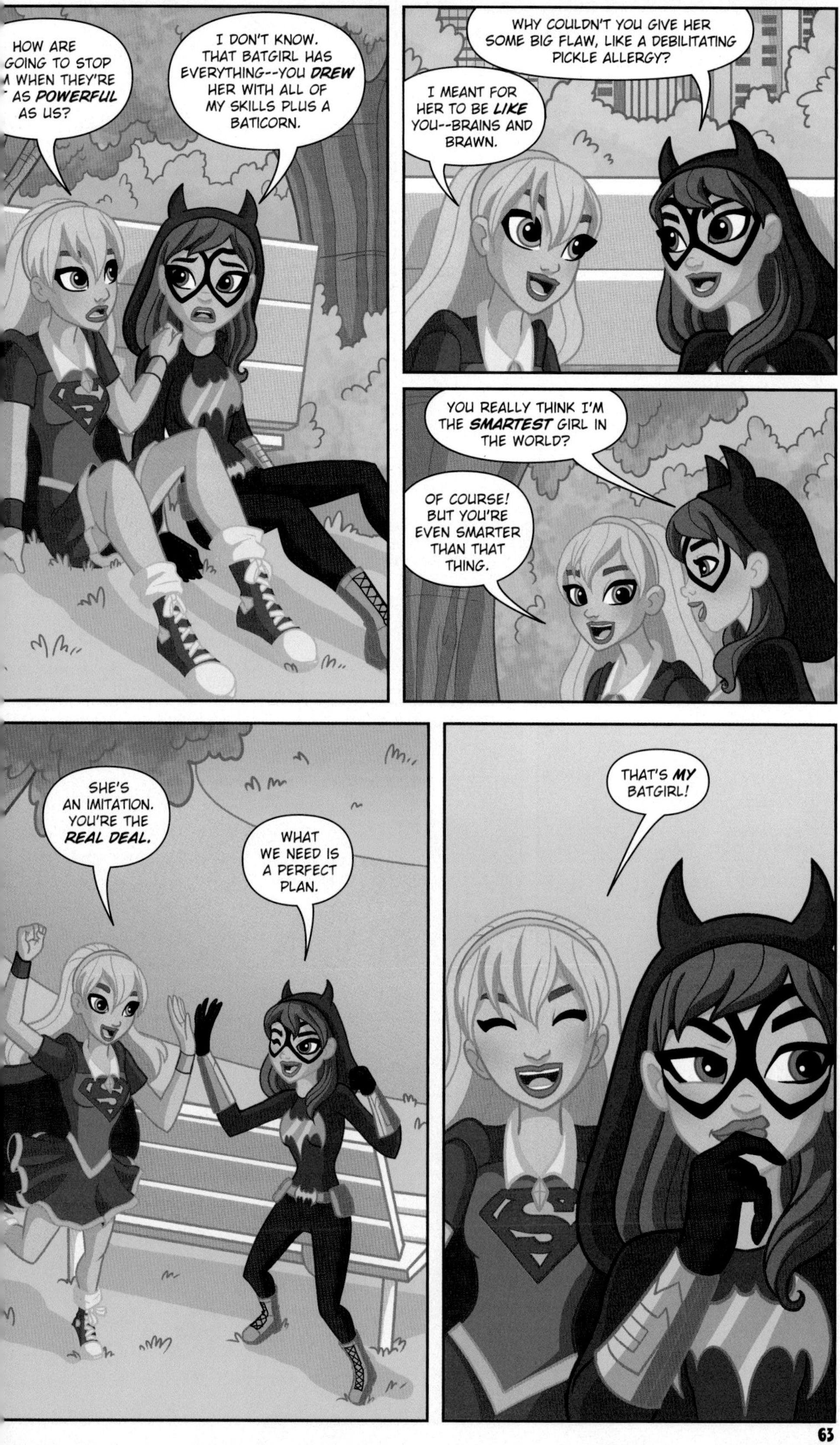
HOW ARE
GOING TO STOP
WHEN THEY'RE
AS POWERFUL
AS US?
I DON'T KNOW. THAT BATGIRL HAS EVERYTHING--YOU DREW HER WITH ALL OF MY SKILLS PLUS A BATICORN.
WHY COULDN'T YOU GIVE HER SOME BIG FLAW, LIKE A DEBILITATING PICKLE ALLERGY?
I MEANT FOR HER TO BE LIKE YOU--BRAINS AND BRAWN.
YOU REALLY THINK I'M THE SMARTEST GIRL IN THE WORLD?
OF COURSE! BUT YOU'RE EVEN SMARTER THAN THAT THING.
SHE'S AN IMITATION. YOU'RE THE REAL DEAL.
WHAT WE NEED IS A PERFECT PLAN.
THAT'S MY BATGIRL!

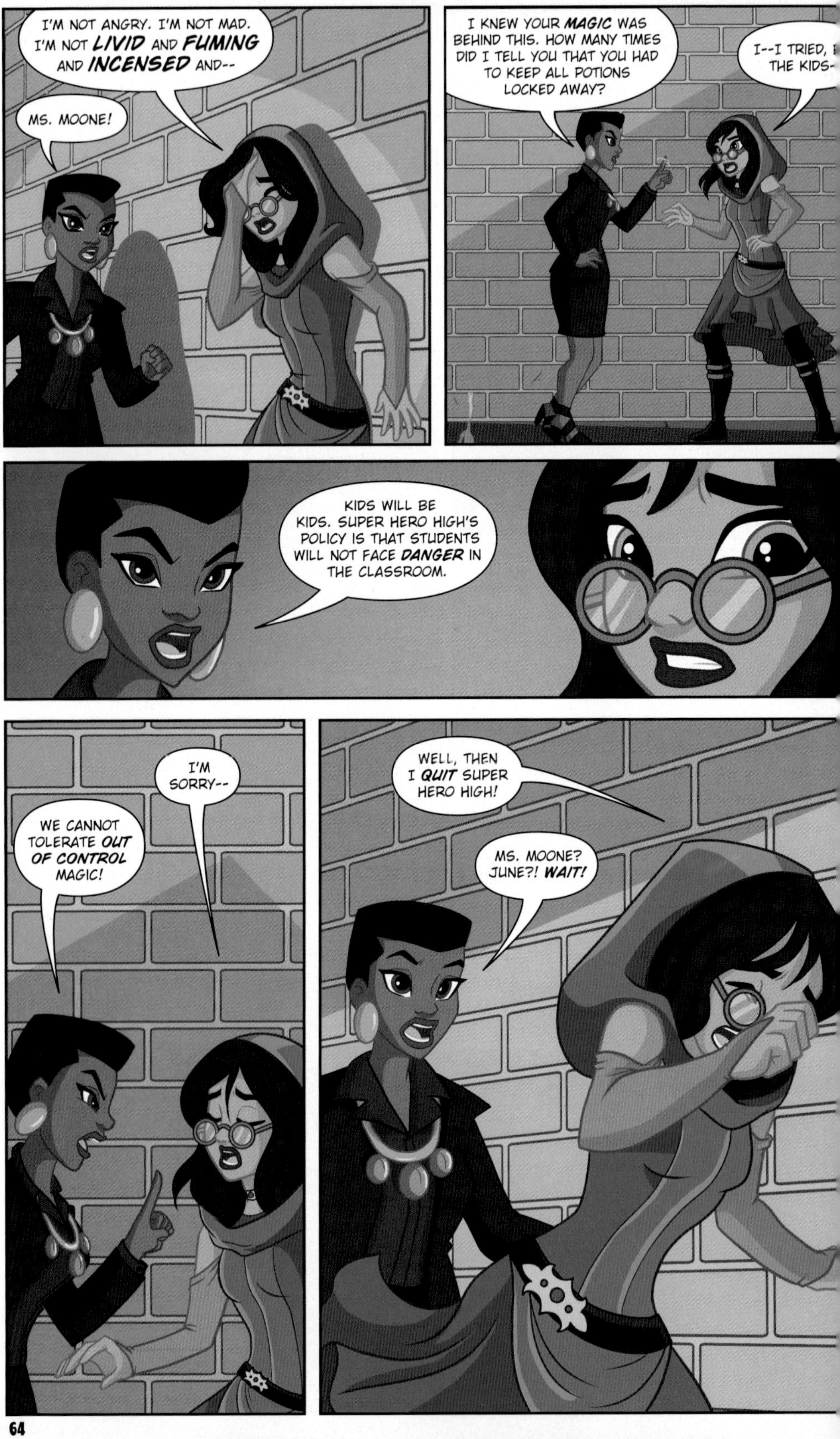
I'M NOT ANGRY. I'M NOT MAD. I'M NOT LIVID AND FUMING AND INCENSED AND--
MS. MOONE!
I KNEW YOUR MAGIC WAS BEHIND THIS. HOW MANY TIMES DID I TELL YOU THAT YOU HAD TO KEEP ALL POTIONS LOCKED AWAY?
I--I TRIED, THE KIDS-
KIDS WILL BE KIDS. SUPER HERO HIGH'S POLICY IS THAT STUDENTS WILL NOT FACE DANGER IN THE CLASSROOM.
I'M SORRY--
WE CANNOT TOLERATE OUT OF CONTROL MAGIC!
WELL, THEN I QUIT SUPER HERO HIGH!
MS. MOONE? JUNE?! WAIT!

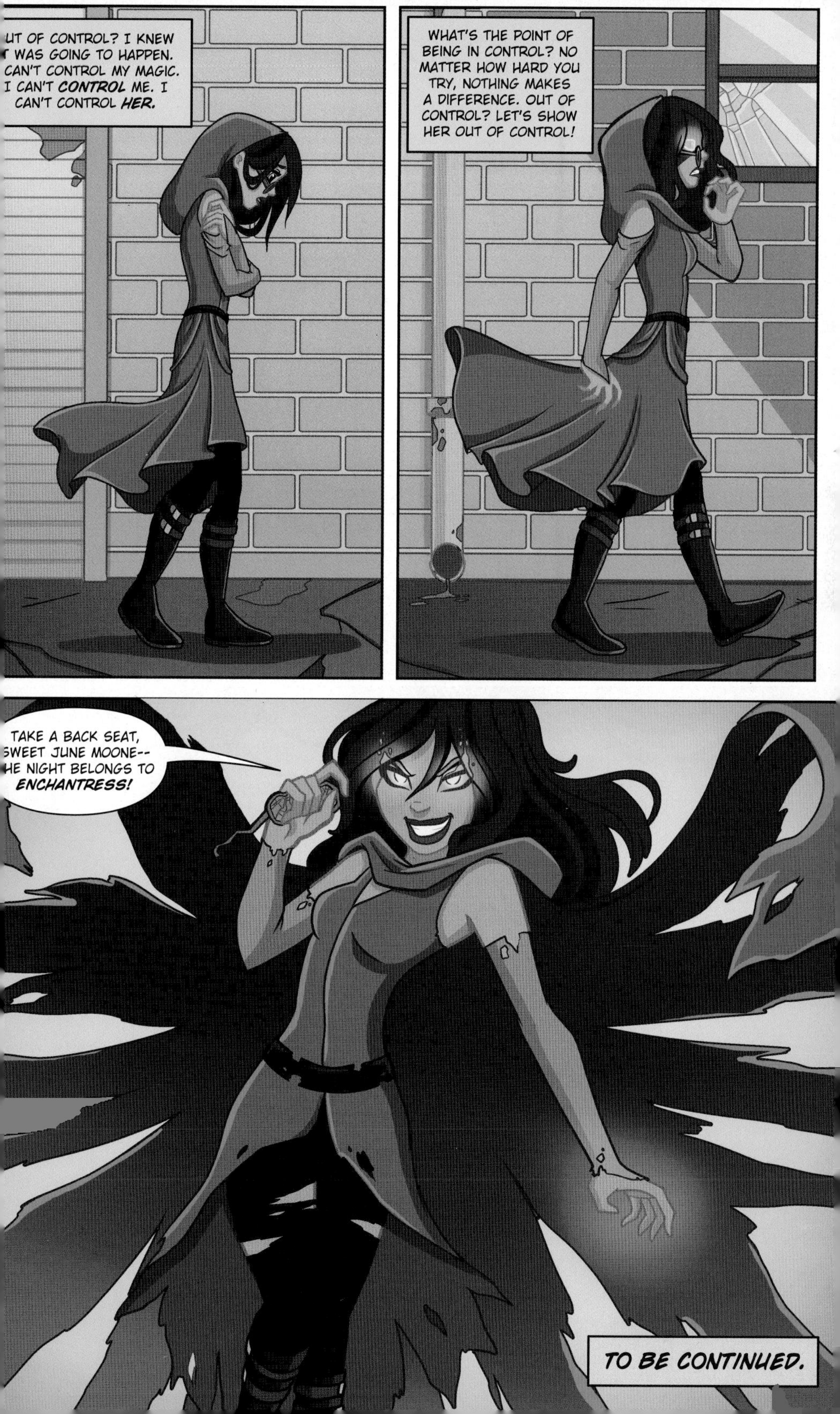
UT OF CONTROL? I KNEW
T WAS GOING TO HAPPEN.
CAN'T CONTROL MY MAGIC.
I CAN'T CONTROL ME. I
CAN'T CONTROL HER.
WHAT'S THE POINT OF BEING IN CONTROL? NO MATTER HOW HARD YOU TRY, NOTHING MAKES A DIFFERENCE. OUT OF CONTROL? LET'S SHOW HER OUT OF CONTROL!
TAKE A BACK SEAT,
SWEET JUNE MOONE--
HE NIGHT BELONGS TO
ENCHANTRESS!
TO BE CONTINUED.

CHAPTER FOUR
THE WRITE STUFF

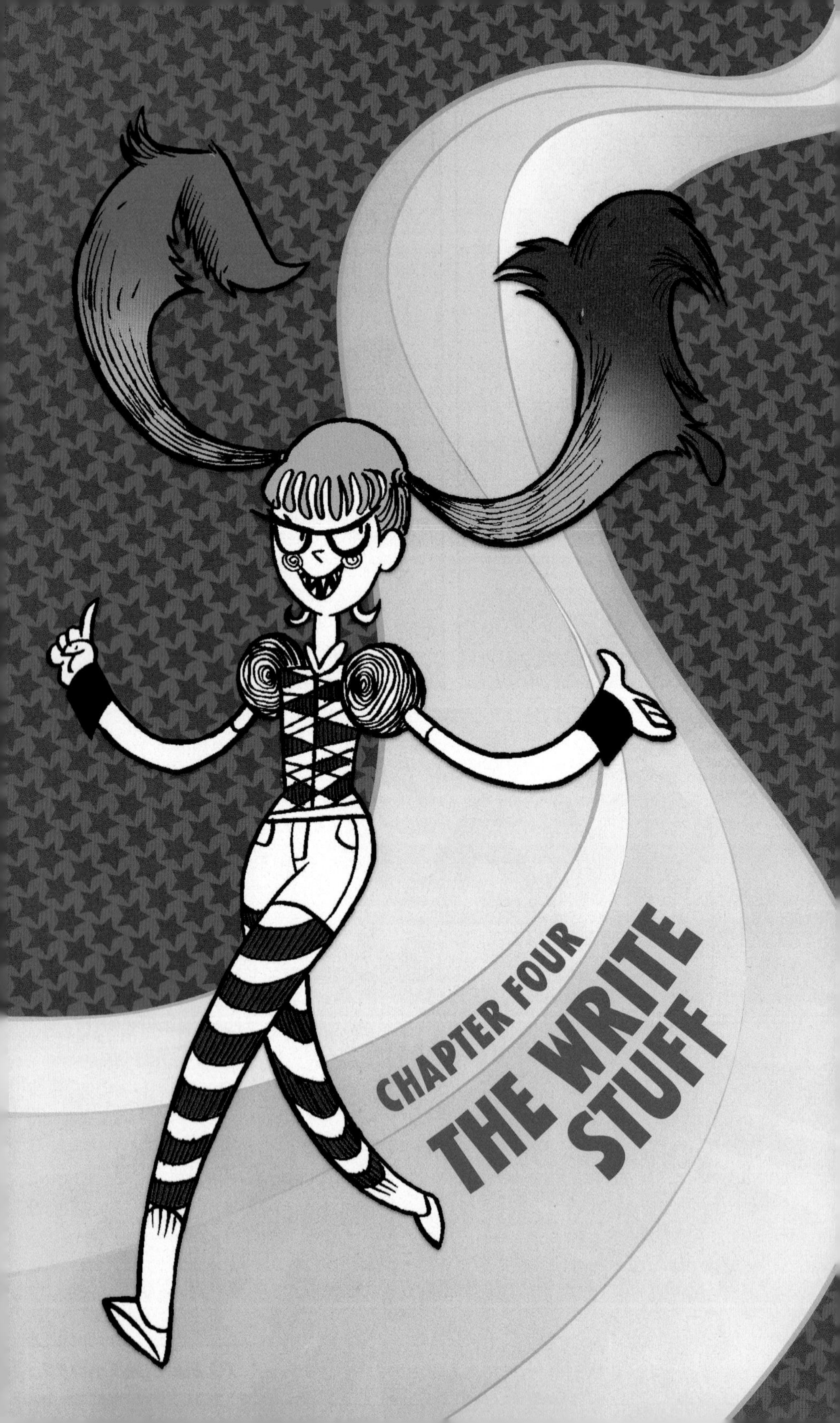

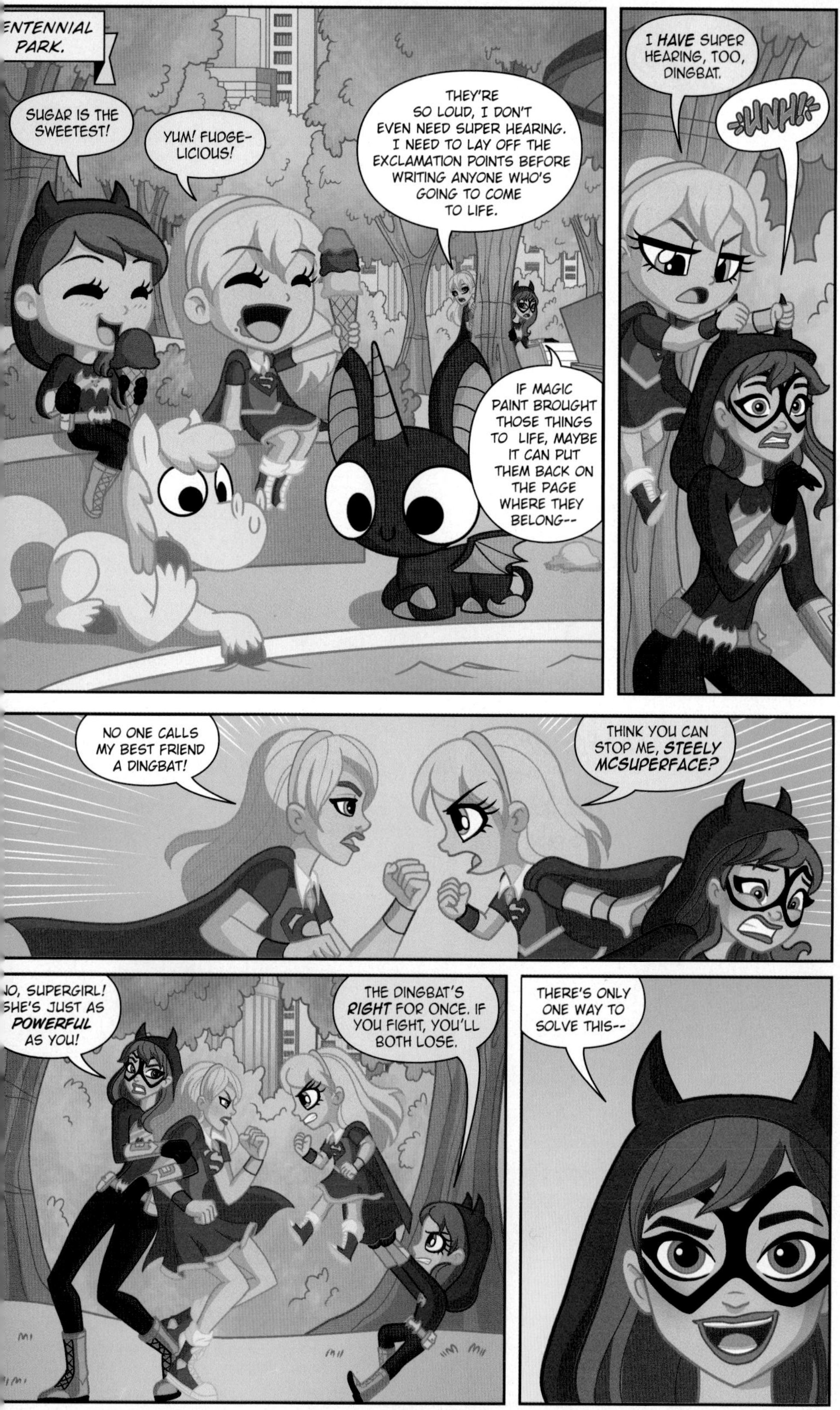

ENTENNIAL PARK.
SUGAR IS THE SWEETEST!
YUM! FUDGE-LICIOUS!
THEY'RE SO LOUD, I DON'T EVEN NEED SUPER HEARING. I NEED TO LAY OFF THE EXCLAMATION POINTS BEFORE WRITING ANYONE WHO'S GOING TO COME TO LIFE.
IF MAGIC PAINT BROUGHT THOSE THINGS TO LIFE, MAYBE IT CAN PUT THEM BACK ON THE PAGE WHERE THEY BELONG--
I HAVE SUPER HEARING, TOO, DINGBAT.
UNH!
NO ONE CALLS MY BEST FRIEND A DINGBAT!
THINK YOU CAN STOP ME, STEELY MCSUPERFACE?
NO, SUPERGIRL! SHE'S JUST AS POWERFUL AS YOU!
THE DINGBAT'S RIGHT FOR ONCE. IF YOU FIGHT, YOU'LL BOTH LOSE.
THERE'S ONLY ONE WAY TO SOLVE THIS--

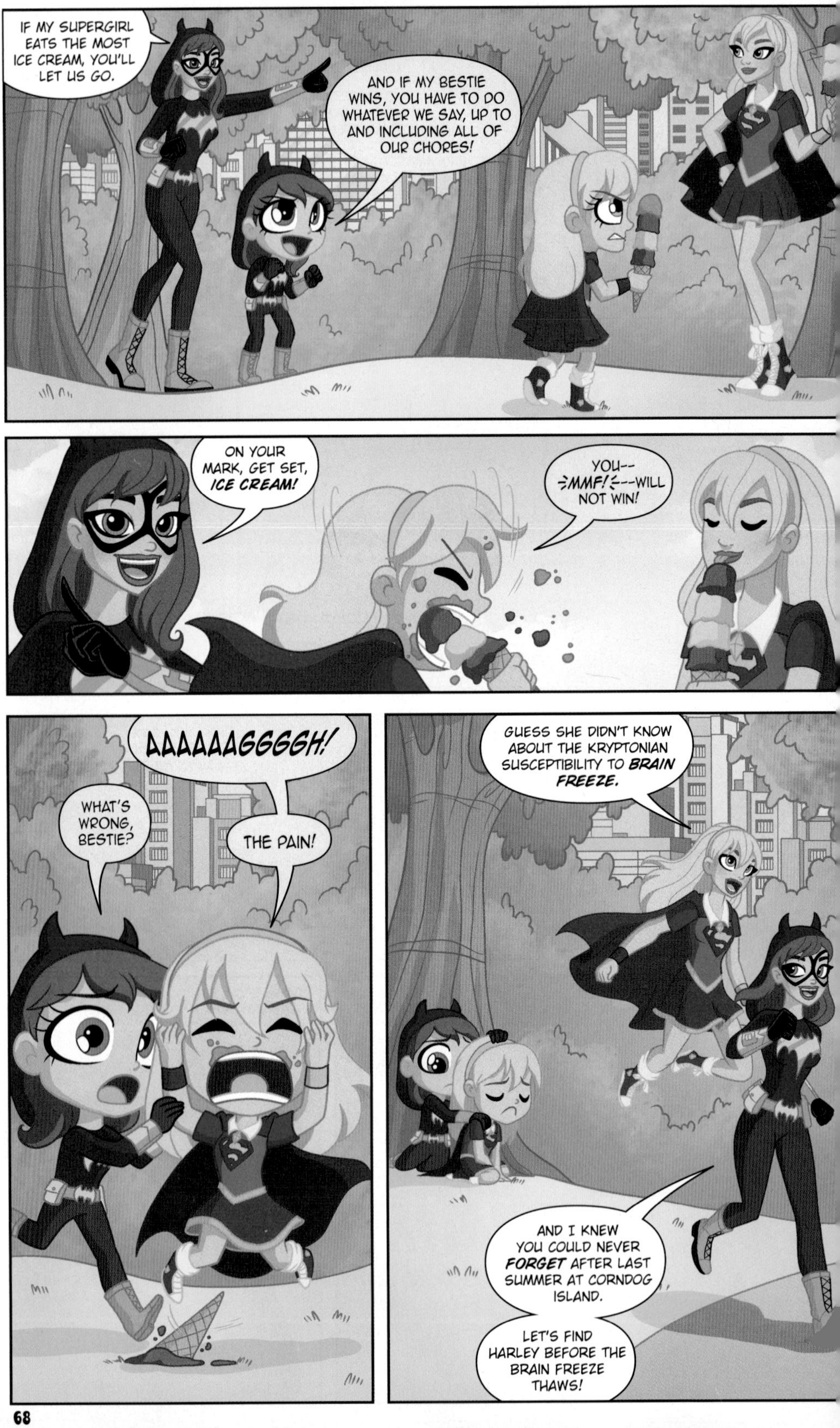
IF MY SUPERGIRL EATS THE MOST ICE CREAM, YOU'LL LET US GO.
AND IF MY BESTIE WINS, YOU HAVE TO DO WHATEVER WE SAY, UP TO AND INCLUDING ALL OF OUR CHORES!
ON YOUR MARK, GET SET, ICE CREAM!
YOU-- MMF! --WILL NOT WIN!
AAAAAAGGGGH!
WHAT'S WRONG, BESTIE?
THE PAIN!
GUESS SHE DIDN'T KNOW ABOUT THE KRYPTONIAN SUSCEPTIBILITY TO BRAIN FREEZE.
AND I KNEW YOU COULD NEVER FORGET AFTER LAST SUMMER AT CORNDOG ISLAND.
LET'S FIND HARLEY BEFORE THE BRAIN FREEZE THAWS!

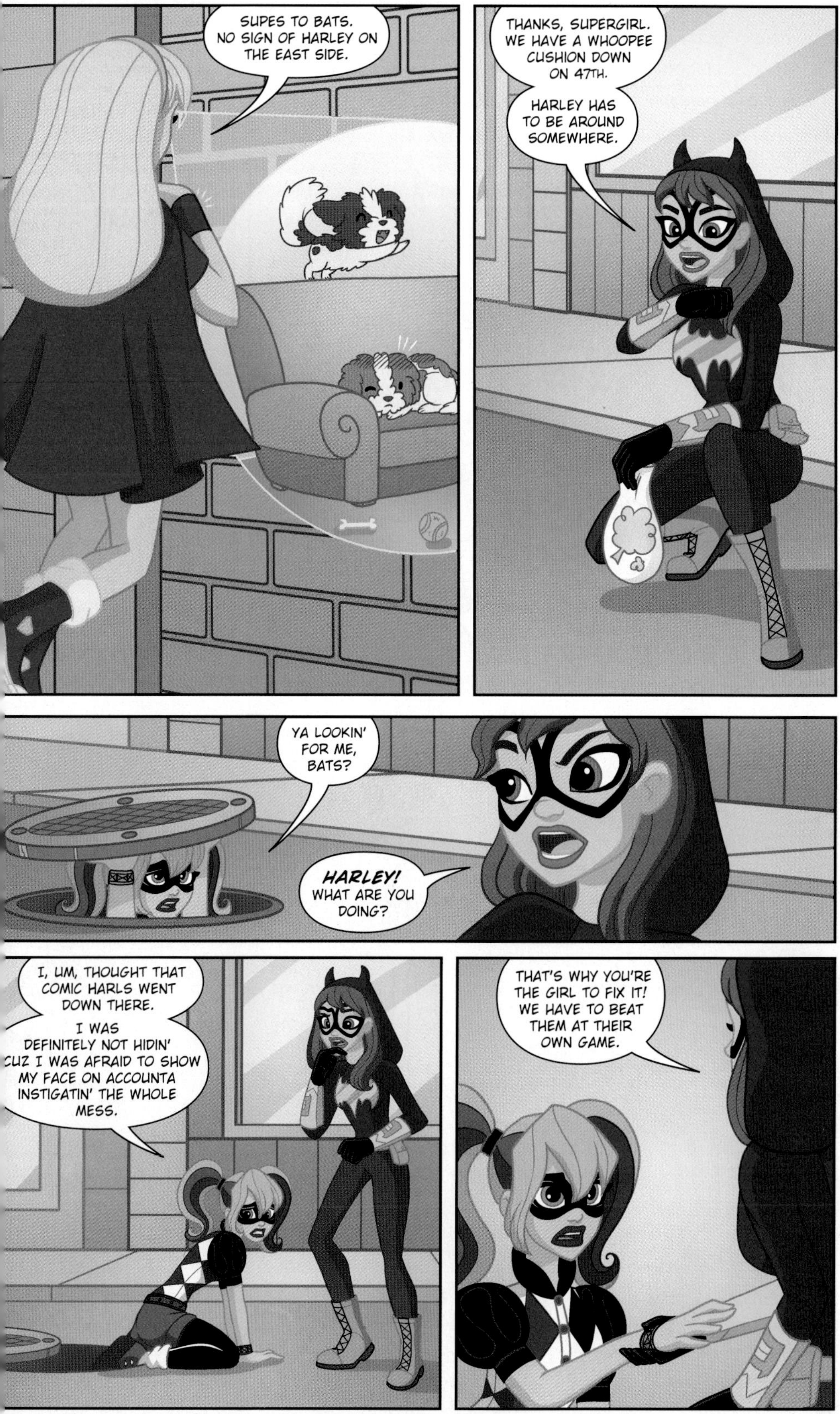
SUPES TO BATS. NO SIGN OF HARLEY ON THE EAST SIDE.
THANKS, SUPERGIRL. WE HAVE A WHOOPEE CUSHION DOWN ON 47TH.
HARLEY HAS TO BE AROUND SOMEWHERE.
YA LOOKIN' FOR ME, BATS?
HARLEY! WHAT ARE YOU DOING?
I, UM, THOUGHT THAT COMIC HARLS WENT DOWN THERE.
I WAS DEFINITELY NOT HIDIN' CUZ I WAS AFRAID TO SHOW MY FACE ON ACCOUNTA INSTIGATIN' THE WHOLE MESS.
THAT'S WHY YOU'RE THE GIRL TO FIX IT! WE HAVE TO BEAT THEM AT THEIR OWN GAME.

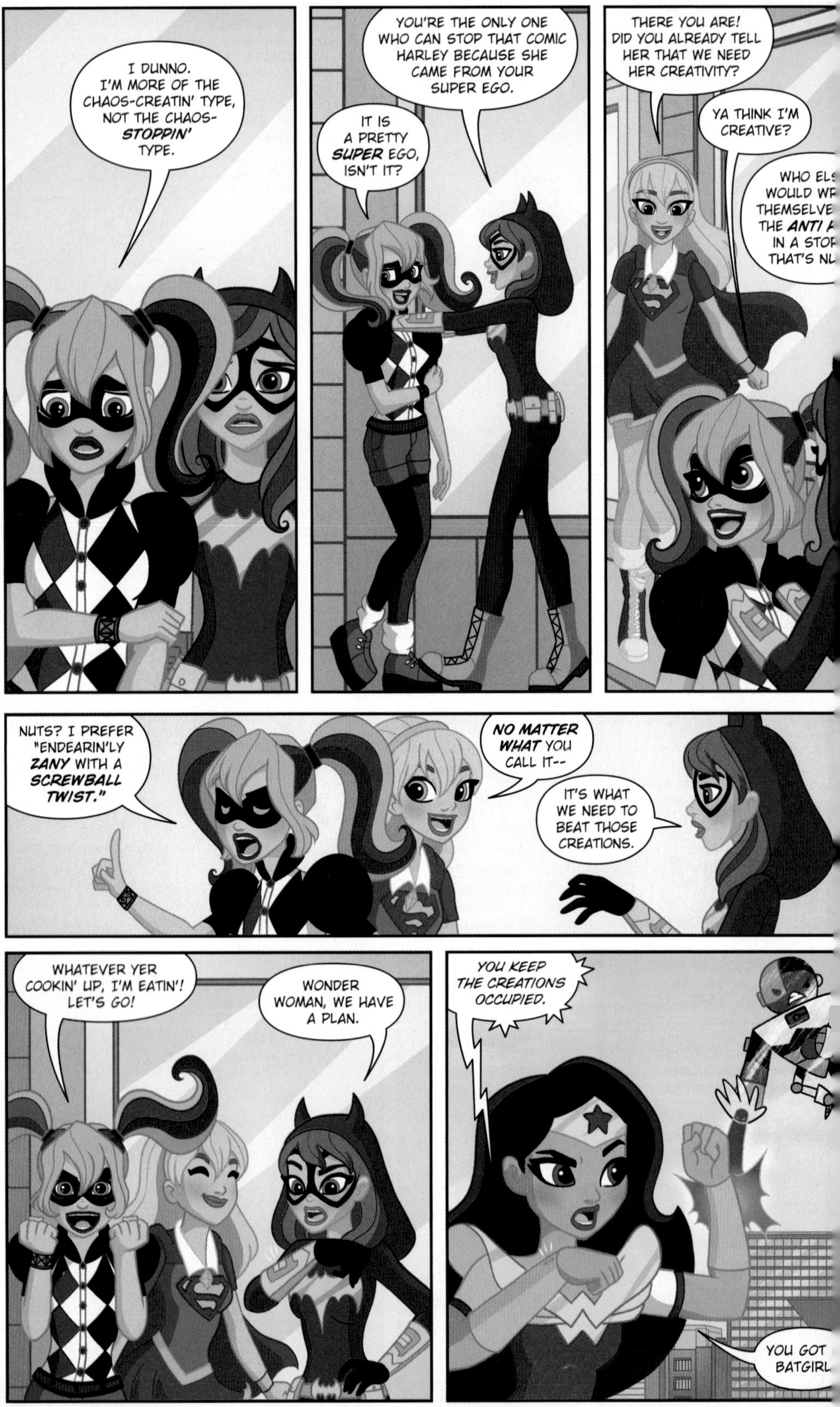

I DUNNO. I'M MORE OF THE CHAOS-CREATIN' TYPE, NOT THE CHAOS-STOPPIN' TYPE.
YOU'RE THE ONLY ONE WHO CAN STOP THAT COMIC HARLEY BECAUSE SHE CAME FROM YOUR SUPER EGO.
IT IS A PRETTY SUPER EGO, ISN'T IT?
THERE YOU ARE! DID YOU ALREADY TELL HER THAT WE NEED HER CREATIVITY?
YA THINK I'M CREATIVE?
WHO ELS WOULD WR THEMSELVE THE ANTI IN A STOR THAT'S NU
NUTS? I PREFER "ENDEARIN'LY ZANY WITH A SCREWBALL TWIST."
NO MATTER WHAT YOU CALL IT--
IT'S WHAT WE NEED TO BEAT THOSE CREATIONS.
WHATEVER YER COOKIN' UP, I'M EATIN'! LET'S GO!
WONDER WOMAN, WE HAVE A PLAN.
YOU KEEP THE CREATIONS OCCUPIED.
YOU GOT BATGIRL

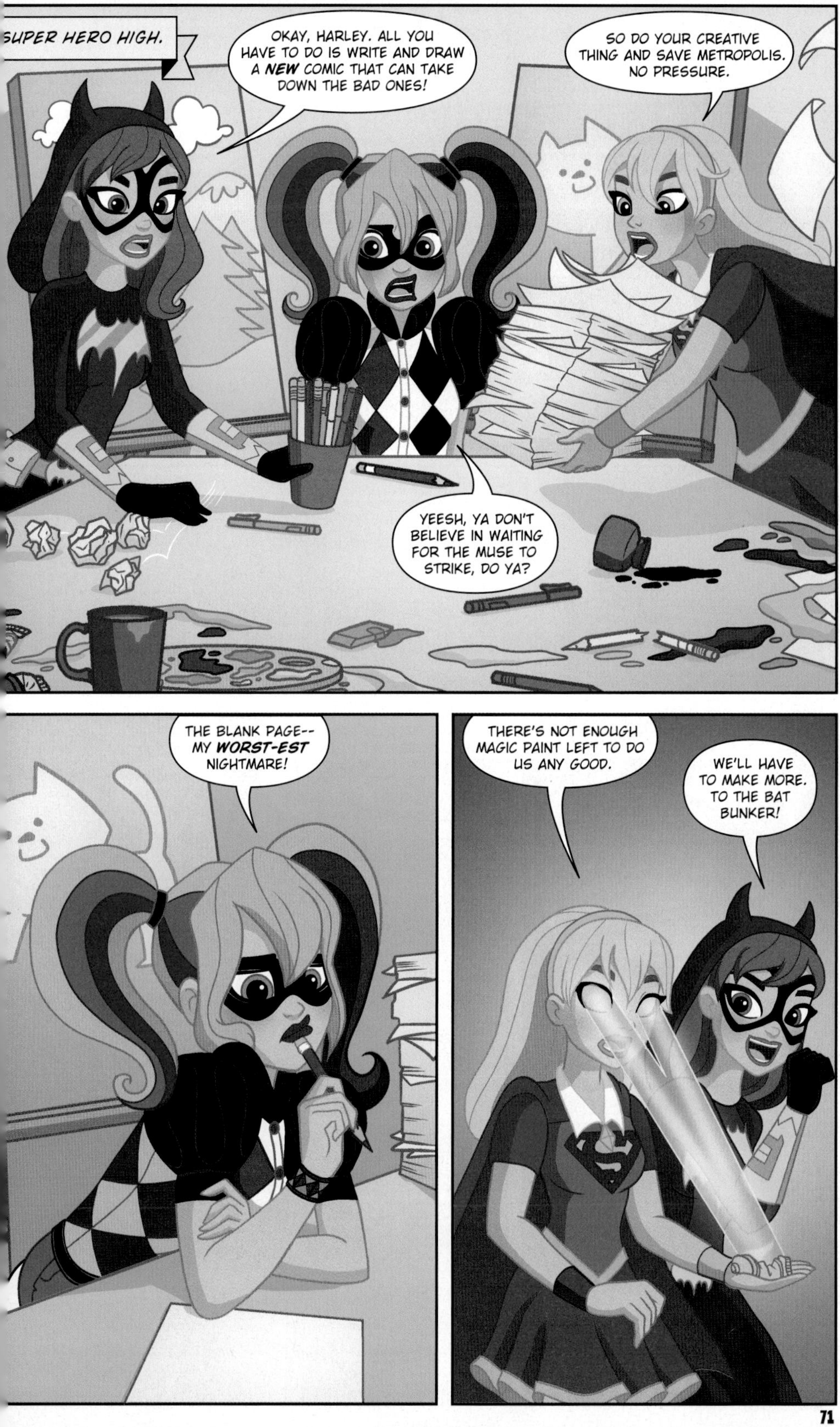
SUPER HERO HIGH.
OKAY, HARLEY. ALL YOU HAVE TO DO IS WRITE AND DRAW A NEW COMIC THAT CAN TAKE DOWN THE BAD ONES!
SO DO YOUR CREATIVE THING AND SAVE METROPOLIS. NO PRESSURE.
YEESH, YA DON'T BELIEVE IN WAITING FOR THE MUSE TO STRIKE, DO YA?
THE BLANK PAGE-- MY WORST-EST NIGHTMARE!
THERE'S NOT ENOUGH MAGIC PAINT LEFT TO DO US ANY GOOD.
WE'LL HAVE TO MAKE MORE. TO THE BAT BUNKER!

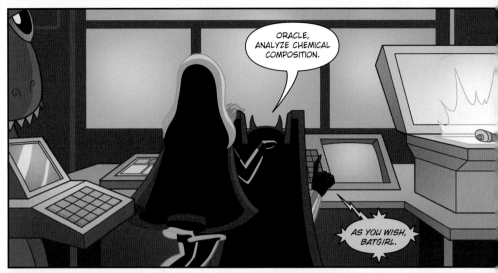

ORACLE, ANALYZE CHEMICAL COMPOSITION.

AS YOU WISH, BATGIRL.

ANALYSIS COMPLETE.

LET'S GET THIS TO FROST. SHE'LL KNOW HOW TO RECREATE IT.

FROST? I THOUGHT YOU WERE THE *OFFICIAL* SUPER HERO HIGH SMARTY-PANTS?

FROST IS A CHEMISTRY *EXPERT* AND THIS SMARTY-PANTS IS SMART ENOUGH TO KNOW WHEN TO ASK FOR HELP.

I CAN PRODUCE PART OF THE REQUIRED SOLUTION WITH THE CHEMICALS I HAVE ON HAND, BUT TO REPLICATE THE ENTIRE FORMULA, WE'LL NEED SOME ORGANIC MATERIALS.

ORGANIC? THAT MEANS WE NEED--

OOH! I KNOW THI ONE! *IVY*

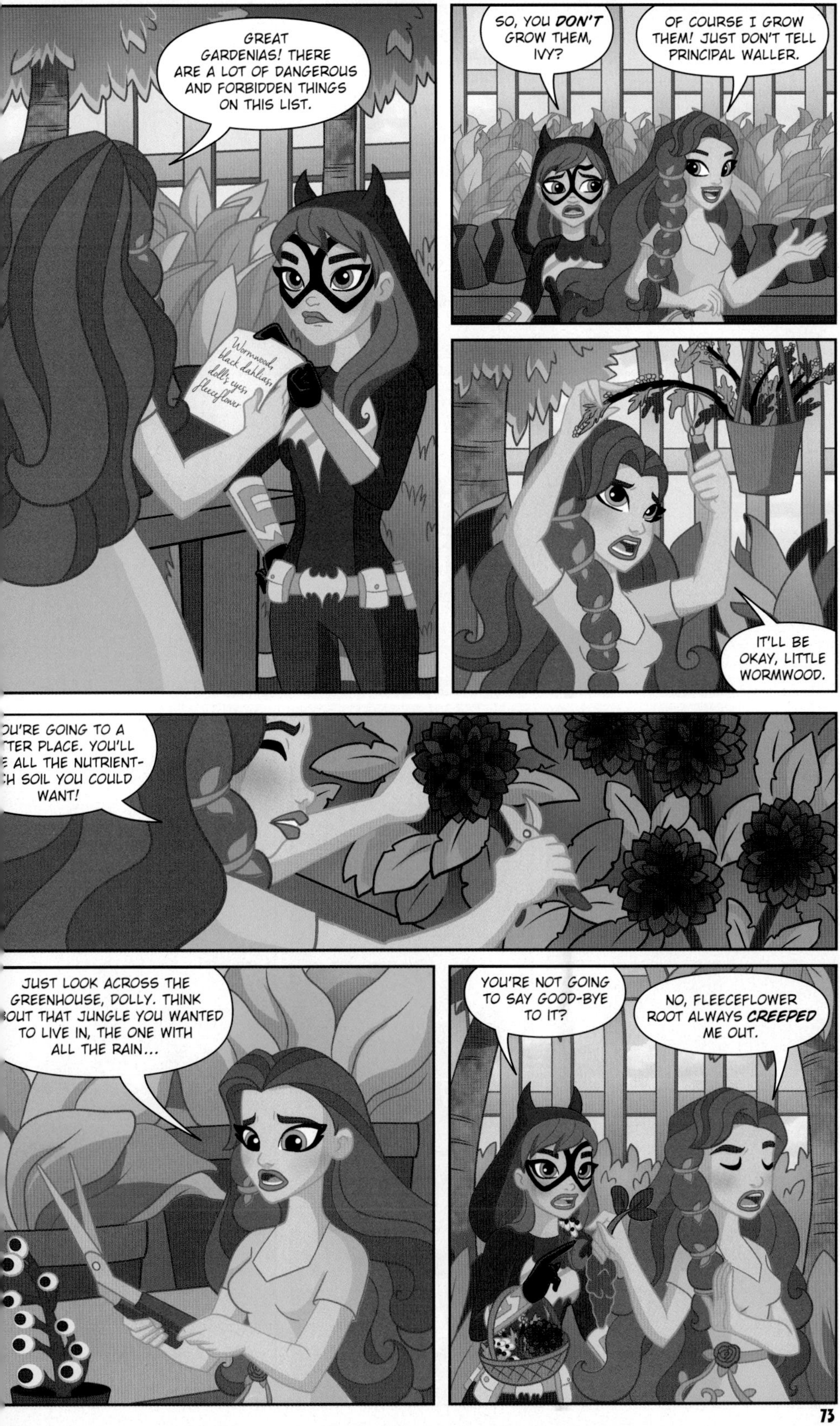
GREAT GARDENIAS! THERE ARE A LOT OF DANGEROUS AND FORBIDDEN THINGS ON THIS LIST.
Wormwood, black dahlias, doll's eyes, fleeceflower
SO, YOU **DON'T** GROW THEM, IVY?
OF COURSE I GROW THEM! JUST DON'T TELL PRINCIPAL WALLER.
IT'LL BE OKAY, LITTLE WORMWOOD.
OU'RE GOING TO A TTER PLACE. YOU'LL E ALL THE NUTRIENT- CH SOIL YOU COULD WANT!
JUST LOOK ACROSS THE GREENHOUSE, DOLLY. THINK BOUT THAT JUNGLE YOU WANTED TO LIVE IN, THE ONE WITH ALL THE RAIN...
YOU'RE NOT GOING TO SAY GOOD-BYE TO IT?
NO, FLEECEFLOWER ROOT ALWAYS ***CREEPED*** ME OUT.

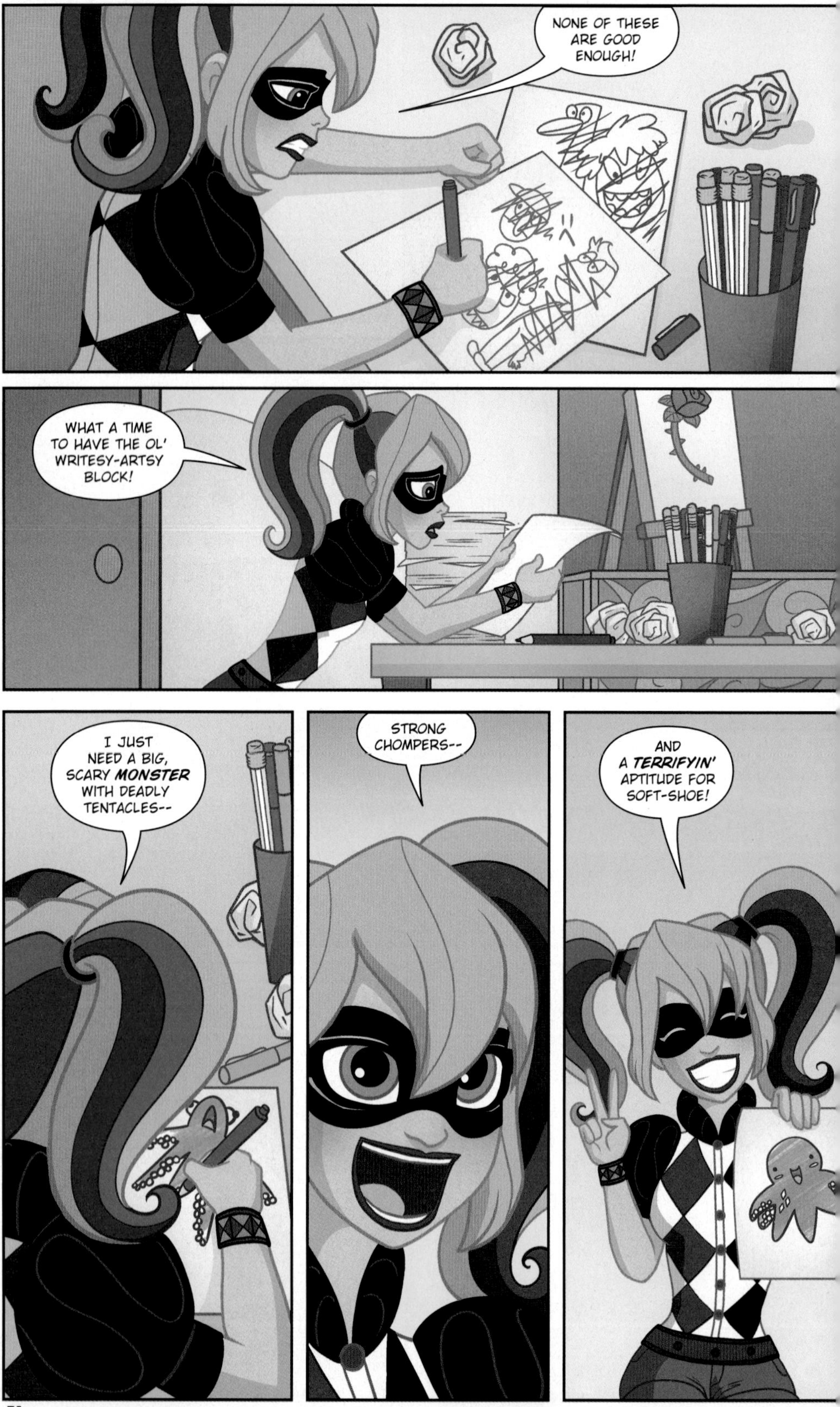
NONE OF THESE ARE GOOD ENOUGH!
WHAT A TIME TO HAVE THE OL' WRITESY-ARTSY BLOCK!
I JUST NEED A BIG, SCARY **MONSTER** WITH DEADLY TENTACLES--
STRONG CHOMPERS--
AND A ***TERRIFYIN'*** APTITUDE FOR SOFT-SHOE!

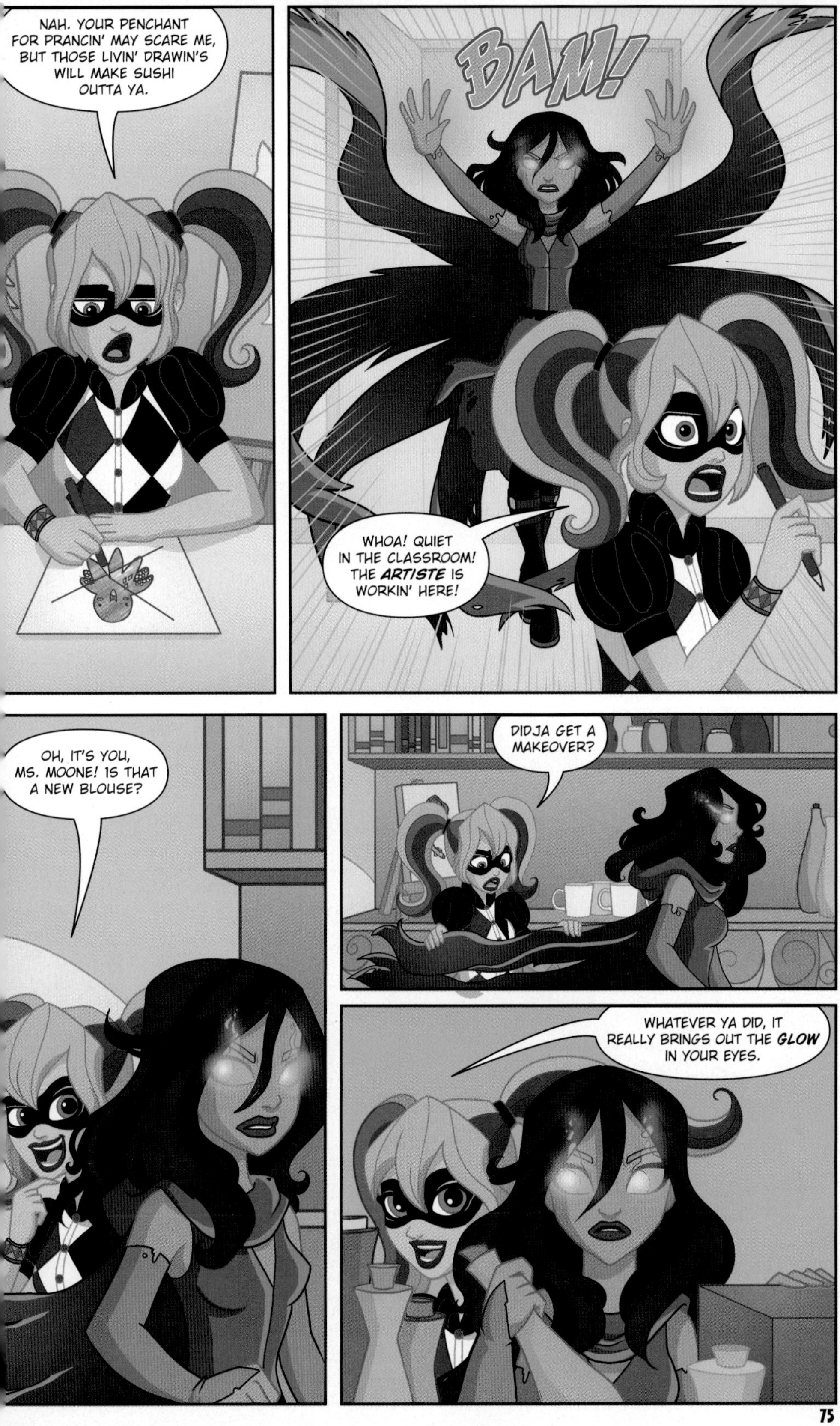
NAH. YOUR PENCHANT FOR PRANCIN' MAY SCARE ME, BUT THOSE LIVIN' DRAWIN'S WILL MAKE SUSHI OUTTA YA.
BAM!
WHOA! QUIET IN THE CLASSROOM! THE ARTISTE IS WORKIN' HERE!
OH, IT'S YOU, MS. MOONE! IS THAT A NEW BLOUSE?
DIDJA GET A MAKEOVER?
WHATEVER YA DID, IT REALLY BRINGS OUT THE GLOW IN YOUR EYES.

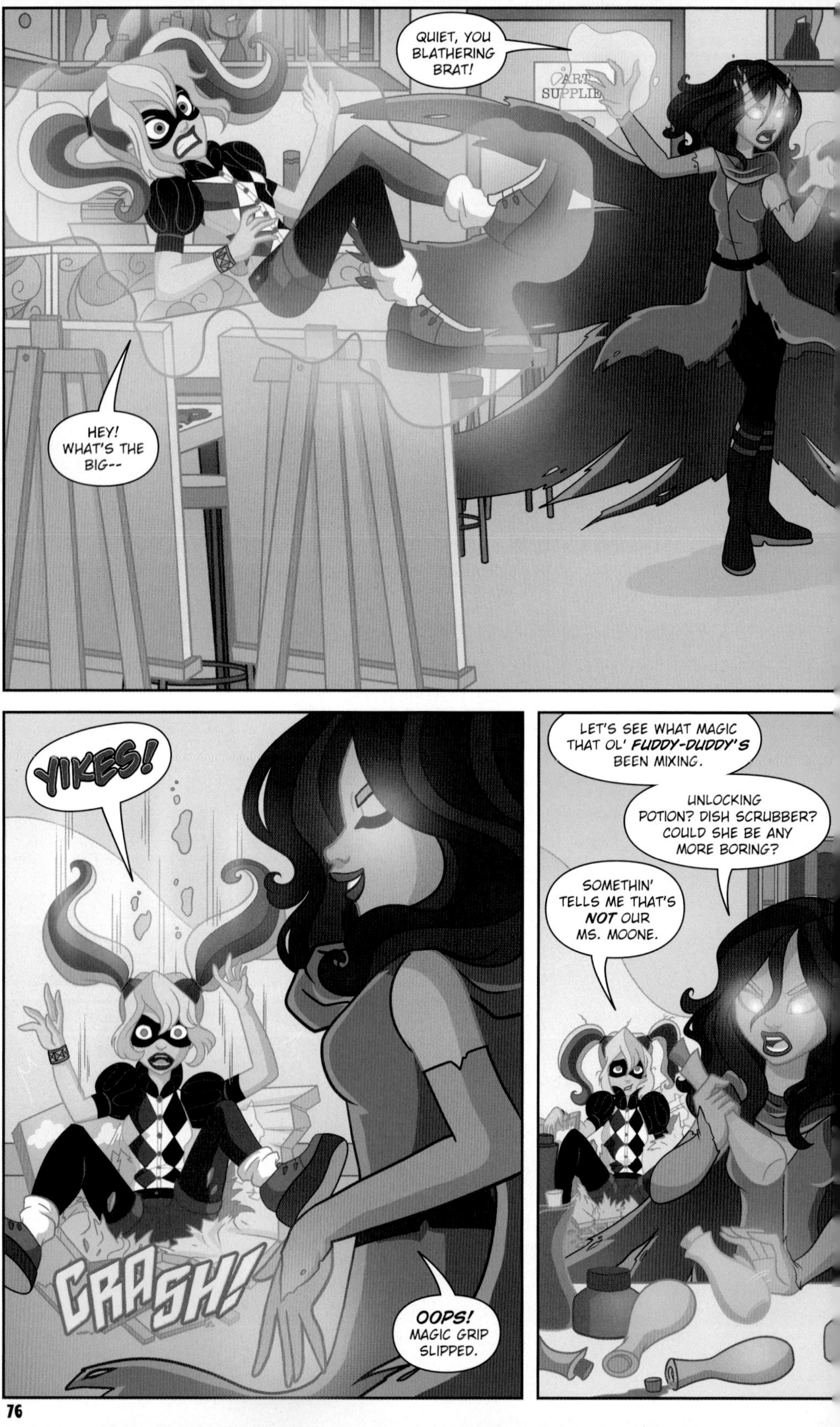
HEY! WHAT'S THE BIG--
QUIET, YOU BLATHERING BRAT!
YIKES!
CRASH!
OOPS! MAGIC GRIP SLIPPED.
LET'S SEE WHAT MAGIC THAT OL' FUDDY-DUDDY'S BEEN MIXING.
UNLOCKING POTION? DISH SCRUBBER? COULD SHE BE ANY MORE BORING?
SOMETHIN' TELLS ME THAT'S NOT OUR MS. MOONE.

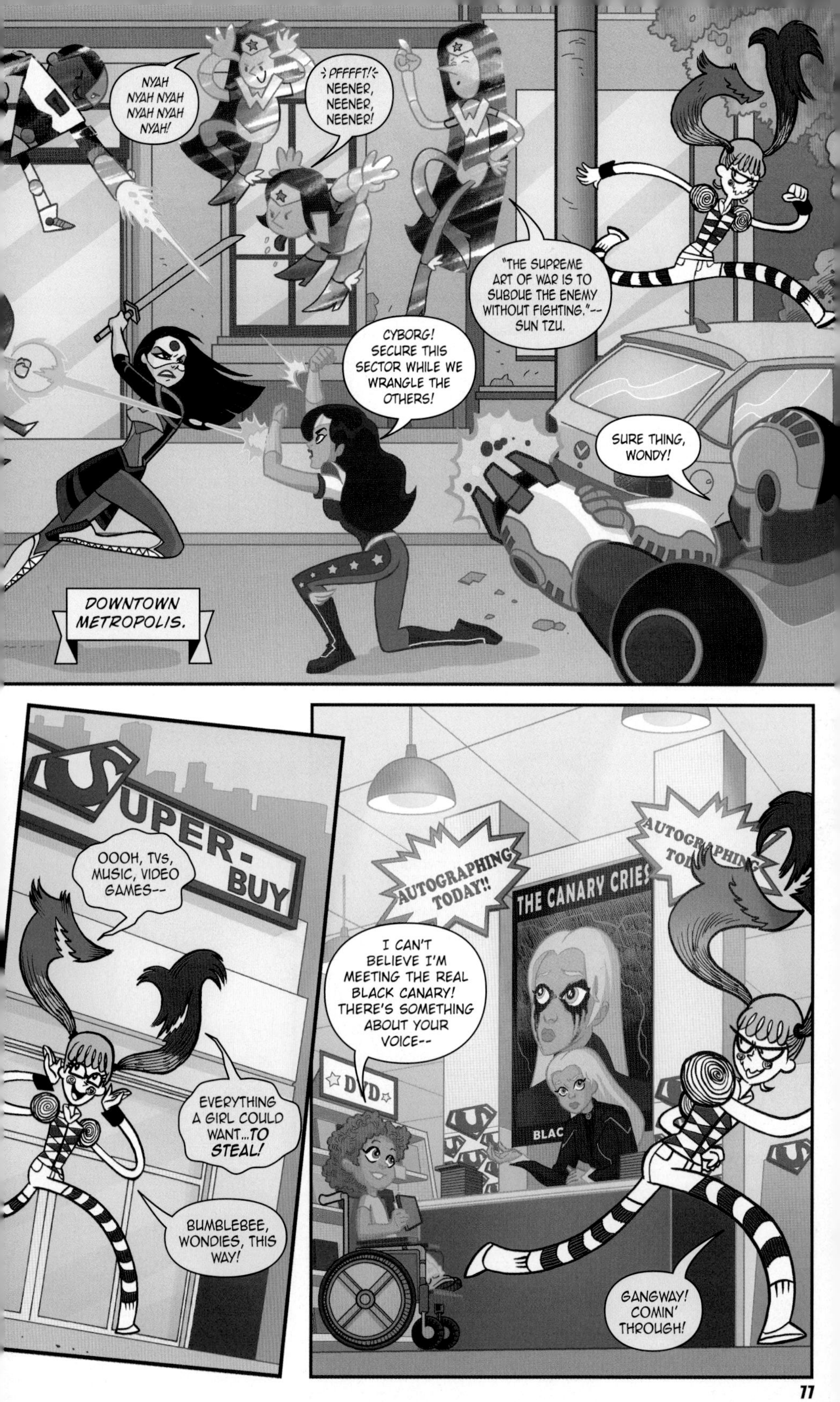

NYAH NYAH NYAH NYAH NYAH NYAH!
PFFFFT! NEENER, NEENER, NEENER!
"THE SUPREME ART OF WAR IS TO SUBDUE THE ENEMY WITHOUT FIGHTING."-- SUN TZU.
CYBORG! SECURE THIS SECTOR WHILE WE WRANGLE THE OTHERS!
SURE THING, WONDY!
DOWNTOWN METROPOLIS.
SUPER-BUY
OOOH, TVS, MUSIC, VIDEO GAMES--
EVERYTHING A GIRL COULD WANT...TO STEAL!
BUMBLEBEE, WONDIES, THIS WAY!
AUTOGRAPHING TODAY!!
THE CANARY CRIES
I CAN'T BELIEVE I'M MEETING THE REAL BLACK CANARY! THERE'S SOMETHING ABOUT YOUR VOICE--
DVD
GANGWAY! COMIN' THROUGH!

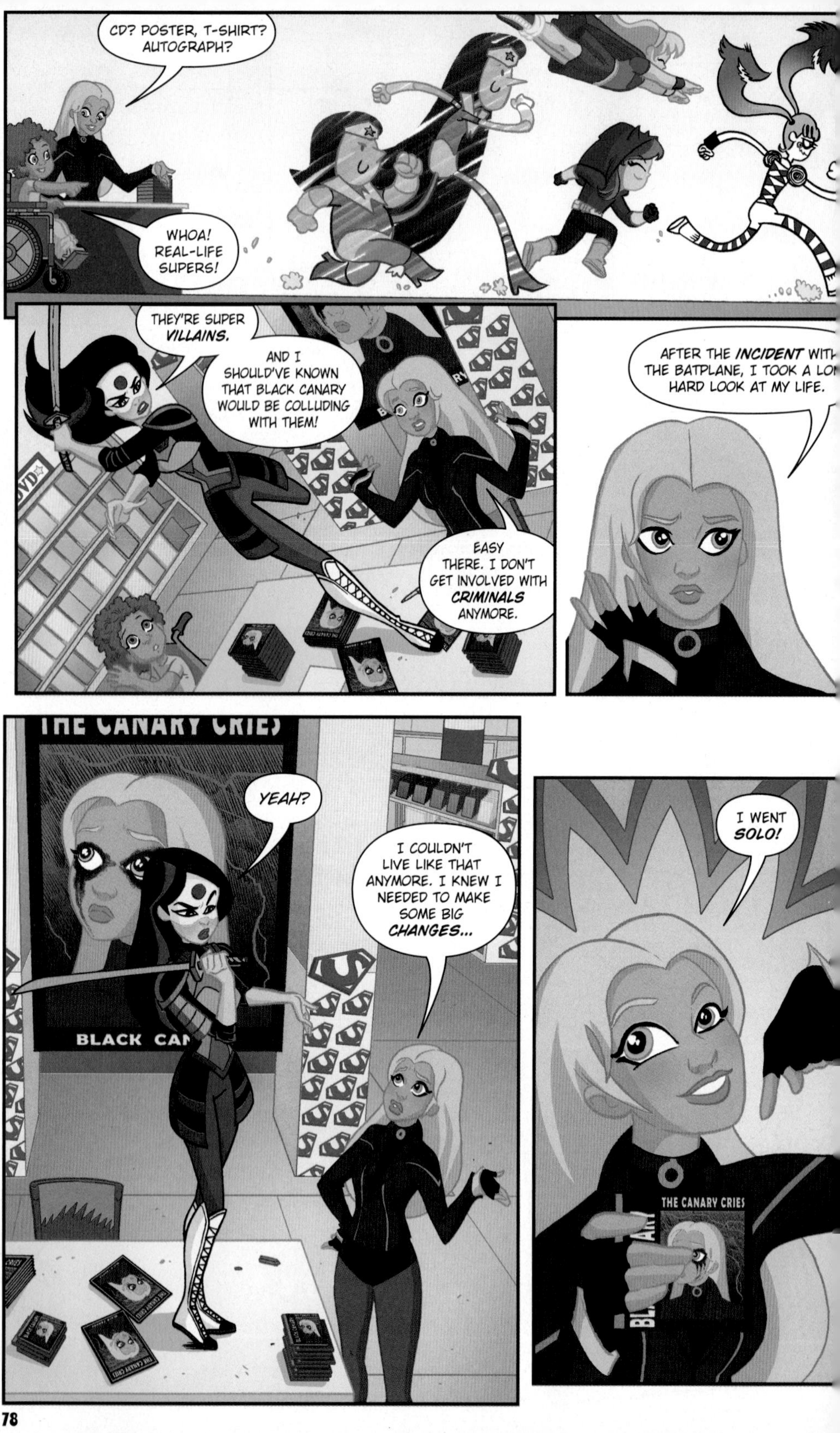
CD? POSTER, T-SHIRT? AUTOGRAPH?
WHOA! REAL-LIFE SUPERS!
THEY'RE SUPER *VILLAINS.*
AND I SHOULD'VE KNOWN THAT BLACK CANARY WOULD BE COLLUDING WITH THEM!
EASY THERE. I DON'T GET INVOLVED WITH *CRIMINALS* ANYMORE.
AFTER THE *INCIDENT* WITH THE BATPLANE, I TOOK A LON HARD LOOK AT MY LIFE.
THE CANARY CRIES
BLACK CAN
YEAH?
I COULDN'T LIVE LIKE THAT ANYMORE. I KNEW I NEEDED TO MAKE SOME BIG *CHANGES...*
I WENT *SOLO!*
THE CANARY CRIES

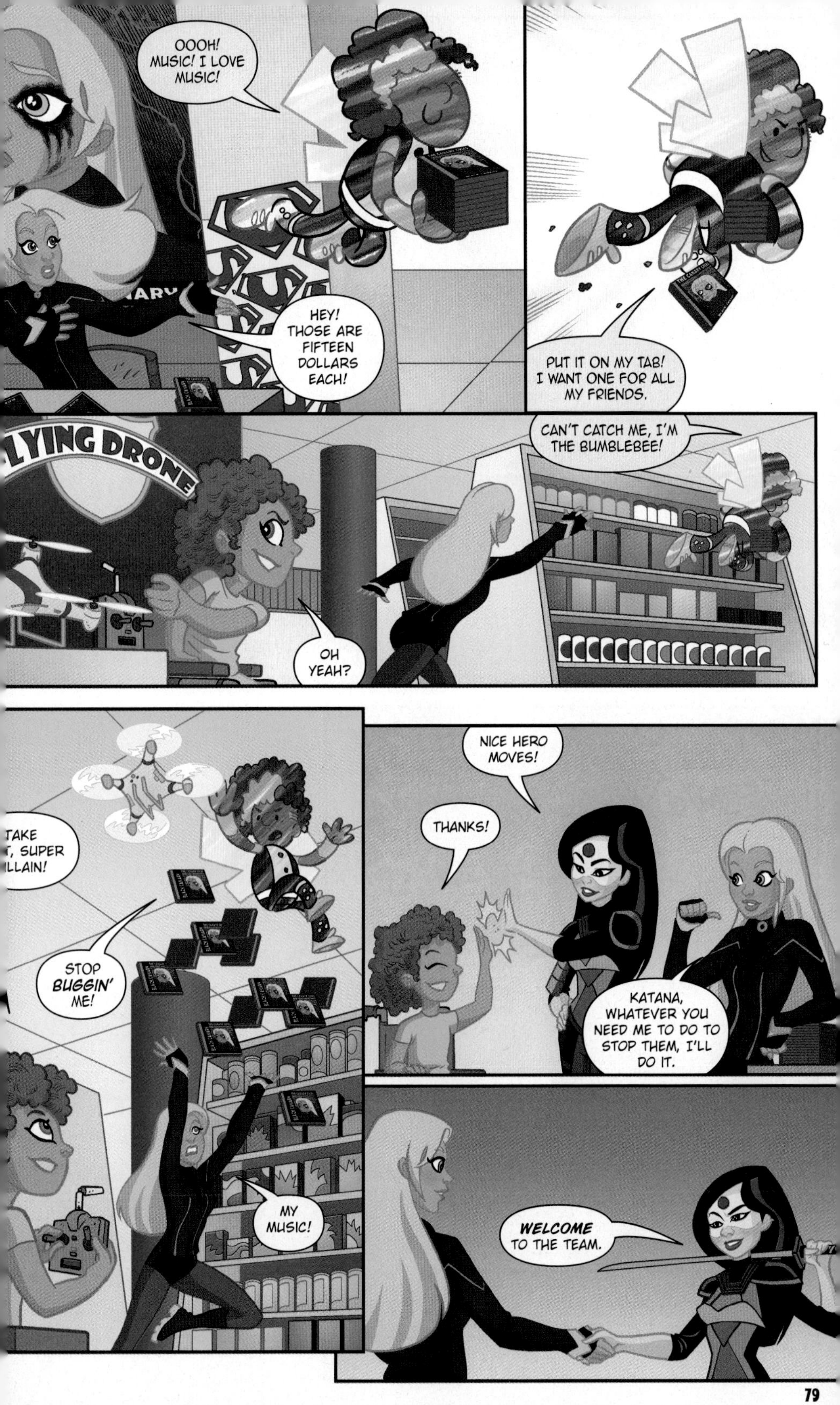
OOOH! MUSIC! I LOVE MUSIC!
HEY! THOSE ARE FIFTEEN DOLLARS EACH!
PUT IT ON MY TAB! I WANT ONE FOR ALL MY FRIENDS.
LYING DRONE
CAN'T CATCH ME, I'M THE BUMBLEBEE!
OH YEAH?
TAKE
T, SUPER
LLAIN!
STOP *BUGGIN'* ME!
MY MUSIC!
NICE HERO MOVES!
THANKS!
KATANA, WHATEVER YOU NEED ME TO DO TO STOP THEM, I'LL DO IT.
WELCOME TO THE TEAM.

WATCH OUT FOR THE TURN, BESTIE!

YOU'RE NOT SUPPOSED TO HELP. WE'RE PLAYING AGAINST EACH OTHER!

LET 'ER RIP, BLACK CANARY!

EEEEEEEE

SUPER LOUD!

OW!

TRAPPED BY TECHNOLOGY!

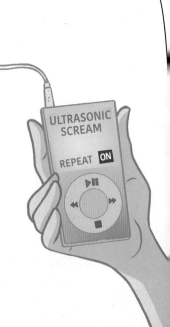

I HAD BLACK CANAR[Y] RECORD A SPE[CIAL] TRACK FOR YOU.

ULTRASONIC SCREAM

REPEAT ON

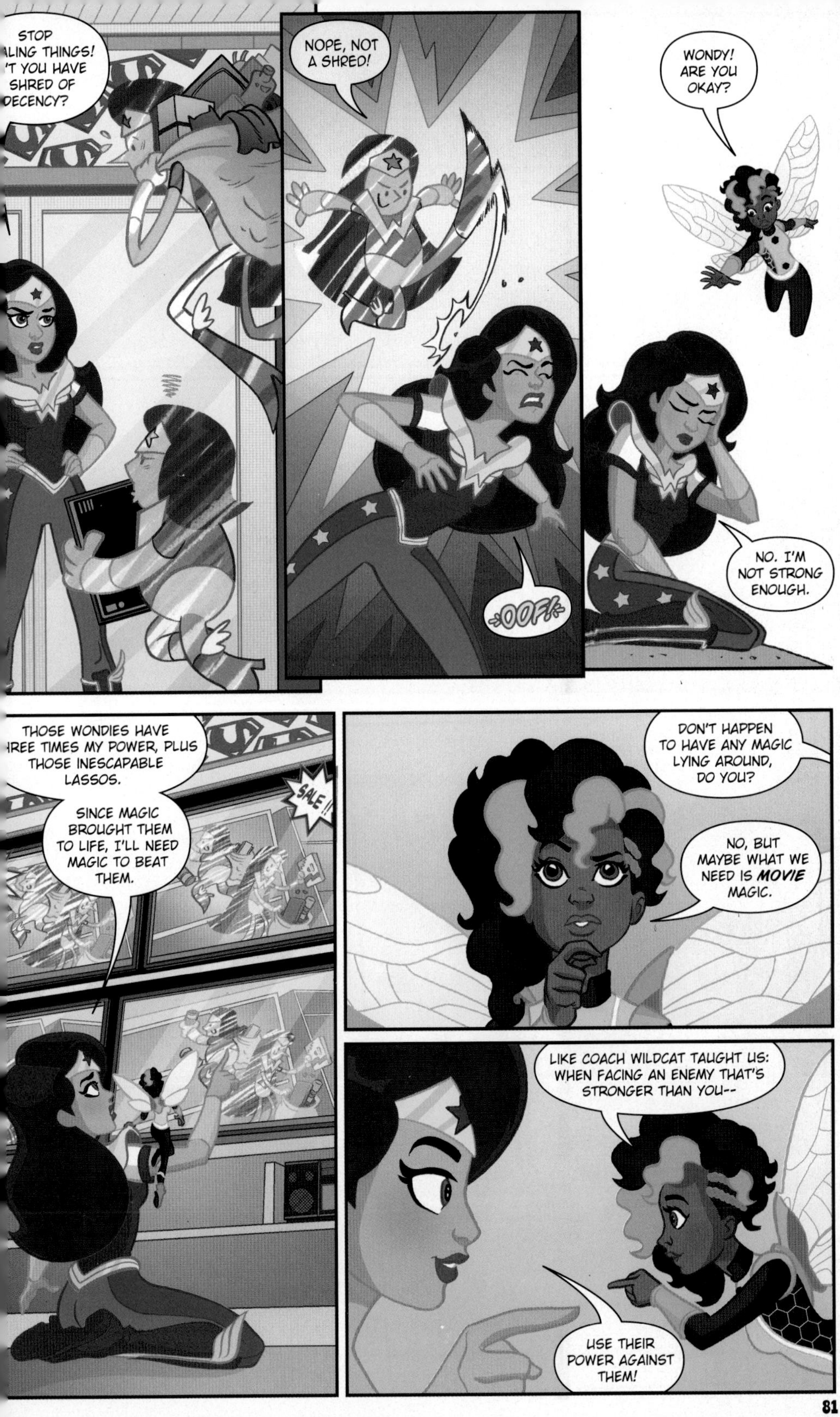
STOP
ALING THINGS!
'T YOU HAVE
SHRED OF
DECENCY?
NOPE, NOT A SHRED!
WONDY! ARE YOU OKAY?
OOF!
NO. I'M NOT STRONG ENOUGH.
THOSE WONDIES HAVE
REE TIMES MY POWER, PLUS THOSE INESCAPABLE LASSOS.
SALE!!
SINCE MAGIC BROUGHT THEM TO LIFE, I'LL NEED MAGIC TO BEAT THEM.
DON'T HAPPEN TO HAVE ANY MAGIC LYING AROUND, DO YOU?
NO, BUT MAYBE WHAT WE NEED IS MOVIE MAGIC.
LIKE COACH WILDCAT TAUGHT US: WHEN FACING AN ENEMY THAT'S STRONGER THAN YOU--
USE THEIR POWER AGAINST THEM!

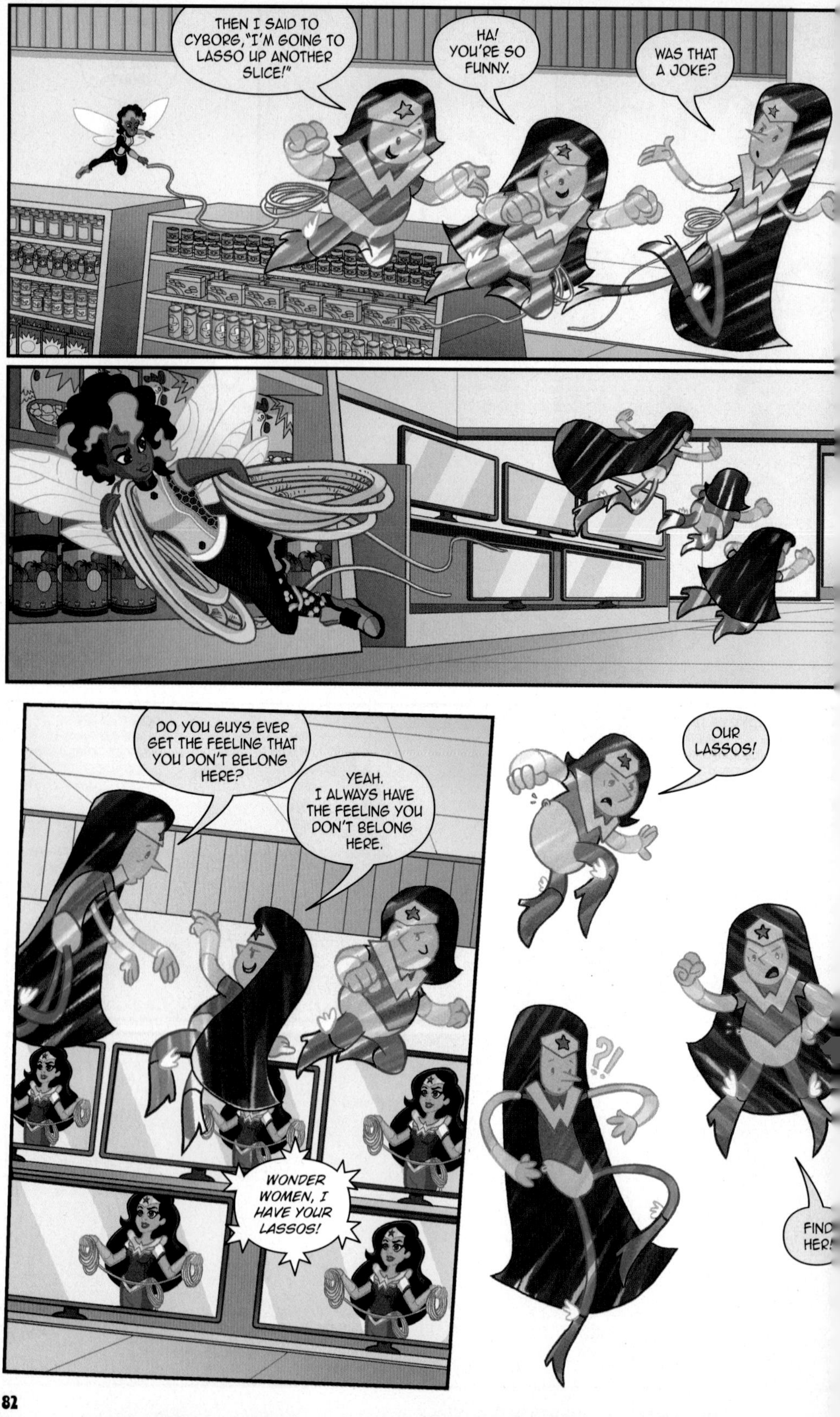
THEN I SAID TO CYBORG, "I'M GOING TO LASSO UP ANOTHER SLICE!"
HA! YOU'RE SO FUNNY.
WAS THAT A JOKE?
DO YOU GUYS EVER GET THE FEELING THAT YOU DON'T BELONG HERE?
YEAH. I ALWAYS HAVE THE FEELING YOU DON'T BELONG HERE.
WONDER WOMEN, I HAVE YOUR LASSOS!
OUR LASSOS!
?!
FIND HER!

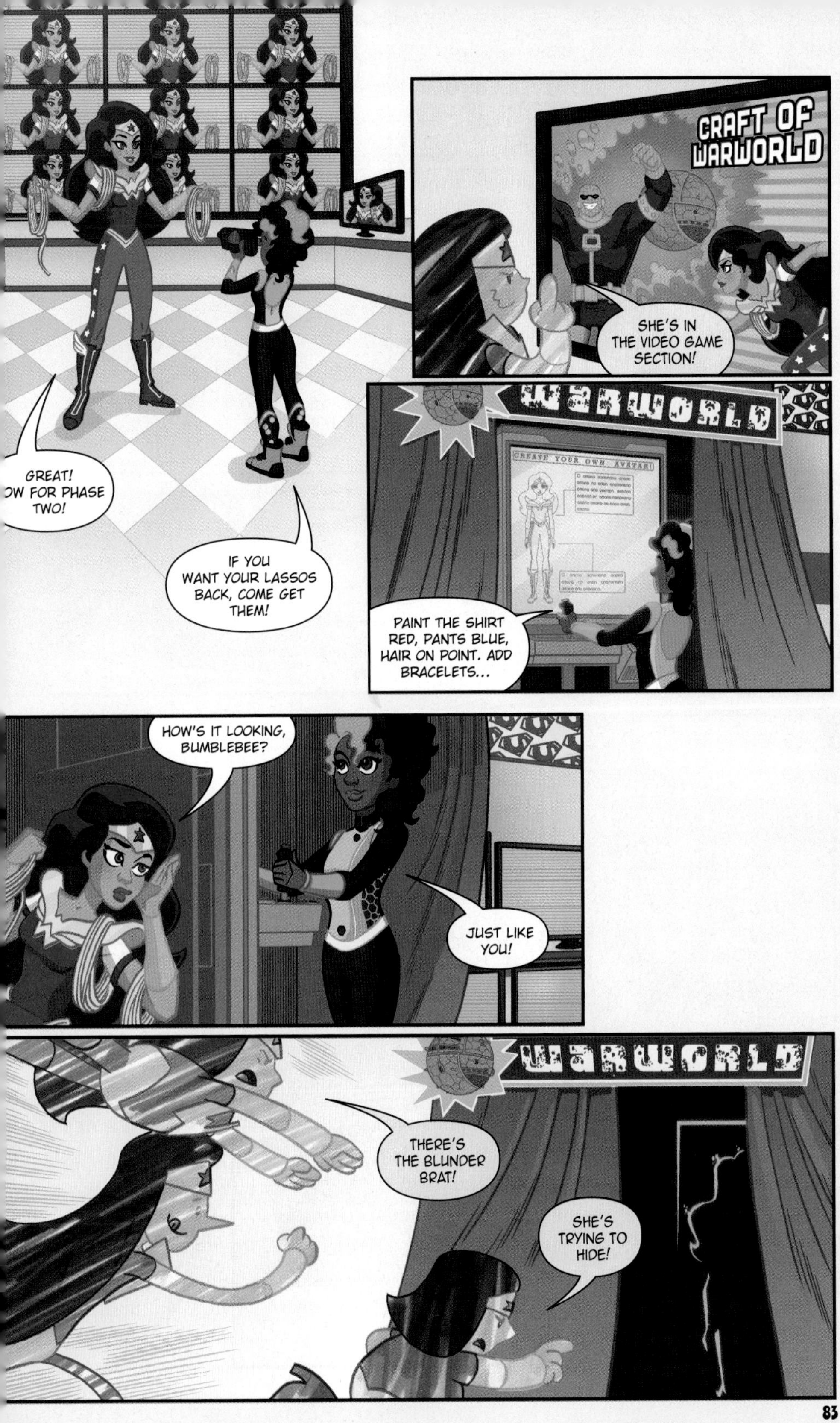
GREAT! OW FOR PHASE TWO!
IF YOU WANT YOUR LASSOS BACK, COME GET THEM!
CRAFT OF WARWORLD
SHE'S IN THE VIDEO GAME SECTION!
WARWORLD
CREATE YOUR OWN AVATAR!
PAINT THE SHIRT RED, PANTS BLUE, HAIR ON POINT. ADD BRACELETS...
HOW'S IT LOOKING, BUMBLEBEE?
JUST LIKE YOU!
WARWORLD
THERE'S THE BLUNDER BRAT!
SHE'S TRYING TO HIDE!

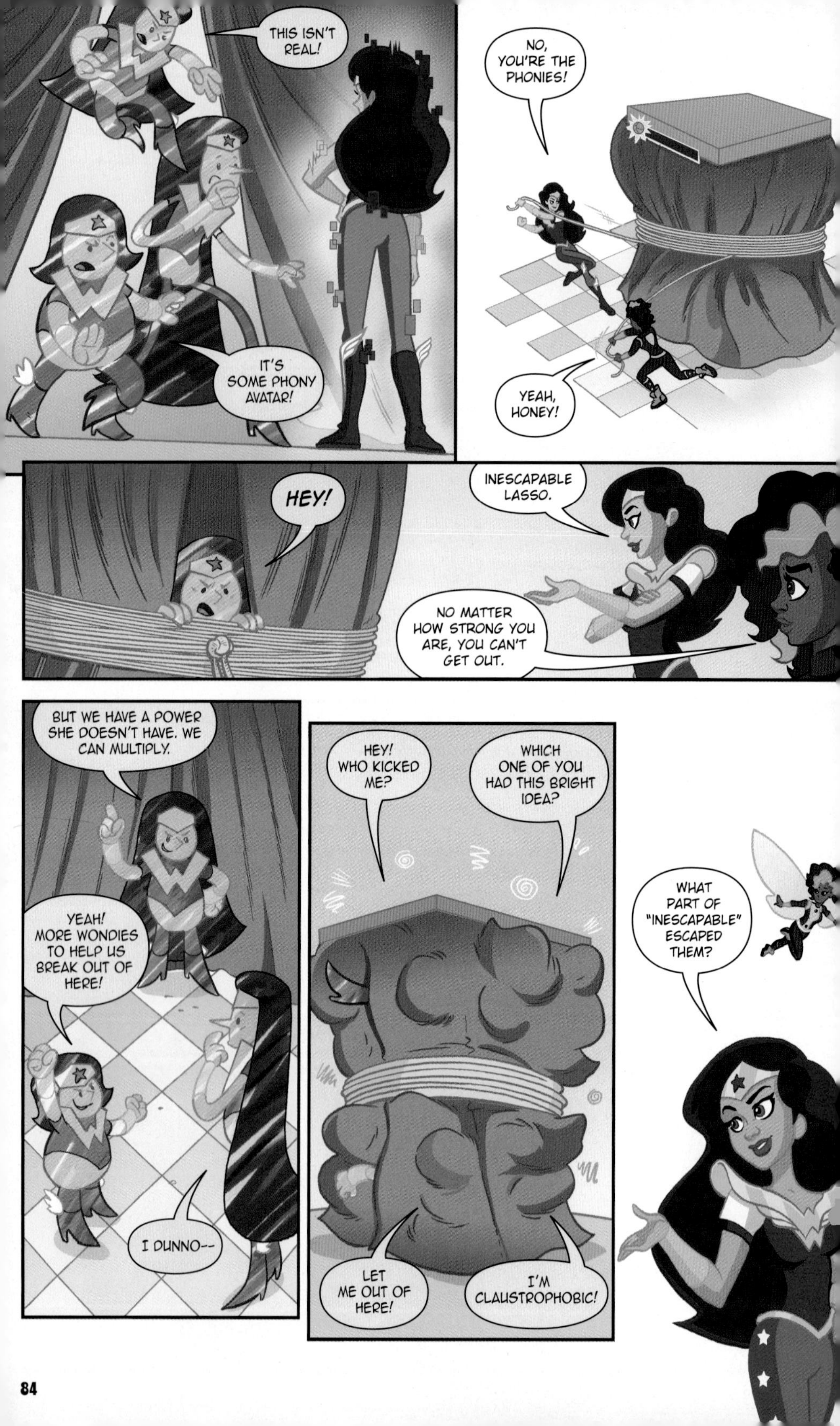

THIS ISN'T REAL!
IT'S SOME PHONY AVATAR!
NO, YOU'RE THE PHONIES!
YEAH, HONEY!
HEY!
INESCAPABLE LASSO.
NO MATTER HOW STRONG YOU ARE, YOU CAN'T GET OUT.
BUT WE HAVE A POWER SHE DOESN'T HAVE. WE CAN MULTIPLY.
YEAH! MORE WONDIES TO HELP US BREAK OUT OF HERE!
I DUNNO--
HEY! WHO KICKED ME?
WHICH ONE OF YOU HAD THIS BRIGHT IDEA?
LET ME OUT OF HERE!
I'M CLAUSTROPHOBIC!
WHAT PART OF "INESCAPABLE" ESCAPED THEM?

SUPER HERO HIGH.

PUT [TH]AT DOWN! [I]T'S PART OF [MS]. MOONE'S [PEA]CE-N-LOVE [S]ERIES.

HARLEY! WE MADE MORE MAGIC PAINT!

NO! GET OUTTA HERE!

OF COURSE THAT *SPINELESS* PEACENIK WOULD WASTE HER TALENT.

OH MY GOOSE GRASS! *SOMETHING'S* HAPPENED TO MS. MOONE!

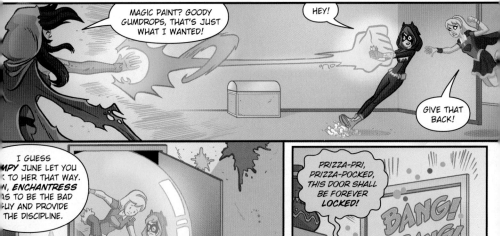

MAGIC PAINT? GOODY GUMDROPS, THAT'S JUST WHAT I WANTED!

HEY!

GIVE THAT BACK!

I GUESS [GRU]MPY JUNE LET YOU [TAL]K TO HER THAT WAY. [THE]N, *ENCHANTRESS* [H]AS TO BE THE BAD [G]UY AND PROVIDE [THE] THE DISCIPLINE.

PRIZZA-PRI, PRIZZA-POCKED, THIS DOOR SHALL BE FOREVER *LOCKED!*

BANG! BANG!

LET US OUT!

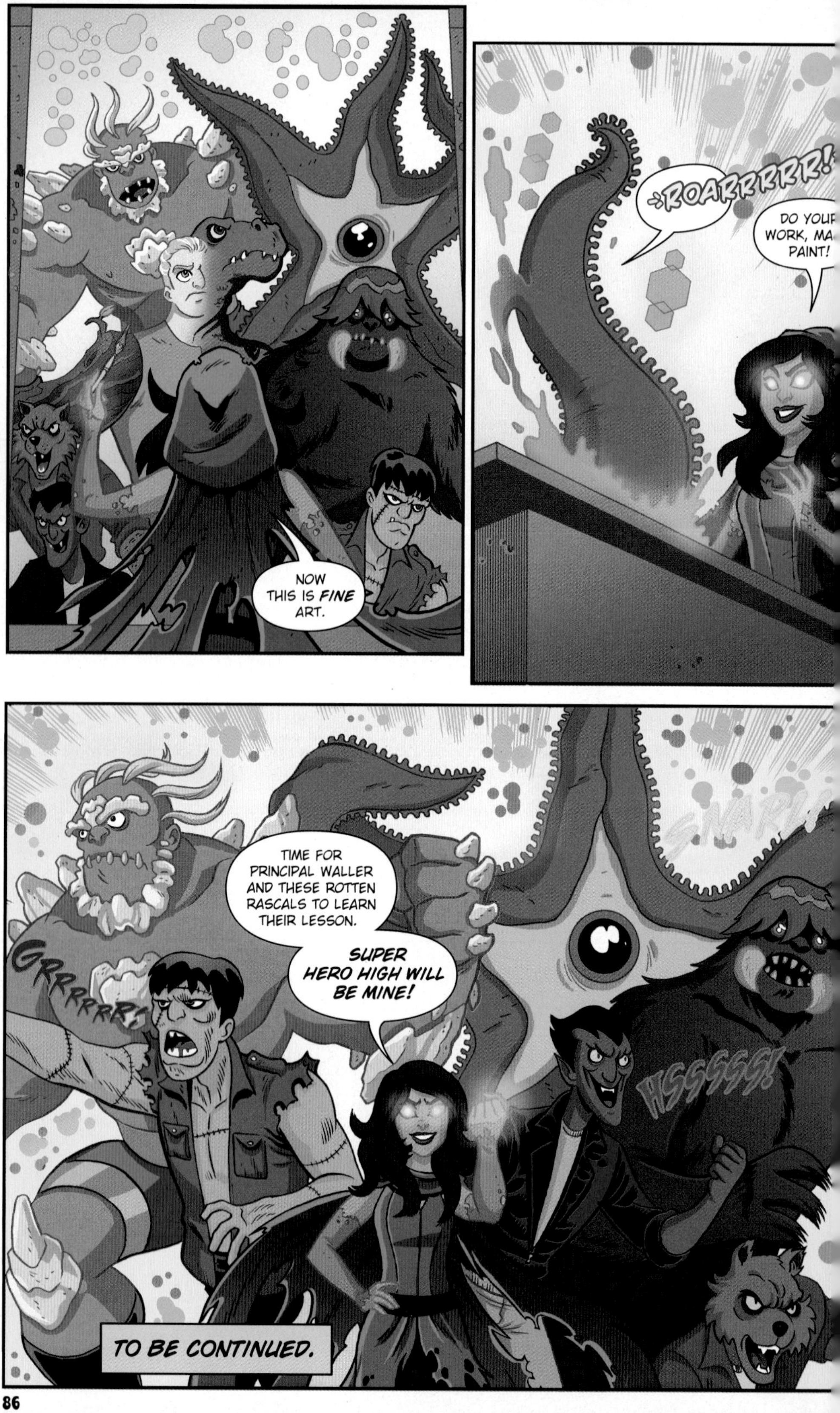
NOW THIS IS *FINE* ART.
ROARRRRR!
DO YOUR WORK, MA PAINT!
SNARL!
TIME FOR PRINCIPAL WALLER AND THESE ROTTEN RASCALS TO LEARN THEIR LESSON.
SUPER HERO HIGH WILL BE MINE!
GRRRRRR!
HSSSSS!
TO BE CONTINUED.

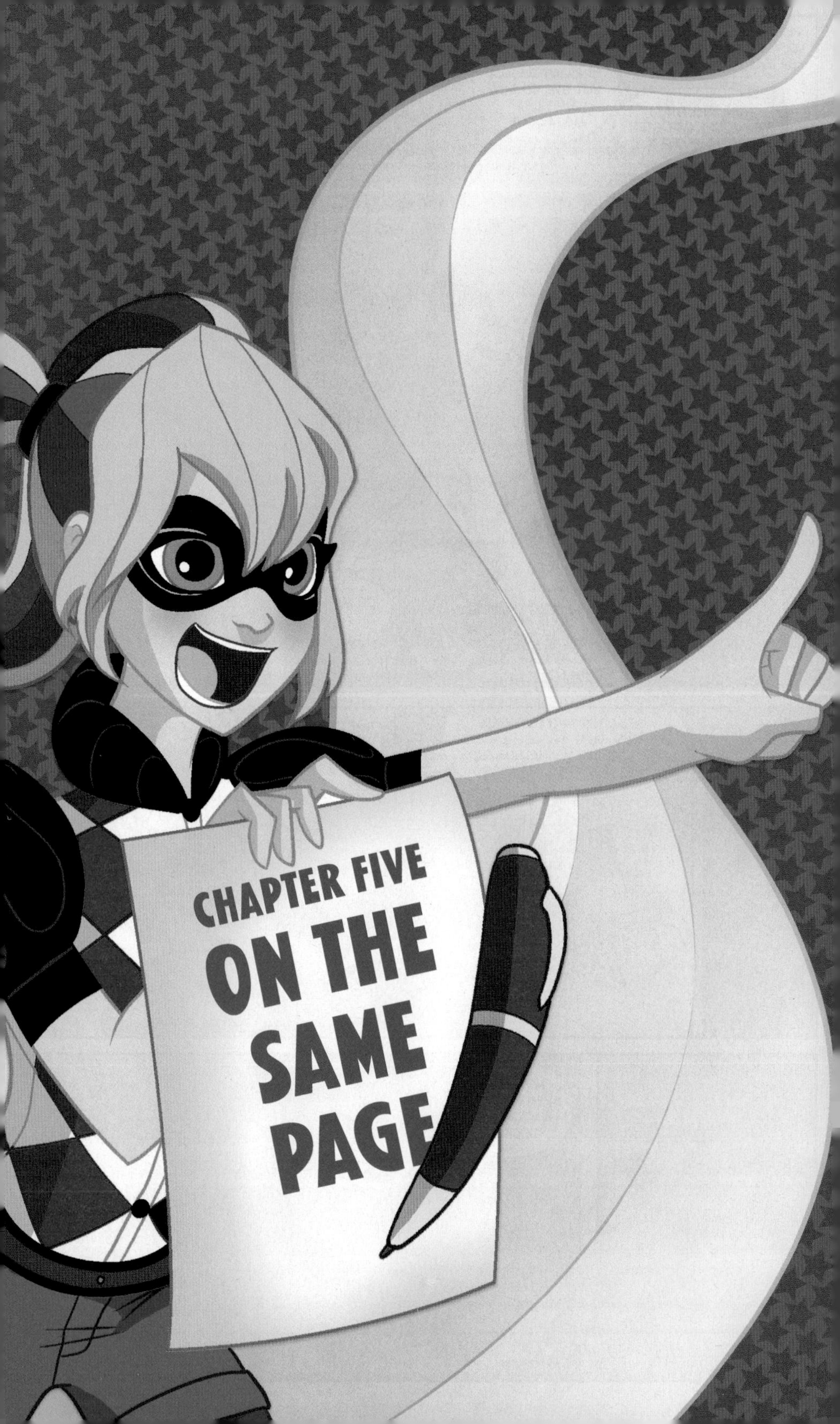
CHAPTER FIVE
ON THE SAME PAGE

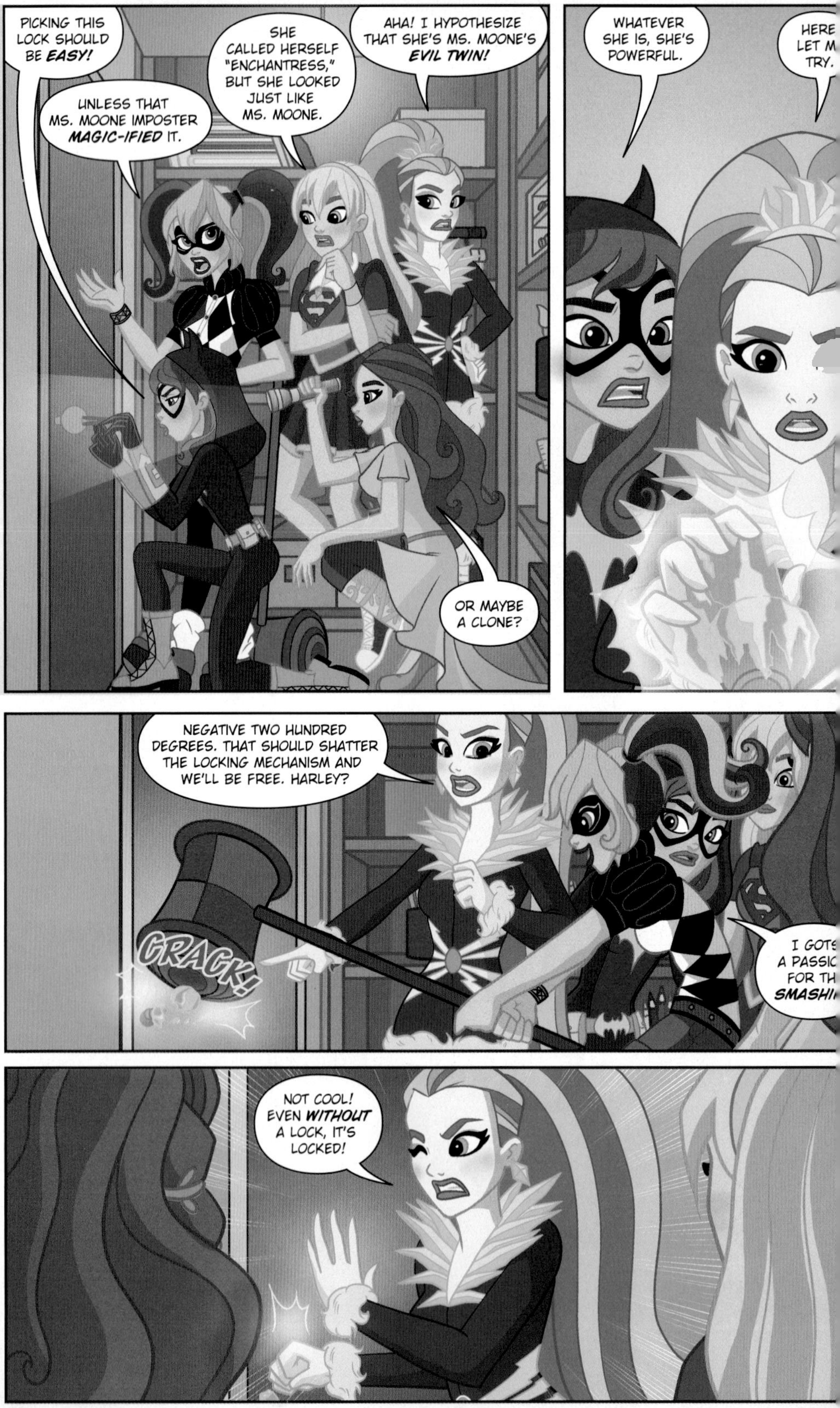
PICKING THIS LOCK SHOULD BE EASY!
UNLESS THAT MS. MOONE IMPOSTER MAGIC-IFIED IT.
SHE CALLED HERSELF "ENCHANTRESS," BUT SHE LOOKED JUST LIKE MS. MOONE.
AHA! I HYPOTHESIZE THAT SHE'S MS. MOONE'S EVIL TWIN!
OR MAYBE A CLONE?
WHATEVER SHE IS, SHE'S POWERFUL.
HERE LET M TRY.
NEGATIVE TWO HUNDRED DEGREES. THAT SHOULD SHATTER THE LOCKING MECHANISM AND WE'LL BE FREE. HARLEY?
CRACK!
I GOTS A PASSIC FOR TH SMASHI
NOT COOL! EVEN WITHOUT A LOCK, IT'S LOCKED!

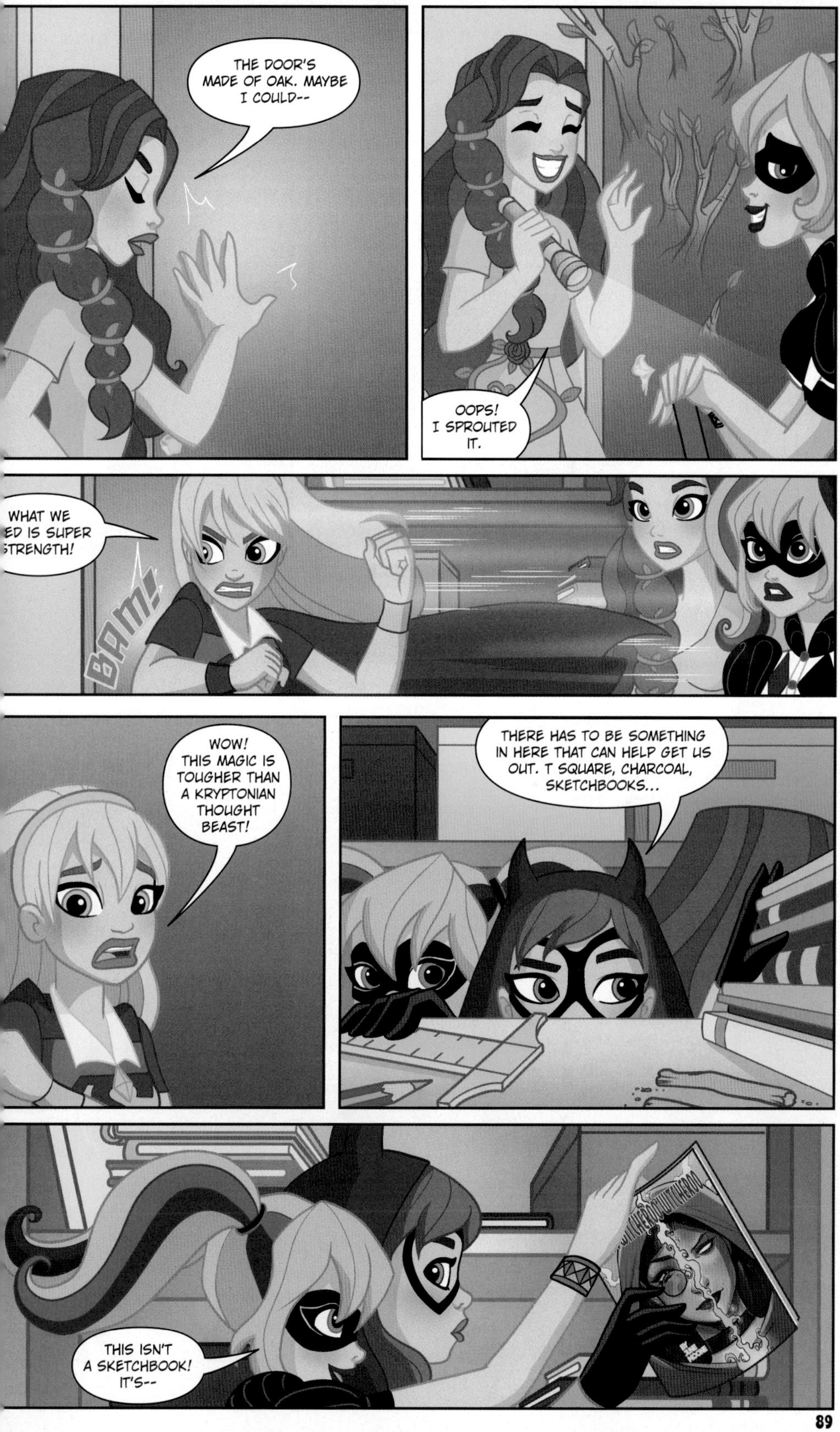
THE DOOR'S MADE OF OAK. MAYBE I COULD--
OOPS! I SPROUTED IT.
WHAT WE ED IS SUPER STRENGTH!
BAM!
WOW! THIS MAGIC IS TOUGHER THAN A KRYPTONIAN THOUGHT BEAST!
THERE HAS TO BE SOMETHING IN HERE THAT CAN HELP GET US OUT. T SQUARE, CHARCOAL, SKETCHBOOKS...
THIS ISN'T A SKETCHBOOK! IT'S--

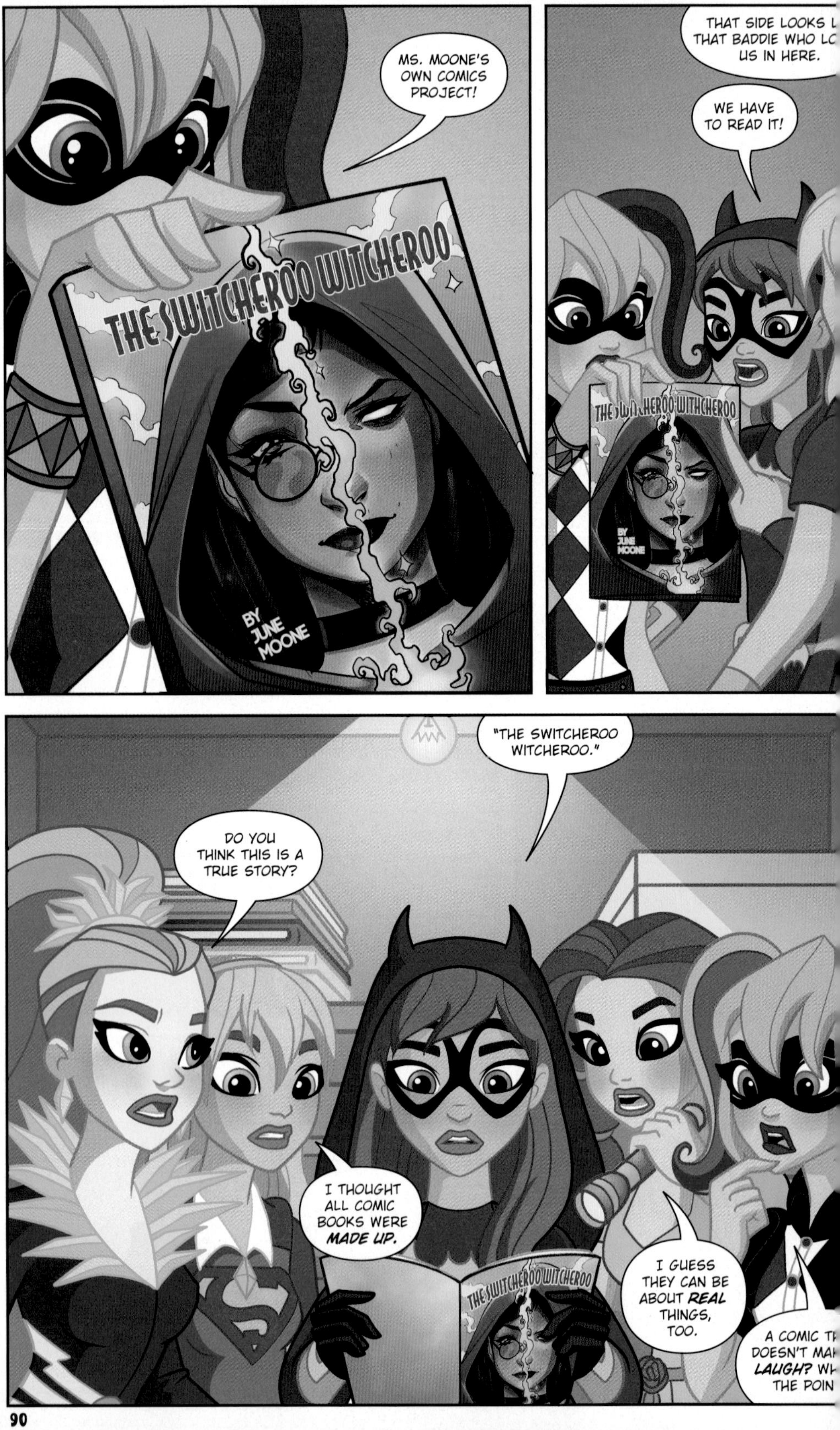

MS. MOONE'S OWN COMICS PROJECT!
THE SWITCHEROO WITCHEROO
BY JUNE MOONE
THAT SIDE LOOKS L
THAT BADDIE WHO LO
US IN HERE.
WE HAVE TO READ IT!
"THE SWITCHEROO WITCHEROO."
DO YOU THINK THIS IS A TRUE STORY?
I THOUGHT ALL COMIC BOOKS WERE ***MADE UP.***
I GUESS THEY CAN BE ABOUT ***REAL*** THINGS, TOO.
A COMIC T
DOESN'T MA
LAUGH? WH
THE POIN

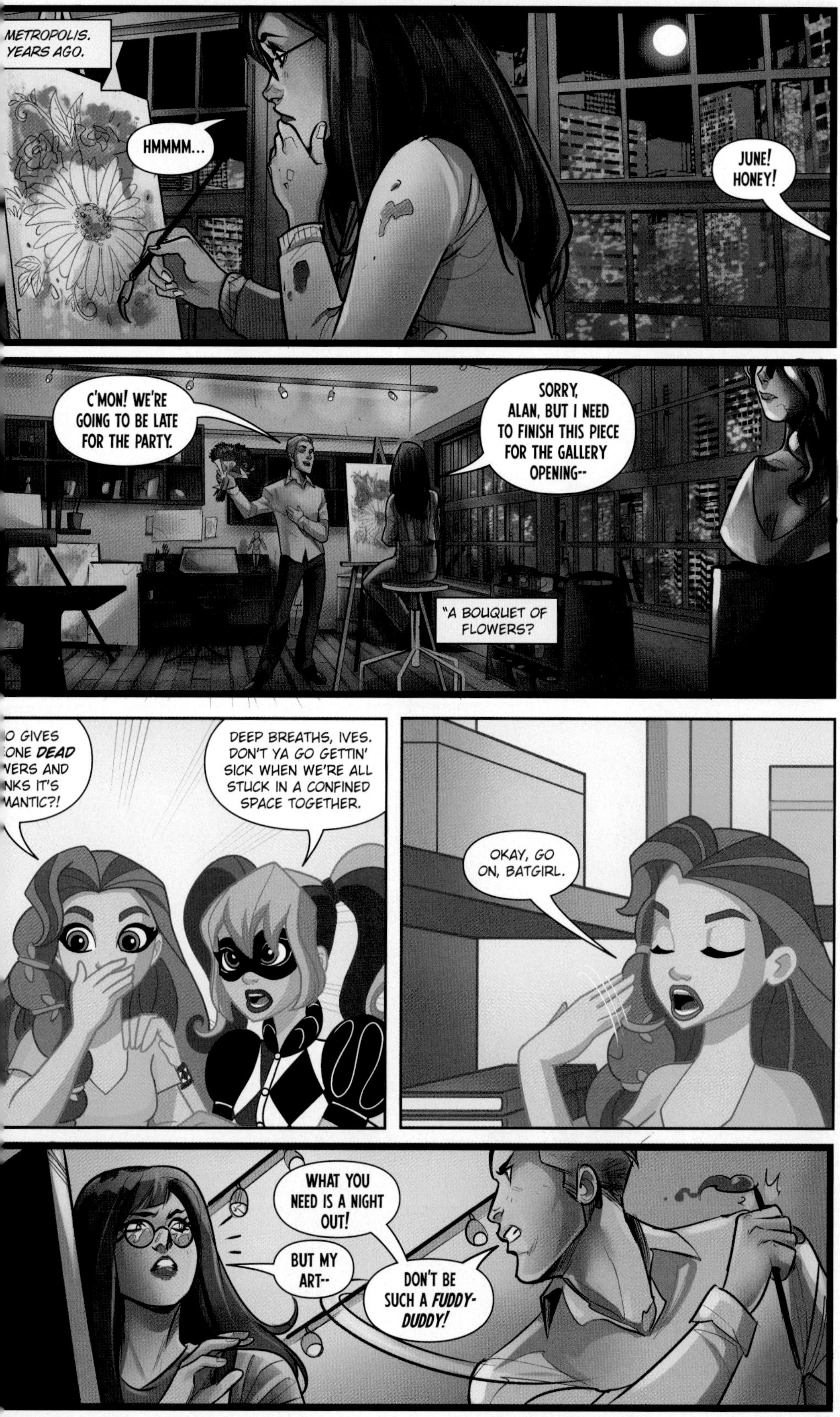
METROPOLIS. YEARS AGO.
HMMMM...
JUNE! HONEY!
C'MON! WE'RE GOING TO BE LATE FOR THE PARTY.
SORRY, ALAN, BUT I NEED TO FINISH THIS PIECE FOR THE GALLERY OPENING--
"A BOUQUET OF FLOWERS?
O GIVES ONE DEAD VERS AND NKS IT'S MANTIC?!
DEEP BREATHS, IVES. DON'T YA GO GETTIN' SICK WHEN WE'RE ALL STUCK IN A CONFINED SPACE TOGETHER.
OKAY, GO ON, BATGIRL.
WHAT YOU NEED IS A NIGHT OUT!
BUT MY ART--
DON'T BE SUCH A FUDDY-DUDDY!

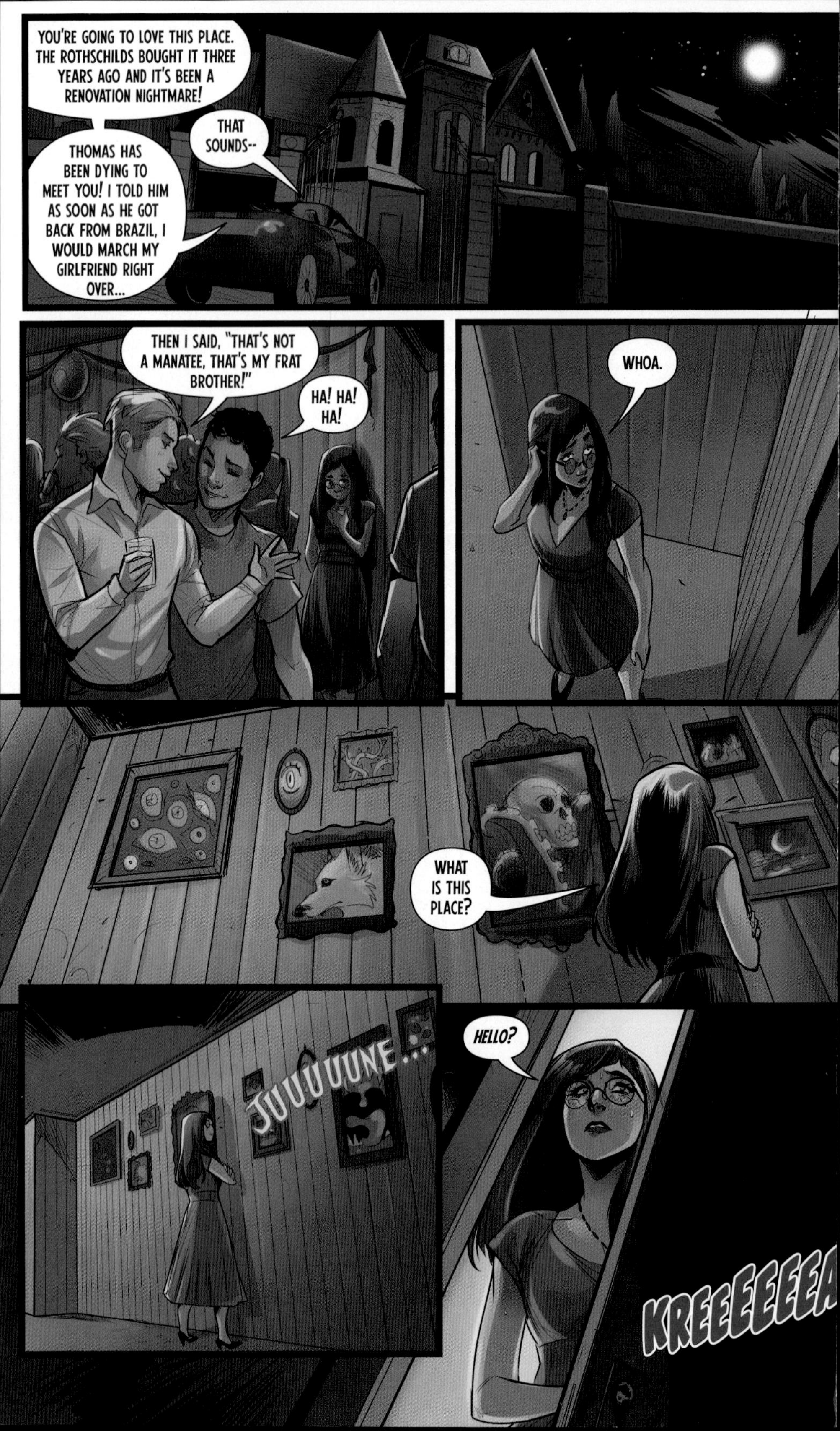

YOU'RE GOING TO LOVE THIS PLACE. THE ROTHSCHILDS BOUGHT IT THREE YEARS AGO AND IT'S BEEN A RENOVATION NIGHTMARE!
THOMAS HAS BEEN DYING TO MEET YOU! I TOLD HIM AS SOON AS HE GOT BACK FROM BRAZIL, I WOULD MARCH MY GIRLFRIEND RIGHT OVER...
THAT SOUNDS--
THEN I SAID, "THAT'S NOT A MANATEE, THAT'S MY FRAT BROTHER!"
HA! HA! HA!
WHOA.
WHAT IS THIS PLACE?
JUUUUUNE...
HELLO?
KREEEEEEA

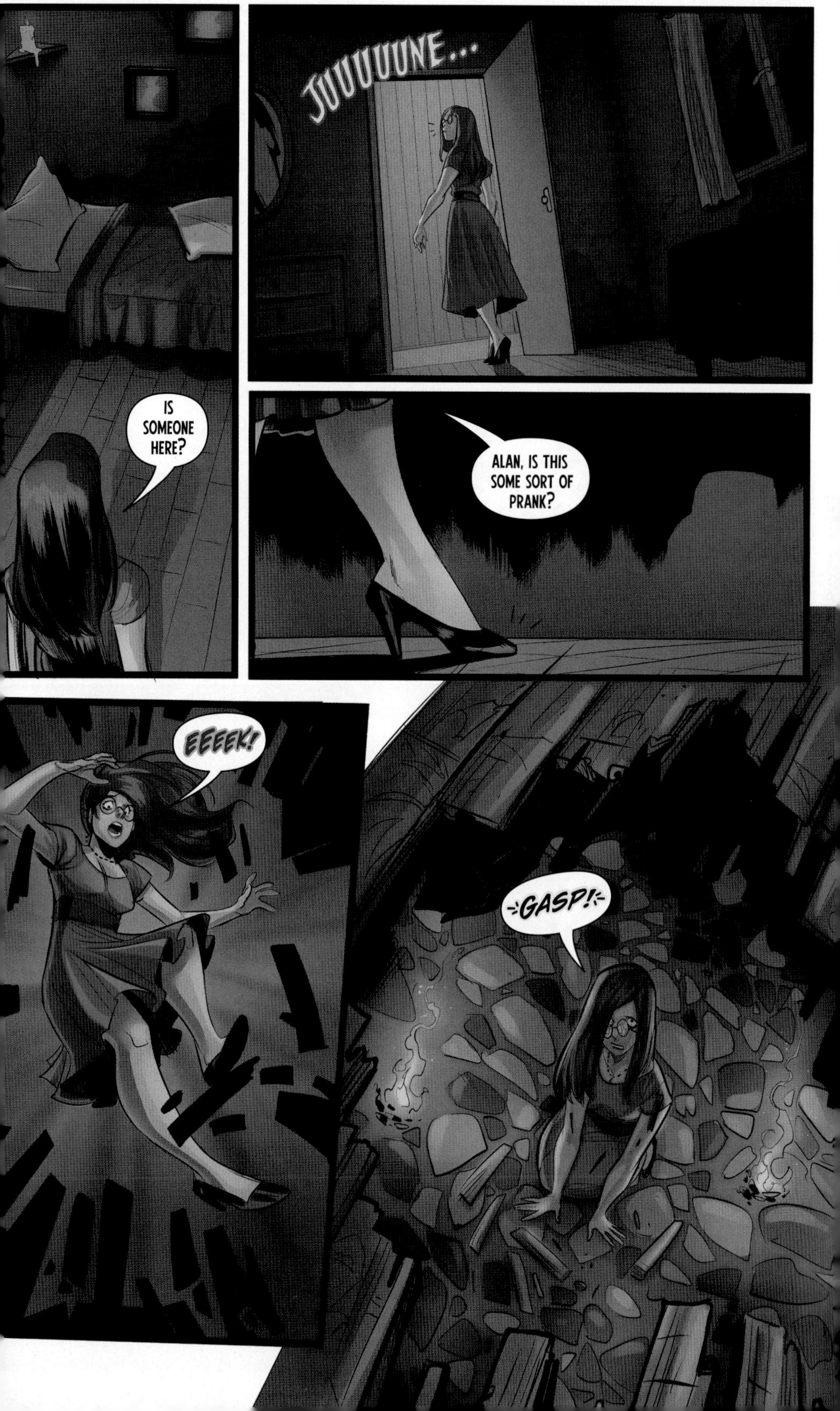
JUUUUUNE...
IS SOMEONE HERE?
ALAN, IS THIS SOME SORT OF PRANK?
EEEEK!
-GASP!-

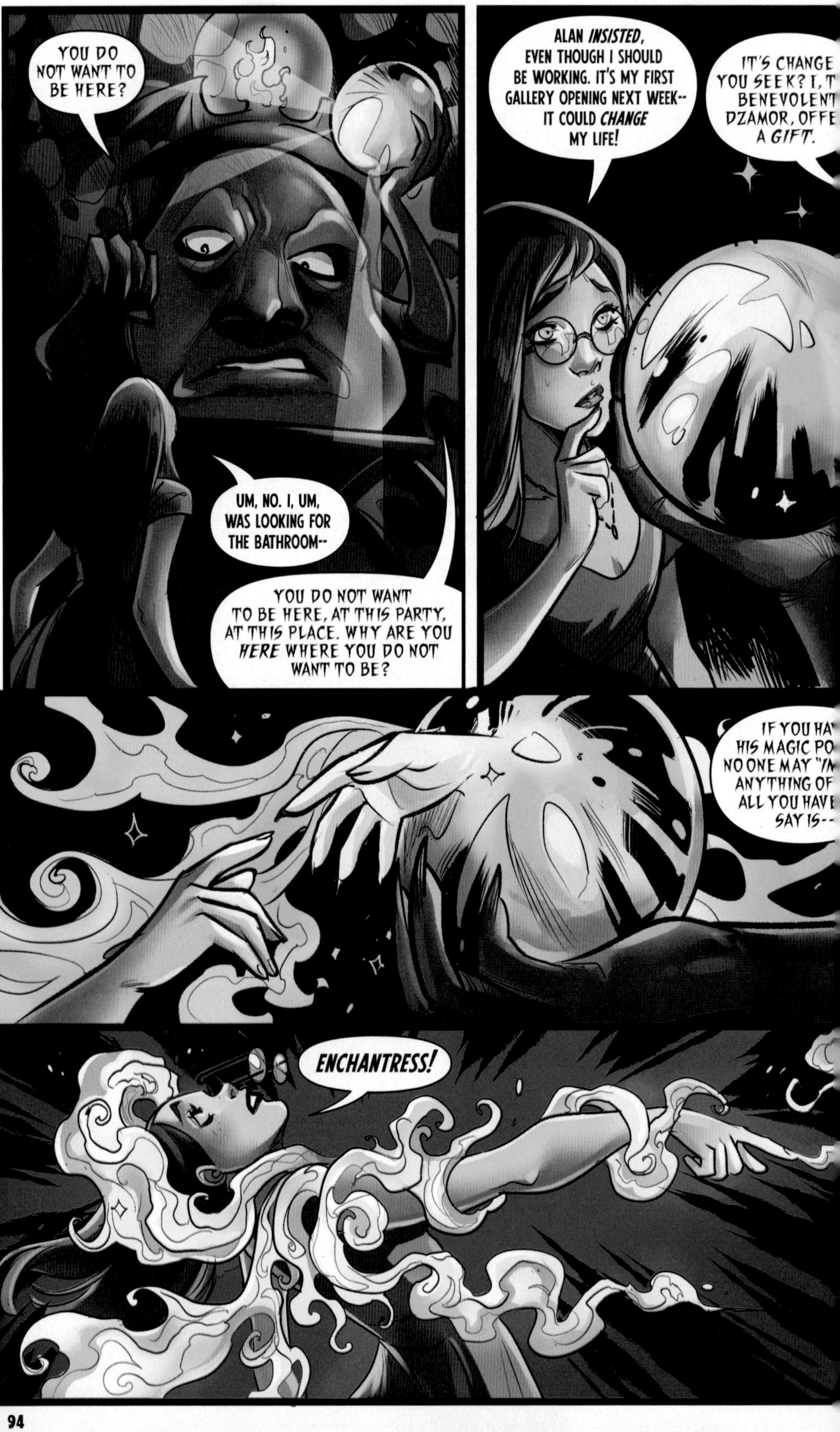

YOU DO NOT WANT TO BE HERE?
UM, NO. I, UM, WAS LOOKING FOR THE BATHROOM--
YOU DO NOT WANT TO BE HERE, AT THIS PARTY, AT THIS PLACE. WHY ARE YOU *HERE* WHERE YOU DO NOT WANT TO BE?
ALAN *INSISTED*, EVEN THOUGH I SHOULD BE WORKING. IT'S MY FIRST GALLERY OPENING NEXT WEEK-- IT COULD *CHANGE* MY LIFE!
ENCHANTRESS!

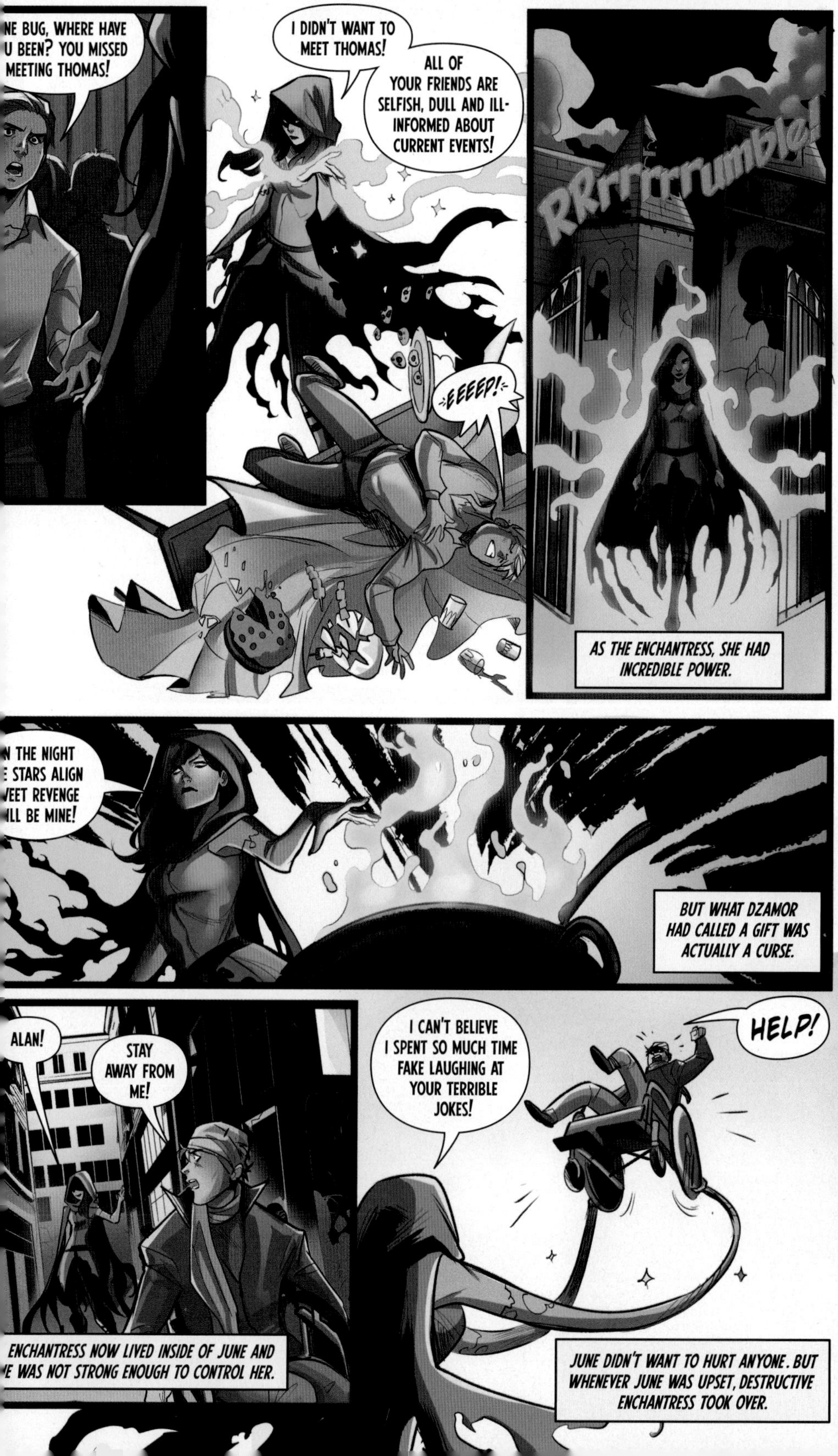
NE BUG, WHERE HAVE
U BEEN? YOU MISSED
MEETING THOMAS!
I DIDN'T WANT TO MEET THOMAS!
ALL OF YOUR FRIENDS ARE SELFISH, DULL AND ILL-INFORMED ABOUT CURRENT EVENTS!
EEEEP!
RRrrrrrumble!
AS THE ENCHANTRESS, SHE HAD INCREDIBLE POWER.
N THE NIGHT
E STARS ALIGN
VEET REVENGE
ILL BE MINE!
BUT WHAT DZAMOR HAD CALLED A GIFT WAS ACTUALLY A CURSE.
ALAN!
STAY AWAY FROM ME!
ENCHANTRESS NOW LIVED INSIDE OF JUNE AND
E WAS NOT STRONG ENOUGH TO CONTROL HER.
I CAN'T BELIEVE I SPENT SO MUCH TIME FAKE LAUGHING AT YOUR TERRIBLE JOKES!
HELP!
JUNE DIDN'T WANT TO HURT ANYONE. BUT WHENEVER JUNE WAS UPSET, DESTRUCTIVE ENCHANTRESS TOOK OVER.

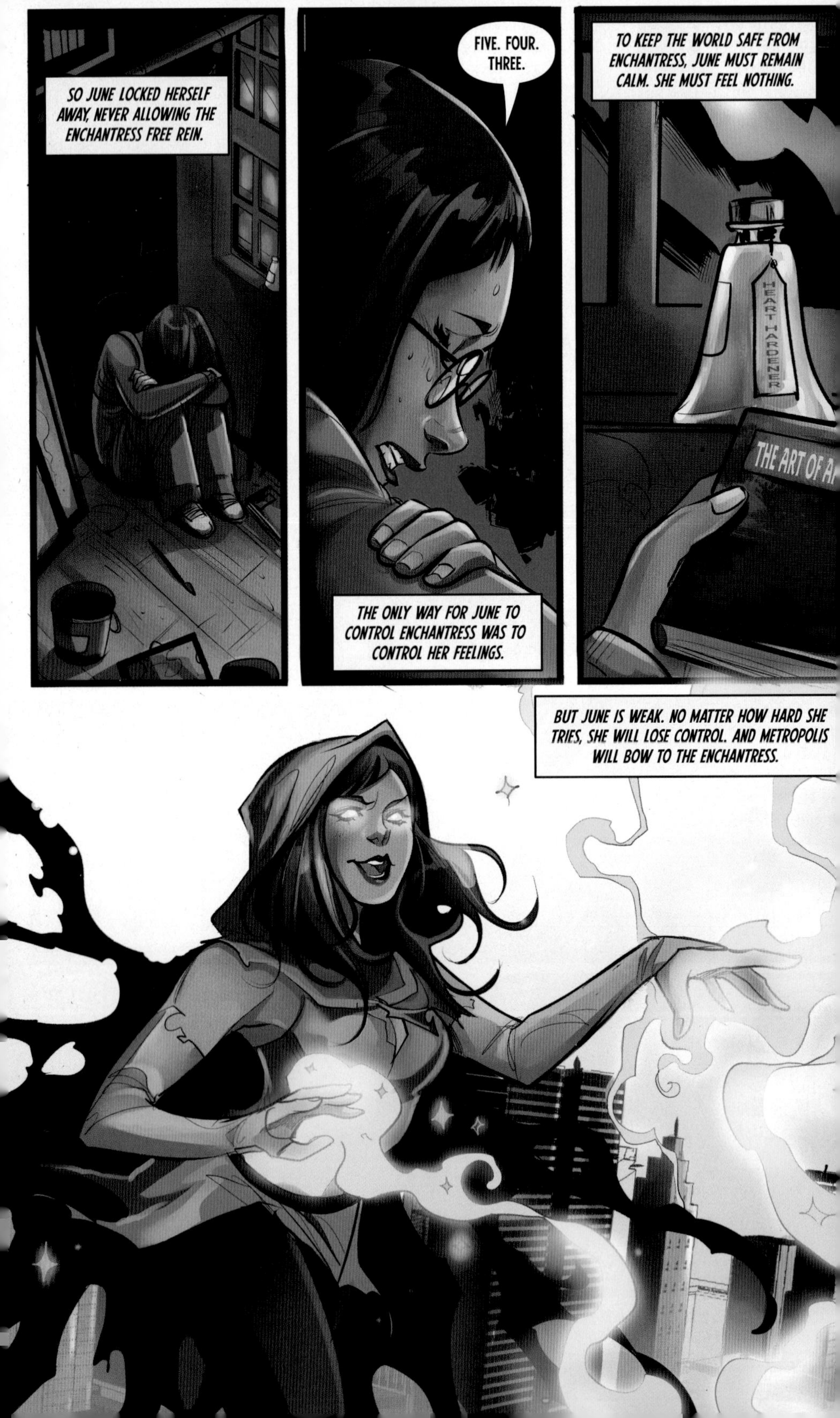
SO JUNE LOCKED HERSELF AWAY, NEVER ALLOWING THE ENCHANTRESS FREE REIN.
FIVE. FOUR. THREE.
THE ONLY WAY FOR JUNE TO CONTROL ENCHANTRESS WAS TO CONTROL HER FEELINGS.
TO KEEP THE WORLD SAFE FROM ENCHANTRESS, JUNE MUST REMAIN CALM. SHE MUST FEEL NOTHING.
HEART HARDENER
THE ART OF A
BUT JUNE IS WEAK. NO MATTER HOW HARD SHE TRIES, SHE WILL LOSE CONTROL. AND METROPOLIS WILL BOW TO THE ENCHANTRESS.

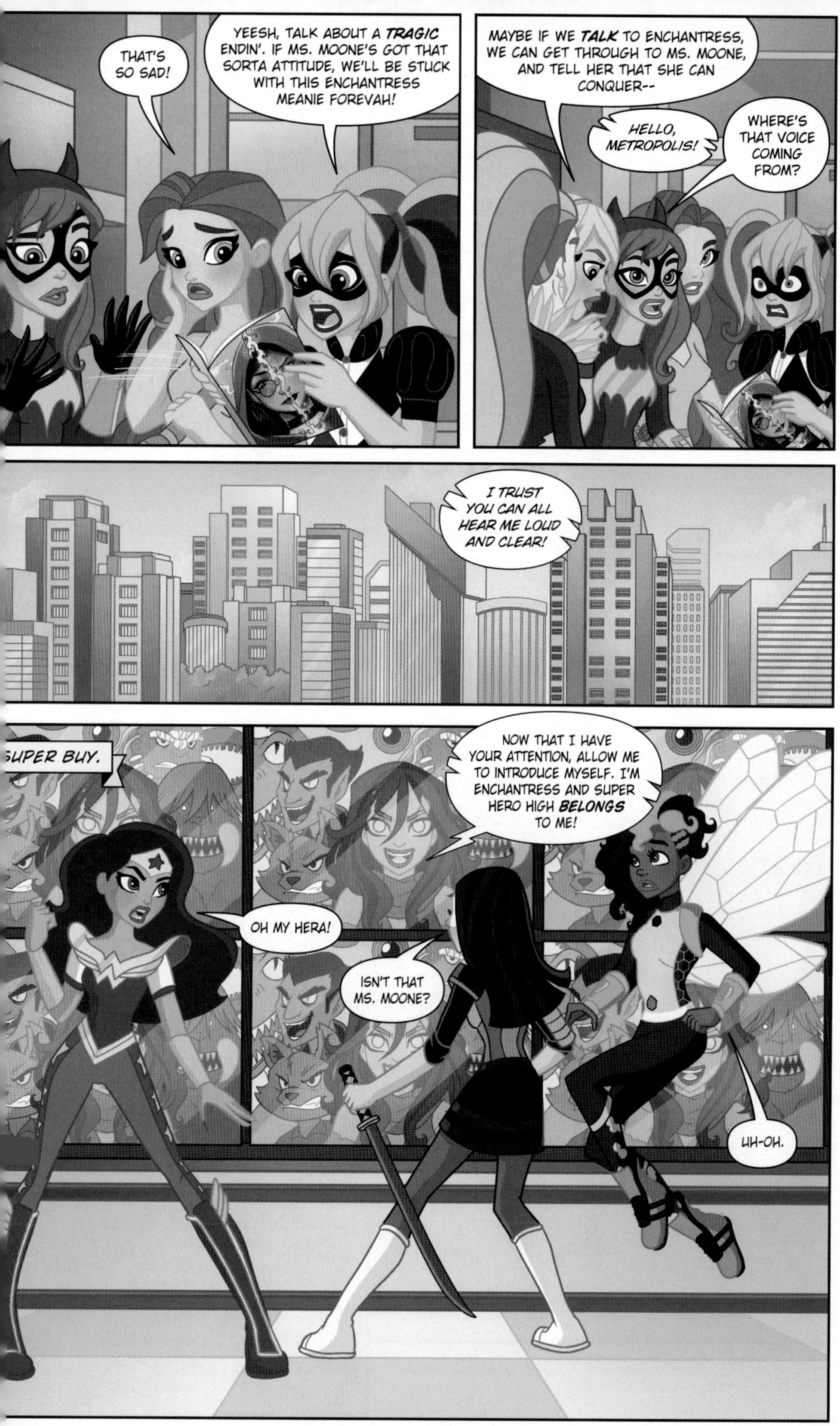
THAT'S SO SAD!
YEESH, TALK ABOUT A TRAGIC ENDIN'. IF MS. MOONE'S GOT THAT SORTA ATTITUDE, WE'LL BE STUCK WITH THIS ENCHANTRESS MEANIE FOREVAH!
MAYBE IF WE TALK TO ENCHANTRESS, WE CAN GET THROUGH TO MS. MOONE, AND TELL HER THAT SHE CAN CONQUER--
HELLO, METROPOLIS!
WHERE'S THAT VOICE COMING FROM?
I TRUST YOU CAN ALL HEAR ME LOUD AND CLEAR!
SUPER BUY.
NOW THAT I HAVE YOUR ATTENTION, ALLOW ME TO INTRODUCE MYSELF. I'M ENCHANTRESS AND SUPER HERO HIGH BELONGS TO ME!
OH MY HERA!
ISN'T THAT MS. MOONE?
UH-OH.

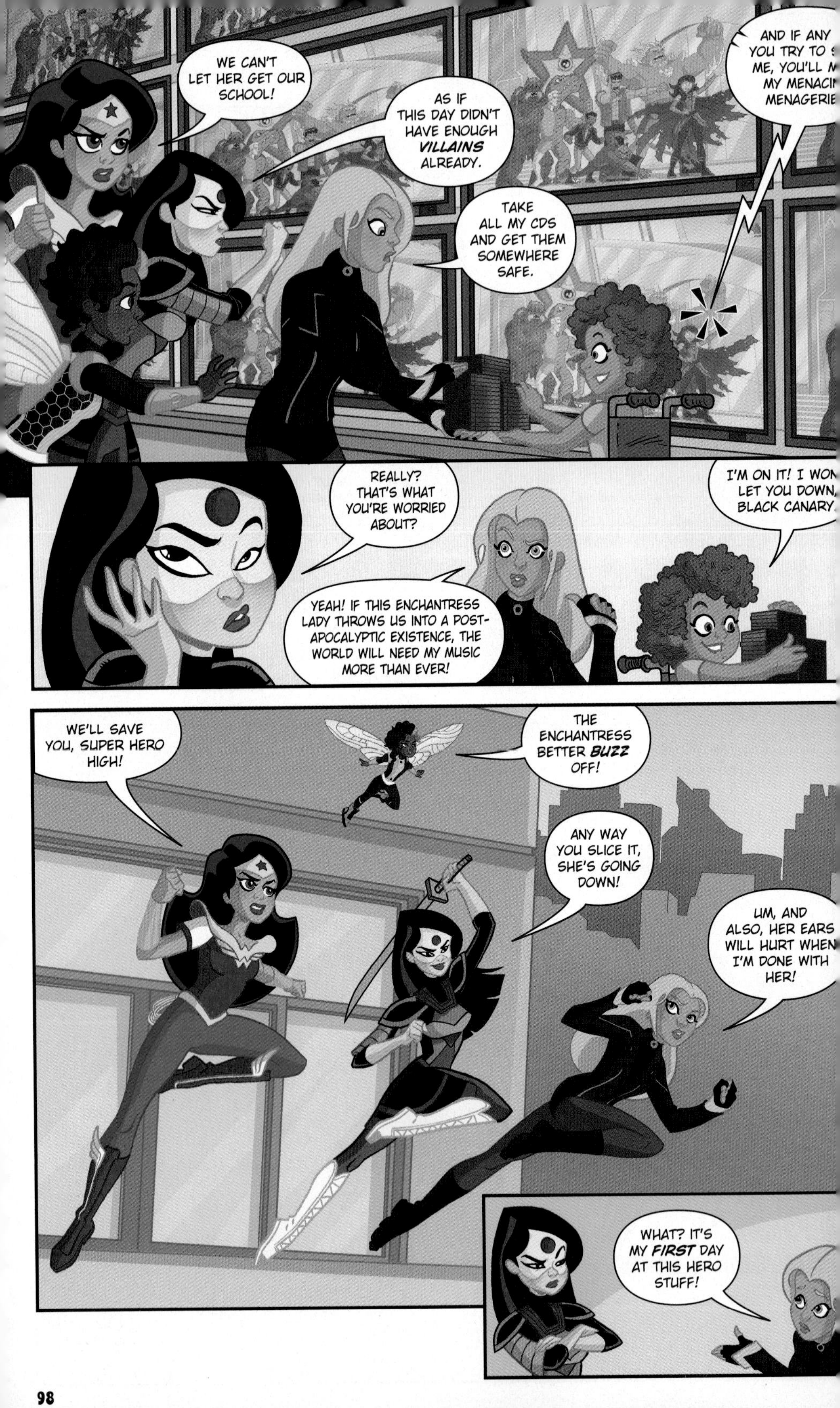
WE CAN'T LET HER GET OUR SCHOOL!
AS IF THIS DAY DIDN'T HAVE ENOUGH **VILLAINS** ALREADY.
TAKE ALL MY CDS AND GET THEM SOMEWHERE SAFE.
AND IF ANY YOU TRY TO S ME, YOU'LL M MY MENACI MENAGERIE
REALLY? THAT'S WHAT YOU'RE WORRIED ABOUT?
YEAH! IF THIS ENCHANTRESS LADY THROWS US INTO A POST-APOCALYPTIC EXISTENCE, THE WORLD WILL NEED MY MUSIC MORE THAN EVER!
I'M ON IT! I WON LET YOU DOWN, BLACK CANARY.
WE'LL SAVE YOU, SUPER HERO HIGH!
THE ENCHANTRESS BETTER **BUZZ** OFF!
ANY WAY YOU SLICE IT, SHE'S GOING DOWN!
UM, AND ALSO, HER EARS WILL HURT WHEN I'M DONE WITH HER!
WHAT? IT'S MY **FIRST** DAY AT THIS HERO STUFF!

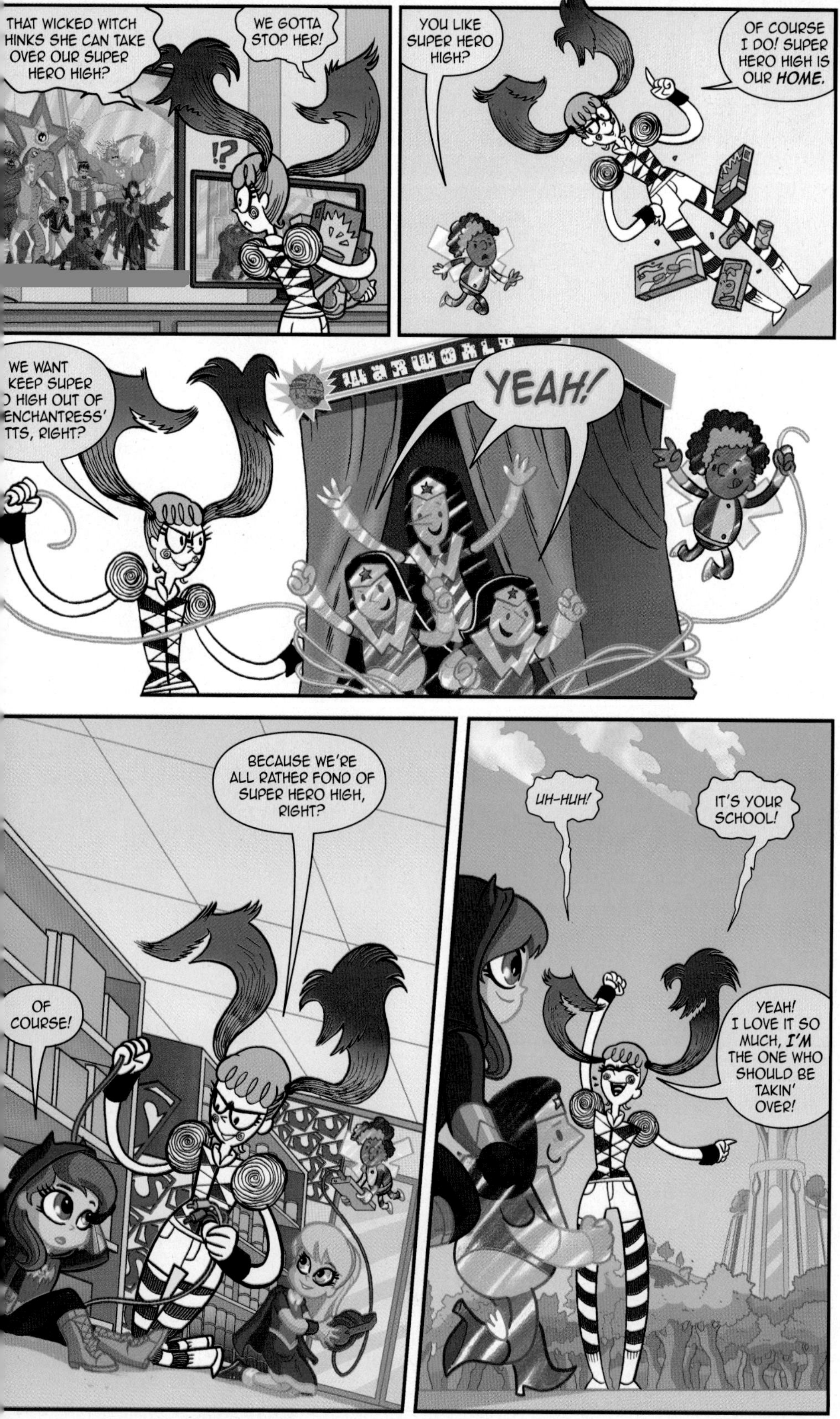
THAT WICKED WITCH HINKS SHE CAN TAKE OVER OUR SUPER HERO HIGH?
WE GOTTA STOP HER!
!?
YOU LIKE SUPER HERO HIGH?
OF COURSE I DO! SUPER HERO HIGH IS OUR *HOME.*
WE WANT KEEP SUPER HIGH OUT OF ENCHANTRESS' TTS, RIGHT?
YEAH!
BECAUSE WE'RE ALL RATHER FOND OF SUPER HERO HIGH, RIGHT?
OF COURSE!
UH-HUH!
IT'S YOUR SCHOOL!
YEAH! I LOVE IT SO MUCH, *I'M* THE ONE WHO SHOULD BE TAKIN' OVER!

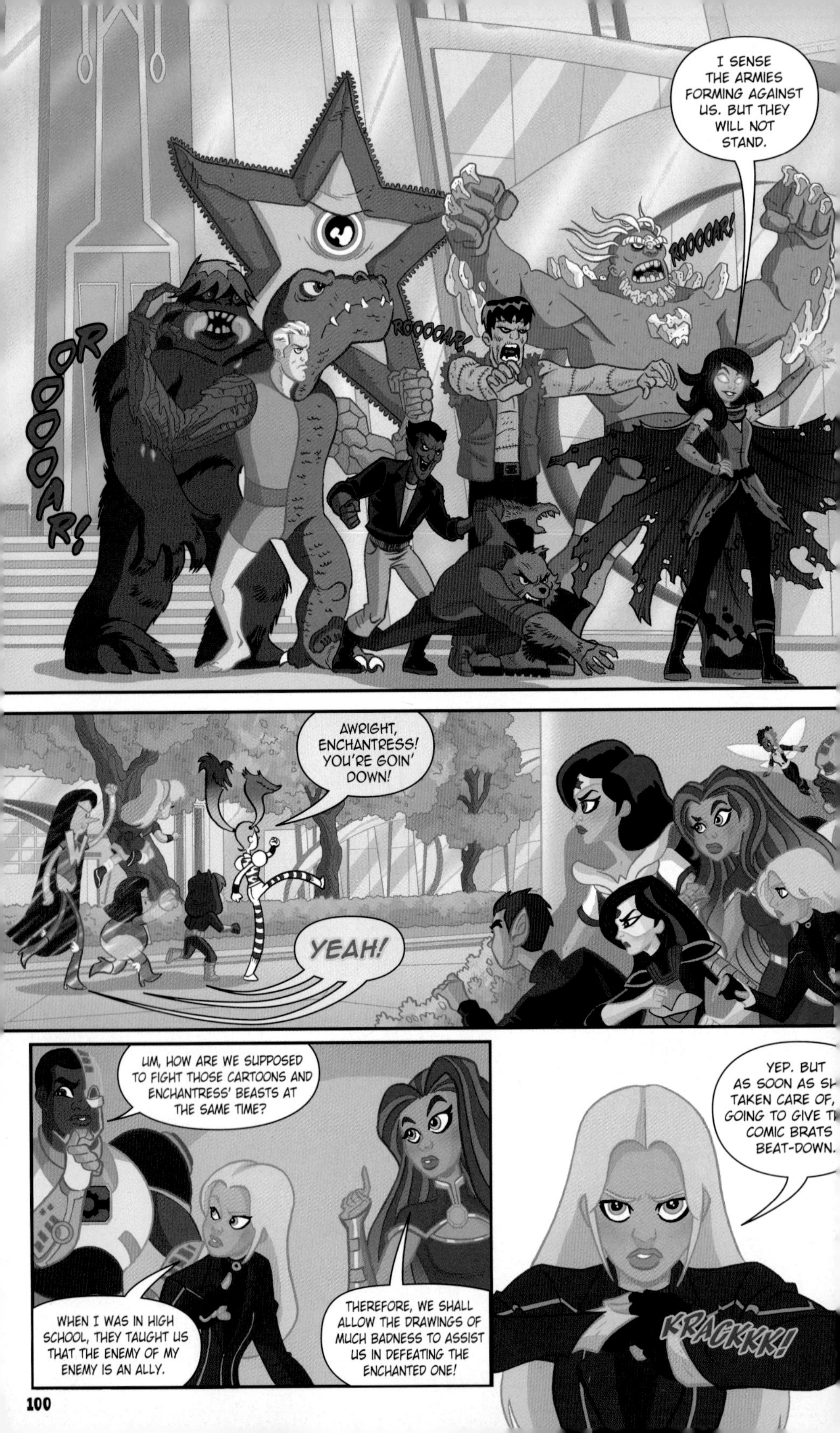
I SENSE THE ARMIES FORMING AGAINST US. BUT THEY WILL NOT STAND.
ROOOOAR!
ROOOOOAR!
ROOOOOAR!
AWRIGHT, ENCHANTRESS! YOU'RE GOIN' DOWN!
YEAH!
UM, HOW ARE WE SUPPOSED TO FIGHT THOSE CARTOONS AND ENCHANTRESS' BEASTS AT THE SAME TIME?
WHEN I WAS IN HIGH SCHOOL, THEY TAUGHT US THAT THE ENEMY OF MY ENEMY IS AN ALLY.
THEREFORE, WE SHALL ALLOW THE DRAWINGS OF MUCH BADNESS TO ASSIST US IN DEFEATING THE ENCHANTED ONE!
YEP. BUT AS SOON AS SH TAKEN CARE OF, GOING TO GIVE T COMIC BRATS BEAT-DOWN.
KRACKKK!

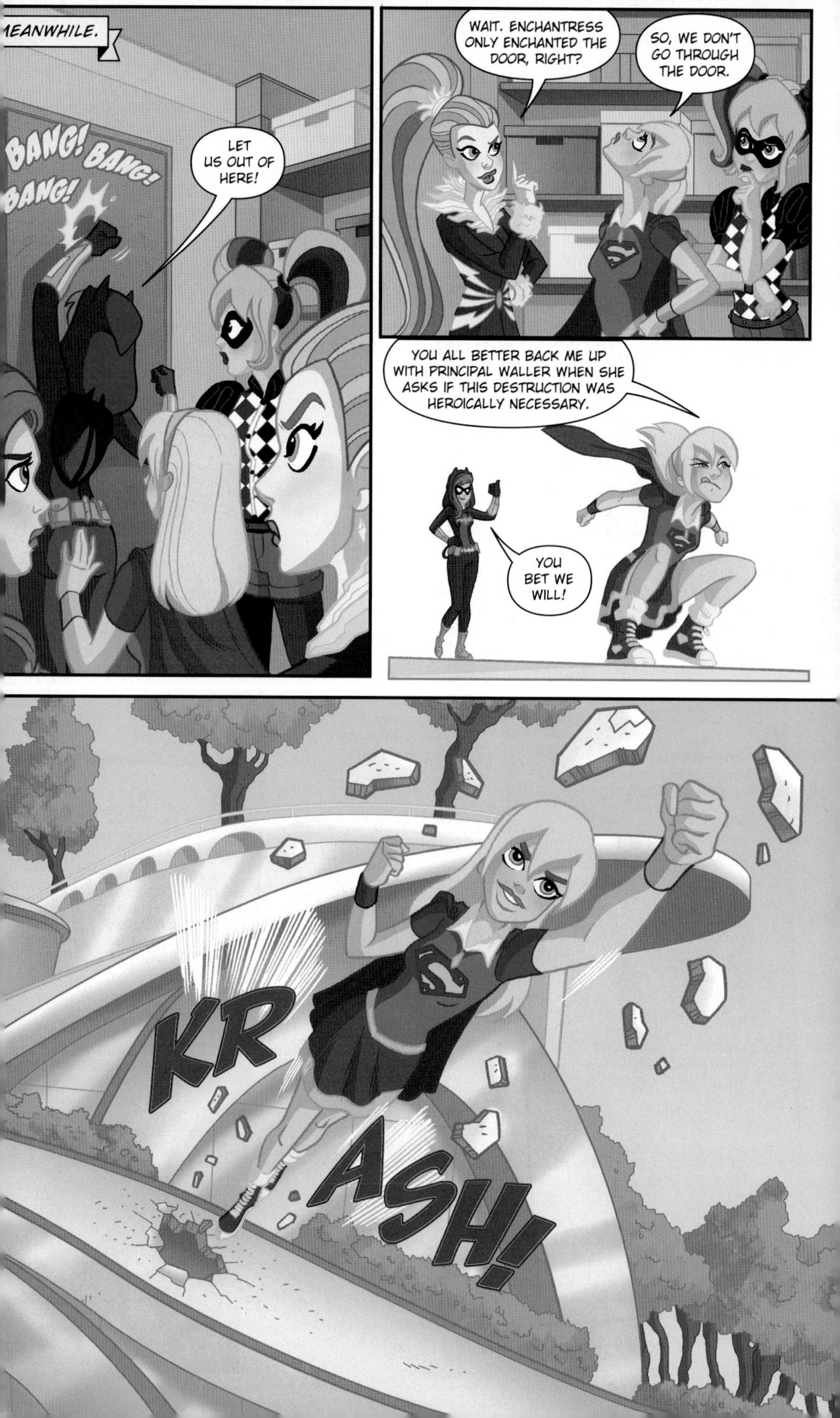
MEANWHILE.
BANG! BANG! BANG!
LET US OUT OF HERE!
WAIT. ENCHANTRESS ONLY ENCHANTED THE DOOR, RIGHT?
SO, WE DON'T GO THROUGH THE DOOR.
YOU ALL BETTER BACK ME UP WITH PRINCIPAL WALLER WHEN SHE ASKS IF THIS DESTRUCTION WAS HEROICALLY NECESSARY.
YOU BET WE WILL!
KRASH!

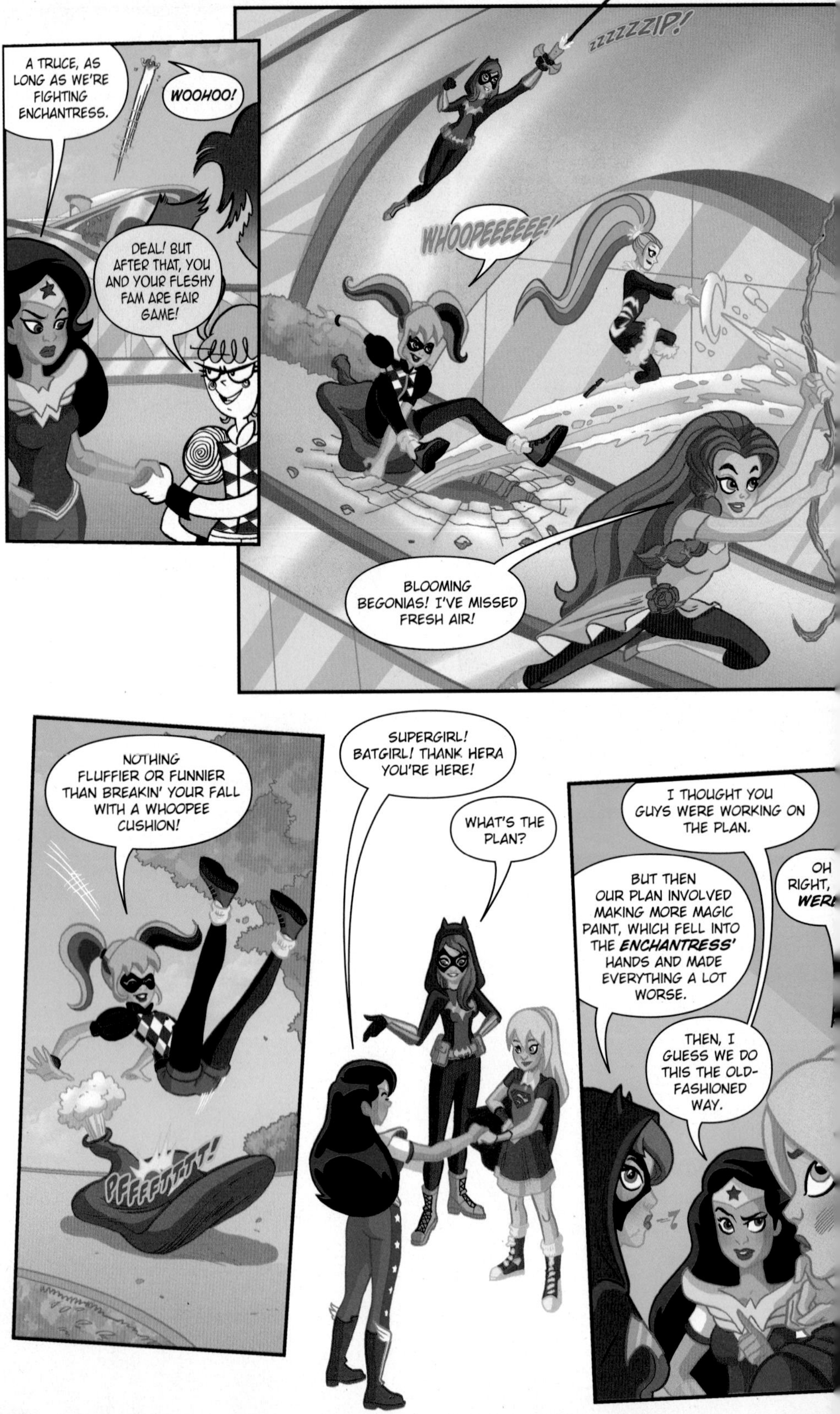
A TRUCE, AS LONG AS WE'RE FIGHTING ENCHANTRESS.
WOOHOO!
DEAL! BUT AFTER THAT, YOU AND YOUR FLESHY FAM ARE FAIR GAME!
ZZZZZZIP!
WHOOPEEEEEE!
BLOOMING BEGONIAS! I'VE MISSED FRESH AIR!
NOTHING FLUFFIER OR FUNNIER THAN BREAKIN' YOUR FALL WITH A WHOOPEE CUSHION!
PFFFFTTTTT!
SUPERGIRL! BATGIRL! THANK HERA YOU'RE HERE!
WHAT'S THE PLAN?
I THOUGHT YOU GUYS WERE WORKING ON THE PLAN.
BUT THEN OUR PLAN INVOLVED MAKING MORE MAGIC PAINT, WHICH FELL INTO THE ENCHANTRESS' HANDS AND MADE EVERYTHING A LOT WORSE.
OH RIGHT, WERE
THEN, I GUESS WE DO THIS THE OLD-FASHIONED WAY.

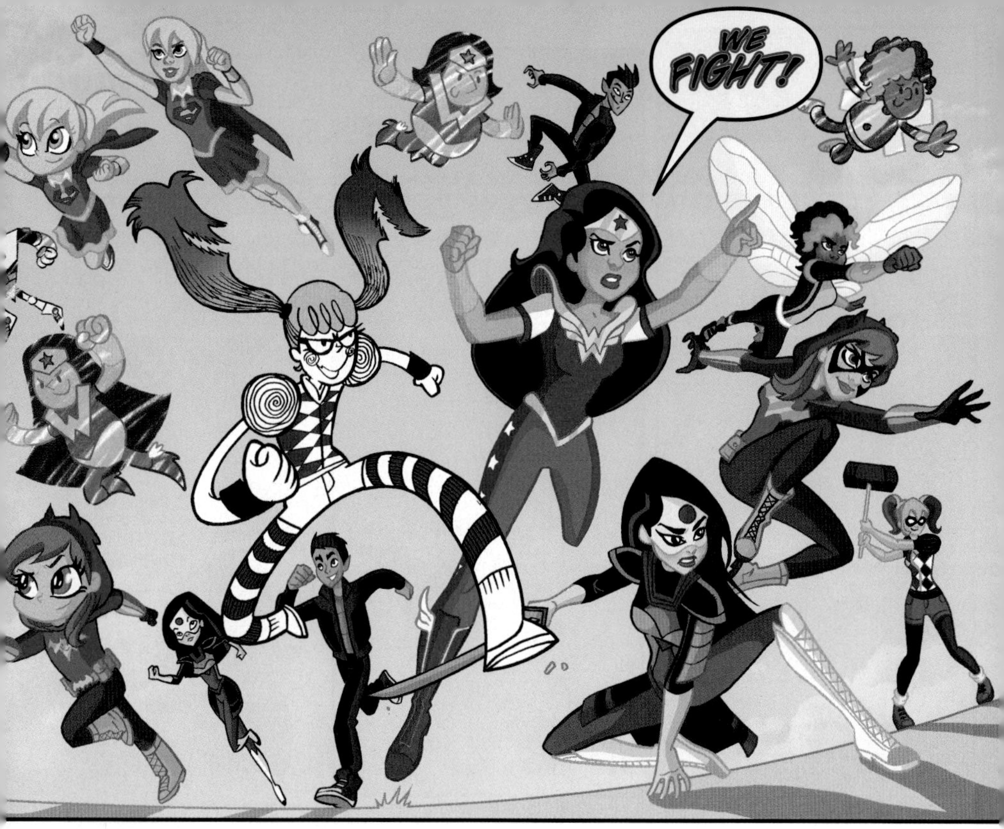
WE FIGHT!

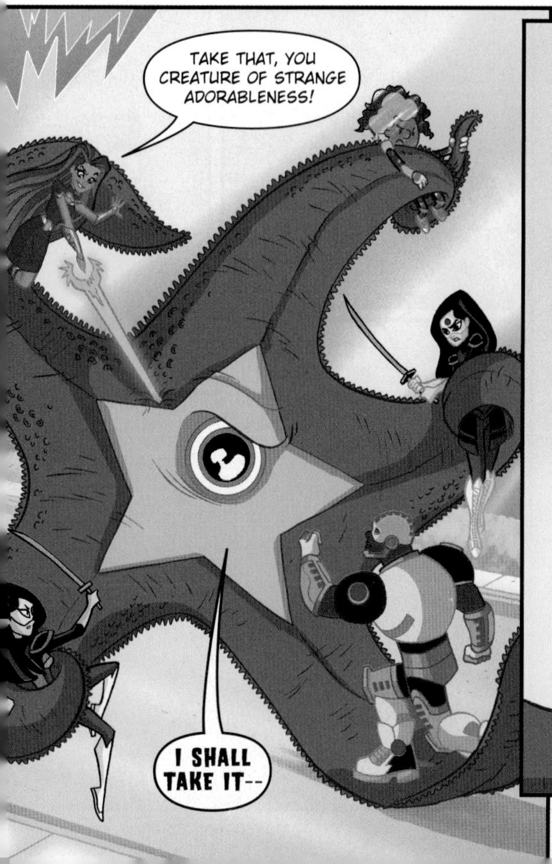
TAKE THAT, YOU CREATURE OF STRANGE ADORABLENESS!
I SHALL TAKE IT--

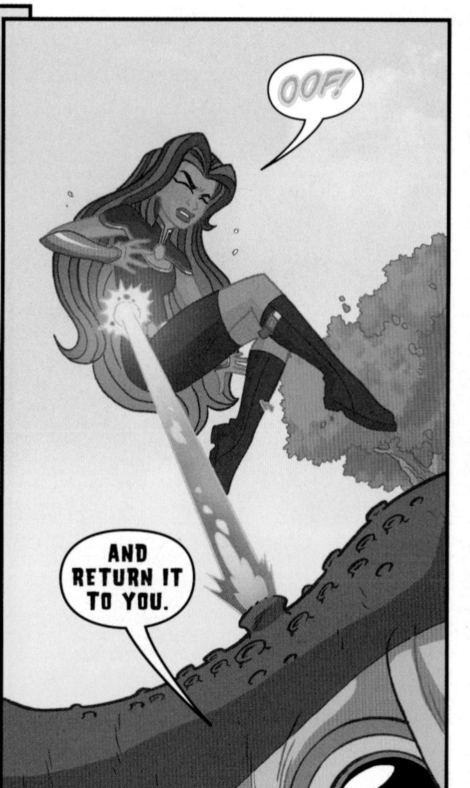
OOF!
AND RETURN IT TO YOU.

THIS IS ÜBER UNCOMFORTABLE!

I AM STARRO, THE CONQUEROR!

PUT DOWN MY DOPPELGÄNGER ON THE DOUBLE!

SHNK!

I HAVE POWERS OF REGENERATI

DION EVEN LO HIS G

UH-OH. I THINK WE ANGERED THE OVERGROWN STARFISH--

~NGH!~

TH WACK!

FFFFEEEEEEEE!

CRY YOUR HEART OUT, CANARY, BUT STARRO DOES NOT HAVE EARS!

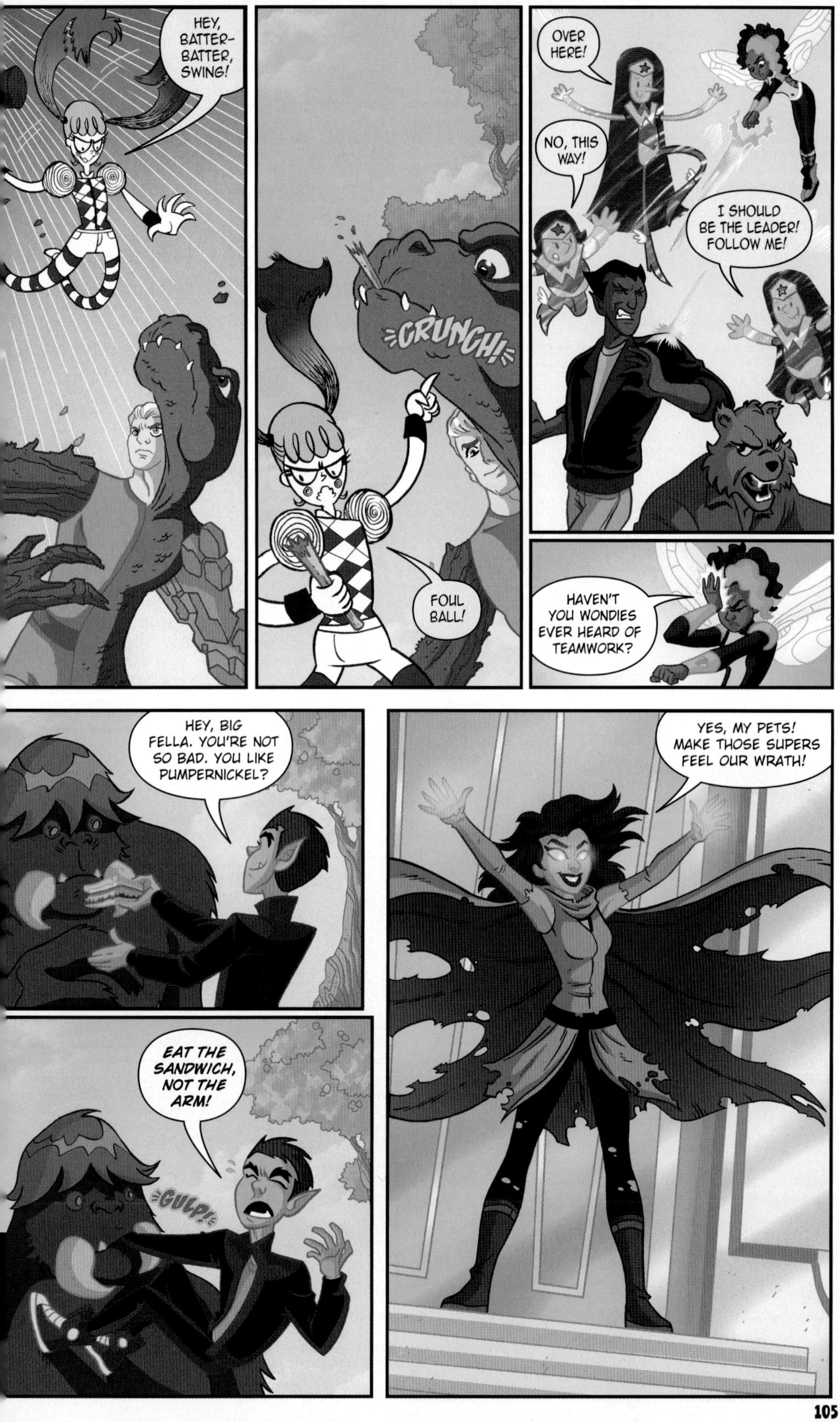
HEY, BATTER-BATTER, SWING!
CRUNCH!
FOUL BALL!
OVER HERE!
NO, THIS WAY!
I SHOULD BE THE LEADER! FOLLOW ME!
HAVEN'T YOU WONDIES EVER HEARD OF TEAMWORK?
HEY, BIG FELLA. YOU'RE NOT SO BAD. YOU LIKE PUMPERNICKEL?
EAT THE SANDWICH, NOT THE ARM!
GULP!
YES, MY PETS! MAKE THOSE SUPERS FEEL OUR WRATH!

TIME TO TURN UP THE HEAT--

PUMP UP THE LASSO--

AN TIE UP MONS

RRRRRAAARGH!

I DO THIN LIK TH

WATCH THE RIBS! I NEED THOSE!

OH MY HERA!

OW!

AAAGH!

Y!!!!

NO ONE'S EVER TOSSED ME AROUND LIKE THAT. I'M WONDER WOMAN!

HOW DO YOU THINK I FEEL? MY OFFICIAL POWER LISTING IN THE YEARBOOK SAYS "INVULNERABLE!"

M MONS ARE WO

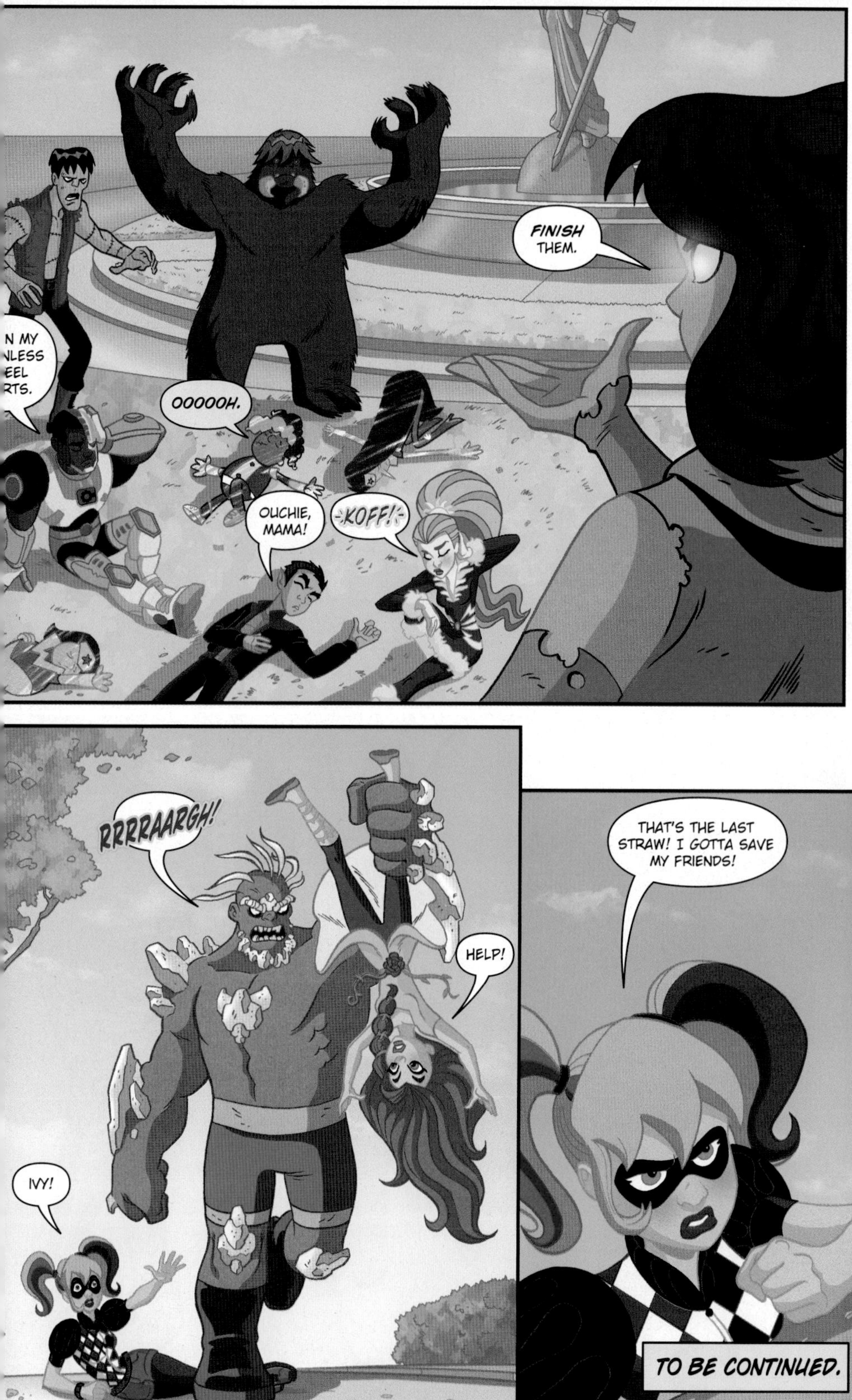
FINISH THEM.
N MY NLESS EEL RTS.
OOOOOH.
OUCHIE, MAMA!
-KOFF!-
RRRRAARGH!
HELP!
IVY!
THAT'S THE LAST STRAW! I GOTTA SAVE MY FRIENDS!
TO BE CONTINUED.

CHAPTER SIX
FINAL DRAFT

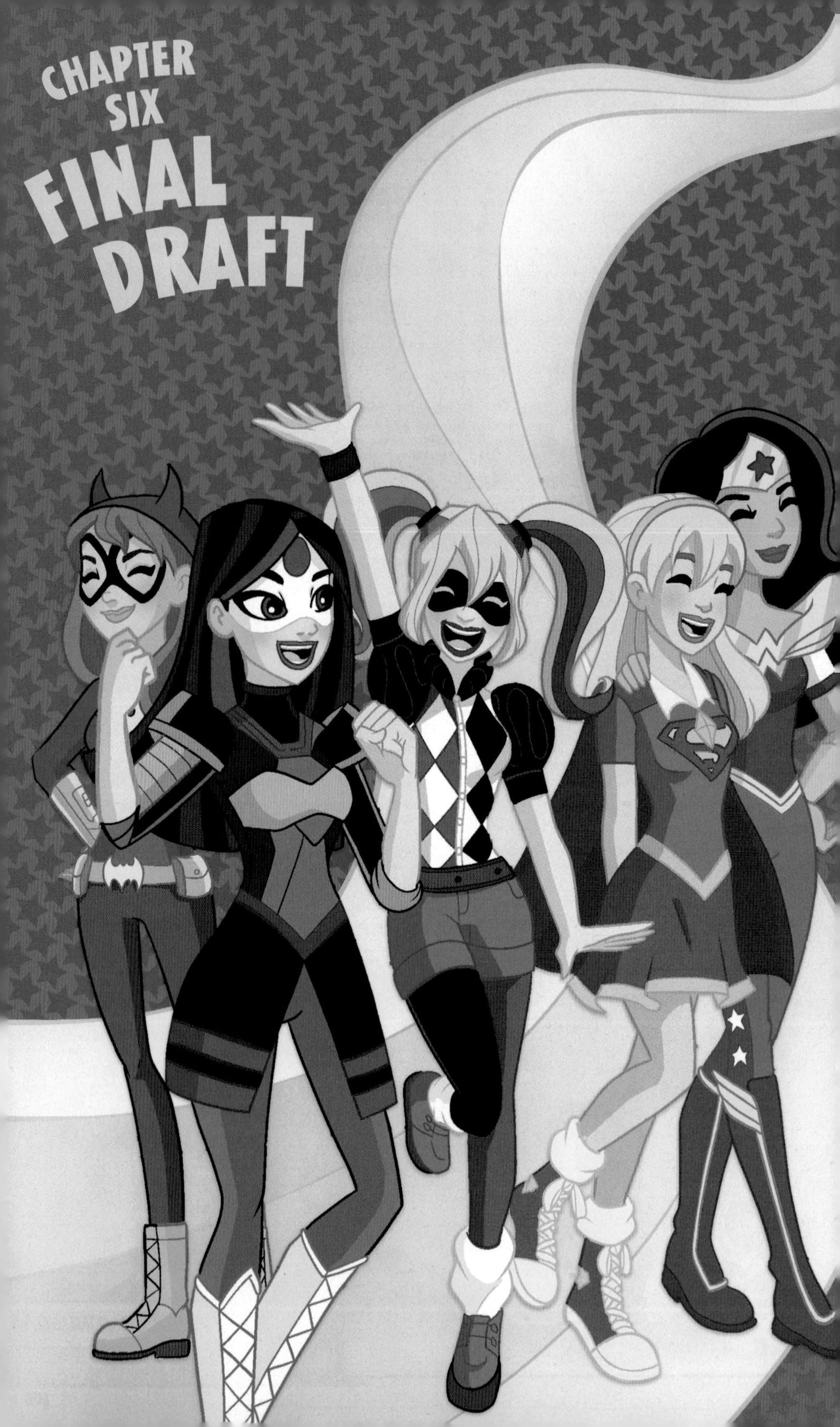

TIME TO THINK MY WAY OUTTA THIS BOX!

I'M THE MOST *CREATIVE* GIRL AT SUPER HERO HIGH AND THESE MONSTERS ARE GONNA EAT MY WEIRD, WACKY DUST!

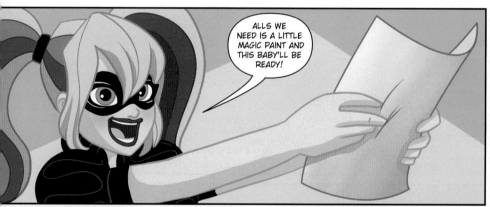

ALLS WE NEED IS A LITTLE MAGIC PAINT AND THIS BABY'LL BE READY!

GH!!

IF THERE'S ANYTHING I LEARNED FROM TOOTHPASTE, IT'S THAT YA CAN ALWAYS SQUEEZE A BIT MORE OUTTA THE TUBE!

ANIMAL-VEGETABLE-MINERAL MAN, HUH? WELL, I CHALLENGE YOU TO A SHAPESHIFT OFF!

MIGHTY MORPHIN' POWER BEAST BOY GOES *BEAR!*

MOOSE!

I SEE YOUR MOOSE, AND I RAISE YOU ELECTRIC EEL!

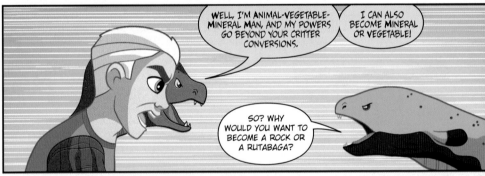

WELL, I'M ANIMAL-VEGETABLE-MINERAL MAN, AND MY POWERS GO BEYOND YOUR CRITTER CONVERSIONS.

I CAN ALSO BECOME MINERAL OR VEGETABLE!

SO? WHY WOULD YOU WANT TO BECOME A ROCK OR A RUTABAGA?

POWER OF *TURNIP!*

EW, STE YOU BRO WI

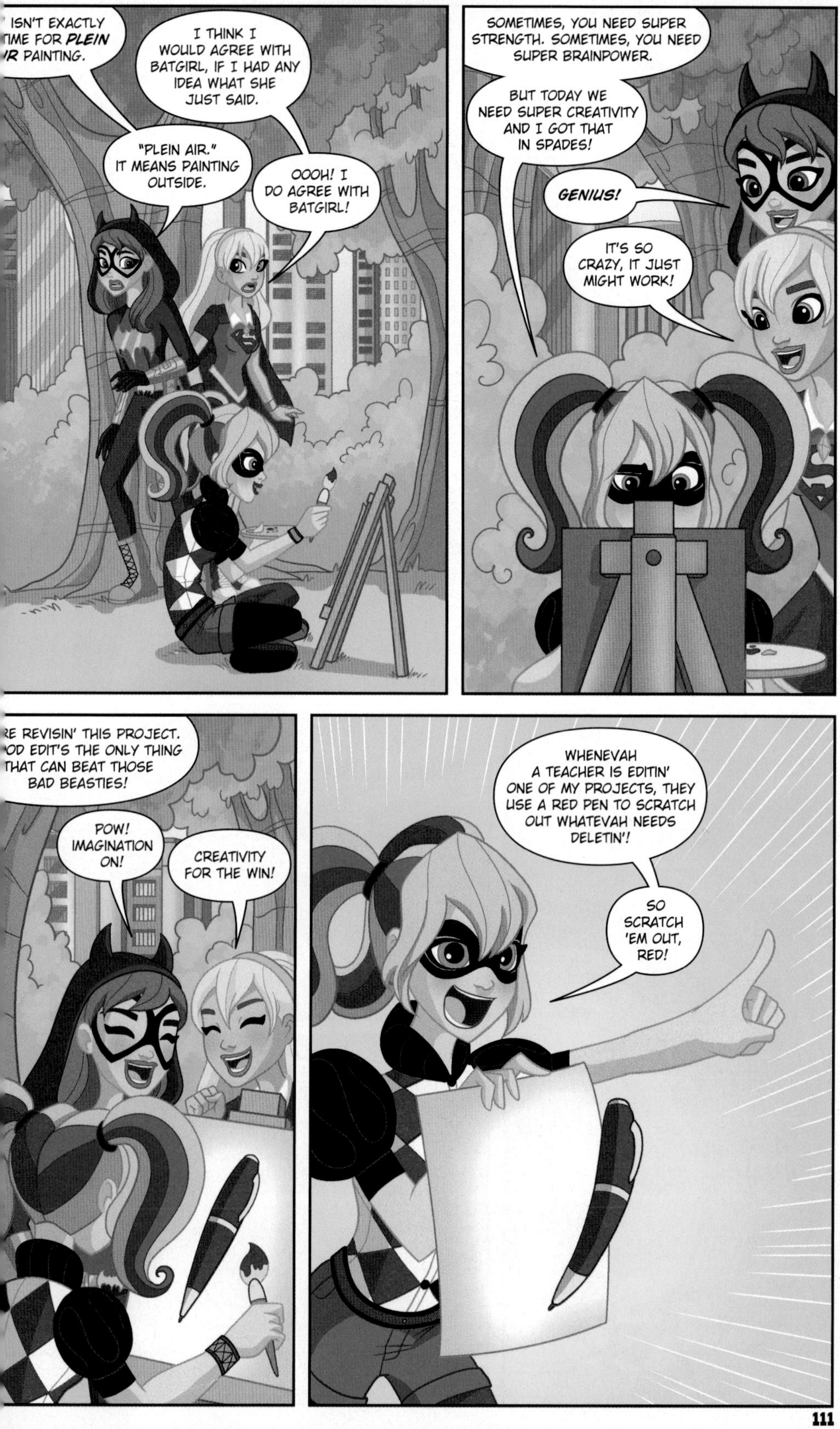

ISN'T EXACTLY
TIME FOR PLEIN
IR PAINTING.
I THINK I WOULD AGREE WITH BATGIRL, IF I HAD ANY IDEA WHAT SHE JUST SAID.
"PLEIN AIR." IT MEANS PAINTING OUTSIDE.
OOOH! I DO AGREE WITH BATGIRL!
SOMETIMES, YOU NEED SUPER STRENGTH. SOMETIMES, YOU NEED SUPER BRAINPOWER.
BUT TODAY WE NEED SUPER CREATIVITY AND I GOT THAT IN SPADES!
GENIUS!
IT'S SO CRAZY, IT JUST MIGHT WORK!
RE REVISIN' THIS PROJECT.
OD EDIT'S THE ONLY THING
THAT CAN BEAT THOSE
BAD BEASTIES!
POW! IMAGINATION ON!
CREATIVITY FOR THE WIN!
WHENEVAH A TEACHER IS EDITIN' ONE OF MY PROJECTS, THEY USE A RED PEN TO SCRATCH OUT WHATEVAH NEEDS DELETIN'!
SO SCRATCH 'EM OUT, RED!

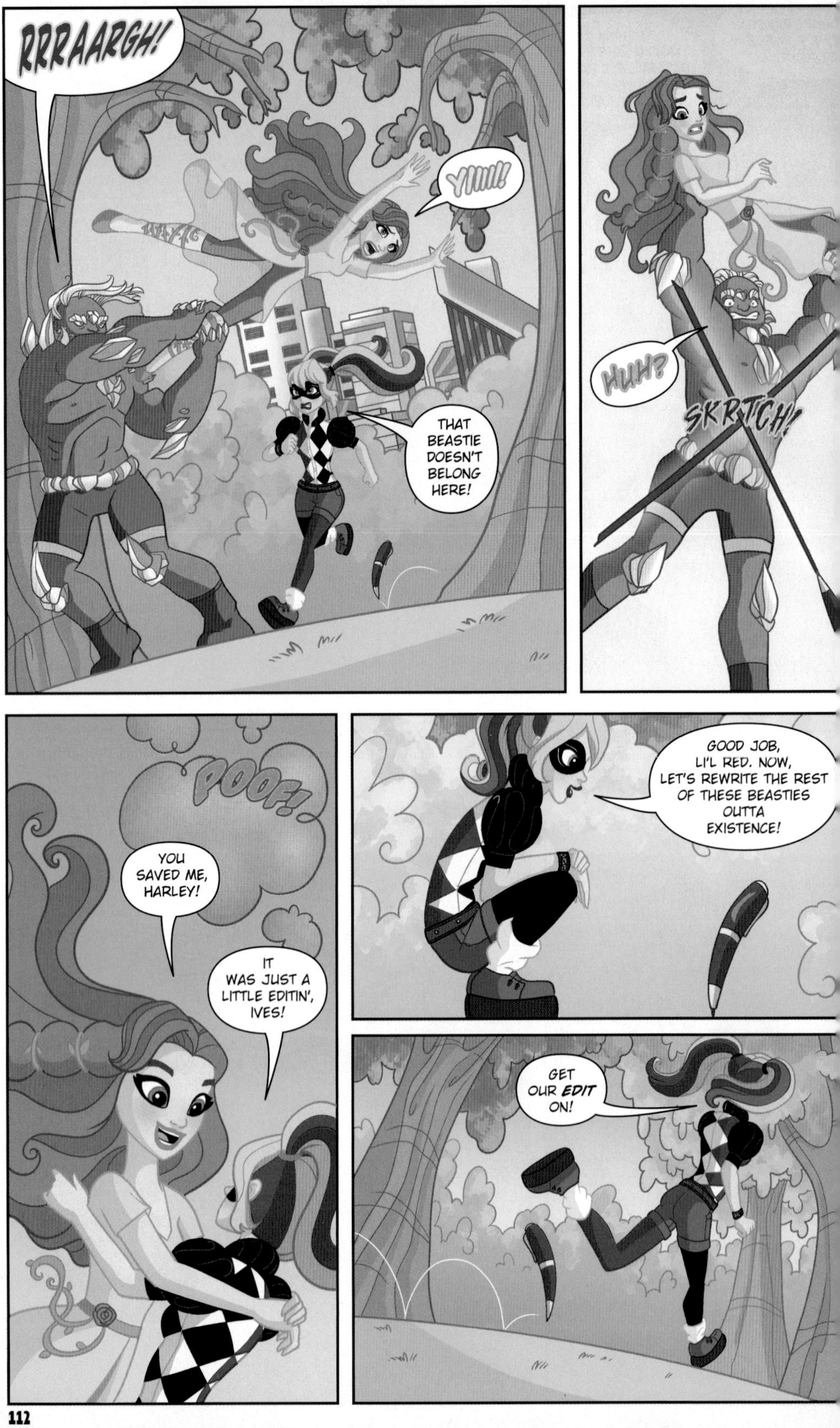
RRRAARGH!
YIIIIII!
THAT BEASTIE DOESN'T BELONG HERE!
HUH?
SKRTCH!
POOF!
YOU SAVED ME, HARLEY!
IT WAS JUST A LITTLE EDITIN', IVES!
GOOD JOB, LI'L RED. NOW, LET'S REWRITE THE REST OF THESE BEASTIES OUTTA EXISTENCE!
GET OUR EDIT ON!

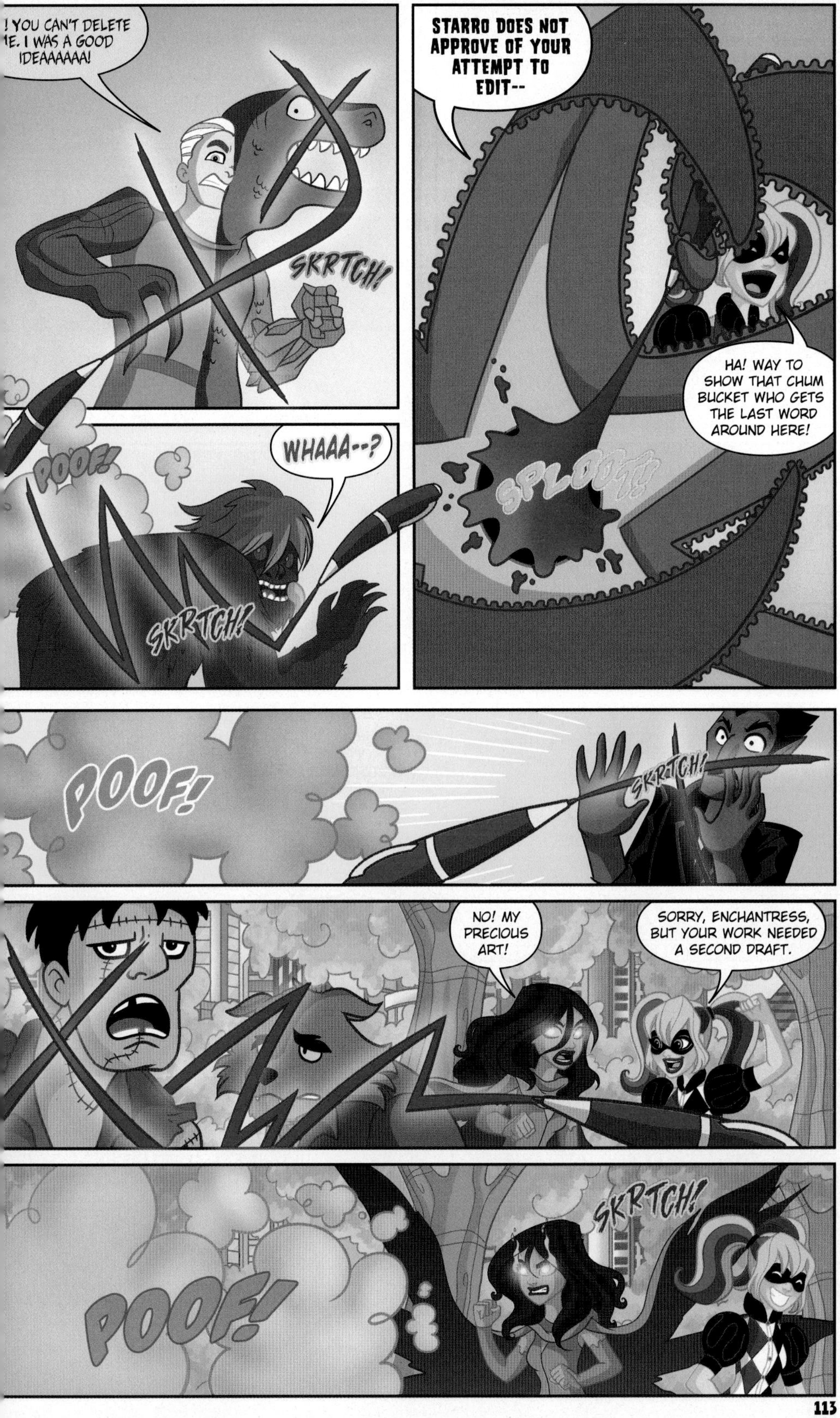
! YOU CAN'T DELETE
ME. I WAS A GOOD
IDEAAAAAAA!
SKRTCH!
STARRO DOES NOT
APPROVE OF YOUR
ATTEMPT TO
EDIT--
HA! WAY TO
SHOW THAT CHUM
BUCKET WHO GETS
THE LAST WORD
AROUND HERE!
SPLOOT!
POOF!
WHAAA--?
SKRTCH!
POOF!
SKRTCH!
NO! MY
PRECIOUS
ART!
SORRY, ENCHANTRESS,
BUT YOUR WORK NEEDED
A SECOND DRAFT.
SKRTCH!
POOF!

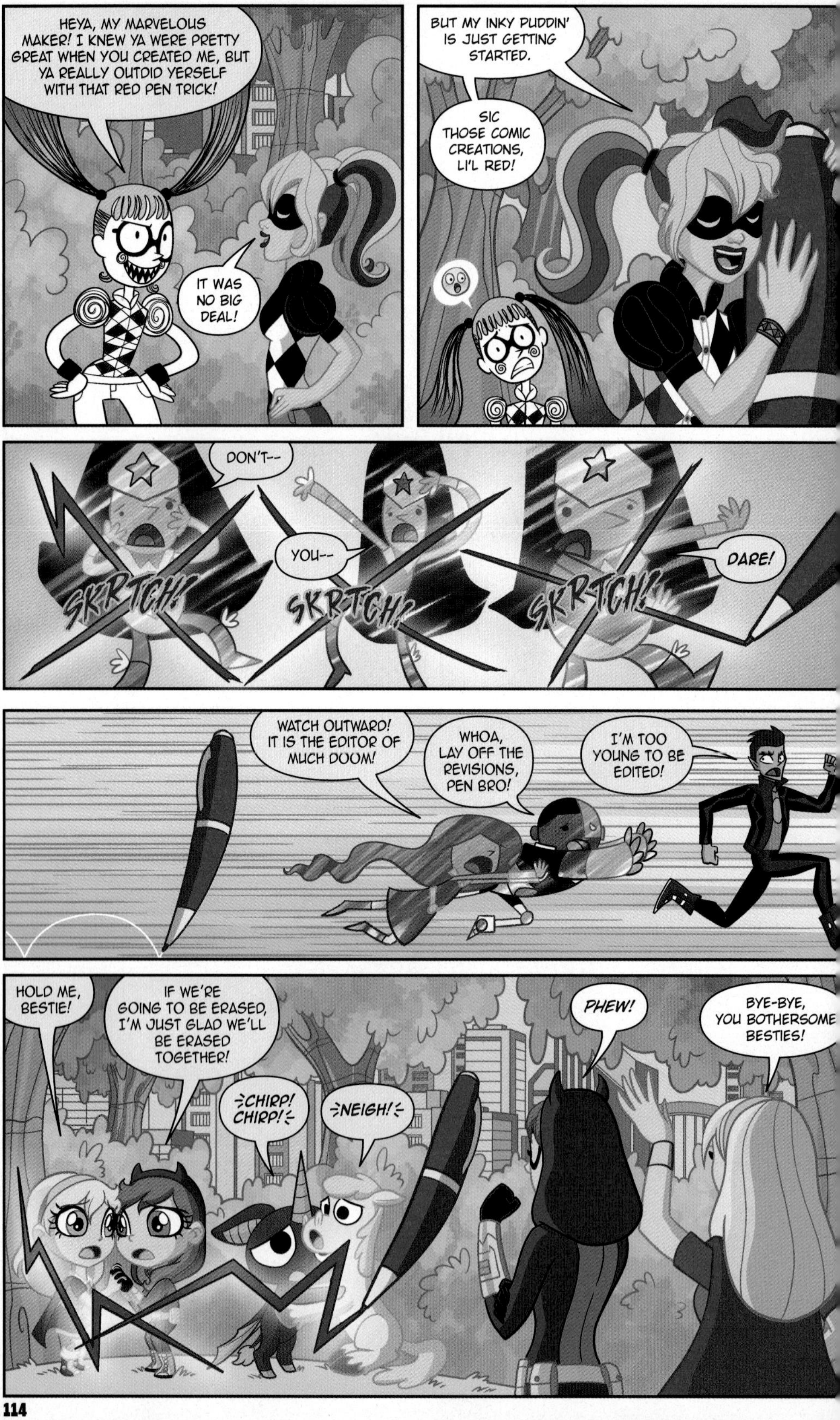
HEYA, MY MARVELOUS MAKER! I KNEW YA WERE PRETTY GREAT WHEN YOU CREATED ME, BUT YA REALLY OUTDID YERSELF WITH THAT RED PEN TRICK!
IT WAS NO BIG DEAL!
BUT MY INKY PUDDIN' IS JUST GETTING STARTED.
SIC THOSE COMIC CREATIONS, LI'L RED!
DON'T--
YOU--
DARE!
SKRTCH!
SKRTCH!
SKRTCH!
WATCH OUTWARD! IT IS THE EDITOR OF MUCH DOOM!
WHOA, LAY OFF THE REVISIONS, PEN BRO!
I'M TOO YOUNG TO BE EDITED!
HOLD ME, BESTIE!
IF WE'RE GOING TO BE ERASED, I'M JUST GLAD WE'LL BE ERASED TOGETHER!
CHIRP! CHIRP!
NEIGH!
PHEW!
BYE-BYE, YOU BOTHERSOME BESTIES!

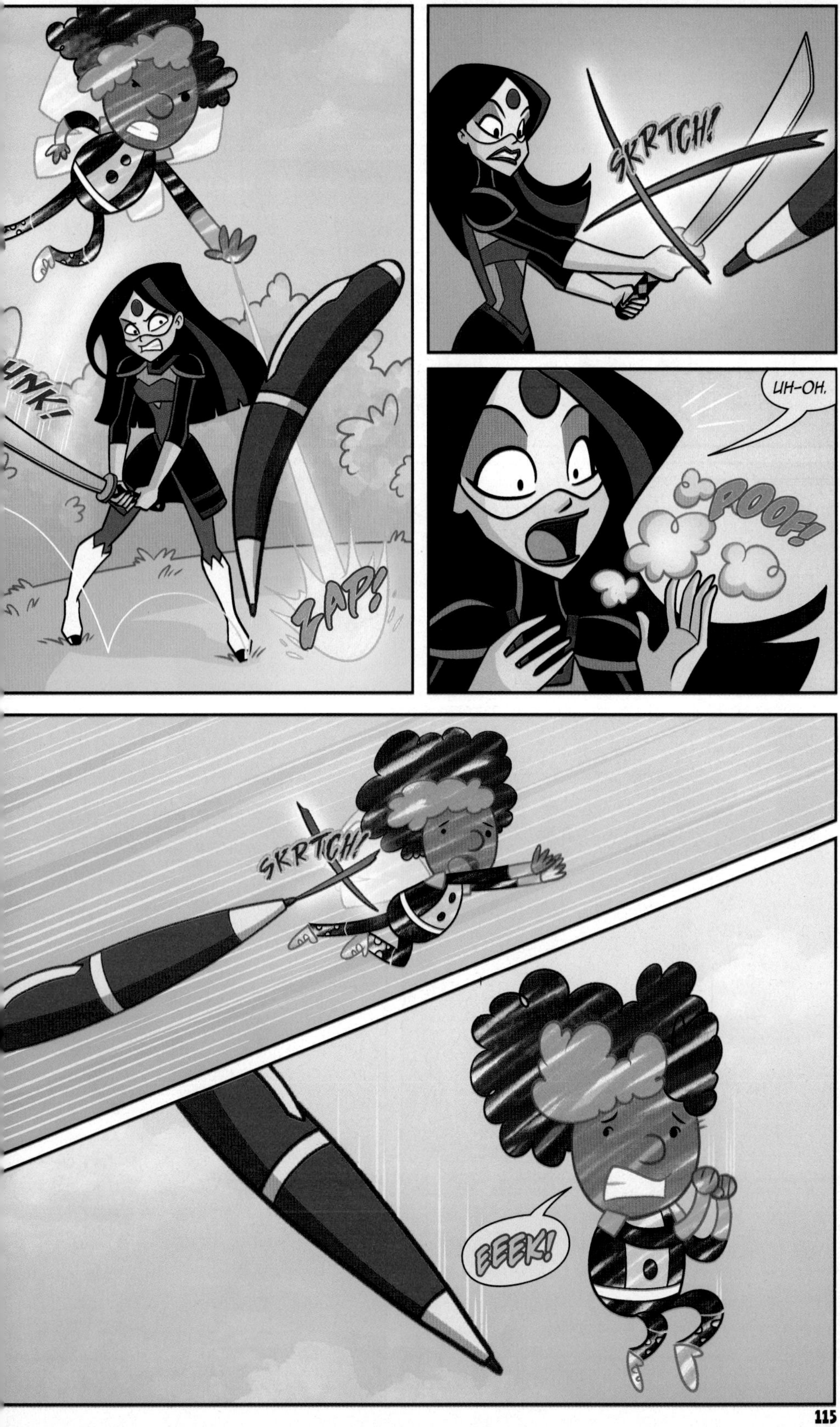
UNK!
ZAP!
SKRTCH!
UH-OH.
POOF!
SKRTCH!
EEEK!

SHE CAN'T DO THIS TO US!

C'MON, HARLS! JUST THINK OF THE FUN YOU AND ME COULD HAVE TOGETHER! WE WERE MADE FOR EACH OTHER!

BEG! APPEAL TO HER CREATOR'S EGO!

DOUBLE THE HARLEY?

I'D INVITE YOU TO TAG ALONG, BUT IT LOOKS LIKE YOU'RE TIED UP!

AND PAY FOR ONE MOVIE, BUT THEN SNEAK INTO ALL OF 'EM!

WE COULD ROB CANDY STORES, BREAK INTO SWIMMIN' POOLS--

I ALWAYS WANTED A PARTNER IN CRIME!

ACTUAL MY DUPLICI DOUBLE, B GOOD IS MORE F

BESIDES, I CAN'T RISK YA TAKIN' MY SPOTLIGHT!

SKRTCH!

AS SOME OLD ENGLISH DUDE ONCE SAID, "THE PEN IS MIGHTIER THAN THE SWORD!"

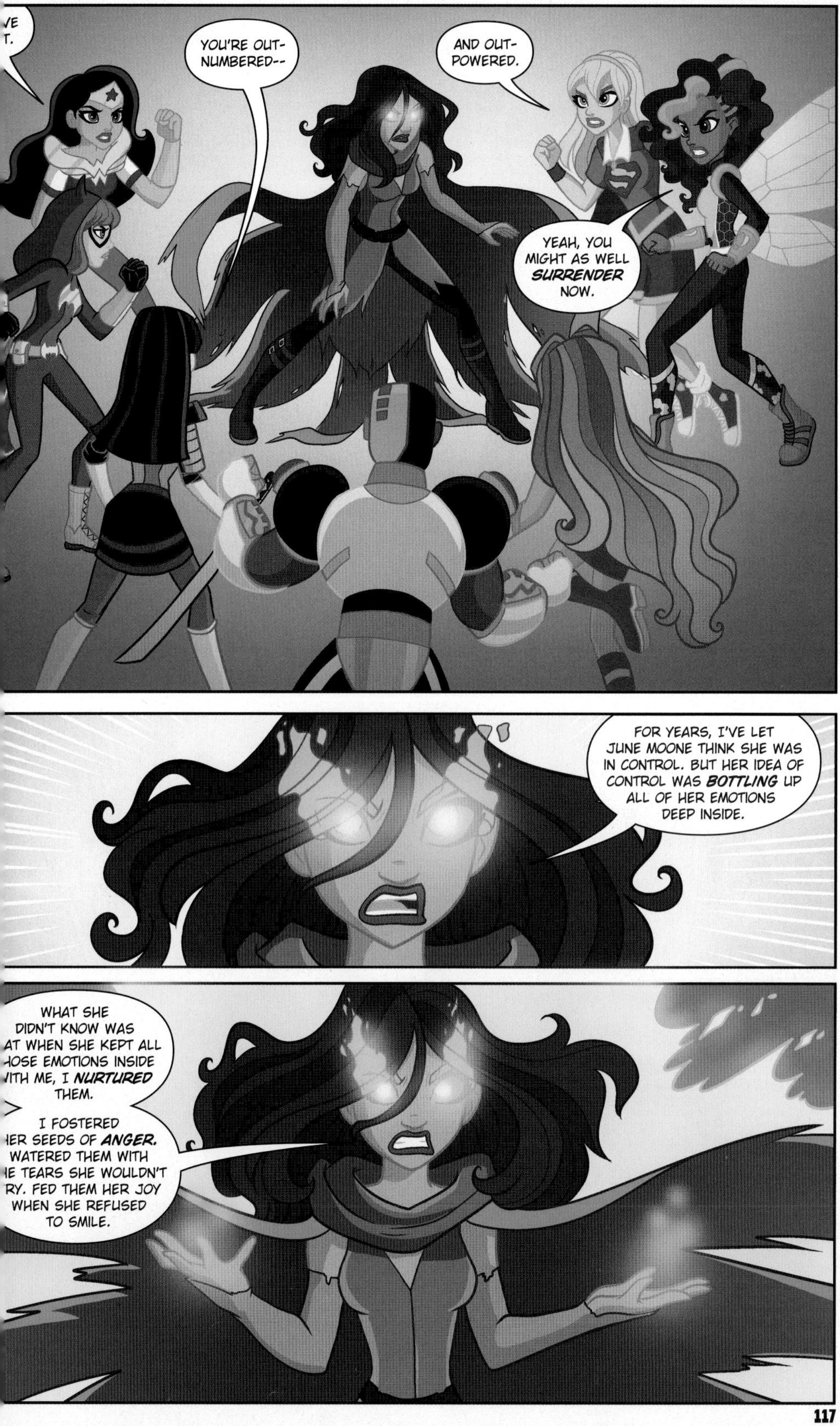

VE
T.
YOU'RE OUT-NUMBERED--
AND OUT-POWERED.
YEAH, YOU MIGHT AS WELL SURRENDER NOW.
FOR YEARS, I'VE LET JUNE MOONE THINK SHE WAS IN CONTROL. BUT HER IDEA OF CONTROL WAS BOTTLING UP ALL OF HER EMOTIONS DEEP INSIDE.
WHAT SHE DIDN'T KNOW WAS AT WHEN SHE KEPT ALL HOSE EMOTIONS INSIDE WITH ME, I NURTURED THEM.
I FOSTERED HER SEEDS OF ANGER. WATERED THEM WITH HE TEARS SHE WOULDN'T RY. FED THEM HER JOY WHEN SHE REFUSED TO SMILE.

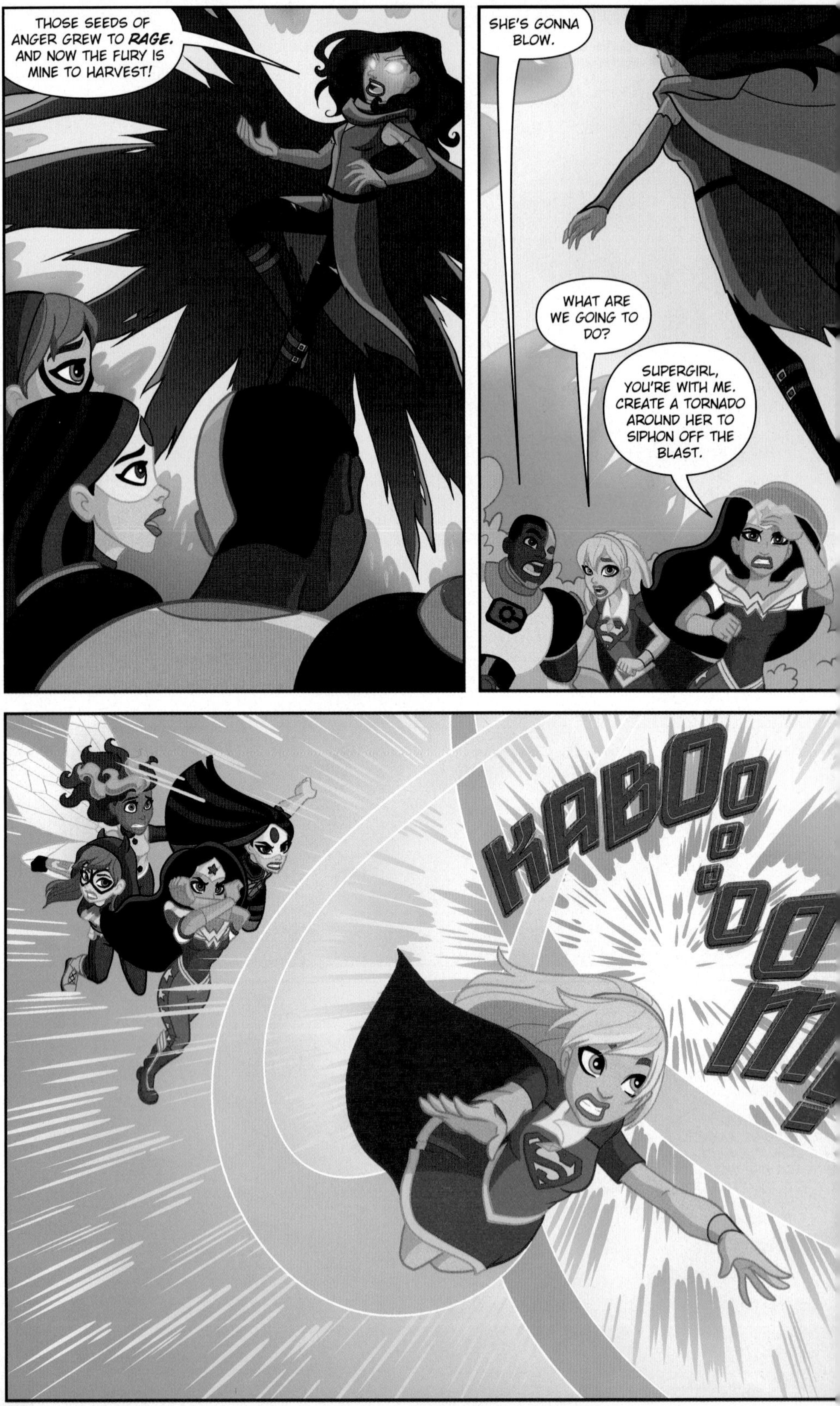
THOSE SEEDS OF ANGER GREW TO ***RAGE.*** AND NOW THE FURY IS MINE TO HARVEST!
SHE'S GONNA BLOW.
WHAT ARE WE GOING TO DO?
SUPERGIRL, YOU'RE WITH ME. CREATE A TORNADO AROUND HER TO SIPHON OFF THE BLAST.
KABOOooOOM!

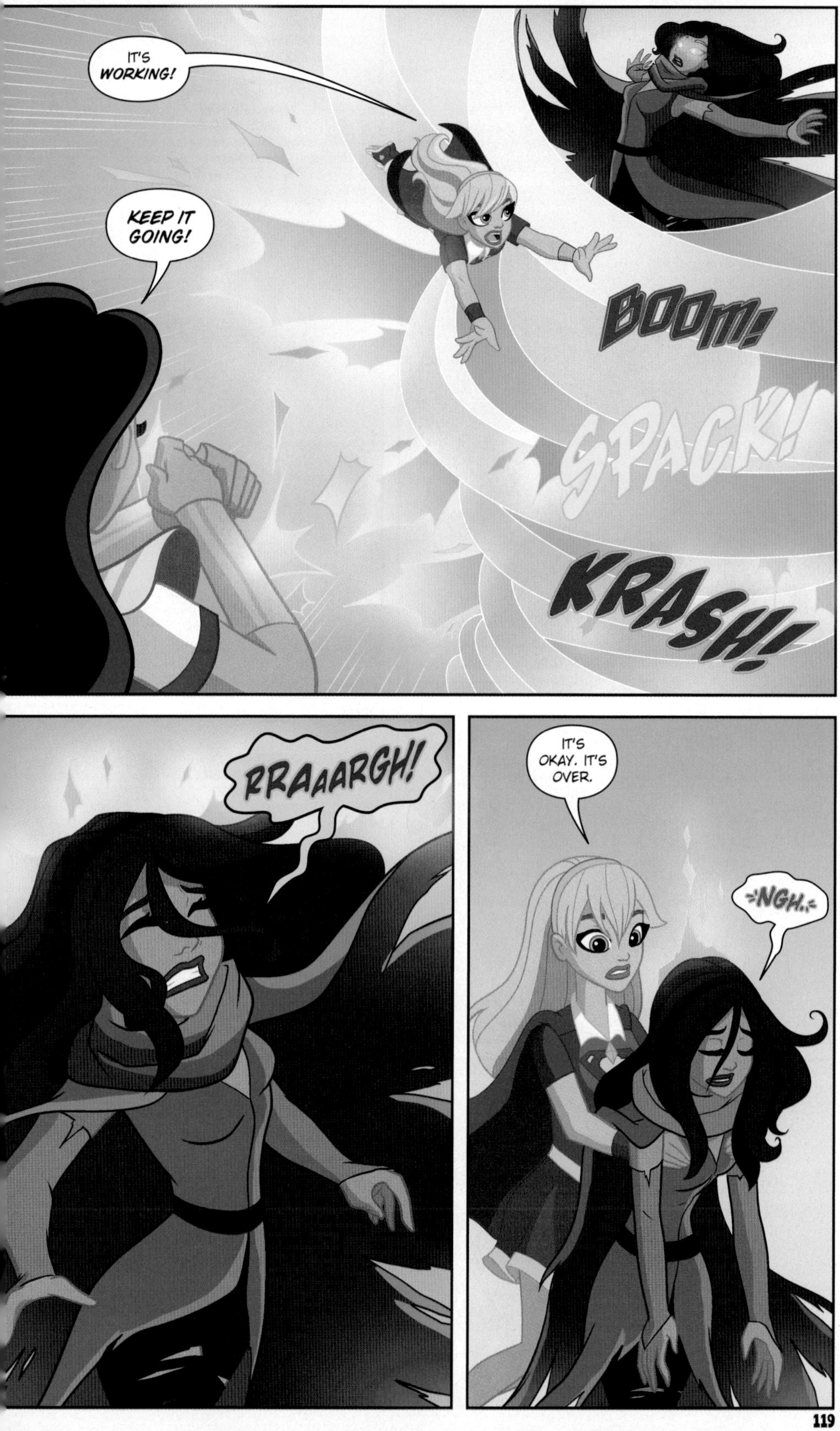

IT'S WORKING!
KEEP IT GOING!
BOOM!
SPACK!
KRASH!
RRAAARGH!
IT'S OKAY. IT'S OVER.
NGH..

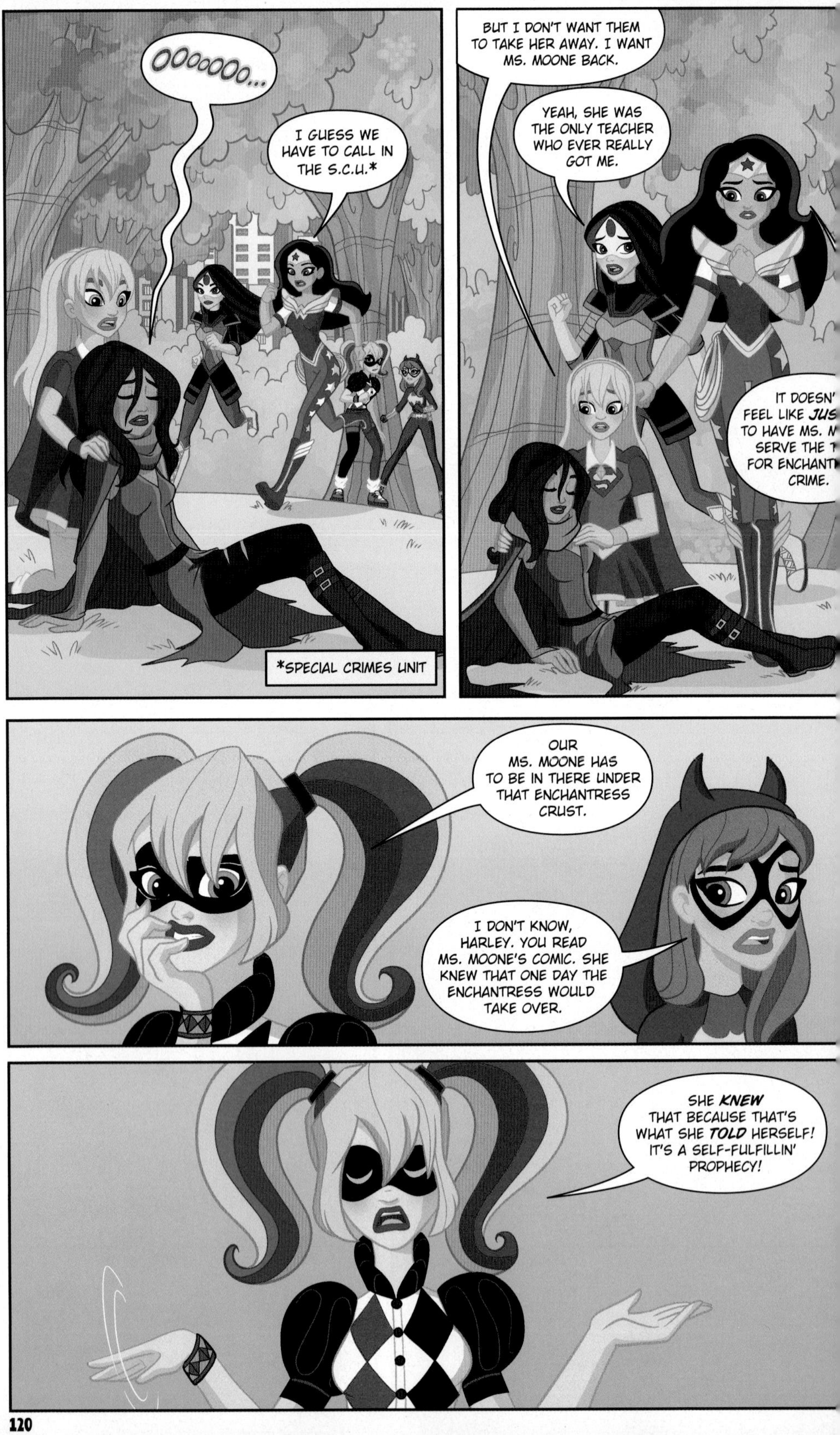

OOOoOOO...
I GUESS WE HAVE TO CALL IN THE S.C.U.*
*SPECIAL CRIMES UNIT
BUT I DON'T WANT THEM TO TAKE HER AWAY. I WANT MS. MOONE BACK.
YEAH, SHE WAS THE ONLY TEACHER WHO EVER REALLY GOT ME.
IT DOESN' FEEL LIKE JUS TO HAVE MS. M SERVE THE FOR ENCHANT CRIME.
OUR MS. MOONE HAS TO BE IN THERE UNDER THAT ENCHANTRESS CRUST.
I DON'T KNOW, HARLEY. YOU READ MS. MOONE'S COMIC. SHE KNEW THAT ONE DAY THE ENCHANTRESS WOULD TAKE OVER.
SHE ***KNEW*** THAT BECAUSE THAT'S WHAT SHE ***TOLD*** HERSELF! IT'S A SELF-FULFILLIN' PROPHECY!

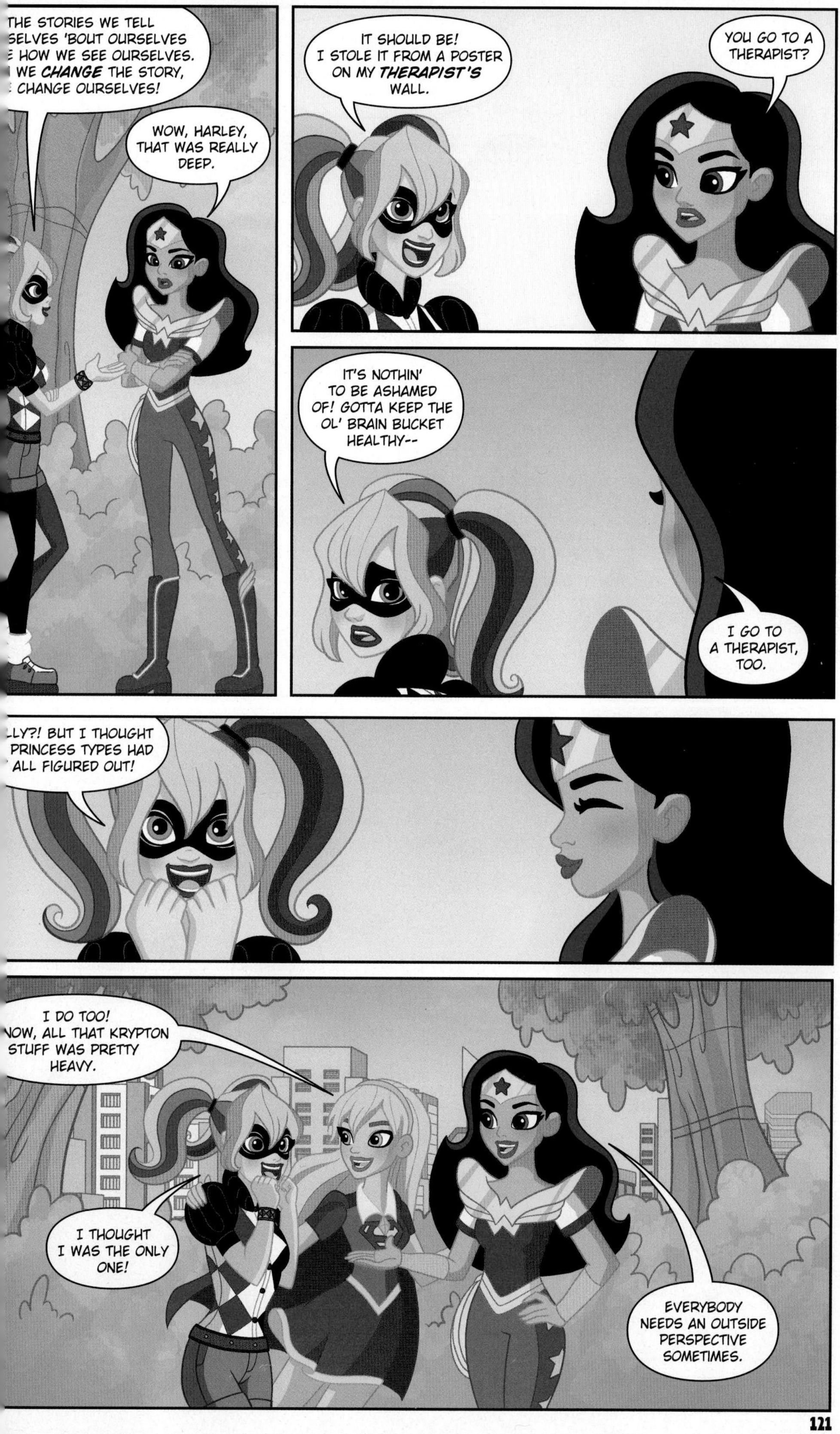
THE STORIES WE TELL
SELVES 'BOUT OURSELVES
E HOW WE SEE OURSELVES.
WE *CHANGE* THE STORY,
CHANGE OURSELVES!
WOW, HARLEY, THAT WAS REALLY DEEP.
IT SHOULD BE! I STOLE IT FROM A POSTER ON MY ***THERAPIST'S*** WALL.
YOU GO TO A THERAPIST?
IT'S NOTHIN' TO BE ASHAMED OF! GOTTA KEEP THE OL' BRAIN BUCKET HEALTHY--
I GO TO A THERAPIST, TOO.
LLY?! BUT I THOUGHT
PRINCESS TYPES HAD
ALL FIGURED OUT!
I DO TOO!
NOW, ALL THAT KRYPTON STUFF WAS PRETTY HEAVY.
I THOUGHT I WAS THE ONLY ONE!
EVERYBODY NEEDS AN OUTSIDE PERSPECTIVE SOMETIMES.

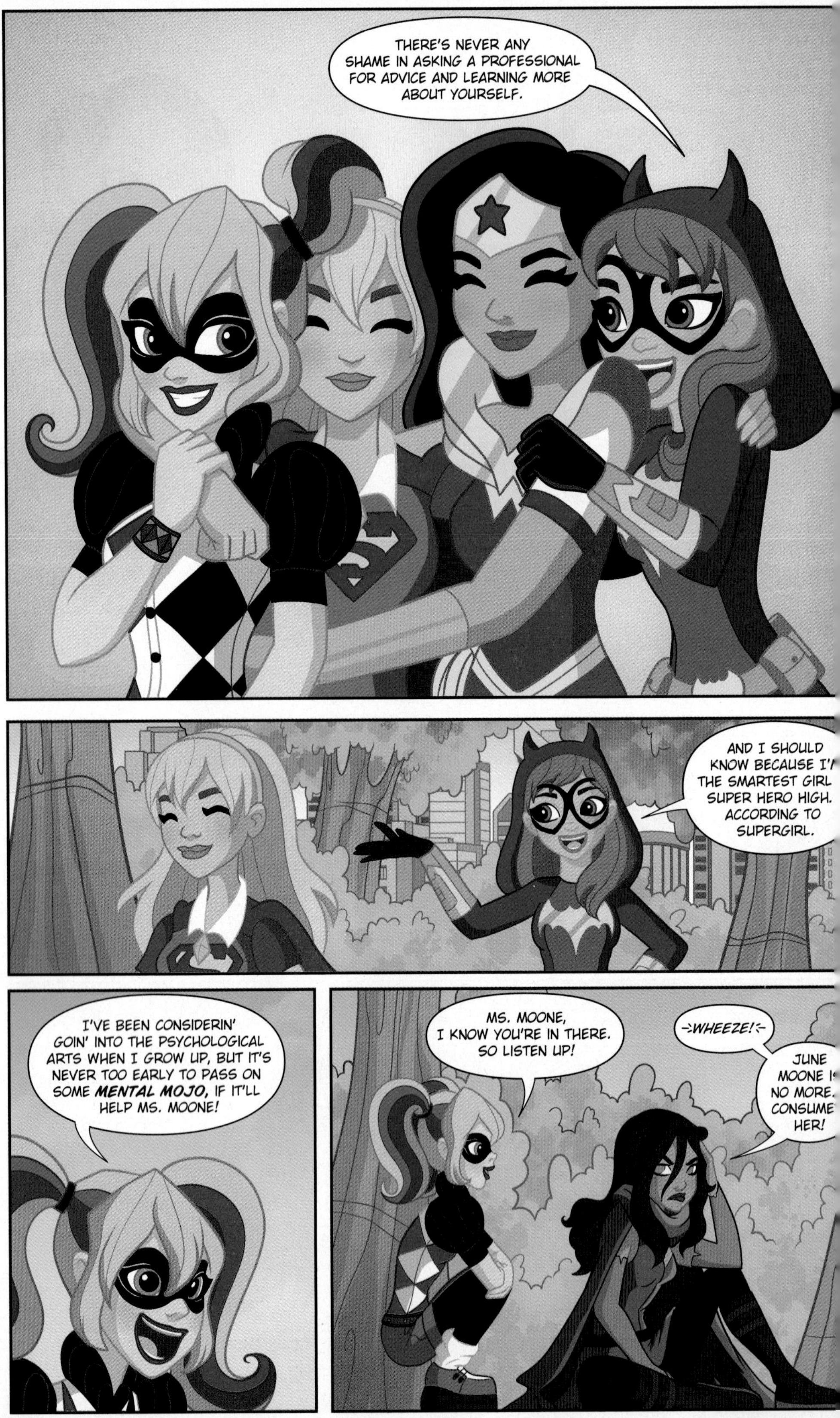
THERE'S NEVER ANY SHAME IN ASKING A PROFESSIONAL FOR ADVICE AND LEARNING MORE ABOUT YOURSELF.
AND I SHOULD KNOW BECAUSE I' THE SMARTEST GIRL SUPER HERO HIGH. ACCORDING TO SUPERGIRL.
I'VE BEEN CONSIDERIN' GOIN' INTO THE PSYCHOLOGICAL ARTS WHEN I GROW UP, BUT IT'S NEVER TOO EARLY TO PASS ON SOME **MENTAL MOJO,** IF IT'LL HELP MS. MOONE!
MS. MOONE, I KNOW YOU'RE IN THERE. SO LISTEN UP!
-WHEEZE!-
JUNE MOONE I NO MORE. CONSUME HER!

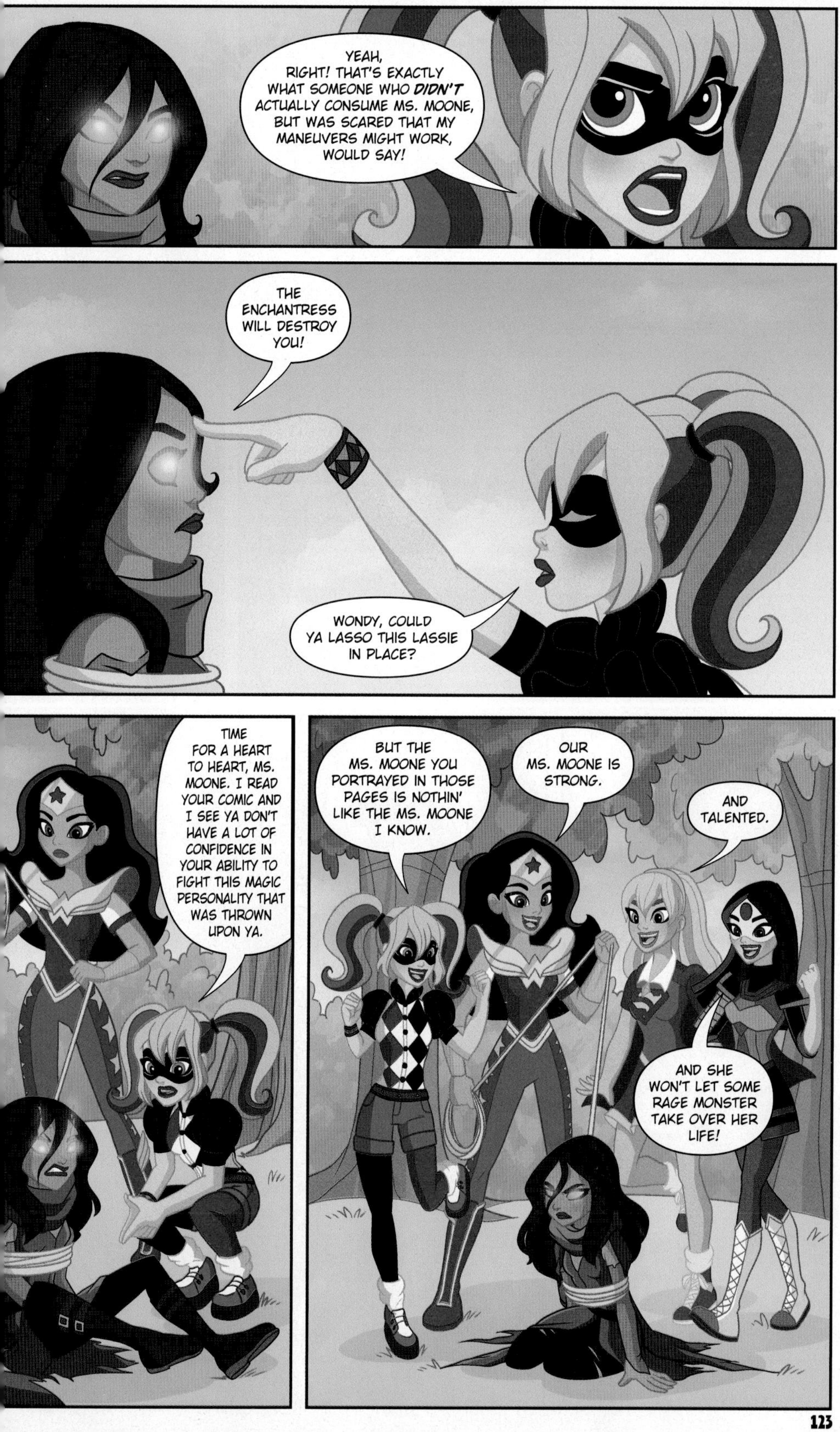
YEAH, RIGHT! THAT'S EXACTLY WHAT SOMEONE WHO DIDN'T ACTUALLY CONSUME MS. MOONE, BUT WAS SCARED THAT MY MANEUVERS MIGHT WORK, WOULD SAY!
THE ENCHANTRESS WILL DESTROY YOU!
WONDY, COULD YA LASSO THIS LASSIE IN PLACE?
TIME FOR A HEART TO HEART, MS. MOONE. I READ YOUR COMIC AND I SEE YA DON'T HAVE A LOT OF CONFIDENCE IN YOUR ABILITY TO FIGHT THIS MAGIC PERSONALITY THAT WAS THROWN UPON YA.
BUT THE MS. MOONE YOU PORTRAYED IN THOSE PAGES IS NOTHIN' LIKE THE MS. MOONE I KNOW.
OUR MS. MOONE IS STRONG.
AND TALENTED.
AND SHE WON'T LET SOME RAGE MONSTER TAKE OVER HER LIFE!

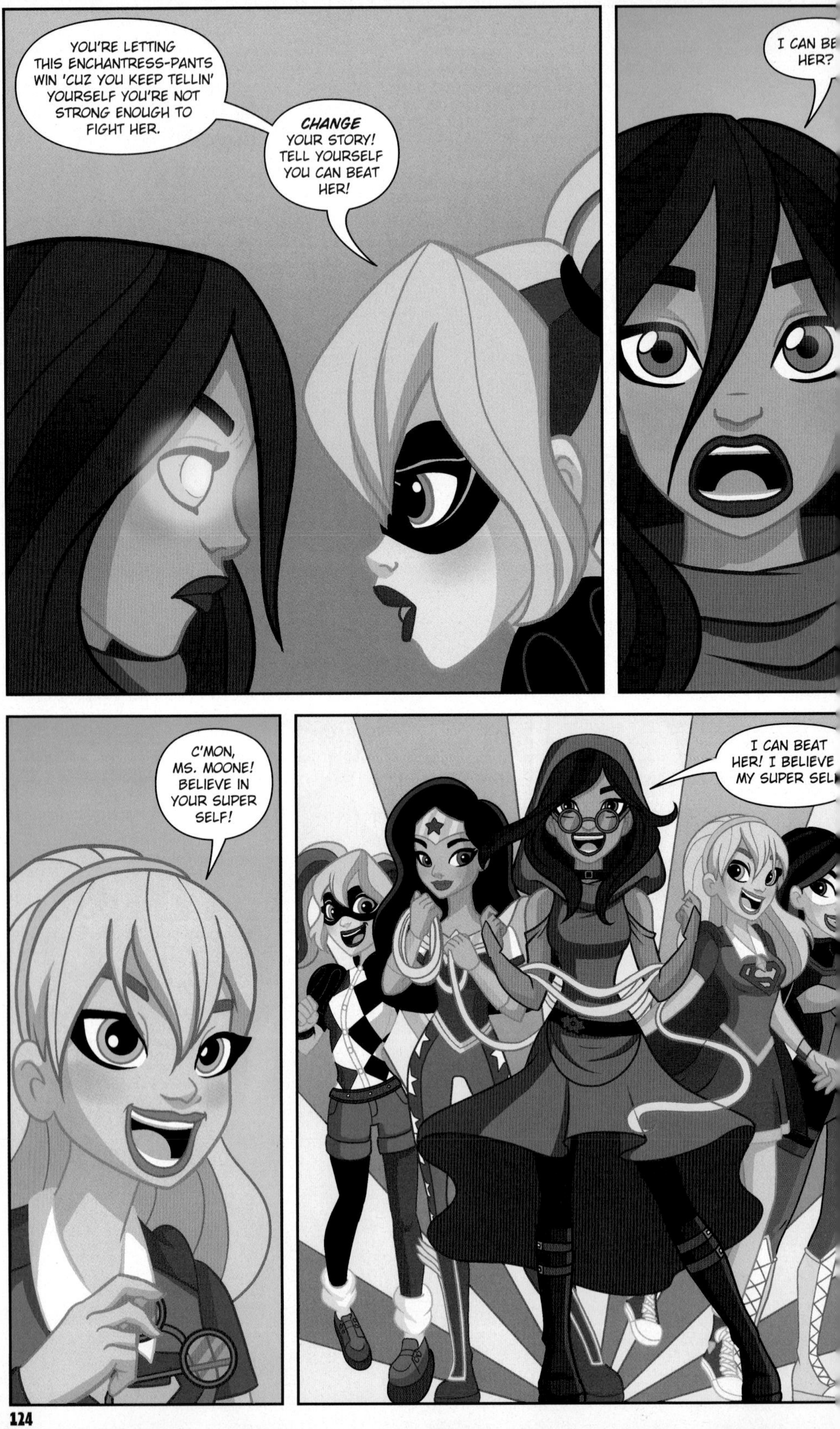
YOU'RE LETTING THIS ENCHANTRESS-PANTS WIN 'CUZ YOU KEEP TELLIN' YOURSELF YOU'RE NOT STRONG ENOUGH TO FIGHT HER.
CHANGE YOUR STORY! TELL YOURSELF YOU CAN BEAT HER!
I CAN BE HER?
C'MON, MS. MOONE! BELIEVE IN YOUR SUPER SELF!
I CAN BEAT HER! I BELIEVE MY SUPER SEL

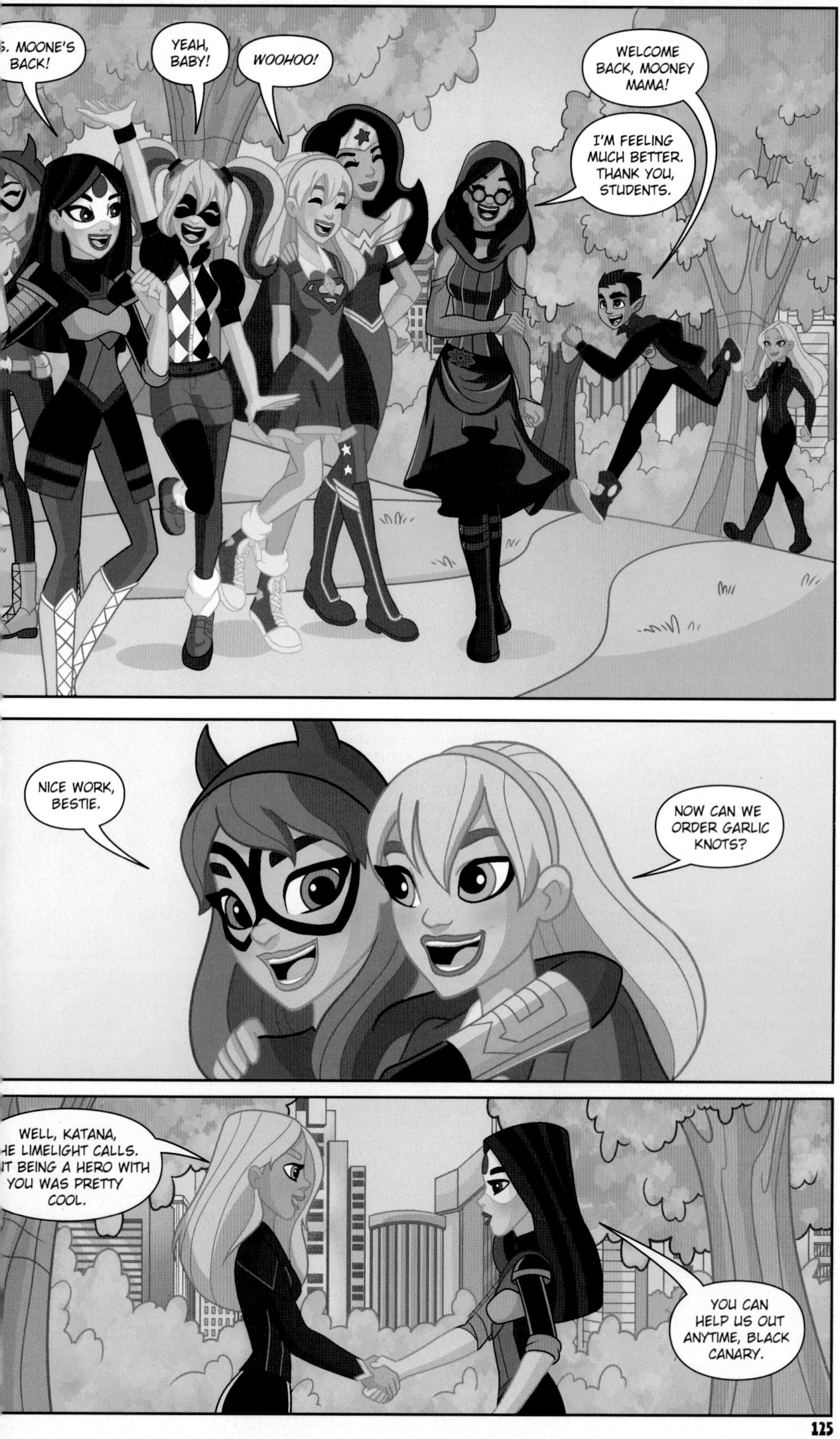
S. MOONE'S BACK!
YEAH, BABY!
WOOHOO!
WELCOME BACK, MOONEY MAMA!
I'M FEELING MUCH BETTER. THANK YOU, STUDENTS.
NICE WORK, BESTIE.
NOW CAN WE ORDER GARLIC KNOTS?
WELL, KATANA, HE LIMELIGHT CALLS. IT BEING A HERO WITH YOU WAS PRETTY COOL.
YOU CAN HELP US OUT ANYTIME, BLACK CANARY.

WHAT IS GOING ON HERE? WERE YOU TRYING TO TAKE OVER *MY* SCHOOL?

NO! WELL, TECHNICALLY, *YES*, BUT IT'S OVER NOW.

PRINCIPAL WALLER, I SUPPOSE APOLOGIZING FOR MY OUTBURST WON'T BE SUFFICIENT.

NO, AN APOLOGY WON'T MAKE UP FOR THE MESS THAT WAS MADE TODAY--

BUT PRINCIPAL WALLER, YOU HAVE TO GIVE MS. MOONE HER JOB BACK!

YEAH, SHE'S GO TO BE EVEN BET TEACHE NOW!

IF YOU'D LET ME FINISH. AN APOLOGY WON'T MAKE UP FOR THE MESS, WHICH IS WHY I EXPECT YOU TO RESUME YOUR TEACHING DUTIES TOMORROW AND MAKE IT UP TO US BY *BEING* THE BEST TEACHER YOU CAN BE.

BUT I CAN'T HAVE YOU BOTTLING UP ALL YOUR FEELINGS LIKE THAT ANYMORE. THAT'S WHAT MAKES YOU *EXPLODE.*

SO, IF YOU WANT TO KEEP YOUR JOB, I EXPECT YOU TO SEE THE SCHOOL COUNSELOR EVERY WEEK AND LEARN TO DEAL WITH YOUR EMOTIONS AS THEY COME ON.

ABSOLUTELY.

IT'S GOOD TO HAVE YOU BACK.

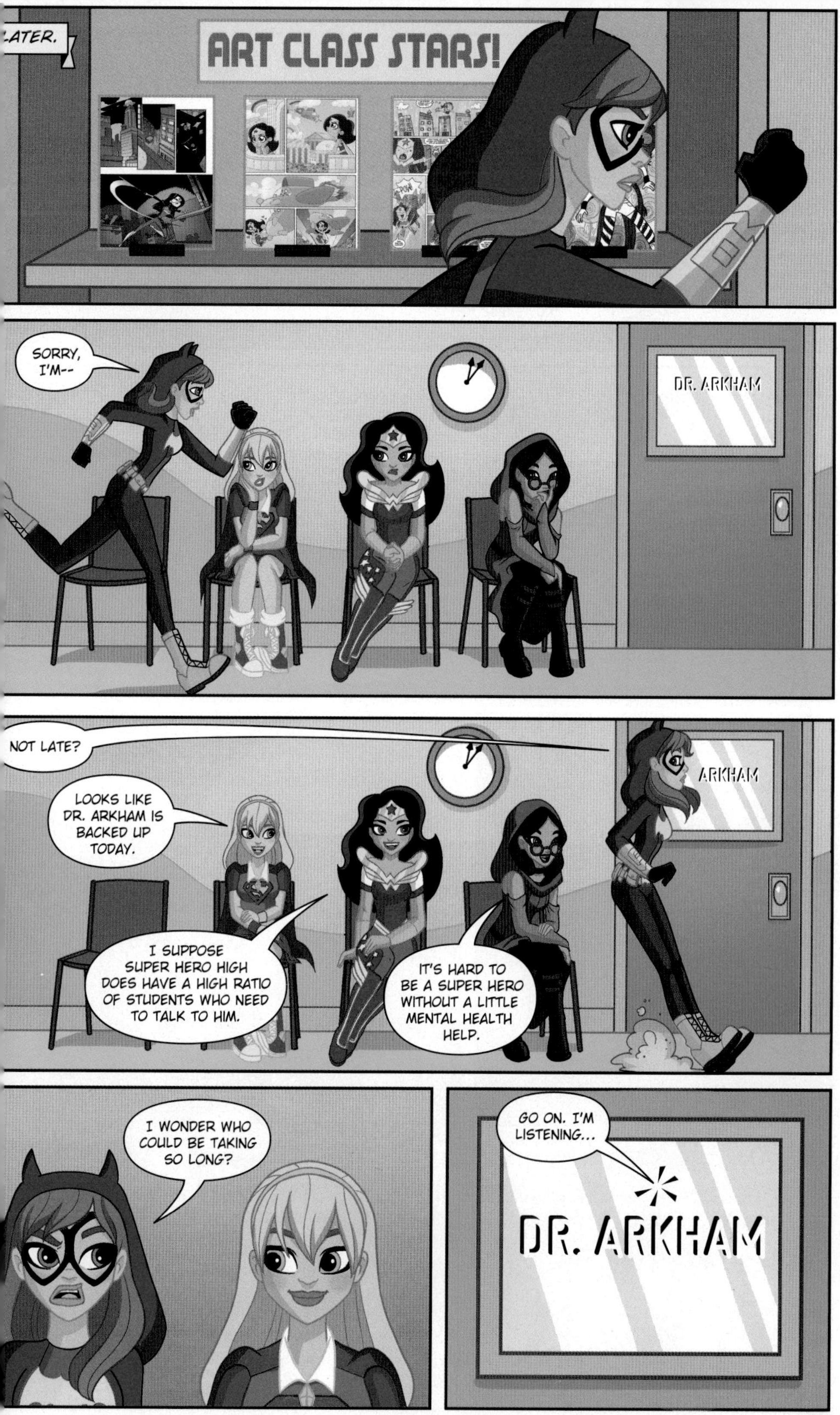
LATER.
ART CLASS STARS!
SORRY, I'M--
DR. ARKHAM
NOT LATE?
LOOKS LIKE DR. ARKHAM IS BACKED UP TODAY.
ARKHAM
I SUPPOSE SUPER HERO HIGH DOES HAVE A HIGH RATIO OF STUDENTS WHO NEED TO TALK TO HIM.
IT'S HARD TO BE A SUPER HERO WITHOUT A LITTLE MENTAL HEALTH HELP.
I WONDER WHO COULD BE TAKING SO LONG?
GO ON. I'M LISTENING...
DR. ARKHAM

WELL, IT'S NOT EASY TO TALK ABOUT, BUT HERE GOES. *AFTER THAT*, THIS *GREEN HAIRED KID* WAS ALWAYS PULLIN' MY PIGTAILS AND TEASIN' ME.

LIFE IS ROUGH WHEN YOU'RE IN KINDY-GARTEN.

KINDERGARTEN?

THIS WAS ALL BEFORE KINDERGARTEN?

PATIENT: HARLEY QUIN
PATIENT: HARLEY QUI
PATIENT: HARLEY QU
PATIENT: HARLEY
PATIENT: HARLEY QU
PATIENT: HARLEY QU
PATIENT: HARLEY Q
PATIENT: HARLEY
PATIENT: HARLE

YEAH, DOC! I WAS A PRECOCIOUS KID. NOW WHERE WAS I...?

THE END.